ARKANA

THE BESTIARY OF CHRIST

Louis Charbonneau-Lassay (1871–1946) was a French Catholic archaeologist/historian with a profound knowledge of medieval Christian art and symbolism. He contributed regularly to leading esoteric journals of the day, including *Atlantis* and *Études Traditionnelles*, and himself edited one entitled *Rayonnement Intellectuel* until the advent of Second World War.

D. M. Dooling, the founder and editorial director of *Parabola Magazine*, is the editor of *A Way of Working: The Spiritual Dimension of Craft* and *The Sons of the Wind: The Sacred Stories of the Lakota*, and co-editor (with Paul Jordan-Smith) of *I Become Part of It: Sacred Dimensions in Native American Life*.

Louis Charbonneau-Lassay

THE BESTIARY OF CHRIST

With Woodcuts by the Author

Translated & Abridged

by D.M. Dooling

A Parabola Book

ARKANA
Published by the Penguin Group
Viking Penguin, a division of Penguin Books USA Inc.,
375 Hudson Street, New York, New York 10014, U.S.A.
Penguin Books Ltd, 27 Wrights Lane, London W8 5TZ, England
Penguin Books Australia Ltd, Ringwood, Victoria, Australia
Penguin Books Canada Ltd, 10 Alcorn Avenue, Suite 300, Toronto, Ontario, Canada M4V 3B2
Penguin Books (N.Z.) Ltd, 182–190 Wairau Road, Auckland 10, New Zealand

Penguin Books Ltd, Registered Offices:
Harmondsworth, Middlesex, England

First published in the United States of America by Parabola Books 1991

Published in Arkana Books 1992

1 3 5 7 9 10 8 6 4 2

Le Bestiaire du Christ originally published by Desclée, De Brouwer & Cie, France, 1940.

LIBRARY OF CONGRESS CATALOGING IN PUBLICATION DATA:
Charbonneau-Lassay, Louis, 1871–1946.
[Bestiaire du Christ. English]
The bestiary of Christ / Louis Charbonneau-Lassay; translated & abridged by D. M. Dooling; with woodcuts by the author.
p. cm.
Translation of: Le Bestiaire du Christ. 1940.
Includes bibliographical references.
ISBN 0 14 019.449 5
1. Christian art and symbolism. 2. Animals—Religious aspects—Christianity. 3. Animals—Symbolic aspects. 4. Animals in art.
I. Dooling, D. M. II. Title.
BV168.A5C4813 1992
246—dc20 91–40422

Printed in the United States of America
Set in Cloister
Designed by James Safati and Kathy Massaro

CONTENTS

PART IV BIRDS

PART V SEA CREATURES

PART VI INSECTS

PART VII FABULOUS BEASTS

FOREWORD

LE BESTIAIRE DU CHRIST was orginally a book of a thousand pages and over a thousand of the author's woodcuts. It was published in Brussels just after the outbreak of the Second World War: one of four volumes planned by Louis Charbonneau-Lassay, all pursuing his interest in religious symbolism. The others were *Le Floraire du Christ*, *Le Vulnéraire du Christ*, and *Le Lapidaire du Christ*. All the material was gathered for them, but he did not live to finish and publish any of the three. *Le Bestiaire* alone has survived, and barely. The firm of Desclée, De Brouwer et Cie. published it in a limited edition of five hundred copies, almost all of which, along with the woodblocks for the illustrations, were lost when a bomb set fire to the warehouse where they were stored. Four other printings of five hundred copies each were printed in Milan from surviving copies of the first edition. That is the entire publishing history of this extraordinary book until its present appearance.

Evidently, not many people have had a chance to read it; yet the rumor of it has spread slowly, almost secretly, as if the magic of the old symbols, reinvested through the love and sensitivity of the author with the power of their ancient meanings, traveled on some unknown wavelengths to reach out, fifty-odd years later, to another audience. Bits and traces of the original book were found here and there; I knew of it long before I held a copy in my hands—and after that, slowly but inevitably, it became necessary to pass it on to others.

Who was Louis Charbonneau-Lassay? A name of importance as it must have been in his lifetime to an inner circle of "les érudits," it was never familiar to the public, and since his death in 1946 it would be forgotten—were it not for *Le Bestiaire*. He led one of those remarkable unremarkable lives that are probably the reason why God does not lose patience entirely with the human race. He was born in Loudun in 1871, and lived in that west central part of France all his life, except for a few years spent at Orly, near Paris. He went to school at the monastery of the Brothers of St. Gabriel, and later of his own wish joined the novitiate of Saint-Laurent-sur-Sèvre, where he pursued his training in history, art, and archaeology. He became a professor and taught at Poitiers and Moncoutant until a throat ailment prevented him from lecturing. But it did not deflect him from his search into the past, for he went into field work and the excavations of the many dolmen sites in the Loudunnaise region. In 1903 the order of St. Gabriel dissolved. Charbonneau had never taken permanent vows, and although he remained all his life a devoted and convinced Catholic, he was now well launched on what was to be his life work and was receiving honors and recognition as an archaeologist and a historian, and it was in this way rather than as a monk that he chose to serve his religion.

In 1933, already in his sixties, he married and moved to Orly where he took full advantage of the libraries and museums of Paris. He was an active member of various historical, archaeological, and religious groups, wrote papers for learned journals, including *Atlantis* and *Études Traditionelles*, and edited one himself: *Rayonnement Intellectual*, until the war loomed as a serious threat in 1939. By this time, he had returned with his ailing wife to Loudun, to a beautiful garden and a house filled with his collections of art and antiquities. Probably he looked forward to a peaceful old age preparing his books for publication. Then came the German Occupation. In Loudun, the commandant ordered all citizens to turn over their firearms. Charbonneau trudged to headquarters with a sack of some of his antique firing pieces. "I have about fifty guns in my house," he told the astonished and suspicious officer, "but as the most recent of them is a hundred years old, I brought you some samples to see if you want them." He must have had a very charming smile. He was allowed to take his guns home again; and although German troops were quartered in his house during the Occupation, not a single item of his collections was lost or damaged.

The *Bestiaire* appeared in 1940, and Charbonneau dedicated himself to finishing his other books and readying them for publication, but circumstances opposed him: the war, the Occupation, his wife's ill health and his own. Mme. Charbonneau died during the war, which he survived by only a year. Never robust, he fought his increasing frailty in unsuccessful efforts to finish his other books. He died the day after Christmas in 1946.

When my love affair with *Le Bestiaire du Christ* began, I thought it would be possible to make a much shorter book out of it that would give a sort of distillation of its essence. I have indeed omitted certain chapters and cut out many repetitions which were probably caused by the strange order in which Charbonneau-Lassay arranged, or jumbled, his creatures, and sometimes even his separate accounts of them. I have changed his arrangement considerably; anyone fortunate enough to have a copy of the original book and attempting to trace in it the path of my abridgement-translation would find it a strenuous gymnastic exercise. I have also omitted some of the detail of the author's research, though including enough, I hope, so that other students may follow up his sources if they wish. But I found it was not possible to make the book as small as I had at first envisaged it. It seemed determined to be a considerable volume, one that must be taken seriously.

All the notes referring to the present text have been included for the sake of the ambitious reader, and they show the astonishingly wide range of Charbonneau-Lassay's own research, as well as his remarkable inconsistency in checking such details as publishing information and even authorship (for example, I have found no one who has ever heard of a book by Xenophon called *Geoponicus*; see note 1 in Part III, "The Deer.") Most of the references, of course, are to French books and journals which I have not had the possibility of rechecking, but wherever I could find Latin or English titles of books or any other relevant facts, I have added them in the bibliographical appendix. These added notes, however, do not pretend to be complete, and I must emphasize that this work, standing firmly on its own merits, cannot be taken for something it is not: a dependable reference book in any scholarly or scientific sense. But unreliable as they are, the notes may contain clues of which I haven't wanted to deprive the researcher.

Although I have corrected typographical errors where it was possible, the French edition contained a great many and I cannot guarantee the accuracy of page or file numbers in books I was not able to check for myself. So I must share with the author the responsibility for all errors of fact or judgment that appear in these pages, at the same time gratefully acknowledging the skillful and enthusiastic help I have received from a number of people better versed than I in their various fields. Among them are John Anthony West whom I consulted on references to ancient Egypt; I am indebted to him for a number of corrections and for several of the editorial notes. Caroline Herrick and Patty Ewing investigated questions about ancient China, and for general research into various obscure terms and references I am deeply grateful for the help of Heather Wolfe and Jane Brooks. Others who have researched, corrected, proofread and in general enormously helped and supported the work of this book are Paul Jordan-Smith, Jean Sulzberger, and Rob Baker. I also wish to thank M. le Comte Élie de Dampierre for supplying me with handbooks on the birds, animals, and insects of Europe, and the Lady Devlin for information about little-known corners of England. Above all, I want to thank Joseph Epes Brown, Henri Tracol, and the late Ilonka Karasz, whose knowledge and appreciation of *Le Bestiaire* were what first led me to it. A special increment of gratitude goes to Joseph Brown for lending me his copy of the rare first edition; he tells me there is only one other in the United States, which was owned by Dr. Ananda Coomaraswamy.

The chapters on the Lion and the Hippogriff were originally translated by Carol Zaleski, and Gabriela Laignel and Linda Daniel helped me with the translation of the early chapters, until I realized that the translating could not be separated from the editing and that both had to be done together by the same hand. The chapter on the Sphinx appeared in PARABOLA, Vol. VIII, No. 2, under the title "Hieroglyph of Life," in Irving Friedman's translation, and several other excerpts of the present work have been seen in PARABOLA since then: portions of the chapter on "The Man" in Vol. VIII, No. 3, entitled "Tongues of Fire"; of "The Weasel" in Vol. XIV, No. 1; of "The Ouroboros" in Vol. XV, No. 1, and an excerpt from "The Horse" in Vol. XIV, No. 4. I have revised all the translations and am ultimately responsible for any cuts or what may be felt as liberties taken with the text.

Finally, I wish to thank the original publishers, Desclée, De Brouwer et Cie., for their patience and cooperation in bringing this wonderful book back into circulation.

D.M. Dooling

INTRODUCTION

"TAKE CARE, ABOVE all, not to reveal the secrets of the holy mysteries, and do not allow them to be indiscreetly exposed to the daylight of the profane world. . . . Only the saints—not everyone—may lift a corner of the veil which covers the things which are holy. . . . Our most saintly founders . . . charged the celebration [of the mysteries] with so many symbolic rites that what is in itself one and indivisible can appear only little by little, as if by parts, and under an infinite variety of details. However, this is not simply because of the profane multitude, who must not glimpse even the covering of holy things, but also because of the weakness of our own senses and spirit, *which require signs and material means to raise them to the understanding of the immaterial and the sublime*[1]."

These words, attributed to St. Dionysius the Areopagite, are a very exact statement of the principal reasons for the use of symbolism. It is to remedy the weakness of our nature and to satisfy its need that all religions and mysteries have felt the obligation to create for themselves codes of symbols kept secret by a strict discipline of caution. It was in this way that the mysteries of Eleusis, of Delphi, of Ephesus and others were protected, and the same practice held in the Mithraic cults and in the Orphic schools. Everyone recognized not only the danger of persecution but also the mysterious, hierarchical authority whose validity Pythagoras affirmed with the words: "It is not good to reveal everything to everyone."

In all the countries where they found themselves, the first Christians—not finding riches enough in their own treasury of sacred images—adapted ancient local religious symbols to their own particular beliefs; and among these, some were dedicated to the representation of the Savior. Others lent themselves to the expression of the great themes of Christian spiritual life, or seemed to represent one of Christ's perfections or roles. There was little modification of the accepted and often conventional forms; so these images of things and of real or imaginary beings are presented in the works of the first Christian artists exactly as one sees them in the decorations of temples, palaces, baths, and other major buildings of Latium or of the Roman provinces. The dolphin in the catacombs, now representing Christ, remained the same image that adorned the palace mosaics and the fountains splashing in the gardens of the Caesars' Rome; the anchor kept the form that it had in the temples of Neptune-Poseidon, and the centaur and the griffin, the hippocampus and hippogriff remained what the artists in Greece and Rome had made of them.

When the early pilgrims to the holy places and the Crusades returned to the West after their sojourns in the Near East and in Egypt, the stories they brought back, as well as the works of art and the products of commerce, such as fabrics, had a strong influence on religious and secular art in our occidental countries. The same thing happened with the first great world travelers who during the second half of the Middle Ages penetrated into the farthest parts of Asia, to Mongolia, to China, or to the African equator. The animals, birds, trees, fruits, and minerals, the fantastic beings who filled their tales, were taken over by the Western symbolists to represent the gifts of God and even Christ himself.

Later the old symbols were to permeate all of European art and the entire heraldic code with the rich essence they contain. "For the Middle Ages," wrote Gevaert, "the whole universe was a symbol[2]." "It knew that everything on earth is a sign, everything is an image, that the visible is of value only in the measure that it covers the invisible. The medieval period, which consequently was not the dupe of appearances, as we are, studied very closely the science of symbolism, and made it the purveyor and servant of mysticism[3]."

A book which goes back to the earliest Christian times, the *Physiologus*, adds to the elements drawn from the old naturalists, with images borrowed from Greek and Oriental writers and from fables and myths from all parts of the world. This work remained in great favor throughout the Christian world, especially during the four or five centuries which followed the peace which Constantine granted to the Church, and a considerable number of somewhat different versions were circulated, so that we no longer know exactly what was the original text. The fourth-century *Commentary of Physiologus*, attributed to St. Epiphanius, contains twenty-six chapters dedicated only to animals. Works of the same kind, in verse or prose, were composed in the Middle Ages under the name of bestiaries, or volucraries when restricted to the symbolism of birds. For plants there were florilegia, and lapidaries dealt with the miraculous properties of precious stones and minerals. Other writers on more general lines, of the same period, gave a good deal of space to the symbolic meanings of animals and objects. These various writings were truly the breviaries of the contemporary artists, and agreed so well with the spirit of the times that Richard de Fournival achieved fame by using them as a model for his *Bestiary of Love*.

Although most of the sacred symbols of great Christian art came from ancient religions and writings and were disseminated by clerics, monks, and other lettered men, the humble country folk, in their fields and gardens, along with these learned ones and feeling with them the same need to see the Savior everywhere, chose for themselves metaphors for Christ that were entirely their own. They saw him as a child in the color of the pale-pink carnation, stained with his own blood in the crimson rose; the first swallow of spring was for them the emblem of his Resurrection, as was also the butterfly; the gray ass whose back is marked with the cross evoked the journey to Calvary; lively legends connected the woodcock, the goldfinch, and the robin to his crucifixion, and the fossilized sea-urchin and certain mineral conglomerates to the Eucharist, which is Christ incarnate.

Besides these mentioned sources of inspiration, an important place must also be given to various factors which at times found fresh interpretations for previous symbolic forms, and even produced new ones. In the front rank of such influences must be placed that of Gnosticism. Another is to be found in the combined efforts of the Hebraic Kabbalah, the ritual formulas of demonic or superstitious practices, astrological and divinatory sciences, alchemy in its pure form or mixed more or less with magic, even with sorcery: which, all grouped together, are commonly (though incorrectly) called hermetism—that is, the secret knowledge, because it was given only to the few initiates. But during the Middle Ages, Christian scholars and clerics, even saints, began to understand that there was nothing whatever wrong in the study of anything which concerned nature or the properties of plants and minerals, including those branches of knowledge hitherto closed to them, such as alchemy; or in astrology, the possible influences of atmospheric conditions, or of the movements and conjunctions of the stars, on the conception and parturition of animals and the germination of plants. Nevertheless, it must be borne in mind that those who taught in the episcopal or monastic schools opened their knowledge only to pupils known to be discreet and of sound judgment, for it was not easy to discern the boundary between what the Church allowed in this domain and what was forbidden. Discretion was a necessity in this period when the suspicion of magic or of sorcery could lead entirely innocent people to torture and death.

From the end of the twelfth century, heraldry with its secular coats-of-arms had become one of the best codified creations that human intellect had achieved during medieval times. By the middle of the thirteenth century, heraldry had its own precise language governed by strict rules, and its own art, also rigidly codified, which remains today one of the most prestigious in the world, and which within its unyielding framework still made room for works of astonishing variety and marvelous zest.

From its birth heraldry was penetrated and dominated by Christian iconography, principally through engravings on coins during the early Middle Ages. Heraldry repaid the debt of its adoption by Christian symbolism by finding new aspects of several of the ancient emblems, and by helping to continue the use of others which would otherwise have fallen into oblivion; and also by guarding the secret of numerous interpretations that we now can understand only by its means, so that in a sense it can very justly be said that he who studies the Christian symbolism of the Middle Ages, especially in the West, will never completely penetrate it if he is not familiar with the science, the art, and the spirit of ancient heraldry in all its various forms—that of the Church, of the nobility, and of the commercial guilds. And we can also invert this proposition, so vividly and so intimately did Christian symbolism and heraldry interpenetrate each other.

Since in those days theology and heraldry ruled both sacred and profane arts, Christian emblems of vices and virtues, like those of the Trinity and of the characteristic attributes of the saints, were not applied thoughtlessly, as happened later much too often; the discipline of symbolism was effectively maintained and respected. In fact, symbols must not be considered as arbitrary. "Faithfully transmitted by tradition," wrote Professor Hippeau in the last century, "they constituted a kind of *artistic orthodoxy* which did not allow them to be considered as solely a product of imagination and whim[4]."

We still have much to learn about the religious thought of the Middle Ages. Many of its symbolic forms are enigmas for us; we can recognize that some are the signs of heraldry, some are workmens' trademarks, others are decorative — and although this may be the case, it is only their outer *raison d'être*, their exoteric side, and they can and almost always do have a hidden significance, which is their esoterism. Formerly this underlying meaning was kept for only a small number of people. There were schools "generally very exclusive and little-known," which were not at all schools of philosophy, and whose teachings were conveyed only behind the veil of certain symbols which must have been quite obscure for those who did not have the key to them. The key was given only to close followers of proved discretion and intelligence, who had undertaken certain commitments. Evidently all this indicates the presence of teachings profound enough to be totally foreign to the ordinary way of thinking, and as this phenomenon seems to have been fairly frequent in the Middle Ages, there is strong reason for caution in speaking of that epoch's intellectual attainments and for taking into account what might have existed outside of what is known to us with certainty. Many things must have been lost because they were not written down, which is also "the explanation for the almost total loss of the Druidic teaching. Among the schools alluded to, we might mention the alchemists, whose doctrine was above all of a cosmological order. . . . One might say that the symbols contained in alchemical writings constitute their exoterism, while their secret interpretation constitutes their esoterism[5]."

The medieval era practiced and glorified the intensive culture of spirituality, and for it, all beauty was beauty only when seen in the divine light; the value of anything was measured by the degree in which it favored the ascension of the soul. But then came the Renaissance and a tragic retreat of the spirit. Human beings left the ethereal atmosphere of God to descend and breathe that of man. REASON EVERYWHERE was inscribed on the portal of a house of that time in Poitiers, not far from the well-known university where learned doctors taught in the fashion of the day. Renaissance art, the direct reflection of a way of thinking no longer imbued with mystical Christian spirituality, could not be anything but the glorification of material beauty. "The symbolism which had been the very soul of art in the thirteenth century," says Émile Mâle, "this beautiful idea that reality is but an image, that rhythm, number, and harmony are the great laws of the universe, this whole world of thought where dwelt the old theologians and the old artists, seems closed off . . . one feels the withering and dying of the ancient symbols[6]."

In fact, not all the symbols died, but many disappeared from the habitual forms of art. And above all, the true meaning of these emblems was forgotten; room was made for arbitrary interpretations and the allegorical ideas applied to some of them changed totally: for instance, the pelican, the old symbol of the purifying Christ who washes the sins of his children with his blood and so returns them to life and grace, became almost solely, in the eyes of all, an emblem of the Eucharist, because the action of *purification* by blood was ignorantly seen as the gesture of *feeding*, which belongs to the vulture in ancient Egypt. And the pelican was not the only one abused in this fashion.

Symbolic representations also suffered, especially those that had not evolved from the iconography of ancient Greece and Rome. The quality of the sacred accorded them by medieval art no longer had the same value, and the symbolic animals lost their ideal character and came closer to the anatomic forms of natural beasts. All they retained were easy, stale, exoteric meanings without depth or substance, without mystery: the lion was *only* the image of strength and courage, the lamb of gentleness, the snake of discretion, the phoenix of immortality, the rose of beauty . . . and it was forgotten that in the beginning their function had been to represent Christ and his gifts on the consecrated shield of the knight.

Other symbols, such as the panther, the stork, the crow, and so on, were no longer understood at all, and the angels of Paradise, the beautiful, ethereal and radiant angels of the Byzantines and the sculptures of Rheims, of Fra Angelico and Jehan Fouquet, were changed in the churches of the Renaissance into chubby, naked cherubs; the goats, rams, doves, storks, and cocks ceased to allude to some of the most fascinating aspects of Christ and became only allegories of a purely sensual and quite inferior order.

Studies of archaeology and sacred art made in the past century have restored to symbolism, for those well-read in the subject, a part of the very high esteem due to it. It merits, however, much greater recognition: it should be known and understood more precisely, first of all by artists, and by all the clergy and serious Christians, at least, since the appropriate use of symbols offers a source of light for the understanding and of substantial nourishment for the spirit.

* * *

In this work, I have tried to present the exact meanings of symbolic images which, in the course of the Christian centuries and in very different places, have been taken as mysterious representations of the person of Jesus Christ in his various aspects. Among these ideograms there are some that could provide material for a whole book. I have had to condense and to keep to the essentials of their Christian and pre-Christian history.

I have listed my sources of information, not to make a childish display, but simply to allow the reader to go back to these sources if he wishes. The images of the artistic examples which illustrate the text in these pages were cut in service-wood with the simple tools used by the fifteenth-century wood engravers: I have not been so presumptuous as to aspire to a work of art, but only to hope that in spite of their imperfections, the crude support they bring to the text will be enough to make a better understanding possible of the passages they accompany.

L. C-L.

NOTES

Title Figure: The Griffin-Christ.

1. *Le Traité de la Hiérarchie* (English: *Celestial Hierarchies*), attributed to St. Denis (Dionysius the Areopagite). Cf. Lecornu, "La mystique de la Messe," in *Revue du Monde Catholique*, 1866, Vol. XIV, No. 115, p. 226.
2. Gevaert, *L'Héraldique*, p. 37.
3. Huysmans, *Le Cathédrale*, Vol. II, p. 297.
4. *Bestiaire divin*, p. 34 (note).
5. Guénon, *Introduction to the Study of the Hindu Doctrines*, Chapter IX.
6. Mâle, *L'art religieux* (1), p. 491.

I

THE TETRAMORPH

THE TETRAMORPH

IN THE SERIES of living beings claimed by Christian symbolism to form the mysterious crown of Christ, a group of four animals is notable for the large place it held, and continues to hold, in sacred art and in mystical literature. We see them represented at times separately from one another and at times united, blended together in the form of a unique being that would be strange indeed and disconcerting to anyone ignorant of ecclesiastical symbolism (Fig. 1).

These celestial animals are the ones that the Hebrew prophet Ezekiel, towards the end of the seventh century B.C., and the evangelist St. John in the first years of the Church, saw come to life in visions, of which they have left us extraordinary and troubling accounts: the lion, the ox, the eagle, and man. They form what sacred art has named the Tetramorph, "the Four Forms."

Fig. 1 Tetramorph in the Louvre Museum.

These are the words of Ezekiel: "Now it came to pass . . . as I was among the captives by the river of Chebar, that the heavens were opened, and I saw visions of God. . . . And I looked, and, behold, a whirlwind came out

Fig. 2 11th-century Tetramorph at Mount Athos.

of the north, a great cloud, and a fire infolding itself, and a brightness was about it, and out of the midst thereof as the colour of amber, out of the midst of the fire. Also out of the midst thereof came the likeness of four living creatures. And this was their appearance; they had the likeness of a man. And every one had four faces, and every one had four wings. And their feet were straight feet; and the sole of their feet was like the sole of a calf's foot: and they sparkled like the colour of burnished brass. And they had the hands of a man under their wings on their four sides; and they four had their faces and their wings. Their wings were joined one to another; they turned not when they went; they went every one straight forward. As for the likeness of their faces, they four had the face of a man, and the face of a lion, on the right side; and they four had the face of an ox on the left side; they four also had the face of an eagle. Thus were their faces: and their wings were stretched upward; two wings of every one were joined one to another, and two covered their bodies. And they went every one straight forward: whither the spirit was to go, they went; and they turned not when they went. As for the likeness of the living creatures, their appearance was like burning coals of fire, and like the appearance of lamps: it went up and down among the living creatures; and the fire was bright, and out of the fire went forth lightning. And the living creatures ran and returned as the appearance of a flash of lightning[1]."

And now St. John:

"And immediately I was in the spirit: and, behold, a throne was set in heaven, and one sat on the throne. . . . And before the throne there was a sea of glass like unto crystal; and in the midst of the throne, and round about the throne, were four beasts full of eyes before and behind. And the first beast was like a lion, and the second beast like a calf, and the third beast had a face as a man, and the fourth beast was like a flying eagle. And the four beasts had each of them six wings about him; and they were full of eyes within: and they rest not day and night, saying, Holy, holy, holy, Lord God Almighty, which was, and is, and is to come[2] (Fig. 2)."

In St. John, as in Ezekiel, these four animals, or rather these four "living creatures," are the epitome of creation, because of all creatures they are the noblest. We shall see how Man, Lion, Ox (or Bull), and Eagle were taken to represent Christ symbolically and how the Christian arts placed them around him to represent the four Evangelists who have transmitted to us his story and his teaching.

NOTES

Title Figure: Byzantine Tetramorph.

1. Ezekiel 1:1, 4-14.
2. Revelation 4:2, 6-8.

End Figure: The wheels of Ezekiel's vision; from a 6th-century illumination.

THE LION

THE KING. BEHOLD the King: the first of those four kings whom God disclosed to the dazzled eyes of Ezekiel on the banks of the Chebar[1], and whom St. John recognized in his resplendent vision on Patmos, when they sang before the throne of the sovereign Lamb, beating their fiery wings: the Lion, awesome king of the beasts; the Ox, king of sacrificial victims; the Eagle, king of the air; and Man, king of the world.

Yet this lion of the prophets of Israel, sovereign though he was, was only a servant. That is why, together with the man, the eagle, and the ox, he stood transfixed with love and adoration, acclaiming the One who occupied the throne, by turns lion and lamb; the One whom John saw ascend to the divine seat, there to open the book sealed with seven seals[2].

Fig. 1 Sekhmet, the lion-headed goddess; from the tomb of Seti I at Thebes.

But many centuries before the time that John rested his head on his master's heart and felt the Spirit descend upon him, the pre-Christian traditions of Europe, Africa, and Asia surrounding Israel and its religion had adopted the image of the lion to represent what they believed to be the various attributes of divinity.

Among the Egyptians, the goddess Sekhmet proudly bore a lion's head (Fig. 1); among the Ammonites, the sun was adored under the name of Camos, the Lion-sun, and in Syria, as we shall see later on, the royal animal had also a divine character. For millennia, Tibet has worshipped the Ka-gro-Mha, goddesses with the heads of lionesses, like Sekhmet of Egypt, divinely beautiful, who dance naked upon the corpses of conquered men and animals.

Among the Greeks, four harnessed lions drew the chariot of Cybele, at a stirring gallop or pacing majestically—Cybele, mother of the gods, the "Good Goddess," image of the divine bounty which gives humanity all the good things which come forth from the earth.

Fig. 2 The heraldic lion of Persia.

In Persia, the lion was one of the animals sacred to the cult of Mithra. The feasts of this god were called the "Leontic rites," and often on the sculptures which depict Mithra sacrificing the bull, the lion and the serpent are shown lying underneath the slain animal. In the Mithraic mysteries, initiates of the Fourth Order were called "lions" and "lionesses"; and Mithra himself, "the Invincible Sun," seems to have been sometimes personified by a lion-headed god. Even today, the heraldic, sword-wielding lion of the Persian state bears on his back the resplendent sun (Fig. 2). In ancient Syria, the god of courage was represented by a crowned lion-centaur endowed with four lion's paws and two human arms.

The lion also lends his claws to the sphinx and his body to the griffin, giving them a part of his nature and of the qualities which are attributed to him: royalty, power, watchfulness, courage, and justice.

Royalty and power: no doubt this was why Alexander the

Great, and after him, Maximilian-Hercules, Probus, Gallienus, and other rulers, appeared on their coins hooded with the skin of a lion's head.

Strength and courage: over and above the Mithraic influence, this accounts for the lion's adoption as insignia by the legions of Rome.

Watchfulness: the age-old belief, sanctioned as well by classical Latin authorities, which shows the lion sleeping in the desert with his eyes wide open, day or night, must surely have seemed significant to the first Christian symbolists. What did it matter to them whether the alleged facts were true or not? St. Augustine, in commenting on a rather strange characteristic attributed to the eagle, tells us that in symbolism "the important thing is to consider the significance of a fact and not to dispute its authenticity[3]." Thus Christian idealism of bygone days always and in everything paid heed to the symbol and not to the thing, to the spirit which gives life and not to the letter which sucks dry. So it sees in the perpetually open-eyed lion the image of the attentive Christ who sees everything, and who guards souls from evil when they truly wish, like a watchful pastor, a good shepherd.

Here, the Far East is in agreement with the Western and Christian Middle Ages in seeing the lion as a vigilant guardian. Since what long vanished epoch have granite lions, crouched and ferocious, like those of Angkor Wat, stood guard in the company of fearsome dragons at the threshold of India's temples? For the symbolists of Asia, as for those of the West, lions and dragons never shut their eyes; they would say, with our Brunetto Latini, "All lions of every kind keep their eyes open even while they sleep[4]."

William of Normandy, who wrote his *Divine Bestiary* at the beginning of the thirteenth century, also underlines the symbolic character of the watchful lion, and gives the following interpretation:

Quer quant il dort, li oil veille;	When the lion sleeps, his eye watches;
En dormant a les euz overz,	In sleep his eyes are open,
Et clers et luisanz et apers.	Clear and gleaming and awake.

Now, he adds, we must understand what this means:

Quand cest lion fut en croiz mis	When this lion was put on the cross
Par les Ieves, ses anemis,	By the Jews, his enemies,
Qui le jugièrent a grant tort,	Who judged him so wrongfully,
L'umanité i soffrit mort	His humanity suffered death then
Quand l'espérit de cors rendi	When he rendered the spirit from the body,
En la saincte croiz s'endormi;	And fell asleep on the holy cross;
Si que la deité veilla.	But the divine nature kept watch.

And here the ancient poet is in accord with St. Hilary and St. Augustine who see, in the lion's way of sleeping, an allusion to Christ's divine nature which was not extinguished in the sepulcher, even while his humanity underwent a real death.

Justice: for the Ancients used to say that the lion will attack his prey only if he is compelled by an urgent need for food, and that, even then, he will never pounce upon a foe who has fallen before the battle can begin. It was also said that the lion knew how to show appreciation for a favor, to the point where he might teach humans some useful lessons in gratitude.

The Middle Ages maintained the connections which had previously linked the lion to the idea of justice. From Italy up to the Loire, ecclesiastical courts were often held in the forecourts of churches between stone lions which framed the portal, and judgments were handed down there in accordance with the well-known expression *inter leones et coram populo*: "between the lions and before the assembled people." One can still see one of these forecourts of justice, flanked by weather-beaten lions, at the grand portal of the church of St. Radegund in Poitiers, and lions appear again at the threshold of several ancient churches in Rome, at St. Lawrence-outside-the-Walls, at the Church of the Twelve Apostles, at St. Lawrence-in-Lucina, and at St. Saba.

The concept which links the lion to the virtue of justice is supported in Christian symbolism by the Bible's description of Solomon's throne of justice, made of ivory and gold, which rested on six steps guarded by twelve magnificent lions[5].

Fig. 3 The lion bringing its cub back to life, 13th century.

The lion was also an emblem of the Resurrection. Émile Mâle explains a stained glass window in the cathedral of Bourges which shows a symbolic lion near the tomb of the risen Christ, by recalling the tradition which made the lion, in Christian art, an emblem of Christ as the risen God-Man.[6] Mâle writes, "In the Middle Ages, everyone subscribed to the idea that the lioness brought forth young which appeared to be stillborn. For three days the lion cubs would give no sign of life, but on the third day, the lion would return and animate them with his breath (Fig. 3)."

The authors of the bestiaries of the Middle Ages certainly found this legend in Aristotle and in Pliny the Elder; yet Plutarch, better informed about the Orient and its creatures, had written that, on the contrary, lion cubs come into the world with their eyes wide open; and for that reason, certain peoples of his time consecrated the lion to the sun[7]. (This would also explain the lion's presence alongside Mithra, the *Sol Invictus.*) Although Cuvier and the modern naturalists confirm Plutarch's opinion, the authors and artists of the Middle Ages, relying on the scant authority of Origen[8] and of the *Physiologus*, followed the opposite view. In such a thoroughly idealistic world, which sought to consecrate every truth by means of symbols, the fable of the lion cubs born dead and brought to life on the third day by their father enjoyed a great vogue; it was favored by St. Epiphanius, St. Anselm, St. Ivo of Chartres, St. Bruno of Asti and many others[9]. As Mâle puts it, "The apparent death of the little lion represented the sojourn of Jesus Christ in the grave, and his birth was like an image of the Resurrection[10]."

Fig. 4 The resurrection of the lion cub, 13th century.

William of Normandy, in his *Divine Bestiary*, might be translated as follows:

Quant la femele foone
Le foon chiet a terre mort;
De vivre n'aura ia confort
Iusque li pere, au tierz iior
Le souffle et leche par amor;

En tel maniere le respire

Ne porreit aveir autre mire

Autresi fu de Ihesu-Christ
L'umanité que por nos prist,
Que por l'amor de nos vesti,

Paine et travail por nos senti;
Sa deité ne senti rien
Issi creez, i ferez bien.
Quand Deix fu mis el monument

Treis iorz i fu tant solement
Et au tierz ior le respira

Li pere, qui le suscita
Autresi comme li lion
Respire son petit foon.

When the lioness gives birth,
Her cub drops to earth, dead;
He lacks the force of life
Until the father, on the third day
Breathes on him and licks him
for love,
In this way, he breathes life into
him;
No other remedy could save him.
(Fig. 4)

So was it with Jesus Christ:
The humanity which he assumed,
And cloaked himself in for love
of us,
Suffered pain and labor for us
Of which his divinity felt nothing
Believe thus and you will do well.
When God was put into the
tomb
He stayed only three days
And on the third day again
received his breath
From the Father who roused him
Just as the lion breathes life
Into his little cub[11].

And the custom which prevailed before Christianity, in Lycia and in Phrygia as in several other regions, of placing the image of the lion on the tombs of kings or illustrious heroes, might have its source, in part, in the fabled power of resurrection which the Ancients attributed to the lion. In the art of antiquity, his image often accompanies the palm tree which throughout the ancient world was an emblem of resurrection still more than of the desert.

The union in Jesus Christ of two natures, human and divine, has been the theme of many allegorical images, including that of the lion, and it is certainly in the lion that the two are the least visibly differentiated. The Ancients were in agreement that all the lion's active qualities were located in his foreparts: in his head, neck, chest, and front claws; for them, the hind quarters served only as the animal's physical support. Thus they made the forequarters of the lion the emblem of Christ's divine nature, and the hindquarters the image of his humanity. Was it not perhaps because of this idea that the heraldic lion, called the "lion rampant," was represented lifting himself on his hind legs, with his foreparts turned to the sky? (Fig. 5).

Fig. 5 Lion from the family coat-of-arms of Cardinal Pasca, 1565.

It is also quite natural that mystical writers saw an image of the potent speech of the Christ in the roar of the lion. The formidable voice which resounds through the immense expanses of the desert served as an image for that of the Teacher of the Word and its unequalled range. Hosea prophesied of this matchless voice: "They shall walk after the Lord: he shall roar like a lion: when he shall roar, then the children shall tremble from the west[12]." And Joel, in turn: "The Lord also shall roar out of Zion[13]." Later on, the Latin liturgy would make use of the same terms in speaking of the Savior: *De Sion rugiet, et de Jerusalem dabit vocem suam*: "The Lord also shall roar out of Zion, and utter his voice from Jerusalem[14]."

Perhaps this is why, in our western regions at least, preaching pulpits often are supported by lions. In Chasseignes, near Loudun (Vienne), and in the same city, at the Church of Martray, the pulpits—dating from the fifteenth and sixteenth centuries—are made in the form of stone fonts, and rest their base on seated lions.

But the lion shares with numerous animals—which are also authentic emblems of Jesus Christ—the negative role of serving equally as an allegorical image for the Antichrist, for Satan.

Since the dawn of the Church, the lion has had this evil significance quite often, on account of St. Peter's words: "Be sober, be vigilant; because your adversary the devil, as a roaring lion, walketh about, seeking whom he may devour[15]." Frequently, in scenes of ancient Christian art where the lion pursues timid does or innocent gazelles, the onlooker sees only the ordinary pursuit of prey by a famished beast, while in reality, these images illustrate the text from St. Peter.

Commentators on the sacred books explicitly recognized the image of the devil in the lion vanquished by young David[16]. The celebrated reliquary of Abbé Bégon, part of the treasure of the ancient ninth-century abbey of Conques-en-Rouergue, which was known as "St. Vincent's Lantern," portrayed

David's combat with the lion; and on the damaged inscription beneath this image, one can still read . . . *sic noster David Satanam superavit*: "Thus our David overcame Satan."

In his infernal role, the lion is often the emblem of one of the "three concupiscences" to which Christian asceticism attributed the downfall of souls: "concupiscence of the flesh"—whence come lust, gluttony, and sloth; "concupiscence of the eyes"—whence lust again, greed, and envy; "concupiscence of pride of life"—whence pride and wrath. In these three filiations of the seven deadly sins, the lion represents pride of life.

NOTES

Title Figure: The Lion of heaven—from the tomb of Seti I.

1. Ezekiel 1:10.
2. Revelation 5 & 6.
3. St. Augustine, *Commentaries on the Psalms, C.II.*
4. Latini, *Li Livres dou Tresor.*
5. I Kings 10:18-20.
6. Mâle, *L'Art religieux* (1), p.29.
7. Plutarch, *Quaestiones Conviviales*, Bk. IV, ch. 5.
8. Origen, Homily XVIII, ch. 49.
9. Cf. Huysmans, *La Cathédrale*, 1920; T II, p. 220.
10. Mâle, op. cit.
11. William of Normandy, *Le Bestiaire Divin*, "La nature de Lion." Hippeau edition, pp. 194-196.
12. Hosea 11:10.
13. Joel 3:16.
14. Breviary of Poitiers, office of 1st Sunday in Advent.
15. First Epistle of Peter 5:8.
16. I Samuel 17:34 *et seq.*

End Figure: The Assyrian warrior god.

THE BULL

ON READING THE Old Testament from beginning to end, one is impressed by the innumerable throngs of victims that the patriarchs and their sons, the Hebrews, sacrificed to God. Exodus and Leviticus liturgically codified these sacrifices where sometimes hundreds of victims were slaughtered at the same time. One of the reasons for these impressive holocausts is given in the sacred text: "For the life of the flesh is in the blood: and I have given it to you upon the altar to make an atonement for your souls: for it is the blood that maketh an atonement for the soul[1]."

Whether as an offering under the knife of the sacrificers of Israel, or in the mythic sanctuaries of the Gentiles where often the victim was a human being, the ritual outpouring of blood flowed in ceremonies of all kinds: of glorification, of initiation and propitiation, of atonement and of gratitude. These are also the functions that Catholic theology attributes to the mysterious sacrifice of the body and blood of Jesus Christ on the altar, which took the place of the abolished sacrifices of ancient Mosaic law.

It is this substitution that brought about the acceptance, in the signs and symbols of Christianity, of the beasts of the holocaust, the ancient "victims," as appropriate symbols of the Savior sacrificed for humanity on Golgotha.

The blood of numerous animals was shed before the altar of Yahweh: the dove, the kid, the he-goat, the lamb, the cow, the heifer, and the calf; but the principal victim was the ox. In the mythological conceptions of ancient Egypt, the ox or bull was one of the symbols through which the supreme god Amon was adored in Thebes; in a hymn of this cult engraved on a piece of pottery in the British Museum, Amon is summoned in the name of the Celestial Bull[2].

In ancient times, because of its universal character as a symbol of fertility, and the symbolic similarity between the shape of its horns and the lunar crescent, the head of the bull was offered and treated separately in Egyptian sacrifices, and its image was worn on amulets. These amulets have been found in many places in Europe, Asia, and Africa[3], and attest to the general character of the ancient connection of the bull and other horned animals to human fecundity and the cult of the moon (Fig. 1).

Fig. 1 Apis, from the tomb of Seti I.

In Egypt, the sacred bull, as well as being the incarnation of the god Amon was also that of the god Ptah, for it was the personification of the divine life force renewing itself unendingly in nature. Perhaps this is why, in the well-known zodiac of Denderah, the ox is portrayed on its knees with the "Key of Life," the *ankh*, around its neck.

The rather complex mythologies of Assyria, Chaldea, Media, and Susiana placed the symbolic bull in relation with celestial influences, and even with the divine nature; and the deified bull was portrayed with a human face[4]. The impressive man-headed oxen, the cherubim of Assyria (Fig. 2), adorned with jeweled tiaras, like the sovereigns and pontiffs of their countries, and provided with great wings like eagles,

Fig. 2 The cherubim, human-headed bull of Nineveh.

Fig. 3
The Assyrian monster, Eabani.

are well-known. The wingless human oxen, however, represent the infernal monster Eabani (Fig. 3). And whatever the ancient commentators on the Bible may have thought, it is completely possible, if not certain, that in Israel, the gold cherubim which covered the Ark of the Covenant with their wings[5], and those in Solomon's temple[6], were oxen more or less similar to those of the Assyrians.

In the Assyro-Babylonian pantheon, the god who was specifically empowered to control thunderstorms was named Adad; he was "the lord of the celestial fire." His symbol was the bull, whose charge is impetuous like that of a storm and whose voice evokes the rumble of thunder. There is a stele that shows us Adad riding on his symbolic ox with one foot on its hindquarters and the other on its forehead[7] (Fig. 4).

Fig. 4 Adad standing on the bull; Louvre Museum.

In his splendid work on the theology of the Greeks, Victor Magnien specifies that oxen were sacrificed to Poseidon, black like his garments, because the noise of the sea, his empire, like the bellowing of the bull, is a result of "powerful breathing[8]."

The mysterious cults of Mithra and Orpheus ascribed to the immolation of the bull such a special power of purification and propitiation that the bull sacrifices took on the form and the sacramental liturgy of a kind of baptism of blood. Consider this impressive rite:

In an excavation hollowed out under a floor made of latticed wood on which the sacrificers slaughter the bound animal, there stands naked the candidate to receive the benefits of the initiation and the purification through contact with the ritual blood.

"Through the slats in the wood," says Prudentius, "the blood falls into the hollow and the initiate turns his head towards the drops that fall; he exposes his entire body to them. He leans backwards so that they may sprinkle his face, his ears, his lips, and his nostrils; he immerses his eyes in the warm liquid and not even sparing his palate, inundates his tongue in the blood and drinks avidly[9]." Then, when the last agonized tremors have emptied the veins of the powerful victim and his life is extinguished, the initiated one emerges from the excavation dripping with blood, and offers himself to the veneration of the people who believe him purified by this scarlet baptism and brought close now to divinity.

Today, near the falls of the Zambezi, a cruel custom still proclaims the belief in the virtues of hot, living, bovine blood; "The bull or ox has a ligature around its neck; a well-directed arrow causes abundant bleeding; the black native fills a horn with the blood and then drinks it with gusto; for other animals, it is from a large cut, with blood gushing from it, that the natives come to drink as they would from a cup; the beast is then sewn up again and frolics once more in the midst of the herd[10]."

Today also in Laos, the buffalo is solemnly sacrificed in order to ask the heavens to foretell the future to humanity. Repeatedly but with lapses of time between each stab, so that death will be slow, the sacrificer plunges a large spear into the flank of the animal, and the way in which the buffalo falls and dies indicates to the people whether the year will be good or bad, peaceful or troubled[11].

One might believe that the domesticated bull, like the male buffalo or the wild bison, earned human respect through the fear it inspired. In the drawings engraved on the walls of prehistoric caves as in the most beautiful Greek works of art, the bull poses as the powerful chief of the herd. These ancient testimonials well portray its strength, the speed of its charge, its fury, its sexual passion, and the imposing gravity of its motionless stance. Nonetheless, it was more as the herd's prolific sire than as its formidable leader that the bull was valued by the people of the first human societies[12]. Throughout Asia, it was always the embodiment of all the psychic and physical energies which constitute the driving force in the lives of all beings. In Egypt the image of the bull was the hieroglyph of the word "fertility" and for the Greeks he was the symbol of the creative force[13].

All the cults of the ancient peoples of Iran and Chaldea, who brought us astronomy, celebrated the ram and the bull, the fathers of the herds, as the spring signs of the zodiac. But is it true, as it has been said, that this symbolism came from these regions of Asia and later spread to Egypt and Europe? (Figs. 5 and 6). I prefer to think, on the contrary, that it was born of itself wherever primitive man became hunter and then herdsman. Before Brahmanism appeared in Tibet and India,

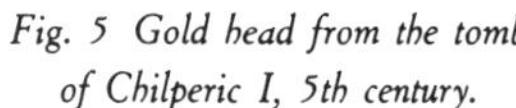

Fig. 5 Gold head from the tomb of Chilperic I, 5th century.

Fig. 6 Spanish amulets, Madrid Museum.

before the Sumerians made their rich amulets, even before the civilizations of Babylonia, Nineveh, or Susa were born, the aborigines of the northern slopes of the Pyrenees modeled the clay bison of the cave of the "Two Brothers," and engraved the superb oxen of the Magdalenian caverns of France and Spain.

Relying principally on the visions of Ezekiel and St. John, our first Christian symbolists depicted the ox and the other three animals, eagle, lion, and man, as hieroglyphs of Jesus Christ (Fig. 7). Other French authors of the Middle Ages who fell heir to their way of thinking are equally explicit on this point: "Taurus, Christus," writes Rabanus Maurus[14]; and after him, St. Bruno d'Asti[15] and St. Yves of Chartres[16] say the same thing. Thus, they saw the ox as the symbol of the redeeming victim which through the complete outpouring of its blood assured the purification of our race and its reconciliation with justice from above. But another less well-known symbolism related the symbolic figure of the ox to the personage of Christ. A close study of the iconography of Jesus Christ in the first thirteen centuries shows that, among many others, there were two dominating ideas that had a considerable influence: one portrays him as the source and hearth of light, and the other as those of life: he is the illuminating Word, the Word which shed the first light onto the chaos of the world[17], the Word whose doctrine illuminates souls; he is also the Word which is the creator of life, and the First Principle whose fertilizing strength spreads and perpetuates physical life in the natural order on earth[18], and whose grace produces spiritual life in the supernatural order. Thus, from him, the initial source, emerges the sensible life of the body and the suprasensible life of the soul.

Fig. 7 The Bull of Ezekiel's vision (from Raphael's painting).

This mystical conception was echoed in the liturgy, in sacred literature and art, and also in Christian symbolism, in the form of the ox, the ram, and the stag.

Here perhaps we should call to mind the Spanish bullfight, which, however imperfectly, compares the bull to the Redeemer marching towards death. In tauromachy, the "Veronica pass" which consists of holding the cape in front of the bull's face, is named for the compassionate woman, in the legend which has sprung up around what was told in the gospel, who offered her veil to the exhausted Savior[19].

It was in compositions of an apocalyptic nature, above all,

that the bull lent his image to Satan and personified the works of hell: a medieval manuscript, for example, shows us Satan in the form of a being with the head of a lion, the body and horns of a bull, bat wings and eagle's claws[20]; in Veniers, near Loudun, a church cornice from the end of the Roman period shows a variation of the basilisk: an ox with the head of a cock. In a superb fourteenth-century book from Count Ashburnham's collection[21], the Babylonian god Bel is represented with a head that is half human, half ox-like, a hairy torso, and the legs of a vulture (Fig. 8).

Fig. 8 The god Bel on the 14th-century Ashburnham manuscript.

This last creation of the Near Eastern imagination coincides, curiously enough, with the sacred iconography of Babylonia in the time of Daniel; the cylindrical seals of other Chaldean documents of this period show us in fact the monster Eabani and other manifestations of evil in the form of horned men with the hindquarters of oxen. Unrelated to this type of iconography, the representations of sea oxen, or dragonlike oxen with snakelike or fish-shaped bodies, are also images of evil monsters which are living vehicles of the Evil Spirit (Fig. 9). To the Ammonites, the Moabites, the Canaanites and their neighbors, Molech was an evil god represented as having a human body with a bull's head. Some of his statues, made of bronze, were colossal and hollow, and his cult ordained that in certain circumstances they should be filled with children, before setting fire to the logs surrounding them and heating the statues to a glowing red. In

Fig. 9 The bull of the sea, from a fresco in the Roman catacombs.

spite of the prohibition of Leviticus: "Thou shalt not let any of thy seed pass through the fire to Molech[22]," it was by subscribing to this abominable cult that Solomon and Manasseh, kings of Israel[23], committed a sin that brought about the apostasy of the Israelites, until Josiah put an end to these horrors.

Long before our era, Aegean mythology had for its own part imagined the Minotaur, a being strangely resembling the ox-headed monsters of Chaldea. Like them, this creature represented the antithesis of the cherubim, the divine winged oxen with human faces of Assyria, in which we can see images of the "divine power uniting material force with intelligence[24]." According to Homer, Minos, king of Crete, was the son of Jupiter and the nymph Europa, but he did not fulfil his obligations to the divine powers. For this, Poseidon punished him by inspiring in his wife, Pasiphaë, a monstrous passion for the miraculous bull which he had failed to sacrifice to the gods. From this unnatural union there was born the Minotaur, who had the head of an ox and the body of a giant man, like the Eabani of the Chaldeans and Baal of the Syro-Phoenicians. The Minotaur became the curse of the island of Crete, and Minos had him locked up in the Labyrinth of Knossos where the Greeks, conquered by the king of Crete, were required periodically to bring him seven boys and seven girls to devour. Finally, the Greek hero Theseus, with the help of the enamored Ariadne, killed the Minotaur, thus delivering his country from the hateful tribute.

Lanoë-Villène sees in the story of the Minotaur a very ancient solar myth[25], and Glotz, in accordance with one of the principal symbolic characteristics of the bull as sire and fertilizer of the herd, presents the Minotaur as the Cretan god of virile strength. "He demanded victims, like all divinities," he wrote, "but it is not the mythology of the Cretans, it is the legend of foreign peoples who made out of him a god hungry for human blood[26]."

Nevertheless, the Cretan monster has continued to be accepted as one of the representations of the Evil Spirit, and Theseus, his conqueror, who delivered Greece from his oppression, was sometimes likened by Christian teachers to Christ, the liberator of souls.

NOTES

Title Figure: The Winged Bull, from the Hortus Sanitatis, *16th century.*

1. Leviticus 17:11.
2. *Inscriptions in hieratic characters.* Plate XXVI.
3. See Schliemann, pp. 69 and 71.
4. Cf. H. Breuil, "Le Bison et le Taureau Celeste Chaldéen" in *Revue Archéolog.*, 4th series T. XIII (1909), p. 250.
5. Exodus 25:20.
6. I Kings 6:23.
7. From Guirond, "Mythologie Assyro-babylonienne" in *Mythologie Larousse*, p. 53.
8. Magnien, "Notes sur l'antique théologie des Grecs," p. 11 & 14, in *L'Acropole*, Jan.-June, July-Dec., 1929.
9. Prudentius, *Peri-Steph. X*, 1011.
10. Paul Achard, *Le Vrai Visage de l'Afrique*, 1931.
11. Alex Aymé, *Une Française au Laos*, 1932.
12. Cf. P. Pierret, *Panth. Egyptien.*
13. Cf. Pomponius Mela, *De Situ orbis*, I, 9.
14. Rabanus Maurus, *In Genesim*, 49, *De Universo*, VII, 8.
15. Bruno d'Asti (Astensis), *De Novo Mundo.*
16. Yves de Chartres, *Sermo de Convenientia.*
17. Genesis 1:3.

18. Numerous symbols interpreted the same idea: the swastika, the rose, the pomegranate, the pine cone and especially the ram, the stag, and the cock, etc.
19. See H. de Montherlant, *Les Bestiaires*, II.
20. Bibliothèque Nationale, no. 501, 6869.
21. Catalog Joseph Boer, Frankfurt, 1912; ch. LVI, p. 300.
22. Leviticus 18:21.
23. I Kings 11:7 and II Kings 21 and 23.
24. F. Lenormant, *Antiquités de l'Assyrie et de Babylone*, III.
25. Lanoë-Villène, *Le Livre des Symboles*, T. II, pp. 151 et seq.
26. Glotz, *Civilisation Égéenne*, L III, 2, p. 292.

End Figure: Old Greek coin.

THE EAGLE

IN THE TWELFTH century the Archbishop of Tours, Hildebert de Lavardin, wrote the following:

> Christus HOMO, Christus VITULUS, Christus LEO,
> Christus est AVIS, in Christo cuncto notore potes[1].

Christus est AVIS... Christ is a bird. He is in fact portrayed, in Christian symbolism, in the forms of a dove, a pelican, a phoenix, a swan, an ibis, a crane, a stork, and in many other less well-known forms. However, here it is the noblest, the king of birds that we are speaking of, the royal eagle, whose characteristics have struck mankind since the beginning of time and won its admiration.

In his day, Ezekiel saw it like burning coals of fire; and on the solitary island of Patmos, when the eyes of John the Evangelist opened to the infinite horizons of the eternal kingdom, he in his turn gazed upon what the old prophet had only glimpsed. The Eagle and the three other animals appeared distinctly, no longer as lightning flashes along the rugged banks of the Chebar while their wings sounded "like the noise of great waters[2]," but beating those quivering wings, on which flamed thousands of eyes, while the whole firmament hailed the triumphant Lamb.

These visions of Ezekiel[3] and St. John[4] are the principal Christian bases for the symbolism of the eagle, as well as for the lion and the ox; all three were already endowed with the riches of the past.

It is in Central Asia, as well as among the peoples of the near East, that we find the most ancient proven documents on the symbolic value of the eagle. The ancient Hindu religion already used the eagle as the emblem of Vishnu[5], and in the art of Chaldea, the eagle is the noble bird that accompanies the king in the royal images, that tames the lion, and that helps the Chaldean Hercules in his battle with the monsters[6].

The same favored place was given to the eagle in the unusual art of the Hittites of Asia Minor, which is mentioned in the Pentateuch and in the Book of Kings, and whose crude artistic patterns seem to have been drawn from the regions of the Tigris and the Euphrates.

It is especially in the religious art of Syria that the eagle appears with the meanings which Christianity later could appropriately transpose to apply to the Lord Jesus Christ.

Fig. 1 Syrian eagle on a tombstone from Menbidj.

The Syrian eagle and its sacred meanings have been illuminatingly studied by the Belgian professor and savant, Franz Cumont. He says that it is in the region of Hieropolis, the holy city of the great Syrian goddess Atargatis, where the eagle shows itself most frequently on funeral monuments, in the role of transporter of souls "toward the celestial gods[7] (Fig. 1)." Perhaps this vision of the eagle was borrowed by the Syrians—as Cumont believes—from the Babylonians. The fable of Etana, one of their most popular myths, seems, in fact, to bear out this opinion. The eagle having devoured the serpent's young, the serpent, in revenge, is on the point of killing the marauding bird which it has managed to entrap in its coils; but Etana fights the serpent and frees the eagle, who then betakes itself up to heaven where it seizes—although it is unable to keep—the insignia of divine royalty.

This tale, represented in numerous Babylonian works of art, could hardly have been unknown in ancient Syria, since the two countries were in frequent contact. Thus by extension the myth of Etana became the image of the soul and the royal bird became a "psychopomp"; that is to say, it was seen as the carrier, the vehicle, bearing blessed souls to their celestial source; for, in accordance with Semitic beliefs, souls came to earth from the Sun and had to return to it after the death of the body. The Syrians must have been all the more willing to accept this symbolism since for them the eagle was already the bird of the sun.

Like the Egyptians, the ancient peoples of Assyria and Chaldea depicted the sun most often in the form of a disc with two outstretched wings, two great eagle wings; and as the Syrians were descendants of the ancient peoples of Assyria and Chaldea, it seems very likely that this is the source of the idea behind the frequent carvings of the eagle on the burial stones of their dead; the soaring eagle, that is, portrayed the movement of the soul's departure from earth into space.

We also find, in the very ancient art of Sumer, the eagle with a lion's head which thus unites the sovereignties of both earth and sky. The recent excavations made by Tello have provided us with several examples of this lion-headed eagle.

In Phoenicia, the god Melkarth, of Tyre, immolated himself for mankind on a funeral pyre, where, metamorphosed into an eagle, he flew off into the sky, the conqueror of death[8].

The Greeks, and then later the Romans when they came to Syria, borrowed from the peoples of this region the oriental belief that the sacred eagle carried souls to the kingdom of the gods; and this is no doubt the reason why, in Greece and in Rome, the eagle became the bird of Zeus and Jupiter. It also explains its presence on Plato's tomb[9], and why a live bird was placed on the summit of the funeral pyre that was erected in Tarsus in honor of Sandan-Heracles, the protector of the city who is portrayed on its coins. From there also stems the special liturgy of the Apotheosis, in the Rome of the Caesars who had been judged worthy of the honor of divinization. From the summit of an immense funeral pyre, built in the shape of a pyramid, which was to consume the body or its effigy, an eagle was made to escape, charged with carrying the soul of the newly deified being in its flight towards heaven[10] (Fig. 2). This rite was not restricted to royalty, and was also used for numerous other individuals.

Fig. 2 Old cameo showing the apotheosis of a Caesar.

The priceless treasure recently discovered in Montalban in Oaxaca, Mexico, along with marvelous objects of gold and precious stones, contains beautiful eagles of gold and jade from very ancient times. These prove that in their time, on the other side of the world which was then unknown to our continent, the eagle had evoked in the human spirit the same thoughts and feelings that it had wakened in our European and Asian ancestors[11].

The establishment of Christianity was followed closely by the creation of its liturgy and symbolism, and in the latter, the eagle became an excellent figure to represent Christ, to whom were applied the words of Jeremiah: "Behold, he shall come up and fly as the eagle, and spread his wings over Bozrah: and at that day shall the heart of the mighty men of Edom be as the heart of a woman in her pangs[12]."

Fig. 3 Christian lamp from Carthage.

The use of the eagle as a symbol of divine power was widespread. Emblem of imperial Rome's triumph and world-wide domination, it also became, for the Christians, following the conversion of Constantine and the liberating edict of 314, the emblem of the triumph of the Christian religion over persecution and of its universal diffusion.

This is probably the significance of the representation of the eagle on Christian lamps in the fourth century in Carthage[13] (Fig. 3) and elsewhere, and also on the beautiful fragment of a sarcophagus at Arles where the eagle appears, its wings in gliding flight, and on its breast a crown in the center of which one can still see half of a "Chrismon" with the I and the X superimposed[14].

The eagle, bird of the sun and conductor of souls to heaven, was to the ancient peoples also the carrier of celestial fire and light. The Greeks, and subsequently the Romans, represented it holding in its claws the lightning bolts of Zeus-Jupiter; the Egyptians and the Assyrians gave its wings to the solar disc. It was believed that the eagle and the falcon were the only creatures that could stare fixedly into the sun's intense light, and that the eagle tested the legitimacy of its young by making them look straight into it from the moment of their birth, throwing out of its nest the eaglet whose eyes blinked under the blinding rays[15] (Fig. 4). The eagle plays with lightning bolts, said the ancient poets, when the most terrible outbreaks of thunder and lightning make all other living beings tremble; and it is no doubt for this reason that the ancient Greeks nailed eagles above their doors, in order to protect themselves from evil forces and from being struck by lightning[16], which, they believed, never touched this bird[17].

Fig. 4 Eagle presenting to the sun a bad eaglet that turns away its head. 13th-century sculpture from Strasbourg Cathedral.

The symbolism of Christ as fire and light penetrated the most ancient Christian liturgy.

The tales of the Orient, which show us the eagle rising towards the sun, into the abode of the gods, said that the bird came so close to the divine star that in its old age its feathers became charred, and its flesh dried up almost completely; but once it returned to the earth, it plunged itself three times in the spring water of a fountain and emerged regenerated, with all the youthfulness of its early years. This fable was already very old when the Church was born, since David was inspired by it: "Bless the Lord," he wrote, "who satisfieth thy mouth with good things; so that thy youth is renewed like the eagle's[18]."

Because of the regeneration that the eagle found in the life-giving fountain, the ancient Orientals made it the emblem not of the resurrection of the body, but of the immortality of the soul, and this was one of the roles in which it was adopted by the Syrians, as the protective spirit of their tombs[19].

The Egyptian eagle sometimes appears carrying in its beak the "Cross of Life," and in the West also the eagle and the idea of life were related. Thus it is that a stone called "the eagle's stone," an iron-oxide geode which encloses a semi-liquid center, was a much sought after talisman. In his *Hortus Sanitatis*, Joannes de Cuba, an author of the latter part of the fifteenth century, wrote that the eagle takes this stone into its nest because it counteracts the great heat that the bird generates to the point of endangering its own eggs; the stone can conquer the heat even of fire[20]. Other ancient authors attributed a solar origin to these stones. Those who believed that they possessed them used to place them in contact with women in labor to aid their delivery.

We have seen in the previous study of the lion that it was an emblem of royalty and the Resurrection of Christ, but also an emblem of Satan the Antichrist, because, according to St. Peter, it is the beast of prey who roars and seeks to devour. The eagle also, image of Christ in many ways, was taken to represent Satan, because it is not only the noble and magnificent bird but also the rapacious destroyer; under this aspect Deuteronomy had already categorized it among the impure beasts, whose flesh the Israelites were not to eat[21].

We know that one of the first emblems chosen to represent Christ was the fish which, by analogy, was taken as the image of the faithful as well. It was in this role that it was associated with the eagle, giving the latter its satanic meaning: the eagle was shown trampling with its talons a fish which it often struck with its beak. It is a fact, it seems, that the eagle dives at times from the heights of the sky on fish that sleep trustingly, near the surface of the water, and carries them off to eat its fill. In the fifteenth century Joannes de Cuba describes the eagle thus: "He has so sharp a vision that from the air, where he is so high he can barely be seen, he spies the little fish swimming in the sea and lets himself fall in like a stone, and takes the fish and carries it to the shore to eat it . . . [22] (Fig. 5)" So the devil does with the soul.

Fig. 5 Baked clay of the Merovingian epoch, in the Musée des Antiquaires de l'Ouest, Poitiers.

Elsewhere in the Christian works of art, the eagle captures a hare, or catches in its claws a young lamb.

A few of the Church fathers have tried to explain away the carnivorous actions of the eagle: when it falls from the clouds like lightning on the fish of the tranquil waters, say the Saints

Bruno d'Asti, Isidore, and Anselm, it is the image of the Savior, fisherman of souls, who takes them from the earth to elevate to heaven. But this kindly interpretation has found little response, and the devouring eagle has remained the image of our relentless enemy.

NOTES

Title Figure: Stylized eagle from the Hortus Sanitatis.

1. De Lavardin, *Opera*, p. 1318.
2. Ezekiel 1:24.
3. Ezekiel 1:5-27.
4. Revelation 4:6-9.
5. Guénon, *L'Ésotérisme de Dante*, p. 25.
6. Mâle, *L'Art religieux* (2), p. 350.
7. Cumont, "L'Aigle funéraire des Syriens et l'apothéose des empereurs," in *Revue Historique des Religions*. T. LVII, No. 2, year 1910, pp. 120-164.
8. See Vellay, *Le culte d'Adonis-Thammouz*, p. 168.
9. Diogenes Laertius, IV, 44.
10. Cf. Iamblichus, *De Mysteriis*, v, 12.
11. See *Excelsior*, March 21, 1932.
12. Jeremiah 49:22.
13. Cf. R. P. Delattre, "Lampes chrétiennes de Carthage," in *Revue d'Art Chrétien*, 1890, p. 48, engraving No. 288, and *Symboles Eucharistiques de Carthage* (1930), pp. 62-65.
14. Cf. Leclercq and Marron, *Dictionnaire*. T. V, vol. I, col. 2,455. No. 4,704.
15. See Pliny, *Natural History*, Book X, 3.
16. Cf. Reinach, Académie des Inscriptions, March 4, 1907.
17. Cf. Pliny, *op. cit.*, Book II, 56.
18. Psalms 103:1-5.
19. Cumont, *op. cit.*, p. 145.
20. Joannes de Cuba, *Hortus Sanitatis*, II, Part III, "Des Pierres," X.
21. Deuteronomy 14:12.
22. Joannes de Cuba, *op. cit.*, Part II, "Des Oyseaux."

End Figure: 12th-century capital at St. Martin de Nevers.

THE MAN

THE SOUL OF Christ was joined on earth with a human body which suffered and died on Calvary, and in whose likeness artists from every Christian era have shown him, in picturing the events of his terrestrial life. But *symbolically* he is represented only in the conventional form attributed to the angel, of a winged man (Fig. 1).

Fig. 1 12th-century sculpture of angel at St. Benigne in Dijon.

The beneficent spirits had already been given this form in Chaldean art and in the art of ancient Greece long before our era. Primitive Christian art adopted it as a convention to represent the angels who, in the Bible, sometimes manifest themselves as handsome young men[1]—and also, sometimes, represent the Christ taken as *Aggelos*, as "Angel": that is to say, as "the one sent," a messenger from the Father, and the bringer of salvation.

We shall see this human body and its wings in the Tetramorph which, like Ezekiel's animals, unites the four faces in one image. The Tetramorph, evoking for the Christian the four Evangelists, represents the "good news," the doctrine unknown till then that Christ brought to the world, and refers to his angelic character as the Father's messenger.

Commentators on the sacred books began very early to designate the angels as manifestations of the divine Word, which Christ was to represent in the course of the coming ages. In the Bible, it is the angels who transmit the word of God to humans—for example, those who appeared to Abraham[2], to Jacob[3], and to Moses in the burning bush[4]; it was the angel of the Lord also who comforted the young Hebrews in the fiery furnace of Babylon[5]. The commentators likened the angel of the Lord to the horseman whom Zechariah saw standing among the myrtle trees[6], and the angel in the Book of Judges who is called "wonderful." It is always the angel of the Lord, who is different from Michael, Gabriel, Raphael, and Uriel: it is the Angel-Word of the beginning of things, who was "with God, and . . . was God," according to the words of St. John[7].

Fig. 2 Center of a small altar cross of the Middle Ages.

Sometimes artists became the interpreters[8] of these theological opinions and gave Christ the conventional appearance of the angel adopted by their era. At other times they substituted Jesus directly for the biblical angel: this was the case with Nicolas Froment, who in his beautiful fifteenth-century painting of the burning bush, in the Cathedral of Aix-en-Provence, placed the Savior in the midst of the flames. Sometimes he even wears wings like the angels, as we see him on the central medallion of an altar cross of medieval workmanship (Fig. 2).

This is not the place for a detailed study of the diverse human forms which Christian art chose to represent angels, and occasionally Jesus Christ as the supreme Angel; let us say only that in the first Christian centuries, the orthodox Catholics as well as the Gnostics showed angels with human bodies dressed in girdled robes and equipped with a pair of bird's wings. The middle of the first millenary was sometimes more idealistic, and in the sixth century, angels appear on a miniature of *Kosmas Indicopleustes*, formed by a human face carried by several pairs of elegantly arranged wings (Fig. 3). During the Romanesque era, western medieval art depicted them in many ways, all of them hieratic and often with multiple wings. In the latter part of the Middle Ages the angel was further humanized, and the marvelous spirits painted by Fra Angelico are radiant apparitions of the most delightfully idealized human type.

Fig. 3 Seraphim of Kosmas Indicopleustes; *6th century.*

At the same time, the custom of portraying St. Michael in the form of a knight in armor caused the representation, at times, of anonymous angels also in war dress, considering angels as the militia of God's celestial armies. At Ewelme in Oxfordshire, the artist who decorated the tomb of the Duchess of Suffolk at the end of the fifteenth century surrounded it with alternating angel-priests and angel-knights, the latter armed from head to toe and carrying great shields; all with folded wings[9].

Fig. 4 Angel from a 13th-century miniature, representing the nine angelic choirs comprised of nine groups of three.

The last three centuries of the Middle Ages saw the adoption of a more immaterial form which reduced the angel to the human face alone, framed by two wings, a very ethereal figure which through the suppression of the body and limbs likens the angel to the "Bird of Paradise" of the symbolists of that time. This creation, still timid and rare in the thirteenth century (Fig. 4) was frequently employed by the end of the fifteenth, as for example on the beautiful angelic circle which surrounds the choir in the church of St. Severin in Paris; but this elevated type was soon lowered by the very earthy use made of it by the Renaissance, which applied it to Eros, or profane love.

But three parts of the human body, the hand, the heart, and the tongue, have been used separately by symbolists to represent the power of the world's redeemer, his love, and the word through which he communicated the "excellent doctrine" to mankind.

Fig. 5 Prehistoric rock paintings in the cave of the Cabreret.

The symbol of the hand is one of those which have been passed down through the millennia since the beginning of time. When used as the sign of divinity, it represented everywhere supreme sovereignty and creative energy, irresistible force, the power of command, of justice and direction, of protection, help, and munificence. Everywhere, when it represented man's soul in the accomplishment of his religious duties, it made the pious gestures of adoration, acclaim, and invocation, fulfilling the requirements of homage and prayer.

Already from the beginning of the Quaternary era, when human beings lived in caverns or dark shelters, in the caves of the Font de Gaume, Gargas, and Cabreret, for example, the outstretched hand is raised palm outwards, as it is still seen on amulets worn today (Fig. 5).

In Central Asia, from the very beginning of the Brahman cult the hand was the representation of Shiva, either as a right hand holding a tambourine or as a left hand holding up the symbolic antelope or a coiled rope[10]. And since far-off times in China, the rays emanating from the face of the sun-god Amida Avalokiteshvara ended in hands distributing gifts[11]. In Egypt, the hand was the sign of the paternal generosity of

Amon; hands dispensing his grace were also found at the ends of the rays of light that fell from the solar disk[12], and we see it thus in the pure art of temple walls and burial places.

The art of those times reveals that among certain oriental peoples, as among the Egyptians, the posture of adoration is one of kneeling and lifting the open hands to the level of the head[13]. This is the position of the hands of suppliants shown in the little votive statuettes of Asia Minor, as well as the figures standing in front of the solar disk on the great carved boulder of Eflatoun in Lycaonia[14] (Fig. 6).

The hand as a symbol of the divine was also the instrument of sacred gestures in the celebrations of the old Babylonian cults, and "among the hymns which often express sublime feelings in magnificent poetry, one of the most beautiful is the hymn to Ishtar which is entitled 'Prayer of the elevation of the hand[15].'" In ancient Caucasia and the region of the Caspian Sea, as it was elsewhere, the hand was the dual symbol of divine bounty and power and of human supplication; and in ancient Greece, in the cults of all such deities as Aesculapius and Hygeia who dispensed the gift of health, divine aid was symbolized by the succoring hand. The hand appears in Carthage on the steles characterized by the mysterious triangle of

Fig. 6 Monument of Eflatoun, in the region of Iconim.

the goddess Tanit[16] (Fig. 7), and this same area would later be familiar with the talisman so widespread today in all of northern Africa, known as "Fatima's hand" (Fig. 8).

Thus in the whole ancient world, the outstretched hand expressed the presence of divinity, somewhat in the way in which in Brahmanist thought "Vishnu's foot" symbolizes his real presence. On the secular level also in those times the open hand was the sign of loyalty, welcome, good faith, and friendship. Another nonreligious usage is shown in the gold hand of an antique clasp that ends in a serpent's body, and tells us, at least in the language of the exoteric, that one must act cautiously at all times[17] (Fig. 9).

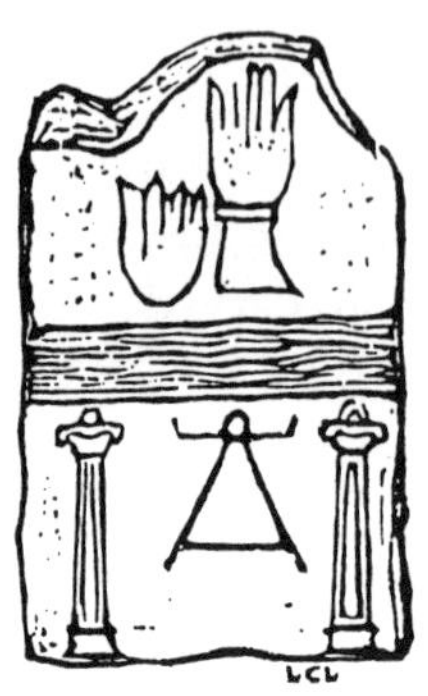

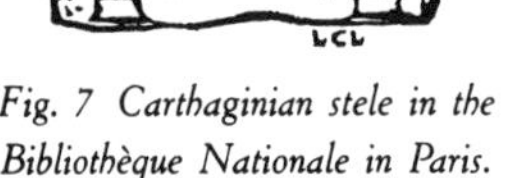

Fig. 7 Carthaginian stele in the Bibliothèque Nationale in Paris.

Fig. 8 Moslem talisman called "Fatima's hand."

Thus, Christian symbolism found that the sign of the hand was honored everywhere by different nations for reasons that the doctrine could easily adopt; so the hand rapidly became one of the symbols used specifically for God the Father and for Christ. As a general rule, when it represents the Son and not the Father, the hand is placed on a cross, between alpha and omega (Fig. 10), or carries a cruciform nimbus (Fig. 11), or appears in some other context that leaves no question of its meaning. There were few exceptions to this rule.

According to St. Augustine and the Fathers of the Church, it was the left hand that the early symbolists consecrated as standing preeminently for the justice of the Christ-King,

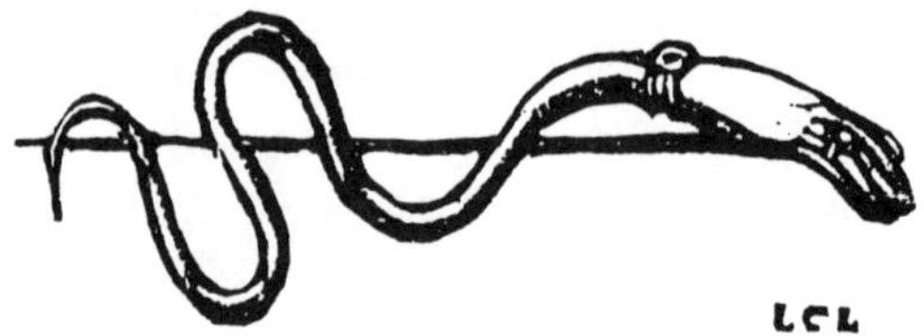

Fig. 9 Antique gold clasp.

whereas the right was the image of his mercy, his goodness, and his generosity. Certain ancient representations show him with the right hand, the "Hand of Mercy," larger than the left, to show that in the Savior's heart mercy is more than justice. In a church in the Hautes-Pyrénées, St. Peter is portrayed in the same manner, no doubt as representing the Catholic Church.

Fig. 10 Christ's blessing hand, between alpha and omega, engraved on a 13th-century funerary medal.

Fig. 11 The hand of Christ, 12th-century miniature in the Bibliothèque Nationale.

It was this divinely rescuing hand that Constantine called upon when, after his conversion, he ordered the striking of new coins. As on those he had issued previously, he was portrayed riding in a chariot drawn by four horses into the heavens; only on the later coins he raises a hand towards another Hand which reaches down to him from the sky, and which can only be the hand of Christ whose divinity he had just recognized[18].

Fig. 12 The caressing hand, from a 4th- or 5th-century tomb.

The laying on of hands is one of the oldest gestures that we know. In Genesis, we see Isaac laying his hands on his sons Esau and Jacob, and Egyptian monuments show us figures in analogous postures. This imposition of the hand or of both hands was also part of a great number of initiations into the mysteries of pre-Christian cults in Asia, Europe, and Africa. In the gospels Jesus is constantly placing his hands on someone to bless and heal (Fig. 12). Following the example of their master after he had left them, the apostles continued the laying on of hands[19], and this custom entered into the first liturgy of the sacraments and into the blessing ceremonies[20]. The origin of this rite seems to be based on an invisible physical reality which has been more or less well-known since the early days of human civilizations, which is that a considerable quantity of magnetic fluid escapes through the fingers of the outstretched hand. The Ancients even then had the firm faith that after having raised their hands to heaven to call and receive the divine influx, it was then concentrated and in turn communicated to others by placing their outstretched fingers on their heads. This divine influx was shown by Christian iconography as light rays coming from the hand (Fig. 13).

The hand of Christ is sometimes shown as blessing and at others as the symbol of his omnipotence and of the universality of his empire. It holds then in its palm the seven apocalyptic stars[21], as images of the immensities of the firmament (Fig. 14), or the globe of the world surmounted by the cross. In this role, the Lord's hand is rarely separated from the whole image of his person. The iconographic image pictured in Figure 14 shows the seven stars together as fire flowers within the circumference of the circle of the firmament. It is borrowed from an illumination in a twelfth-century manuscript[22].

The frequent saying in Christian literature: *Digitus Dei est hic*: "the finger of God is here," refers as often to Christ as it does to the Father. Ordinarily the finger thus described does

Fig. 13 The hand of Christ on a 13th-century tryptich in Nôtre Dame de Chartres.

Fig. 14 The hand of Christ upholding the seven stars.

not imply the idea of benediction but rather that of action and power. In iconography, the hand which represents this *Digitus Dei est hic* of the sacred writings must be a right hand with only the index finger extended, the other fingers being folded (as in the pointing hand), because the extension of the index finger alone is the natural gesture of imperative command allowed only to the one in authority.

Among all the ancient peoples whose civilizations are known to us, especially those of Asia, Europe, and North Africa, and up to modern times, the image of the heart is used much more as the ideogram for knowing, for reasoning, and for understanding, than for affective or physical love[23]. The sages of Egypt affirmed that the heart is the source of all that man knows, and all that he can do; and from it, they said, human activity receives its inspirations and its force in the realm of thought as well as in that of physical action.

Fig. 15 The heart and truth weighed in the scales of judgment.

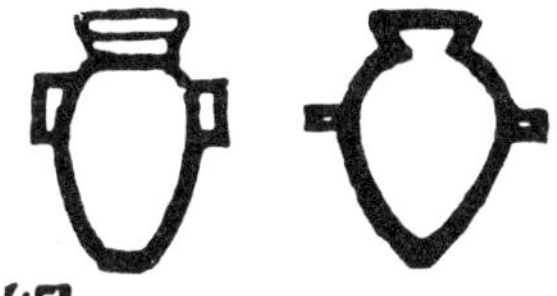

Fig. 16 The vase, hieroglyph for heart.

The whole point of view of ancient times, both in the Orient and Occident, was summed up by Pliny in the words: "Inside itself, the heart in its winding passages provides the first home of the soul and the blood . . . there the Intelligence resides[24]." Starting with such concepts, the religious thought of the ancient Egyptians quite naturally also made the heart of the supreme God the seat and source of divine perfections. And consequently we see old texts expressly evoking the divine Heart. Ramses II, after being ill-supported by his officers in a battle, ended his reproaches to them by saying: "I will no longer carry you in my heart"[25] (Figs. 15 and 16).

In one of the hymns composed by the Pharaoh Amenhotep IV (Akhenaten) and his lovely wife Nefertiti to Aten, the image of the Divinity symbolized by the solar disc, we read in the course of a long text: "Thou hast created the earth in thine heart, when thou wast alone . . . thou hast made the seasons to give birth and growth to all thou hast created . . . thou hast made the distant sky that thou mightest rise up into it and see from there all that thou hast created, thou alone. Thou appearest in the form of the living Aten; thou risest shining, thou goest away and returnest, thou art in my heart. . . .[26]"

The same concept is expressed in the funerary inscription of a priest of Memphis, the text and meaning of which have been established by Maspéro, Breasted, and Erman. From this it appears that the theologians of the Memphis school made a distinction, in the work of the Author of all things, between the role of creative thought, which they called the *action of the heart*, and that of creation's instrument, which they called the *action of the tongue*, the Word[27]. Another theological school that we learn about from the monuments of the time of the Ramses pharaohs (nineteenth dynasty, about 1200 B.C.) expresses a theory according to which God, the supreme God whose nature (literally, name) is mystery, is presented as being formed of three distinct entities which make up a true Triunity: Ptah, Horus, and Thoth. Ptah is the Supreme Person, the perfect intelligence; Horus, according to a belief which was already ancient at that time, is the comprehensive and affective Heart of the divinity, the spirit that animates all of life; Thoth is the Word, the instrument of the divine works.

Ptah is delineated as the Supreme Being, because in a way the whole triad comes from him. According to the evidence mentioned above, he is "He who becomes Heart, he who becomes Tongue."

Horus, the divine Heart, was represented in sacred art in the form of a falcon. From the time of the fourth dynasty, about 2575 to 2465 B.C., he appeared under this symbol; for instance, on the beautiful statue of Chephren in the Cairo museum, the sacred bird leans his heart, his whole body, against the nape of the pharaoh whom he protects and inspires, and whose head he enfolds with his spread wings (Fig. 17). The singular attitude of the falcon god means very much more than just an attendance on the pharaoh, the back of whose neck he covers and warms at the very sensitive spot which neurology calls the "Bridge of Varolius," which puts him into almost immediate contact with the cervical nerve ganglion that certain anatomists have named the "Tree of Life." Could it not be said that by means of this warm touch the divine Bird, symbol of the heart of the deity, in some way fecundates Chephren's spirit in the brain, in that hostelry where, according to the sages of that epoch, the thoughts conceived and born in the heart stay a while before they can be sent out into the world by the movement of the tongue and the opening of the lips, in the utterance of words?

Fig. 17 The pharaoh Chephren and the divine Falcon.

The sublime hymn in honor of the eternal Word with which St. John begins his Gospel has been inscribed in the Christian liturgy since its inception and forever after: "In the beginning was the Word, and the Word was with God, and the Word was God. . . . All things were made by him . . . In him was life; and the life was the light of men . . . . That was the true light, which lighteth every man that cometh into the world. . . . And the Word was made flesh, and dwelt among us . . . And of his fullness have all we received. . . .[28]" At the close of each celebration of the Mass, the church acclaims and recalls the gifts of the Word, and its dues.

In symbolic terms, it is the human tongue that represents this eternal Word, the Christ; but in fact, in literature as well as in art, the tongue is identified with the lips which are more visible, more expressive, even more important because they form the chief gate of the breath, which is aspiration and expiration; they call forth or put a stop to this factor that is necessary to life. Only through them can pass exhalations charged with the particular influences that have such specific roles in various liturgies, as well as in magic. The Catholic Church sanctifies breathing from the first moments of the baptismal liturgy[29], and introduces it into her exorcisms; and in the rites of Holy Saturday, the celebrant begins by breathing three times on the water that he blesses in the name of God, to whom he says: *Tu has simplices aquas tuo ore benedicito*: "Thou thyself, O God, with thy mouth bless these pure waters." Then he calls upon Virtue, the power from on high, and again breathes three times on the water, adding: "May the Virtue of the Holy Ghost make this water fruitful and give it the power to regenerate[30]."

Here, the lips of the priest, by means of words and breath, can take the place of the divine mouth and breathing whose image and interpreters they are. This same role devolves upon them when they pronounce the sacramental words of the consecration of the bread and wine in the canon of the Mass: "This is my Body; this is my Blood."

In the human mouth, the lips guard the door, for they stop the breath or let it pass as they do speech. Acting with the tongue and the vocal cords, it is they who give the word its form, its clarity, its beauty, its power to act. It is they who seal the vows of love or faith with the kiss of loyalty, giving them their supreme consecration; and when they betray, an echo is heard of Gethsemane: "Forthwith he [Judas] came to Jesus, and said, Hail, master; and kissed him[31]."

There are many passages in the scriptures that praise pure lips. David prayed that his might be opened by the Lord himself, so that he might praise him fittingly[32]; and he attributes the privilege of perfect praise to the lips of innocent children: *Ex ore infantium et lactentium perfecisti laudem*: "Out of the mouth of infants and of sucklings thou hast perfected praise[33]." Our illuminators of the first fifteen centuries of the Christian era, especially in Byzantium and the Orient[34], reproduced a number of times the scene where Yahweh's seraphim place a burning coal from the altar on the lips of the prophet Isaiah, saying to him: "Lo, this hath touched thy lips; and thine iniquity is taken away[35] (Fig. 18)."

Fig. 18 Seraphim purifying Isaiah's lips with fire, 10th century.

It is the divine Word, expressing itself through human lips, that our forefathers honored by giving the name *Chrysostom*, "golden mouth," to John, holy bishop of Constantinople, who lived in the fourth century, and that of *Chrysologus*, "golden word," to St. Peter, archbishop of Ravenna, a century later.

To symbolize Jesus Christ under the aspect of the divine Word, the artists of antiquity sometimes made use of animal and other forms that had been chosen by the writers of Scripture: the lion roaring in the desert, the bellowing bull in the pasture, the eagle crying in the cloud, the swan singing its final song, the cock saluting the dawning day, the nightingale's nocturnal melodies—and also, the thunder that follows lightning, and the trumpet, the conch, and the bell, which call and command. The anatomical shape of the tongue does not lend itself at all to such images, so in most cases, when artists have tried to show the Savior as the Word, they have done so, following the text of the Apocalypse, with a sword blade between the lips: "And out of his mouth goeth a sharp sword; that with it he should smite the nations[36]." The word strikes and penetrates like a sword. Few artists have risked using the image of the tongue itself, and the results of their daring have not been happy. About the end of the fifteenth century the symbolists of *L'Estoile Internelle* showed it as a sort of oval form inscribed with a V, probably alluding to the "lingual V" formed by the thick, chalice-shaped papillae on the human tongue, and to the initial letter of the accompanying inscription, taken from St. John: *Verbum caro factum est:* "The Word was made flesh[37] (Fig. 19)." This image is very similar to the wax tongues which mothers offer at the tomb of St. Radegund in Poitiers so that their children may speak readily and clearly.

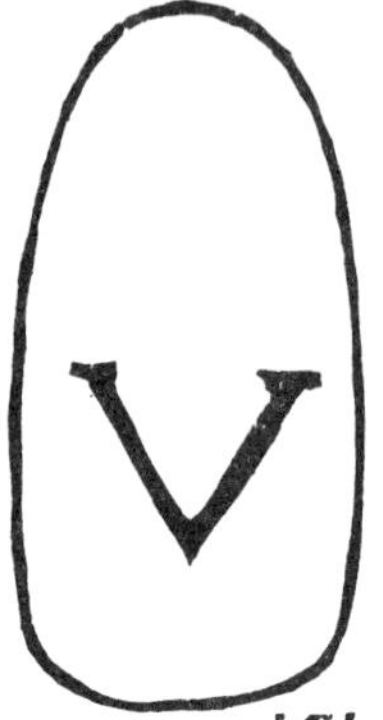

Fig. 19 The tongue, symbol of the Verbe, *the divine Word.*

The Kabbalah and several hermetic groups of the Middle Ages preferred to make use, for their initiates, of the Hebrew letter *yod* reversed and doubled—an arrangement which produces a form quite like that of human lips (Figs. 20 and 21). The letter *yod* has always been considered a divine symbol, here applied to the Eternal Word. "*Yod*," said René Guénon, "besides being the first letter of the Tetragrammaton, constitutes in itself a divine name, whether alone or repeated three times[38]." St. Jerome says that *yod* is "the symbol of the principle of goodness[39]."

Fig. 20 The Hebrew yod *and two pairs of* yods *reversed in the form of lips.*

Fig. 21 The human face with lips formed by two yods.

The two *yods* together mirror the "heraldic" or "gliding flight" made by two wings outstretched and joined together; and this resemblance reinforces the symbolic idea, for the Word flies with the power and speed of the most agile spirit. Like the tongue, the "flight" created by the two *yods* put together sometimes stands for the Holy Ghost—when pictured above the terrestrial sphere, for example, or above the image

Fig. 22 Tongues of fire coming as straight rays from the Holy Spirit; a 14th-century diptych from the Vatican.

of the sea. Then it evokes the creating and fecundating Spirit which, the Bible says, moved over the first waters among the shadows covering the abyss, "in the beginning," when "God created the heaven and the earth[40]."

The description of the descent of the Holy Ghost upon the Apostles in the feast of Pentecost was naturally symbolized by tongues of flame. The sacred text tells how, when the Apostles were assembled, "there appeared unto them cloven tongues, like as of fire, and it sat upon each of them. And they were all filled with the Holy Ghost, and began to speak with other tongues, as the Spirit gave them utterance[41]." Artists of the Middle Ages represented the fiery tongues, in which dwelt the Holy Spirit, by straight rays coming from the hand of the All-Powerful or from the beak of the divine bird[42]. Sometimes the flames undulate like blazing swords that spring from a cloud or from the beak of the holy dove[43] (Fig. 22). With the dawning of the Renaissance, artists gave these tongues the form of fiery drops or tears placed on the Apostles' brows, something like the flames that the illuminators and the even earlier painters—the Byzantines, for instance[44]—put on the brows of certain angels, or on those of some of the ideal personifications of great virtues, such as Giotto's Charity[45].

At about this same time another symbol was added, that of the inner fruit, the edible nut, of the almond tree, whose shape is like that of the human tongue. Like the tongues of fire, this symbol referred to the gift of tongues that the Apostles received at Pentecost. These tongues of fire which descended upon the Apostles only after Christ's death seem not to refer to him; however, it must be remembered that he had said "But the Comforter, which is the Holy Ghost, whom the Father will send in my name, he shall teach you all things. . . .[46]"

Truly the best and worst of all things, as Aesop says, is the human tongue. The spirit of the old Phrygian fabulist still lends itself to the game of contraries so dear to former symbolists. We have just seen how the word of salvation came to

Fig. 23 The Holy Spirit casting undulating tongues of flame on the Apostles.

us by the tongue and lips of Christ; nevertheless, speaking in the name of the teacher of the whole world, his disciple St. James affirms that "the tongue is a fire, a world of iniquity[47]." Under this aspect it symbolizes the Evil Spirit; and Christian symbolists then show it as forked like that of a serpent or headed with an arrow or harpoon, a shape they attribute to the tongues of dragons. It is supposed to wound like a dart or to carry a mortal poison, for evil speech always causes pain or corruption.

From the eleventh to the sixteenth centuries, medieval sculpture often placed in the symbolic decoration of churches the faces of men, women, or devils, exhibiting monstrous tongues. A Satan on the towers of Notre Dame de Paris sticks out a long, pointed tongue over the city; one of the devils on the Cathedral at Bourges has one that is wide and pendulous. At Santa Maria Formosa de Venise, at Rheims, strange figures loll out their tongues to one side. Very different feelings are expressed by these hideous faces. We read in them despondency or breathless anguish, as the case may be, and often mockery and scorn, as at Magdalen College at Oxford. Elsewhere the protruding tongue may be the symbol of greed or even of the most repugnant lust[48].

Yet, in its other aspect, the tongue represents the *Logos*, the creative Word, which has remained above the world since its beginning like a gliding bird, if one may so describe it, to ensure the continuation of life, its perpetual fecundation, and to inspire the wise. It is in fact by means of it that chosen souls lift themselves as far as it is possible to go toward the unknowable mysteries, which they know to be the necessary cloak in which divinity must hide itself from our eyes while we live on earth.

NOTES

Title Figure: The blessing hand; La Reau Abbey in Poitou.

1. Genesis 18, 19, passim.
2. *Ibid.* 22:12; cf. Tertullian, *De carne Christi*, V.

3. *Ibid.* 31:11.
4. Exodus 3:2.
5. Daniel 3:24-28.
6. Zechariah 1:8-11.
7. St. John 1:1-3.
8. Didron, *Histoire de Dieu*, and de Saint Laurent, *Guide*, T. III, p. 270, fig. 30.
9. Cf. P. Biver and F. Howard, "Les chantry-chapels anglaises," in *Bulletin Monumental*, T. LXXII, (1908), p. 338, No. 220.
10. Cf. Jouveau-Dubreuil, *Archéologie*, T. II, p. 20, fig. 3.
11. Cf. Doré, *Recherches*, Part II, T. VI, p. 150.
12. Tomb at El-Amarna. Cf. E. Amélineau, "Histoire de la sépulture et des funérailles dans l'ancienne Égypte," in *Annales du Musée Guimet*. 1896. T. II, p. 650 and plate C.II.
13. Moret, *Mystères*, IV, p. 200, Pl. VII, 2.
14. *Editor's note*: Now the area around Konya in Turkey.
15. Cf. H. Corat in *Pro Alesia*, XXXVII-XXXVIII (1924), p. 123, fig. 3.
16. Cf. Perrot & Chipiez, *Histoire de l'Art dans l'Antiquité*, p. 325, fig. 168.
17. H. de Montant, *Album de la vie de César*, p. 35.
18. Cf. Cohen. *Médailles impériales*, VIII, p. 318, no. 760; and Eusebius, *Life of Constantine*, IV, 73.
19. Acts 8:17-18; 9:12-17; etc.
20. Leclercq and Marron, *Dictionnaire*, fasc. LXVIII-LXIX, col. 391-413.
21. Revelation 1:16.
22. Cf. de Saint-Laurent, *op. cit.* (see note 8 above), T. IV, p. 463 and *Manuel*, p. 429.
23. Cf. Virey, *La Religion* and Guénon, "La langage secret de Dante et des Fidèles d'Amour," in *Voile d'Isis*, T. XXXIV, (1929), III.
24. Pliny, *Natural History*, Bk. XI, 69.
25. Virey, *op. cit.*, p. 117.
26. Cf. Moret, *Rois et dieux*, p. 64.
27. *Idem.*, *Mystères*, II, "Le Mystère du Verbe Créateur," pp. 103-138.
28. St. John 1, 1-16.
29. Cf. Leclerq, *op. cit.*, T. II, Vol. I, col. 276 and passim.
30. Roman breviary, office for Holy Saturday.
31. St. Matthew 26:49.
32. Psalms 51:15.
33. Psalms 8:2, Douay-Rheims version.
34. See Diehl, *Justinien*, p. 265; also Leclercq, *op. cit.*, fasc. 74-5, col. 1578-80.
35. Isaiah 6:5-7.
36. Revelation 19:15.
37. St. John 1:14.
38. Guénon, *op. cit.* in note 23 above, T. XXXVII, fasc. 147, p. 149.
39. St. Jerome, "Letter to Eusebius," in *Opera*, translated by A. Martin, p. 549.
40. Genesis 1:1.
41. Acts 2:3-4.
42. Cf. de Saint-Laurent, *Manuel*, p. 141, fig. 33.

43. *Ibid.*, p. 142, fig. 34.
44. Cf. *idem*, *Guide*, T. III, p. 279, pl. XIV, 2.
45. *Ibid.*, pl. XXII, 3.
46. St. John 14:26.
47. Epistle of James 3:6.
48. Cf. Dr. P. Fricand-Lebaupin, "La décoration monstrueuse dans l'Art chrétien," in *Autour du Clocher*, T. II, no. 10 (May 1933), pp. 175-178.

End Figure: The Hand of Justice of the French kings, in the Louvre Museum; 12th century.

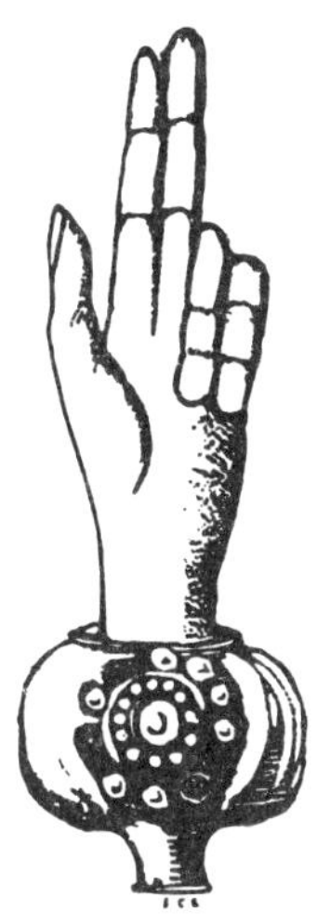

II

DOMESTIC ANIMALS

THE HORN

THE ANCIENT SYMBOLISM of a number of the horned animals—the bull, the ram, the wild sheep, the buck goat, the deer, the oryx, the unicorn—presents a common character in addition to aspects peculiar to each one; the horn expresses active force, strength, domination, the power of command. This is indeed one of the earliest known manifestations of symbolism: in the oldest human societies that we know of in the epochs known as Aurignacian, Chellian, Magdalenian, and Solutrian, the staff of authority, at once magic wand and scepter, was made of reindeer horn, and Déchelette mentions that during the period when the last great dolmens were built "symbolic bulls' horns had an importance in European fetishism equal to that of the axe[1]" with which it is sometimes associated[2] (Fig. 1).

Fig. 1 Animal skull surmounted by sacrificial axe.

A recently-discovered piece of Elamite pottery worked more than three thousand years before our era carries the stylized image of an ibex[3]; the animal's horns are so huge that their exaggeration can only mean to express their symbolic importance (Fig. 2). Much later, the Gauls of

Fig. 2 Symbolic ibex on an Elamite pottery of the 3rd millenary B.C.

western France put the horns of roebuck and beef animals in the tombs of their dead, along with the ritual lamp, and their warriors' helmets were adorned with animal horns[4] (Fig. 3).

Even earlier, in the same symbolic spirit, the potentates of ancient Asia wore horned crowns, as shown on the stele of Naram Sin, king of Assyria. On another monument, this horned crown is called "the crown of domination, characteristic of the divinity[5]." This idea was found everywhere in the ancient world, as well as amulets or talismans shaped like bovine heads, which have already been spoken of[6]. Hermetic signs[7] or schematic figures of horned heads (Fig. 4) are also found, frequently carved on rocks[8] or on the most ancient monuments. Often these drawings suggest a symbolism close to that of the chalice, whose function is to receive, contain, and preserve; by their bowl-shapes, like cross-sections of cups, they seem to indicate the reception of higher influences, divine or magnetic forces coming from above.

Fig. 3 Gallic helmets with horns.

The horned skulls of bovines, of the male goat, and the deer, were associated with the lunar cult, and the Greek poet Nonnus (to quote only one writer) drew attention to the more or less precise similarity in shape between the horns or antlers of these animals and the crescent moon[9]. It is claimed by some with apparent reason that while for the Ancients of the West the bull's horns had a connection with the moon, those of the ram were linked with the sun, because they curled like the solar spirals of the ancient symbolism.

Fig. 4 Prehistoric rock carvings.

In any case, in all the old civilizations, the horn was the

symbol of the active, dominant force; and for the Hebrews, among others, the horn expressed the power both of good and evil. In the Tabernacle of Yahweh, God of Israel, the altar of the burnt offerings was built of acacia wood, and Moses placed at its four corners horns covered with brass[10]; and in the special liturgy of certain sacrificial rites, the priest marked these horns with his finger dipped in the warm blood of the sacrificed victim[11]. Between these brazen horns, prayer mounted with the smoke of the burnt offering toward the All-Powerful whose blessings then descended on the people or on the suppliant. An ancient Mycenaean altar, reproduced by Déchelette, shows the arrangement of the horns on the altars during the two thousand years preceding the Christian era[12] (Fig. 5).

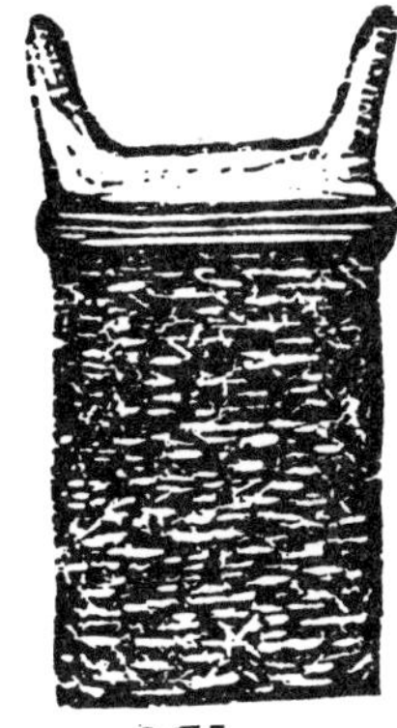

Fig. 5 Ancient horned altar from Mycenae.

It was with a horn filled with consecrated oil, kept in the Tabernacle, that the kings of Israel were anointed[13]. And in the First Book of Kings, in St. Jerome's translation of the Bible, the Vulgate, we read these words: *Dominus judicabit fines terrae, et dabit imperium regi suo, et sublimabit cornu Christi sui*: "The Lord shall judge the ends of the earth, and he shall give empire to his king, and shall exalt the horn of his Christ[14]." In the description of his prophetic visions, Daniel speaks first of a monster armed with ten horns, of which one, the largest, makes war upon the saints of God. Then in another vision a young he-goat fights with a ram; their horns break and immediately grow back again; all these horns are the powers which animate the Spirit of Evil[15]. Christian symbolism, like that of the Hebrew Bible, also accepted the horn as the symbol of the active power of both good and evil. The lid of a tomb in the Abbey of St. Gall shows two armed and horned personages, representing two opposing moral forces: Vice and Virtue in bitter combat[16] (Fig. 6). And often, as in the case of St. Nizier of Troyes,

Fig. 6 Horned combatants from the antiphonary of St. Gall.

medieval Christian art shows the deadly sins as horned personages[17].

Except for rare exceptions, abundance goes hand in hand with power. So this idea of power which the Ancients connected with the animals' horns resulted in the later connection with the symbol of Fortune, the horn of plenty. The origin of this latter, according to Ovid[18], was linked by the Greeks with the goat Amaltheia, whose milk, they said, was given by the two nymphs Adrasteia and Io to nourish the infant Zeus. The supreme god in gratitude placed Amaltheia among the stars, and gave the two nymphs one of her horns which he endowed with the power of filling itself in abundance with all the earth's good gifts.

The Hellenized Egyptians of Alexandria, in the last centuries before our era, borrowed the symbol of the horn of plenty from the Greeks, relating it to the generosity of their divinities; it was in this role that it was attributed to Isis, goddess of all good things. An Alexandrine statuette of baked clay, now in the museum of Lille, shows the "god of the Word" pointing with his finger at his lips, the organs of speech, and holding in his left hand the cornucopia filled with grapes[19]. Another little statue shows the god Amon, the Zeus of Egypt, clothed in a ram's hide and holding the horn of plenty in his hand[20].

In the Far East, the equivalent of the cornucopia has always been and still remains the gourd[21].

Dom Leclercq states that the horn of plenty, which appeared quite often in the art of the early Church, never had any symbolic value there and played a purely decorative role[22]. This is true in most cases; however, when the horn is surmounted with a crown of flowers carrying the monogram of Christ, with a dove supporting it on either side[23] or when it is placed on the cross[24] (Fig. 7), it certainly seems allowable to see in it a symbol of the blessings from on high coming to the soul through the Eucharist. At the end of the fifteenth century, the symbolist of *L'Estoile Internelle* accompanied an image of the cornucopia with words from the Magnificat: "He hath filled the hungry with good things[25]." The horn of plenty, then, the horn of the goat Amaltheia in the charming old fable, becomes an emblem of the munificence of Christ. And it is interesting that the cornucopia of the *Estoile Internelle* contains, among the fruits of the earth, three crosses (Fig. 8) which can only mean that the sufferings of this life are often in themselves providential gifts whose mysterious value is not recognized at once but which generate future happiness. This is precisely the view that Catholic spirituality has always held.

Fig. 7 18th-century horn of plenty.

Fig. 8 The blessings and trials of life in the horn of plenty.

It must be added that since every coin has its other side, the horn of plenty is also a symbolic image of heresy "when it pours forth evil things in the form of scorpions, reptiles, and dragons[26]."

NOTES

Title Figure: The caduceus of peace and prosperity, from a 17th-century etching.

1. Déchelette, *Manuel*, T. I, p. 671.
2. Cf. de Morgan, *L'Humanité préhistorique*, p. 271.
3. From *Le Miroir du Monde*, T. II, 1931, #49, 174.
4. Findings from the excavations of Allaire de Lepinay and L. Charbonneau-Lassay at Châteliers-Châteaumur (Vendée), and in the valley of the Sèvre-Nantaise, 1892-1901.
5. Cf. Tabouis, *Nabuchodonosor*, p. 322.
6. See above, Part I, "The Bull," page 16.
7. There are numerous examples in the Louvre, Salle de la Suziane Mission de Morgan, Salle du Mastaba, etc.
8. See Déchelette, *op. cit.*, T. II, Part I.
9. Nonnus, *Dionysiaca.*
10. Exodus 38:1-2.
11. Leviticus 4:34.
12. Déchelette, *op. cit.*, T. II, Part I, p. 470.
13. I Samuel 16:1, 13; I Kings 1:39.
14. I Kings 2:10, Douay-Rheims version; cf. KJV, I Samuel 2:10.
15. Daniel 7 and 8.
16. See Auguste Demmin, *Guide de l'amateur d'armes et d'armatures anciennes*, p. 178.
17. On the symbolism of the horn, see René Guénon in *Études Traditionelles*, #203, November 1936.
18. Ovid, *Fasti*, V.
19. Cf. Moret, *Mystères*, p. 120, plate II.
20. Cf. L. Heuzey, *Catalogue des figurines de terre cuite au Musée du Louvre*, p. 56, #190.
21. Cf. Dumoulier, *Symboles, emblèmes et accessoires du culte chez les Annamites*, p. 118.
22. Leclercq and Marron, *Dictionnaire*, T. III, vol. II, col. 2,966.
23. *Ibid, loc. cit.*
24. Ancient tabernacle door preserved by the Abbé Bergeron, curé of Le Petit-Boissière, 1895.
25. St. Luke 1:53.
26. Barbier de Montault, *Traité*, T. I, p. 120.

End Figure: Signs relating to the symbolism of the animal skull and the cup.

THE BOVINES

AMONG THE BEEF animals, first of all we have the barnyard ox, the bullock or steer, which is no other than the bull adapted by the countryman to the role of servant for what an old monastic rule calls "the holy work of the hands." Among sacrificial animals, it was the pure victim, which must perforce lead a life of chastity, even as Christ by his very nature did in his life on earth.

Briefly, we can say that the ox was at times taken as the image of the saints; for example, the twelve brass oxen who upheld the immense vat, the "molten sea," which Solomon placed in the temple of Yahweh in Jerusalem[1], were seen by commentators on the sacred books as excellent representations of the twelve apostles who supported the Church in its infancy[2]. The ox was also taken as the image of all those who worked "in the field of God," especially of the teaching pontiffs and the preachers, because of its continence and the strength of its voice (Fig. 1). This symbolism was common enough among literary circles in the Middle Ages to explain how the words of the illustrious Dominican Albertus Magnus, speaking of his silent, hardworking disciple Thomas Aquinas, could be understood by everyone: "Let this ox be; his bellowing shall echo through all the world[3]."

The first Christian commentators and symbolists recognized various symbols of the Redeemer in each different form of bovine offered as sacrifice in the ancient religion of Israel. The calf, image of Christ— "Vitulus Christus," as the Archbishop of Mainz, Rabanus Maurus, wrote in the ninth century[4]—represents the Savior as a victim free from sin, because its youth makes it a virgin animal, and also because the conditions of its sacrifice, specified in the Book of Numbers[5], require that it be without spot or blemish. The representation of the mystic and Christlike calf is not frequent in Christian art, but we nonetheless find some beautiful examples (see Title Figure, p. 61).

Fig. 1 Calf on the façade of the church of the Celle-Briére.

It is generally believed that Christianity from the very beginning forbade its followers to sacrifice animals during a liturgical ceremony. Although this is true in a general sense, the ritual sacrifices of animals persisted for a long time in several countries of the Christian Near East[6]. In Armenia, especially, at least until the time of the Crusades, the bishops and priests gave their blessing to the slaughter of animals which then provided banquets where the clergy and the faithful met and ate together. The immolation of the victim was called *matal*, "sacrifice," or *patarag*, a word whose usage was otherwise restricted to the sacrament of the Eucharist. Besides the lamb, which was a requirement on Easter Day, the ox, calf, cow, sheep, and even pig were sacrificed, as well as those wild animals and birds which Mosaic law classified as pure. These sacrifices were quite frequent: they took place every Sunday and on the principal saints' days, on days on which a church, an altar, or a Christian monument was consecrated, and the third, ninth, and fortieth day following the death of a believer.

For the Sunday *matal* the victim was brought to the door of the church, to the foot of a cross, where it was covered with a scarlet cloth; the priest then blessed some salt and recited four chosen psalms and some passages from Leviticus, from the Second Book of Kings, from the Epistle of St. Paul to the

Hebrews, and from the Gospel of St. Luke; then followed several long prayers evoking the sacrifices of ancient law and that of Jesus Christ on Calvary. Finally the victim was fed the salt, and then its throat was cut[7]. The meat was then cooked and eaten by everyone together. This meal, like the first meals which Christians ate in common, was named *agape*, that is, feast of love. The blood of the victim was not collected and the remains of its flesh could not be saved in people's houses with other unblessed, ordinary foods. The *matal* and the ritual banquet of friendship had to follow immediately the eucharistic sacrifice of consecrated bread and wine. By its very liturgy and by its denomination of *patarag*, the whole *matal* and banquet could be considered a sacramental ritual. The victim of the Sunday *matal* had to have been born during that same year[8] and be sufficiently large to provide the meal, which allows one to think that it was most often either a bull or a heifer calf.

In telling us of the apostasy of the Hebrews at the foot of Mount Sinai, as they turned away from Yahweh to prostrate themselves before the sacred calf of the country of Canaan, the book of Exodus made this animal one of the symbols of the spirit of evil[9]. The calf of cast gold, this "golden god,"

Fig. 2 The golden calf; 18th century.

became in fact the image of the "demon of riches" in Christian symbolism. And at times the golden calf does not represent cupidity but simply idolatry, in remembrance of the apostasy of Israel[10] (Fig. 2).

The symbol of the heifer as the flawless virgin victim, sacrificed for the remission of sins outside the camp of Israel, is the same as that of the calf; but the red heifer or the cow of the same color which is mentioned in the Book of Numbers had a very specific meaning in Christian symbolism. The Lord said unto Moses: "Speak unto the children of Israel, that they bring thee a red heifer without spot, wherein is no blemish, and upon which never came yoke: And ye shall give her unto Eleazar the priest, that he may bring her forth without the camp, and one shall slay her before his face: And Eleazar the priest shall take of her blood with his finger, and sprinkle of her blood directly before the tabernacle of the congregation seven times[11]." Then the biblical text goes on to say that the ashes of the red heifer, which was to be consumed by the fire after its slaughter, are to be mixed with "a water of separation," water that "is a purification for sin[12]."

In all these liturgical applications, which were commented on at length by the Alexandrian Philo Judaeus in the first few years of our era, the mystics of the Middle Ages saw prophetic allegories in the Passion of Jesus Christ, during which his body was drenched with blood. They made of the red heifer "the image of the Redeemer's bleeding flesh. The heifer is the flesh of Christ," proclaimed Rabanus Maurus, in the ninth century, and he explains this by the animal's color[13].

In India the red cow symbolizes the dawn, and the black cow, the dusk, the seeming birth and death of the sun[14]. An orientalist once told me that it also symbolizes the two extreme ends of human life: the beginning of life by its milk—which represents all maternal milk, as it is the best of all wet-nurses—and the end of life because when man pronounces the onomatopoetic sound that imitates the lowing of a cow: moo! .. he advances his lips in a movement of exhaling breath, the image of death which comes with the last breath. This very oriental concept is related to that of the sacred AUM of the Hindus, and we know how important everything is that relates to breath in the metaphysics of several of the great Asiatic nations[15].

In ancient Egypt the cow was one of the psychagogic animals: Ra-Sun rose into the sky on the back of a cow, and it was often red cows that dragged the mummies to the tombs before being sacrificed; the divine cow, like the divine bull, carried souls to the other world[16].

Fig. 3 The cow Hathor; an Egyptian bronze.

In another connection, the divine cow Hathor, goddess of the Theban mountains, whose name is similar to Horus, the heart of divinity, was also the goddess of dawn and dusk, of the appearance and extinction of light, as in Asia[17] (Fig. 3). Was it as the ancient goddess of sunset in Asia, Egypt, Cyprus, and Phoenicia that the medieval iconography of the West, influenced by old traditions, attached the cow to the triumphal chariot of the personified Moon[18]? (Fig. 4). Practices as old and of the same origin, concerning the cow as well as the bull, are still in use even now in the religious lives of certain Mediterranean countries[19]. On the other hand, the horns of the cow as well as those of the bull recall the shape of the lunar crescent.

Fig. 4 The Moon chariot; 12th-century sculpture from the baptistry of Parma.

The thoughtless frolicking of the young calves and heifers in the pastures was regarded by the ancient masters of spiritual life as a symbol of dizzy recklessness, "the impulsiveness that throws youth in the path of violent passions[20]." From another angle, the cow was at times taken as the symbol of lack of intelligence, of stupidity; and when seen walking after a bull who refuses the yoke, it is the symbol of the soul that follows blindly the instigators of schisms and heresies, which rebel against the yoke of the Church. It has also been one of the signs for abject passions[21].

NOTES

Title Figure: Calf on the façade of the church of the Celle-Briére.

1. I Kings 7:25.
2. Cf. Hugh of St. Victor, *Miscellanea*, IV, 11.
3. Cf. St. Bruno D'Asti, in *Levitic.*; Hugh of St. Victor, *op. cit.*, III, 59, etc.
4. Rabanus Maurus, *De Univers.*, VII, 8.
5. Numbers 19.
6. See Leclercq and Marron, *Dictionnaire*, section CXIV, col. 2660-2668.
7. Nersès Shnorhali, library of Saint-Lazare à Venise, Mss. 457, VIII, 6.
8. *Rituale Armenorum*, Oxford, 1905, p. 54.
9. Exodus 32.
10. Cf. Barbier de Montault, *Traité*, T. I, p. 236.
11. Numbers 19:2-4.
12. *Ibid.* 19:9.
13. Rabanus Maurus, *Allegoria.*
14. De Gubernatis, *Mythologie*, T. I, p. 187.
15. Cf. Rama Prasad, *La science du Souffle et la philosophie des Tattras* (1910).
16. Cf. Maspéro, in *Mem. mission, arch. française au Caire*, T. V., pp. 440-453; Virey, *Religion*, p. 140.
17. See Lepage Renouf, *The Life Work*, Vol. 2, p. 256.
18. See Barbier de Montault, *op. cit.*, T. I, p. 111, & plate VII, fig. 75.
19. See H. de Montherlant, *Les Bestiaires*, VI.
20. Fel. d'Ayzac, in *Revue de l'Art chrétien*, 2d series. T. XII, (1880), p. 26.
21. Hugh of St. Victor, *op. cit.*, Book IV, 9.

End Figure: From a 10th-century Anglo-Saxon evangilary, in the Bibliothéque Nationale, Paris.

THE SHEEP

THE IMAGE OF the ram, inherited from primitive peoples, was one of the favorite religious symbols of ancient civilizations. In Egypt, from the time of the most ancient Pharaonic dynasties, the god Amon-Ra, the all-powerful Sun, was worshipped in the form of a ram, crowned with the solar disk (Fig. 1). The ram was the symbolic animal of Kneph, one of

Fig. 1 Head of the ram of Amon, from a painting in the catacombs of Thebes.

Fig. 2 The ram-headed god Kneph, the temple of Ramses II.

the oldest representations of the creator-god[1], who was generally pictured with a ram's head (Fig. 2). The image of Osiris had four heads and four horns, one head and one horn for each of the cardinal points[2]. Later the ram became, like the bird, the sign of the idea of human survival, and hence of the soul[3].

The Greeks borrowed the symbolism of the ram from the Egyptians; their highest expression of the divinity, Zeus, was likened to the god Amon of Egypt and is portrayed with a human torso with ram's horns; on the coins of Lysimachos, Alexander the Great was thus represented as Zeus Amon[4].

For the ancient Mazdeans of Persia in the old cults of Turan and in the most ancient Brahmanism, the ram was the symbol and the vehicle of Agni, one of the two great principles: the pure spirit, the fiery principle as opposed to Soma, the watery principle. Today vulgar Buddhism has debased Agni (Akkini), the god of pure and purifying fire of the ancient ages, to the simple role of the god of the hearth, with two heads and four hands; but often (so tenacious is tradition) this monstrous personage is mounted on Agni's ram of older times.

Fig. 3 Chinese paper talisman for a happy and fruitful marriage.

In China, the ram is still connected with the idea of the propagation of life, which it had in the oldest European civilizations: the ritual talisman used to ensure the happiness of a marriage, in the sense of its fertility, shows a person with a ram's head, printed in black ink on yellow paper[5] (Fig. 3).

In Gaul, the ram played an important role in the still largely unknown cult of the Druids: a ram's head was an attribute of the three-headed god, as we see in the tricephalous divinity in the Carnavalet Museum in Paris, as well as on a stele of the Duquenelle collection in Rheims, and on two other Gallic steles found in the same city. In the familial cult of the Gauls the ram was the god of the hearth. The ram also plays a part in the pre-Christian archeology of Germany, Iberia, Italy, and North Africa[6].

The marks of favor with which this animal was perceived in all of the ancient world were too obvious to be overlooked by Christian symbolists, who followed suit by admitting it to the hieratic fauna of Christ with almost all the meanings which had been ascribed to it by their predecessors. Like certain other male creatures such as the bull, the stag, and the cock, the ram also was for the fathers of the primitive Church one of the emblems of Christ's spiritual fertility. The idea of uniting it with the idea of the propagation of life was not new in the first Christian centuries. In Egypt the sacred statue of the ram in the temple of Mendes was said to make women fertile, as it was believed in a certain way to contain the soul of Osiris; his name, Ba, is in fact a synonym for the word "soul[7]." Sometimes the Greeks and Latins placed the head of a ram, or that of a lion, on the end of certain phallic amulets to represent the force of the reproductive principle with which man is equipped by the grace of Providence[8].

We must not forget that on the circle of the zodiac, which it would seem was transmitted from the Chaldeans to the Phoenicians, to the Greeks, and to the Egyptians[9], the sign of the Ram, Aries, bestrides the months of March and April, and that of the Bull, Taurus, rules the months of April and May, thus endowing by successive parts the three months of spring which compose the season when life stirs most strongly in all nature. And over all this love and all this life, whose manifestation is a resurrection as well as a birth, presides the great feast of the Resurrection of Christ.

The way in which rams fight head-on, striking their adversaries with their foreheads, made them in the eyes of the Ancients an emblem of courage and warlike strength. And with the ram as with the bull, the unicorn, the buck goat, and the rhinoceros, the idea of strength and power has been connected by age-old symbolism to the horns on its head. It was these traditional and already very old ideas which gave the name "ram" to one of the most useful instruments that the military genius of the Ancients used in sieges, in Asia[10] as well as among the Greeks and the Romans. It was essentially a heavy wooden beam armed at one end with a ram's head made of cast iron or bronze, and hung from its center. It was swung back and forth to batter down the walls or gates of cities under siege.

The ram was also taken as the hieroglyph of the divine voice of the eternal Word, because, says St. Ambrose, the ewes follow its voice. It is possible in fact that the docility of the flock in following the voice of the ram, their chief, leader, and father, made of it even for the ancient pre-Christians the emblem of the guide of souls towards their eternal destinations; and this is perhaps why the very same St. Ambrose says elsewhere that the ram "is taken as the symbol of the divine Word even by those who do not believe in the coming of the Messiah[11]."

The ram, like the lamb and the ewe, was offered as a bleeding sacrifice to God, and to the gods of all the ancient peoples; and like the majority of the victims offered in the ancient sacrifices, it became for the Christians the image of Christ as victim. This symbol persevered throughout the Middle Ages, according to the testimony of Rabanus Maurus and the anonymous writer of Clairvaux, who saw in the ram the Word incarnate offered in sacrifice for our redemption[12].

Much earlier, in the mystical commentary on Abraham's sacrifice on Mt. Moriah, where a ram was substituted for the patriarch's son[13], the animal sacrificed in Isaac's place was suggested as the figure of Christ slain instead of sinful humanity.

I would add that in Muslim Morocco, under the name of "Abraham's Sacrifice" a feast is still celebrated which includes the slaughter of a ram under a tent located two or three minutes from the mosque; as soon as the victim has received the death blow it is thrown onto the saddle of a horseman who dashes off at a gallop to the mosque: if the ram is still alive when it arrives, the people of the Maghreb say it is a sign of good fortune for the coming year[14].

Phrixus, the son of the king of Orchomenus, is the Joseph of Greek mythology. Invited to her bed by Demodice, the wife of his uncle, the king of Iolcos, Phrixus refused to give in to her guilty desires, and was then accused by her of having attempted to force her. Soon thereafter a horrible plague ravaged the kingdom of Orchomenus, and the oracle, mistaking the signs, pronounced that the plague would not cease unless Phrixus and his sister Helle were sacrificed. But the great Zeus took pity on the innocents, and as they were being led to their deaths, he caused a cloud to envelop them, and within the cloud was a celestial ram, covered with a resplendent golden fleece. Phrixus and his sister seized the beautiful animal with all their strength, recognizing it as their savior; and the ram rose, slowly at first, above the earth and finally, as swiftly as the kite carrying off its prey, it soared away with its human cargo toward the country of Colchis.

Fig. 4 17th-century trademark of the Golden Fleece.

But as they were passing over the Euxine Sea, the young Helle, terrified by the noise of a storm which was making the waves boil, let go and fell into the water: this part of the sea has been called the Hellespont ever since. Phrixus, who held fast, was let down gently in Colchis and in a gesture of pious gratitude, he offered the marvelous ram as a sacrifice, on the altar of Zeus. He hung the golden fleece as homage on a tree consecrated to the god Ares, the war god of the Greeks, and placed nearby a fearful monster, the Dragon of Colchis, to guard the rich treasure (Fig. 4).

The gods were satisfied with the gratitude of Phrixus and willed that henceforth the fleece be a pledge insuring abundance and good fortune for the place in which it was found. The ram itself was placed by them in the constellations of the zodiac, at the head of the months bringing life and joy to the earth. It was the golden fleece of this savior ram that the hero Jason and his companions, the Argonauts, would later succeed in taking from Colchis, by killing, with Medea's help, the dragon which guarded it.

In the days when troubadours and minstrels sang our great epics, the Golden Fleece of the Greek story symbolized, for "those who knew," two treasures apparently very different. The search for it by the Argonauts was seen as foreshadowing the "quest for the Holy Grail," by the Knights of the Round Table. The Holy Grail was in fact the Eucharist; it was Christ. On the other hand, for the alchemists the same enterprise of the Argonauts stood for the search for the philosopher's stone; and this unique stone, so powerful to knowledgeable alchemists, was also Christ, hidden within a symbol.

About 1447, Pope Eugene IV represented the conquest of the Golden Fleece by the Argonauts on the bronze doors of Saint Peter's in Rome. Christian spirituality saw in Phrixus and Helle the image of human souls, and in the celestial ram, that of Jesus Christ who offers them the possibility of salvation by lifting them above the earth by means of its fleece, that is to say his doctrine and his law. Phrixus holds onto his savior untiringly, with all his might, and reaches the happy shores of Colchis; Helle weakens, is discouraged and lets go of the divine ram, and falls into the abyss where death receives her.

But in Christian art, of all the creatures which have had the honor of symbolizing Christ, it is the lamb that has been the most popular, just as in all the sacrificial cults it was the virginal victim par excellence; its white color, its grace, its youth all marked it for this role, and in the biblical account of the beginnings of the human race, the lamb on Abel's altar was the first sacrificial offering that the Creator looked upon with favor. We shall see later how its protective and expiatory roles were defined by Moses for the Hebrews; but we quote here the words of Isaiah and Jeremiah that were applied to the person of Jesus Christ as prophecies of his role as redemptive victim: "The Lord hath laid on him the iniquity of us all. He was oppressed, and he was afflicted, yet he opened not his mouth; he is brought as a lamb to the slaughter, and as a sheep before her shearers is dumb, so he openeth not his mouth[15]." "But I was like a lamb or an ox that is brought to the slaughter[16]."

Fig. 5 The Lamb with seven horns and seven eyes; 13th century.

Later, recalling these ancient texts, John the Baptist was to say of Jesus as he drew near him in the valley of Jordan, "Behold the Lamb of God[17]."

Here are the words of another John, on Patmos:

"And I beheld, and, lo, in the midst of the throne and of the four beasts, and in the midst of the elders, stood a Lamb as it had been slain, having seven horns and seven eyes, which are the seven Spirits of God sent forth into all the earth. And he came and took the book out of the right hand of him that sat upon the throne. And when he had taken the book, the four beasts and four and twenty elders fell down before the Lamb, having every one of them harps, and golden vials full of odours, which are the prayers of saints. And they sung a new song, saying, Thou art worthy to take the book, and to open the seals thereof: for thou wast slain, and hast redeemed us to God by thy blood out of every kindred, and tongue, and people, and nation; and hast made us unto our God kings and

Fig. 6 The Lamb and the anchor in the catacomb of St. Calistus in Rome.

Fig. 7 The Lamb crowned with the cross in the art of the catacombs.

priests: and we shall reign on the earth[18] (Fig 5)."

As expiatory and propitiatory victim, the lamb was in the first place among the symbols and emblems of Jesus Christ. The earliest artists to picture it in the catacombs seemed to prefer the aspect of the suffering earthly victim to the triumphant heavenly one, for these oldest images show him lying down rather than standing. Before anyone dared to represent the cross in the art of the catacombs, the lamb appears lying by a ship's anchor, a mysterious hieroglyph for the cross. We see it thus on a cemetery stone in Rome[19] (Fig. 6) and we find it again by the cross itself as soon as it appeared in Christian iconography; almost at the same moment, the cross crowns the head of the divine Lamb (Fig. 7). However, in this period and even long after it had been freed by Constantine to emerge into the light of day, the Church did not yet dare to represent the body of its deity on the Roman instrument of execution. The lamb was the symbol chosen to take its place; and this was the first crucifix, one might say the pre-crucifix, for Christians. This custom of placing the lamb on the cross persisted, in the East as well as the West, long after the Church had accepted the representation of the cross bearing the body of Christ (Fig. 8).

As the slain victim, the lamb appears also in other postures—sometimes standing, or stretched on the ground, with blood flowing; at others it is on an altar at whose foot lies the Book spoken of in the Apocalypse[20]. In the symbolism of Freemasonry, the Lamb lying on the sealed book represents the Shekhinah, that is, the presence of the glory of God on the Ark of the Covenant[21]. At other times, it is the lance instead of the cross that proclaims the triumph of Christ's love, since it is the heart that is pierced (Fig. 5). We see it carved like this in ivory on the beautiful Roman crozier at Metten, "the divine Lamb, returned to life, pulls out from its wound the iron that had pierced its heart[22] (Fig. 9)."

The symbolic compositions which link the lamb's image with the idea of the Eucharist quite naturally take the mind back to another lamb which, since the time of Moses, the Hebrews consume according to special rites and whose blood ransomed their lives. Scripture recounts how on the eve of the Hebrews' departure from Egypt, Moses ordered them at the Lord's command to sacrifice a lamb for each family. Each was to take a male yearling without blemish and kill it in the evening of the fourteenth day of the month, and mark with its blood the doorposts and the lintel of the door of the house within which the roasted flesh of the lamb was to be eaten, with unleavened bread and bitter herbs. "And thus shall ye eat it; with your loins girded, your shoes on your feet, and your staff in your hand; and ye shall eat it in haste: it is the Lord's passover." And that night the Lord passed over Egypt and smote the first-born of the land, but the houses of the

Fig. 8 The symbolic Crucifixion, from the Ravenna Museum.

Fig. 9 12th-century crozier from Metten, in ivory and metal.

Hebrews were spared because of the blood of the lamb that marked their doors. And that very day the children of Israel went out of Egypt[23].

On the eve of that day which is unique among days, Jesus with his companions had eaten the ritual Passover lamb, the prophetic symbol of himself; and taking the place of the symbol, he had said while he blessed the bread and wine, "Take ye and eat. This is my body. . . . Drink ye all of this. For this is my blood. . . .[24]" This is why the Church since its earliest days has seen a connecting link between the Paschal lamb and the sacrament of the Eucharist, and St. Paul declared to the Corinthians, "Christ our passover is sacrificed for us: therefore let us keep the feast[25]."

Fig. 10 The divine Lamb on the book sealed with seven seals; 12th century.

The divine Lamb is an inexhaustible source of life and also of light. St. John of Patmos speaks of this in his book of Revelation; after describing the walls of the heavenly Jerusalem made of precious stones, and the twelve gates of pearl, he adds: "And I saw no temple therein: for the Lord God Almighty and the Lamb are the temple of it. And the city had no need of the sun, neither of the moon, to shine in it: for the glory of God did lighten it, and the Lamb is the light thereof. And the nations of them that are saved shall walk in the light of it[26]."

This is undoubtedly the reason why the lamb was sometimes represented in the midst of the sun, or crowned with a halo of rays, or also why a star was sometimes placed before it.

The lamb, then, was considered as a source of light; and the light perceptible to the vision is only the image of that which illumines the soul and gives it wisdom. This is how it has been explained by some learned commentators that the lamb is sometimes seen bearing the lance instead of the cross, as the lance was a symbol of wisdom among the ancients, being associated with Pallas Athena[27]. On the other hand, one can also see in this image simply the evocation of the lance which wounded the Redeemer's side on Calvary, and in Christian iconography both cross and lance evoke above all the Passion of Christ (Fig. 10).

As well as representing the redeemer of humanity and its divine illuminator, the lamb in Christian symbolism also fills the role of purifier of the world and king of virgins. St. John presents it at the head of the hundred and forty-four thousand chosen ones "which were not defiled with women, for they are virgins. These are they which follow the Lamb whithersoever he goeth. These were redeemed from among men, being the first fruits unto God and to the Lamb. And in their mouth was found no guile: for they are without fault before the throne of God[28]."

Fig. 11 The Lamb in a crown of flowers, fruits, corn, and grapes; 5th-century ivory from Milan.

King of those who have remained pure, the Lamb is king also of those who having been defiled "have washed their robes, and made them white in the blood of the Lamb[29]." This is perhaps what St. Peter was referring to with the words: "Forasmuch as ye know that ye were not redeemed with corruptible things, as silver and gold, from your vain conversation . . . but with the precious blood of Christ, as of a lamb without blemish and without spot[30]." The whole iconography of the purifying lamb rests on these texts and similar ones, and they explain the presence of the lamb's image on liturgical furnishings connected with the rites of purification, such as some medieval holy water basins and baptismal fonts.

Fig. 12 The Lamb raising Lazarus from the dead; from the 4th-century tomb of St. Peter in Rome.

The apotheosis of the lamb described by St. John in Revelation, standing on Mt. Zion in the midst of the army of virgins, provided fruitful themes for the Christian artists. In the first centuries, almost the only image showing the Lamb Triumphant was that of a lamb standing in the center of the laurel crown of glory (Fig. 11), or on the mountain from which issued the four, or five, sources of the river of life. These representations became much more elaborate later.

The triumph of the Lamb had to be followed in Christian picturing by the recognition of its absolute power, and this was celebrated by portrayals of the Lamb armed with the rod of authority. On a tomb of 358 A.D., the Lamb is shown with a rod making water gush from a rock, blessing or multiplying the miraculous loaves, and raising Lazarus from the dead (Fig. 12).

The celestial power of the Lamb seems concentrated in the Apocalyptic description of it with "seven horns and seven eyes, which are the seven Spirits of God[31]." As we have already seen, in the language of scripture, and in general in sacred iconography, the horn is always the sign of force and of power; and the number seven is a mysterious number denoting fullness.

The Lord himself used the symbol of lambs and sheep to mean his followers—even the Apostles, to whom he said, "Behold, I send you forth as lambs among wolves[32]," and in committing the care of his flock to Peter: "Feed my lambs . . . Feed my sheep[33]." The sheep as well as the lamb certainly often stands for the Christian soul, in addition to being incontestably the image of the sacrificed Savior. Like the ram and the lamb, the ewe was sacrificed on all the altars of the pre-Christian cults of Europe and Asia, including China, where in the Shan dynasty it was already an old established custom to bury a ewe in honor of the Sun on the mound called "The Royal Palace[34]." A similar offering was made to the Moon on the other mound called "Light of the Night[35]."

It would seem that the ewe is the animal whose milk became the symbol for the Eucharist. Certainly it is always a member of the sheep family who carries the vessel of milk, or lies beside it, on many works of art of the first six Christian centuries. To represent milk allegorically in painting and sculpture, the artists of that time made use of the image of

Fig. 13. Christ the Shepherd with the milk jar and crook; painting from the Roman catacombs.

Fig. 14 The milk jar hung on the shepard's crook.

the rustic container used by shepherds for milking the ewes in the pasture, the *mulctra* of the Latins. It was made of metal or wood, depending on the locality, and had a carrying handle. To identify it in its symbolic sense, the artist usually placed near the vessel one or several lambs or sheep, or the *pedum*, the shepherd's crook of the ancient world (Figs. 13 and 14). It is interesting to note that on the early monuments the vessel of milk is accompanied by no other animal than a sheep; so the milk that in its vessel represents the Eucharist is specifically the milk of the ewe, not that of the cow, or the she-goat, or the doe.

Among all the pre-Christian people that we know anything of, milk was a revered and precious liquid, and nearly all the ancient religions used it as the perfect ritual substance; it was poured in libations before the altars more often than blood, or oil, or liquid honey, and quite as often as wine. From one end of the ancient world to the other, it was related with the idea of prosperity and happiness. The book of Exodus says that when God commanded Moses to lead his people out of Egypt, he described the country he intended for them as "flowing with milk and honey[36]." Much later, in the last century of the pre-Christian era, telling the Romans of the imaginary Golden Age and the delightful region where dwelt its fortunate people, the poet Ovid said, "What are now springs of water were then nearly all fountains of milk, and honey ran down the trees[37]." The same allegorical idea prevailed in Central Asia, where the Mongols and Tartars tossed libations of milk toward the sky as offerings to the spirits[38]; and also in Chaldea, Persia, and Arabia, where later it would be told how an angel offered three cups to Mohammed: one of wine, another of milk, and the third of honey; the Prophet selected the second and was praised by the angel for his wise choice[39].

We might note that butter, made from the cream of milk, also became a symbol of abundance and good fortune. In many places in the Bible, the prophets designate butter and honey as food for the future Messiah and his saints; and the sacred books of the Hindus mention it even oftener: "O powerful gods," says the Rig-Veda, "drop your butter on our cows and your honey on all the worlds[40]."

For the early teachers of the Christian faith, milk had two principal symbolic meanings: for one, it was the emblem of the excellent doctrine which nourishes the Christian's mind, and for the other, it stood for the Eucharist, the necessary food for his soul. At one moment of the Church's early life, some of its priests adopted milk as a true sacramental substance, and celebrated the holy mysteries with bread and coagulated milk. They were known by the name of Artotyrites, (*artos*, bread, and *tyros*, dried milk, cheese): they are known to us through St. Epiphanius, St. Augustine, and Theodorus Lector[41]. The Church forbade the consecration of milk and its derivatives as a sacrament; however, the *Apostolic Tradition*, by St. Hippolitus, who was martyred in 240 A.D., prescribed an exceptional communion rite that was accepted, at least for a certain time in Greece. In addition to bread and wine and the mixture of milk and honey that many churches made use of at this time, this rite offered a cup of water. The communicants were given successively three cups: first, after the consecrated bread, the cup of water; then that of milk and honey, and finally that of wine.

NOTES

Title Figure: The triumphant Ram on the town seal of Tirlemont in Brabant; 13th century.

1. Maspéro, *Études*, T. II, pp. 273-275.
2. *Idem*, "Le Livre des Morts," in *Revue de l'Histoire des Religions*, 1887, p. 278.
3. Maspéro, "Les Hypogées royaux de Thèbes," in *Revue Historique des Religions*, 1888, p. 279, and Strinilbert-Oberlin, *Les Hiéroglyphes*, p. 23.
4. Cf. Louis Menard, *Histoire des Grecs*, T. II, p. 726.
5. Cf. Doré, *Recherches*, 1st part, T. I, Vol. II, p. 214, Fig. 150 bis.
6. Cf. Déchelette, *Manuel*, T. II, 3rd part, p. 1401, and *Revue archéologique*, 1898.
7. Cf. Lefébure, "Bulletin critique des Religions de L'Égypte" in *Revue historique des Religions*, T. LXVII, no. 1, 1913, p. 3.
8. Cf. H. Roux, *Herculaneum et Pompeii*, T. VIII, plate 46.
9. Abbé Moreux, *La science mystérieuse des Pharaons*, p. 106.
10. For Assyria and Chaldea, see Gustave le Bon, *Les premières civilisations*, p. 545.
11. St. Ambrose, *Epistles*, LX, c. III.
12. Dom Pitra, *Spicilège de Solesmes*, T. III, p. 24.
13. Genesis 22:1-13.
14. Cf. A. Chevrillon, "L'Aid-Kebir à Rabat" in *L'Illustration*, T. XCI, no. 4.703, April 1933.
15. Isaiah 53:6-7.
16. Jeremiah 11:19.
17. St. John 1:29.
18. Revelation 5:6-10.

19. Cf. de Rossi, *Rome souterraine*, T. II, p. 1, XX, no. 1.
20. Cf. de Saint-Laurent, *Guide*, T. I, plate IV, no. 2.
21. *Les plus secrets mystères des plus hauts grades de la Maçonnerie dévoilés*, Vth grade, Jerusalem; p. 94.
22. A. Martin, S.J., "Des crosses pastorales," in *Mélanges archéologiques*, T. IV, 1856, pp. 200-201, fig. 62.
23. Exodus 12.
24. St. Matthew 26:26-28, Douay-Rheims version.
25. I Corinthians 5:7-8.
26. Revelation 21:22-24.
27. Cf. Martian Capel, *Sapient*, VIII; also Martigny, *Dict. antiq. chrét.*, p. 21, and A. Lerosey, *Histoire et symbolisme de la Liturgie*, p. 85.
28. Revelation 14:4-5.
29. Revelation 7:14.
30. I Peter 1:18-19.
31. Revelation 5:6.
32. St. Luke 10:3.
33. St. John 21:15-17.
34. The *Li Chi*, XX.
35. Cf. Doré, *op. cit.*, Part I, T. II, vol. IV, p. 365.
36. Exodus 3:8.
37. Ovid, *Metamorphoses*, Book I, ch. 3.
38. Ross, *Les Religions du Monde*, p. 52.
39. Cf. Savary, *Le Coran* (*Vie de Mahomet*), p. 21.
40. Cf. Sanglès, *Le Rig-Véda*, Vol. II, VII: 3-4.
41. Theodorus, *Historia Tripartita*.

End Figure: The Lamb on an 18th-century seal.

THE GOAT

IN COUNTRIES UNDER Greek influence, the he-goat was connected with the popular cult of the goddess Artemis, and a buck was offered to her in the ceremonies celebrated every five years in her honor. On the fringe of the Artemis cult, representations of the god Pan, regarded as the universal generator of the procreative power, showed him with the legs, feet, and horns of the he-goat, and sometimes with its whole body[1].

The actors who distinguished themselves on the stages of the Greek theater, as well as the winners of certain athletic contests, were commonly rewarded with the prize of a goat, and from this came the names *tragodos*, by which actors were generally called, and *tragodia*, tragedy, given to the most popular form of theater[2].

It is interesting that the ancient Scandinavians attached the goat to the chariot of Thor, the god of thunder and lightning[3]. Some people have thought that the foul odor which is sometimes produced at the moment when lightning appears has something to do with this association; and, perhaps by another association connected with it, it was the former practice in some northern countries to place a goat's horn, or even a fragment of the animal's skin, in the top floor of dwellings to protect them from lightning. In the Orient, it was thought that wineskins made from goat hide lent the wine special health-giving properties; and in the eastern Mediterranean region, certain plants, including fennel, anise, and cumin, which were sought so eagerly by goats that they were named for the animal[4], were equally sought out by people who used their seeds for religious and magical rituals.

But rich as the goat's past history has been in its symbolic, hieratic, and sacrificial uses, its role in Christian symbolism stems almost entirely from biblical sources. In many places in the Pentateuch, Moses orders the immolation of the goat. The only chapter in the Book of Numbers that codifies several important liturgies specifies the sacrifice of a goat before Yahweh[5], on ten different occasions, not as an act of adoration or of petition, but for the remission of sins. This expiatory character, clearly defined for each ritual sacrifice of a goat, has quite naturally made the animal appear as a prophetic figure of the Redeemer.

But it is especially in the role of the scapegoat and its companion that the goat has entered into the symbolism of Christ. According to Leviticus, Moses says that after sacrificing a bullock, Aaron, the high priest, is to take two goats, one for Yahweh, the Lord, the other for Azazel, whose name means "the prince of the demons who have been cast out." Then he is to place the two goats before the Lord at the door of the tabernacle of the congregation. Aaron is to cast lots upon the two goats, one lot for the Lord and one lot for Azazel; and he is to bring the goat on which Azazel's lot has fallen and present it alive before the Lord to make an expiation upon it and to let it go for Azazel into the desert.

"Then shall he kill the goat of the sin offering, that is for the people, and bring his blood within the veil, and do with that blood as he did with the blood of the bullock, and sprinkle it upon the mercy seat, and before the mercy seat.... And he shall go out unto the altar that is before the Lord, and make an atonement for it; and shall take of the blood of the bullock, and of the blood of the goat, and put it upon the horns of the altar round about. And he shall sprinkle of the blood upon it with his finger seven times, and cleanse it, and hallow it from the uncleanness of the children of Israel. And when he hath made an end of reconciling the holy place, and the tabernacle of the congregation, and the altar, he shall bring the live goat: and Aaron shall lay both his hands upon the head of the live goat, and confess over him all the iniquities of the children of Israel, and all their transgressions in all their sins, putting them upon the head of the goat, and shall send him away by the hand of a fit man into the wilderness. And the goat shall bear upon him all their iniquities unto a land not inhabited: and he shall let go the goat in the wilderness[6]."

The commentators and exegetes of all times have seen in the first of these two animals the emblem of Christ sacrificed to God his Father as ransom for the world, and in the second, the emblem of this same Redeemer become a sort of universal receptacle of evil, the terrible mass of human sin, which he carries away into the desert—that is, into the solitude of his tomb, or, according to another interpretation, toward heaven where the unseen God awaits. Theodorus, Bruno of Asti, Thomas Aquinas and many other writers give this passage from Leviticus mystical interpretations that substantially agree with what I have just said[7].

Since the beginning of Christianity, the scapegoat, upon which, for the good of the people, rests the accumulation of all their sins, has struck the popular imagination, and we can trace its influence in the customs of our French country folk. The peasants of the western provinces (and doubtless others) often put goats into their stables and barns because, they say, they attract poisonous vapors and the germs of animal maladies, which collect around them without doing them any harm, and thus are kept away from the larger animals. I have observed that several times when the livestock has been decimated by foot-and-mouth disease, the presence of a goat in the stable has in no way prevented the other animals from dying. Nevertheless, when the epidemic is over the peasant simply replaces the goat with another, claiming that the other animal was in bad condition.

Although the young he-goat is a delightful and attractive animal, as it becomes sexually mature it becomes lustful and a vile odor begins to emanate from it; soon it becomes a disgusting and repugnant creature which one wishes to avoid. In the same way, according to the mystics, as long as the Christian keeps his heart young and pure, as long as he resists the lower instincts insofar as nature allows, he remains morally beautiful; but when the human being abandons himself to the vices of his lower nature, his inner corruption shows itself and points the finger of blame at him in one way or another. Among the ancient Greeks, it was said of libidinous people that they "smelled of goat."

Fig. 1 Kabbalistic star of bestiality.

The Gospels also portray the goat as symbol of the accursed. Several centuries earlier Ezekiel had written— "Thus saith the Lord God— Behold, I judge between cattle and cattle, between the rams and the he-goats[8]." But Christ was even clearer: "When the Son of man shall come in his glory, and all the holy angels with him, then shall he sit upon the throne of his glory: And before him shall be gathered all nations: and he shall separate them one from another, as a shepherd divideth his sheep from the goats: And he shall set the sheep on his right hand, but the goats on the left." Then, after welcoming the just, he turns to those on his left, and says— "Depart from me, ye cursed, into everlasting fire prepared for the devil and his angels. . . .[9]"

The he-goat is the special emblem of the King of Hell. All medieval demonologists show Satan almost exclusively in the guise of a buck goat, and if they are to be believed, it is in this form that he presides over his devil's sabbaths. In the hermetic groups of the Middle Ages, which very often remained in perfect harmony with the purest concepts of Christian mysticism, the buck was at once the symbol of Satan and of animality. It is on this account that its head still adorns the five-pointed star that is directed downward[10]— "the black fallen star" which is the antithesis of the pentagram, the star of spirituality, whose point is toward heaven (Figs. 1 and 2).

But as we have said, the goat was not doomed from birth to be scorned by human beings. Among the ancient Greeks, on the contrary, the young he-goat, *tragiskos*, was one of the symbols of purity, of "whiteness," whatever the color of its coat. It was only when it became an adult buck, *tragos*, that it lost the esteem of others along with its innocence.

Fig. 2 Head of the Beelzebub-buck.

It seems also that the same favorable regard, and the same sacrificial rites on the altars of the gods, were accorded to the young of sheep, goats, and even deer; that is, to all the young of the small, horned quadrupeds; further, in the sacred arts of the pre-Christians it was not often possible to distinguish between kids, lambs, and other similar animals.

In the ancient cults and mysteries—those of Ishtar and Tammuz among the Assyrians, for example, and later in the mysterious theories of the Pythagoreans and the Orphists and in the rites of Dionysus—the kid was the image of the believer initiated into the secret teachings. There was a sacred formula in Orphism, which testified to this, which the Pythagoreans also adopted; the mysterious words that can be read on the two gold plates of Thurii[11] (between the fourth and the third centuries B.C.): "Goat, I have fallen in the milk" —or according to Wolgraff— "Goat, I have thrown myself upon the milk," that is, upon the nourishing breast of divinity[12]. Here, "milk" surely means the hidden doctrine, issuing directly from the masters without being seen by the profane, as milk passes invisibly from the mother's breast into the mouth of her young. In the decoration of the Pythagorean basilica of the Porta Maggiore, in Rome, we see a bacchante standing with a kid in her arms which she holds out to another woman who is baring her breast for it[13]. In the same way, in the Dionysiac paintings of the villa Item, in Pompeii, we see a priestess suckling a fawn[14]. It is because of instances of this kind, or of rites unknown to us that were practiced in Assyria in the mysteries of Ishtar and Tammuz, much earlier than Pythagorism or Orphism, that the Pentateuch imposed on the Hebrews (neighbors of the Assyrians) the several-times repeated precept— "Thou shalt not seethe a kid in his mother's milk[15]." The law of Moses does not contain any similar edict in relation to the young of any other animal.

In the Far East, the blood of the kid was and still is believed to protect children from night-walking evil spirits. In China, the kid was always the favored sacrificial victim—Tzu-Fong, in the century before the birth of Christ, offered the sacrifice of a yellow goat to the god Hantzu-kuo, who had appeared to him in a vision; and after that his fortune increased to the size of a king's[16].

In the Pentateuch, nothing is specified in regard to the sacrificial killing of the kid; it follows the rites indicated for other small livestock. But a particular idea of innocence is connected with it, as with the other young victims; and it is this idea of a purity that has remained untouched since its beginning that in earlier times caused the kid's skin to be chosen instead of other leathers or fabrics for making the pontifical gloves for ritual use[17]. The liturgical texts clearly established these gloves as one of the special symbols of Christ's inviolable purity. This same idea of purity served to make the young goat the symbol of Jesus Christ as a virginal victim.

The religious history of the kid in Europe before our era presents it as symbolizing the soul that seeks the divine doctrine; but I have not seen any instance of its being regarded as a direct image of divinity. But for Christians, the kid symbolizes the figure of Christ the expiator, substituted for us; and this idea of substitution is expressed also in Exodus. In the first law stipulated for the Passover, Moses allows the Hebrews to substitute a kid for the paschal lamb: "Ye shall take it out from the sheep, or from the goats[18]." In all the rest of this same law of the Passover, the text speaks only of a lamb; the kid is named at the beginning merely as a victim that, lacking a lamb, could replace it. But in this case, the same virtue of preservation from "the Destroyer" promised for the blood of the paschal lamb is implicit in the blood of the kid. And if the lamb prefigures Christ, so does the kid, since the blood of one and of the other had the same value and the same meaning, being consecrated by the same Mosaic rites.

The imagination of the Ancients generously gifted the blood spurting from the kid's heart with a very unexpected property—it had the power to soften the hardest stones, not excepting diamonds. Up until the middle of the medieval period, the lapidaries took account of this property in their corporate theories; we have incontestable proof of this from the pen of the monk Theophilus who wrote at the beginning of the eleventh century— "If you wish to carve crystal, take a young he-goat, tie its legs, and make an incision between the chest and stomach, in the region of the heart, and let the crystal soak in the blood until it is warm. Carve it then as you wish, and when it begins to get cold, and to harden, put it back in the blood. . . .[19]" As one may well believe, medieval spirituality seized upon this belief of the craftsmen to enrich the symbolism of the Savior.

In Greek mythology, as we have seen, the white she-goat Amaltheia was the glorious nurse of the supreme god, Zeus; and it was one of her horns that Zeus gave to the nymphs. It was "the horn of plenty" which became the symbol of all good things of a spiritual as well as a material nature[20], and the symbol also of their divine source.

It was with a goatskin that Hephaestus covered Pallas-Athena's shield[21]; and it was with the help of the goats of Parnassus that Apollo showed the devotees of his sanctuary at Delphi the generative source of the vapors that caused the ecstatic trance states in which the Pythonesses received their inspirations and transmitted the divine oracles[22]. In ancient Cretan art, the Mother Goddess appeared in the form of a she-goat suckling a child[23]; she is the Earth-Nourisher. In Syria and Chaldea, the celestial she-goat plays an important and favored role in opposition to the invisible evil forces which she puts to flight; an Assyrian bas-relief shows her chasing a lion-centaur spirit. And under the aspect of Capricorn, in these same countries, the goat takes a leading place in the symbolism of the sky and of the air[24].

Fig. 3 The goat climbing the mountain; from a 13th-century miniature in Bibliothèque de l'Arsenal.

Christian symbolists took advantage of the beliefs of the naturalists of the ancient world, which endowed the goat with an extraordinary and increasing power of vision: and like the pre-Christian, included in this privilege both domestic goats and the wild creatures of the mountains. They said that in proportion to the heights they attained in climbing the peaks, they acquired not only a greatly extended field of vision, but also an extraordinary increase in its power and acuteness, to such a degree that no other creature on earth could equal their ability to embrace with one glance the most immense spaces and to distinguish perfectly all the details (Fig. 3).

In the same way, the inner vision of the seeker becomes more penetrating as his understanding attains higher degrees of the mysteries. Thus on the northern and eastern shores of the Mediterranean, the Ancients made the she-goat a symbol of initiation. Thus also St. Gregory of Nyssa, who died about 400 A.D., described the she-goat as a symbol of the total perfection and the universality of the searching look with which Christ, in his divinity, sees everything in the past, present, and future[25]. The *Physiologus*, and the medieval bestiaries that derive from it, always relying on the sayings of Pliny and the Ancients, also took the she-goat as an emblem of Christ's omniscience. And with the same viewpoint, the mystics of that era also made the goat the image of Christ observing from the heights of heaven the actions of the just and the wicked, for the sake of future rewards and punishments[26].

Fig. 4 4th-century painting from the Roman catacomb of Calistus.

The characteristics of the goat which attract it to the heights could provide other reasons than the excellence of its vision why the goat should be taken as the symbolic image of the Lord. Origen, writing at the beginning of the third century, said that not only is the goat endowed with marvelous vision, but that it carries in its breast a liquid that can give the same advantage to human beings. "Thus," he said, "Jesus Christ not only sees God, his Father, but makes him visible also to those whom his word enlightens[27]."

On a fresco of the fourth century, in the catacombs of Calistus, a leaping gazelle or wild goat carries the caduceus of Hermes, the god of knowledge, that is hidden from the vulgar, and mysterious in itself. Who will explain to us the thought of the artist who sketched this astonishing motif? (Fig. 4).

The medieval hermetists also connect the goat with the person of Christ, applying to it the old pagan meaning, which they christianized, of the zodiacal Capricorn. In ancient esoterism, this was the *Janua coeli*, the Gate of Heaven, as op-

Fig. 5 Urn of Pesaro.

posed to *Cancer*, which is *Janua inferni*, the Gate of Hell, and which is represented in hermetic art by crabs and crustaceans of all sorts.

In the art of the catacombs in Rome, the goat often appears in a purely decorative role; but it is also found with the sheep around the Shepherd guarding his flock, as is the case in one of the big frescos of the catacomb of Domitilius; or again, when it is shown on each side of the Good Shepherd. There is no doubt that in both cases the goat is a symbol of the faithful. In the same way, on an urn of Pesaro, which is of the seventh century and probably was for baptismal use, two gazelles drink from the same vessel, a symbol of baptism or of the Eucharist (Fig. 5). In the Roman catacomb called "Priscilla's Cemetery," the Good Shepherd carries on his shoulders not the lost sheep, but a goat (Fig. 6).

Fig. 6 The Good Shepherd and the goats, from the Roman catacomb of Priscilla.

I do not know of a single example of a goat represented in heraldry as a certain image of Jesus Christ; the animal had on the whole a bad reputation in "the noble science." In his great work, published in 1699, Vulson de la Colombière speaks of it thus— "The goat gnaws the buds of the best trees with poisonous teeth, ruining the countryside, and for this reason the Athenians banished it from their territory, and even today it is forbidden to enter several provinces in France." He adds that the she-goat denotes the woman of evil life[28]. But it could well be also that the goat and its relatives, which love to be in high places, sometimes signified something quite different, especially in the heraldry of mountainous regions. It seems certain that in the time of St. Bernard and St. Louis—the cycle of the pure idea—members of the goat family must have been shown on the seals or coats of arms as symbols of the aspirations of souls in love with the atmosphere of spiritual heights, whence heaven can be looked upon from less far away than in the bottom lands of the valleys.

NOTES

Title Figure: The androcephalic buck goat; antique bronze statuette.

1. Cf. Herodotus, *History*, II, 46.
2. Greek *tragos*, goat.
3. See Lanoë-Villène, *Le Livre des Symboles*, Vol. IV, p. 24.
4. "Boucages" from *bouc*, buck or he-goat.
5. Numbers 29.
6. Leviticus 16:15, 18-22.
7. Cf. Theodorus, *In Leviticus*; St. Thomas Aquinas, *Biblical Commentary*, Question XXIII, etc.
8. Ezekiel 34:17.
9. Matthew 25:31-33, 41.
10. Cf. Oswald Wirth, *Le Livre du Compagnon*, p. 40.
11. *Editor's note*: A city of Magna Graecia on the Gulf of Tarentum, near the site of the older Sybaris.
12. Cf. Carcopino, *Basilique*, p. 34.
13. *Ibid*, p. 156.
14. Cf. Rizzo, *Mythes*, Pl. III, 1 and pages 70-71.
15. Exodus 23:19, 34:26, Deuteronomy 14:21.
16. Cf. Doré, *Recherches*, Vol. XI, part 2, p. 906.
17. Cf. Barbier de Montault, "Les Gants pontificaux," in *Bulletin monumental*, Vol. XLII, p. 461.
18. Exodus 12:5.
19. Theophilus, *Diversarum artium schedula*, or *De Diversis artibus*, Book III, 94.
20. See Ovid, *Fasti*, V. Also see above, "The Horn," p. 58.
21. Homer, *The Iliad*, V.
22. Diodorus Siculus, *Bibliotheca historica*, XVI.
23. See Glotz, *Civilisation égéenne*, Book III, p. 280.
24. See Macrobius, e.g.: *Saturnalia*, XVII. See also Creuzer, *Le Symbolisme d'Eleusis et ses traditions*, T. III, Part 2, p. 699.
25. Cf. St. Gregory of Nyssa, *Homily*, V.
26. Corblet, "Vocabulaire des Symboles," in *Revue de l'Art chrétien*, T. XVI, p. 461.
27. Origen, *Op.* in Migne, *Patrologie grecque*, Vol. XI-XVII. See also *Le Bestiaire divin*, p. 137.
28. De la Colombière, *La Science heroique*, p. 299.

THE HORSE

THE ROLE PLAYED by the horse in Greek mythology was such a large one that I cannot hope to set it forth here in full within the limits of this book. Let us simply take note that the horse was so closely allied with Poseidon-Neptune that god and noble animal were often identified with one another. The learned Victor Magnien quotes an inscription from Laconia, thought to be of the fifth century of our era, composed in honor of the horse-god Hippios, whose cult was widespread in Greece[1].

Poseidon, "god of horses," as Servius calls him, created the horse, because the movements of its energy are as rapid and fluid as the sea waves. The Cretan ships of long ago usually carried figureheads in the shape of horses, which according to Reinach represented Poseidon-Hippios[2].

In Greek mythology, all the divine horses were sons of the Winds; for example, Mars' steeds were born of Boreas and one of the Furies. And the light of the sun acting on the earth's atmosphere, through whose agency the winds are formed, also enters into these tales. Thus it is that the divine sun-horse sires offspring as swift as himself, which sometimes carry mortals toward the sky. All these marvelous stories began as symbols by means of which ancient humanity expressed its tremendous need for greater light, for a wider and more direct knowledge of God.

In Hellas, as it was in many other nations, the horse was often sacrificed to the divinity. Its blood flowed not only in honor of Poseidon but also in the temples of Cybele—the Kybele of Berecynthus, the horse-headed goddess, counterpart of Poseidon, who hides perhaps behind the appearance of the forequarters of a horse printed on many Greek coins (Fig. 1).

The horse was one of the victims offered to Phoebus Apollo, the divine charioteer of the Sun. And it is a remarkable fact that one of the mystery cults of the Hellenistic region, a little after the seventh century before Christ, sacrificed a horse in a mystic ceremony in which each initiate covered himself with a horsehide before taking part in the ritual consumption of the victim's flesh, in order to identify himself more closely with it and the deity it represented.

Fig. 1 Coin of Heraclea.

Many Greek coins, and some others, carry the horse's whole image, some placed under a star with rays[3] (Fig. 2). Coins of the Carthaginian armies in Sicily, showing Greek influence, represent the horse with the palm tree, which was a symbol of life and of resurrection for the ancient world in general, as it was in primitive Christianity (Fig. 1).

Fig. 2 Greek coin from Arpi.

Greek metaphysics and theologies considered the earth, the universe, and the human being as formed on the same model, with their thought, *nous*, their ardor, *thymos*, their principle of life and passion, *epithymia*, and their various breathings, *pneumata*. Their theology supplied the Greeks with an image of the soul symbolized by a team of horses, as Plato expresses it in the *Phaedrus*; but Hermias says that Plato took this symbolic comparison from older poets who were inspired by the Divinity, such as Homer, Orpheus, and Parmenides. The driver of this team represents the directing Thought, and the two horses are spiritual Ardor and human Desire[4].

Rudolph Steiner, commenting on Plato, explained the symbolic team in this way: One of the horses is patient and wise, the other wild and rebellious; if the chariot meets an obstacle, the rebellious horse makes use of it to hinder his teammate and go against the driver. If the disobedient one is the stronger of the two, the chariot cannot follow the direction of the gods; but if the obedient horse is the stronger, the chariot will be able to enter the suprasensible world. So it is that the soul can never reach the kingdom of heaven without a struggle.

More simply, the informed Catholic sees in the symbolic equipage the picture of his soul borne along all his life by the two horses, the good and evil tendencies in himself; one that wishes to follow the way that is right and good, the other that wishes to turn aside into the paths of perdition. He looks to the driver, his conscience, to direct and maintain the chariot always according to that impartiality that is the sum total of human duty: the spiritual health and saintliness that he wishes to acquire are formed only from that.

It is well known that the horse played a very big role in religion and symbolism among the Gauls, as it did in all the western and northern countries. The data of prehistoric archeology shows that the ancient tribes of our part of the world believed that a principle of the divine nature existed in the horse. Did they think, as the people of Asia thought, that the sacred horse like a divine Messiah "descended straight from heaven to be sacrificed[5]"? How can we explain the bones of more than forty thousand horses heaped together at the foot of the rock at Solutré?

Gaul also recognized a goddess *Epona* whose characteristics were similar to those of Cybele, the counterpart of the Greek Poseidon, who is equivalent to Demeter, the universal Earth-Mother. Some statuettes discovered at Alesia (near Dijon) show Epona seated, with her hand on the head or neck of the figure of a horse smaller than herself[6]. There were certainly points of contact between the Druids and the high priesthood of the Greeks which declared themselves in exchanges of more or less strong religious influences.

In Spain, the beginning of the Iron Age gave us ornaments in the shape of a horse, with or without a rider, devouring a human head or a small indefinable monster (Fig. 3). The suggestion that has been made that this is the image of a horseman-god peculiar to the Iberians[7] seems fanciful, since some of them are riderless; and it would perhaps be less risky to suppose that they might represent the light of the sun destroying the darkness of night.

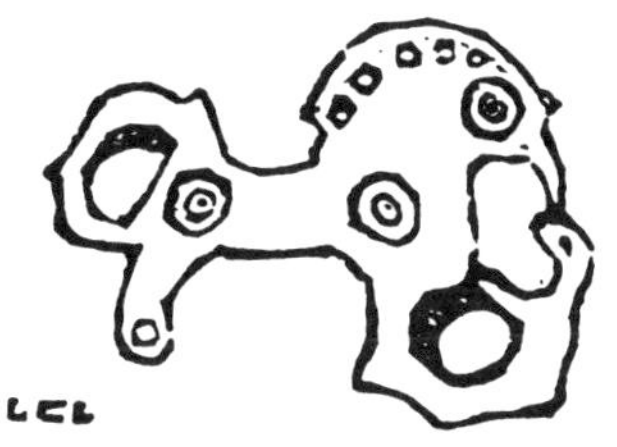

Fig. 3 Prehistoric Iberian ornaments.

Esaias Tegner says that among the Scandinavian countries, the preferred victim for auguries was the horse, whose still-quivering entrails were anxiously examined for omens[8]. Well before Christianity, the horse was worshipped among the Slavs, and survivals of this cult lingered on in the region of Triglaw and Volyn where the living animal was considered a national god and whose states were taken as oracles. This cult was definitely abolished only by the apostolate of the holy Bishop Otto of Bamberg[9].

In Tibet, to this day, the cult of Kwan-on, the horse-headed god, is widespread—it can be found from Mongolia to Japan; and Hayagriva, the god with a horse's neck, is sometimes shown with a small horse-head in his hair[10]. In the mythology of China, heaven is populated by a number of horses of higher and lower grades of divinity.

It is worth noting that the conventional idea of the old-world symbolists was that the mounted horse was one of the ideograms for Wisdom, represented by the horseman, and Intelligence, in the image of the horse; in Egypt, Portal says, the symbol was translated as: to bestow Intelligence[11]. In Gallic mythology, horse and rider were joined as a huge snake-tailed monster symbolizing the earth, carrying the sky on its shoulders.

In Christian iconography, it is rare to find representations of the horse alone that is given the attributes of Christ. The symbolic horse usually has a rider, and here also the two together form one image. Our forefathers connected them all the more readily because of the close association of the two in their daily life; very often, especially in the first millennium of our era, one grave received both horse and master. I have seen this with my own eyes in many different places. But in the Church's symbolism in medieval times, at least in the West, the mounted horse represented Jesus Christ, God and man, the animal corresponding to his humanity and the rider to his divinity. The iconographers Cloquet and Monsignor Barbier de Montault echo this symbolism[12] which we find again in the centaur, and which was expressed by Rabanus Maurus, the ninth-century Archbishop of Mainz; he said that the white horse of the Apocalypse represents the humanity of Christ, whose radiance extends over every blessed being:

Equus est humanitas
Christi: ut in Apocalypti,
Ecce equus albus
Id est, caro Christi omni
Sanctificate fulgens[13].

Here it might be remarked that among the Ancients almost all the sacred or miraculous horses were white. In circumstances of great solemnity it was a white horse that was sacrificed, as was a black bull. And Chinese poetry tells of the miracle of the horsehide and the heavenly lady with a horse's head[14]. The holy books of Judaism describe as "horses of fire" those who carried the prophet Elijah the Tishbite up to heaven[15]; but probably the horses dedicated to the Sun by the kings of Jerusalem which Josiah took away[16] were white, as were those that the classic arts have always represented hitched to the chariot of Apollo the Sun. In Samaria and Phoenicia were the divine horses Anamelech and Adramelech.

The color of the horse's coat was also given a special meaning in the mysticism and hermeticism of the Middle Ages: the white horse is ridden by the virgin heroes of spotless conscience, and also by the glorious saints. When it carries Christ it presents him as the victorious king ruling over the world, hell, and death in an atmosphere of triumphant apotheosis.

In all medieval art, the color russet is equivalent to bright red, the color of blood. The russet or sorrel horse seen in the illuminated manuscripts and stained glass windows of this time has two meanings: it is the mount of Christ as redeemer and victim, whose blood was shed for mankind, and also of Christ the judge, avenger of divine rights abrogated by the forces of evil. In both cases, the Savior is dressed in red and his horse is russet, stained with the blood of the victim, and also because the red robe has been for centuries that of the sovereign judge who has the power to inflict death. Symbolism gives pale and black horses a negative meaning[17]. Angelo de Gubernatis says that in various traditions of Europe and Asia the black horse indicates the demonic. In the West, it signifies Satan, or any influence that draws man down toward hell[18]. In medieval legends, Satan always bestrides a black charger when he puts on the aspect of an evil knight. In the old paintings, the horses of traitors and magicians are also black; and very often, so is the rearing horse which represents Intractability; its rider, which it throws off, personifies Presumption[19].

We find again the representation of the infernal horse in one of the poems which the Middle Ages dedicated to the Holy Grail. In *La Queste del Saint Graal*, attributed to Walter Map, the naiveté of the hero Percival prevents him from recognizing Satan who comes to him in the guise of a huge black charger.

We read in the first chapter of the prophecy of Zechariah:

"I saw by night, and behold a man riding upon a red horse, and he stood among the myrtle trees that were in the bottom; and behind him were there red horses, speckled, and white. Then said I, O my lord, what are these? And the angel that talked with me said unto me, I will shew thee what these be. And the man that stood among the myrtle trees answered and said, These are they that the Lord hath sent to walk to and fro through the earth. And they answered the angel of the Lord that stood among the myrtle trees, and said, We have walked to and fro through the earth, and behold, all the earth sitteth still, and is at rest[20]."

Commentators on the scriptures have seen the prophetic image of Jesus Christ in the man on the red horse who stood among the myrtle trees at the head of a company of angels, whom the prophet himself calls "the angel of the Lord."

In one of St. John's visions on the island of Patmos, a book appeared to him that was sealed with seven seals, which only the divine Lamb could break. And at the breaking of the first of the seven, "behold a white horse, and he that sat on him had a bow, and a crown was given unto him, and he went forth conquering, and to conquer[21]."

At the breaking of the second seal, a red horse appeared, mounted by a man armed with a sword to whom was given the power to spread warfare over the earth. The third seal revealed a black horse whose rider carried a balancing scale; and the fourth seal brought a pale horse ridden by Death, and Hell followed him[22].

Of the four mounted horses appearing in the terror of this vision Christian symbolism has kept only the first, the white horse, as the image of the victorious Christ. Astride his white steed, he carries a bow, and this projecting weapon, along with its accompanying arrow, in the literary symbolism of the holy scriptures, stands for the Word of the Lord.

In another vision, St. John again describes a horseman on a white horse: "And I saw heaven opened, and behold a white horse; and he that sat upon him was called Faithful and True, and in righteousness he doth judge and make war. His eyes were as a flame of fire, and on his head were many crowns; and he had a name written, that no man knew, but he himself. And he was clothed with a vesture dipped in blood: and his name is called The Word of God. And the armies which were in heaven followed him upon white horses, clothed in fine linen, white and clean. And out of his mouth goeth a sharp sword, that with it he should smite the nations: and he shall rule them with a rod of iron: and he treadeth the winepress of the fierceness and wrath of Almighty God. And he hath on his vesture and on his thigh a name written, KING OF KINGS, AND LORD OF LORDS[23]."

It is the grandest of all the symbolic pictures of the powerful and triumphant Christ, and much loved by all the illuminators of medieval copies of the Apocalypse. I reproduce here (Fig. 4) the beautiful miniature from the *Commentary on the Apocalypse* by Beatus of Liebana, from the twelfth or thir-

Fig. 4 Christ the Conqueror on the Apocalypse of Beatus; 12th-13th century.

teenth century. The artist has added a lance, the favorite knightly weapon of those days, to the sword of the Word, which is fashioned like those of good King Philip's barons; and the huge, multiform halo which crowns the divine horseman replaces to advantage the multiple crowns which other artists have piled upon his head.

Fig. 5 Éliphas Lévi's Anamelech.

The white horse also reminds us of the Anamelech of the hermetists. Éliphas Lévi tells us that there is a connection of allegorical meaning with "the Word of beauty." And even for many of the kabbalists, the generating Word of true beauty, of radiant celestial light, is the Messiah, is Christ. Lévi represents Anamelech (Fig. 5) with forepart raised on the globe of the world, the whinnying head lifted and crowned with a globular diadem circled with acanthus leaves. His body is mysteriously veiled in a rich drapery with a clasp at the breast in the shape of the symbolic marguerite of the East and the North, which after playing an analogous role in the ancient religions became one of the Christian emblems of the divine Word and its radiating beams on earth[24]. Lévi does not state the origin of the strange drawing of Anamelech that he shows[25], nor the basis of the symbolic meaning he attributes to him. One of its less enigmatic aspects is that, like the arrow that in the scriptural books, in Christian symbology and in the Kabbalah of the Jews, was one of the most frequently used symbols of God's Word, the horse also is one of the emblems of speed, of the outgoing force of the Word. Every thought, whether human or divine, needs a word, a voice, to express it; this voice carries it as a courser carries its rider; when one appears, it manifests the other. The very name Anamelech can be translated by the words: "the king's oracle."

Historically, the horse-god was worshipped in the Syro-phoenician region, at Sepharvaim and in Samaria, long before our era, conjointly with his brother Adramelech, "the king's robe[26]."

Long before the Christian era, the imagination of the Cretans and the people of Hellas conceived of an evil monster with the head of a horse, the body of a bird, and the paws of a lion. It was one of the emblems of the evil spirit. A number of stone engravings show this creature carrying off to its infernal den a lion that it has killed or perhaps a deer, an antelope, or a mountain sheep[27]. Christian symbology also, when it looked on the dark side of the horse, made it an image of Satan, the Lord of Evil; St. Augustine already in the fourth century saw in it one of the personifications of pride; St. Gregory looked upon it as the symbol of impurity and of a disorderly life, and St. Jerome agreed and made the horse the representative of men "who whinny after the wives of others." This explains the strange compositions of Romanesque art which show the man-horse or the woman-mare in the series picturing the demons of the deadly sins. A sculpture from the church at Montivilliers, in the diocese of Rouen, offers one of the most beautiful examples of these libidinous monsters (Fig. 6).

Fig. 6 The woman-mare on a capital in the church at Montivilliers; 12th century.

I said before that the Phoenician amulets shaped like bulls' heads were connected with an ancient cult of the Moon, on account of the crescent shape of the bulls' horns. I must add here that the talismanic character given in some countries to horseshoes comes from the same lunar cult. A little-known religious idea was also related to horseshoes in western Gaul in the time of the Roman conquest. Parenteau and I have found horseshoes, some whole and some broken, in the burnt and probably pre-Roman tombs of the Gallic necropolises of Bournigal and of Bourbelard de Pouzauges, in Vendée, and elsewhere in Poitou (Fig. 7). At Bernard, in Vendée, the head of a Gallo-Frank had been placed on a horseshoe supplied with nails[28]. Several times I have found half a horseshoe with its nails in a funerary urn, along with human ashes. In its normal use, the horseshoe gives security to the horse's step and hence to its rider; it is possible that in the tomb, broken in half, it pictures a life broken off, an existence stopped in mid-course.

Fig. 7 Horseshoe with six holes and horseshoe nail from a Gallic necropolis in Vendée.

NOTES

Title Figure: Horse engraved on a romanesque Christian epitaph at Tharos.

1. Victor Magnien, *Notes sur l'antique théologie grecque*, p. 15. Also, extract from *l'Acropole*, 1927.
2. Reinach, "Le disque de Phaistos," in *Revue archéologique*, 4th series, T. XV, 1910, p. 367.
3. Cf. Menard, *Histoire des Grecs*, T. I, p. 261, No. 163.
4. Magnien, *op. cit.*, p. 3.
5. Argos, in *Le Voile d'Isis*, T. XXV, 131, November 1930.
6. See Paul le Cour, "Alesia," in *Atlantis*, T. V, No. 42, July 1932, p. 160.
7. Déchelette, "Chronologie Préhistorique de la Péninsule Ibérique," in *Revue archéologique*, 4th series, T. XII, 1908, p. 403.
8. Tegner, *Frithiorf*, III.
9. Cf. L. Léger, "Études de Mythologie slave," in *Revue historique des Religions*, 1899, p. 6.
10. See *Le Voile d'Isis*, "Le Dieu au cou de Cheval," T. XXXVII, 145, January 1932, pp. 56-57.
11. Frédéric Portal, *Les Symboles Égyptiens comparés à ceux des Hébreux*, p. 143 *et seq*.
12. Cloquet, *Éléments d'Iconographie chrétienne*, p. 316.
13. Revelation 6:2; and Rabanus Maurus, *Allegoria*.
14. See Doré, *op. cit.*, Part 2, T. XI, p. 926.
15. II Kings 2:11.
16. II Kings 23:11.

17. See especially Fél. d'Ayzac, "Le Cheval," in *Revue de l'Art chrétien*, 1872, p. 242.
18. De Gubernatis, *Mythologie*, T. I, pp. 314 *et seq.*
19. See A. de Caumont, *Abécédaire archéologique*, (Architecture religieuse), p. 302.
20. Zechariah 1:8-11.
21. Revelation 6:2.
22. Revelation 6:4-8.
23. Revelation 19:11-16.
24. Éliphas Lévi, *Les Mystères de la Kabbale*, p. 56.
25. Above all, it resembles certain interpretations or imitations of Oriental art made in France in the time of Louis XIII and Louis XIV.
26. Cf. Ross, *Les religions du Monde*, p. 50.
27. Cf. Reinach in *Revue archéologique*, 3rd series, T. I, 1883, p. 369.
28. Cf. Abbé Baudry, *Le Cimétière chrétien de Bernard*, p. 14.

End Figure: Pierced bronze buckle from Ginvry (Meuse); between the 7th and 9th centuries.

THE ASS

NOTHING IS MORE arbitrary than the scale set up by human beings of the degrees of dignity of animals. These vary to such an extent in different countries and in different times as sometimes to contradict each other completely. Thus, in the Occident the ass was at all times too little valued, while in the ancient Orient it was always held in very high esteem.

The ancient Greeks linked the ass to the cult of Ceres, and then to that of Dionysus, who was carried by donkeys to Thebes from Boeotia[1]; hence the stone statue dedicated to the donkey in the town of Nauplia[2]. Ritual immolations of the ass in honor of the divinity, although rare, were practiced since very early times. Initiates of the participating cults, like the worshippers of the lion and the horse, wore the skin of the venerated animal during the sacrificial ceremonies[3]. A Mycenaean painting shows a procession of personages with donkeys' heads, and Glotz says that these are not monsters created by the artist's fantasy, but men costumed in sacred animal skins for the enactment of a holy rite. On a plaque from Phaistos, these same ass-headed figures hold in one hand the cross with a handle (the *ankh* or key of life of the Egyptians), and with the other hand make a gesture of adoration[4]. At Lampsacus, the Greeks sacrificed asses to Priapus[5].

In Rome, the ass played an honored part in the liturgy of the cult of Vesta, where it appeared crowned with flowers and little loaves made of wheat flour[6]. In Egypt, it had an important role in the religious myth of Set. The sacred books of the Hindus, the Rig-Veda, for example, praise the asses of Indra, and in India as in China this animal is often the mount of celestial individuals, princes, saints, and heroes[7]. And it should be remembered that Homer compares Ajax to an ass, and Paris to a horse[8]!

In the injunctions of the Mosaic law the ass is the only animal whose firstborn, like that of the human being, can be ransomed at birth by the sacrifice of a lamb. We read in Exodus: "All that openeth the matrix is mine, and every firstling among thy cattle, whether ox or sheep, that is male. But the firstling of an ass thou shalt redeem with a lamb: and if thou redeem him not, then shalt thou break his neck. All the firstborn of thy sons thou shalt redeem. And none shall appear before me empty[9]."

The Bible presents the donkey as the mount of princes: "Speak, ye that ride on white asses, ye that sit in judgment, and walk by the way," sang Deborah to the leaders of Israel[10].

It was as he went in search of the she-asses of the herds of his father, Kish, that Saul learned from Samuel that he was to reign over Israel[11]. Zechariah presents the Messiah as the King of Peace in these ardent terms: "Rejoice greatly, O daughter of Zion: shout, O daughter of Jerusalem: behold, thy King cometh unto thee: he is just, and having salvation: lowly, and riding upon an ass, and upon a colt the foal of an ass[12]." This prophetic text was recalled by the Evangelists themselves when they described Jesus' triumphal entry into Jerusalem.

More than any of the domestic animals, the ass seems to have been close to the person of Jesus Christ. *The Gospel of the Infancy*, the apocryphal *Gospel of Pseudo-Matthew*, and other writings of the first Christian centuries depict it as being present with the ox at the birth of Christ in the stable at Bethlehem. It seems that this specific mention comes from the concern to bring into the account of Christ's birth this verse from Isaiah: "The ox knoweth his owner, and the ass his master's crib: but Israel doth not know, my people doth not consider[13]." From the fourth to the sixth centuries we see the ass and his companion represented on sculptures dedicated to the Nativity.

Around the same time, other works of art show us the donkey carrying Jesus and Mary on the flight to Egypt; and finally, history tells us how Jesus' triumphal entry into Jerusalem, mounted on a she-ass, fulfilled the prophecy made by Isaiah that was just quoted.

Fig. 1 St. Christopher with an ass's head, from the Historical Museum in Moscow.

Simple Christians have had no difficulty in making the ass a sympathetic emblem of Christ, and have warmly honored the donkey of the Bethlehem stable, the mount of the journey to Egypt, and the she-ass and her foal of the triumph of the Day of Palms. Very ancient legends in France, Spain, and Italy, tell how the Savior rewarded the latter by allowing their offspring to become that kind of gray donkey that has two lines of dark hair in the form of a cross on its back and shoulders. In the tradition of our western French provinces, the gray ass marked with the long, dark dorsal cross is a symbol of the Savior carrying the cross of Calvary on his shoulders. A similar idea in the early church in Egypt related to the beetle, on whose back the separate lines of the corselet and wing sheaths trace a Tau, T[14]. Hungarian legends put a great strain on the gospel texts by claiming that the cruciform dorsal stripes on the gray ass were made by spurts of the divine blood at the scene of the Crucifixion. It should be added, on the other side of the picture, that in certain parts of Ireland folk say that the donkey's stripes are vestiges of the whiplashes that Jesus had to give his disobedient mount.

Because of its historical role of carrying Christ, in some countries the ass has received the title of Christophore, Christ-Bearer, from which comes the name Christopher. The same name was given in very ancient times in these same places to holy men who maintained among their fellows the teaching and the spirit of Christ (Fig. 1).

Although it has been so stated, the Western Middle Ages were far from being the inventors of the grotesque motif with which many of their important churches were adorned: an ass playing a lyre, a harp, or a viol. The ancient Egyptians had long ago drawn on their papyri asses standing on their hind legs and playing the harp[15]. Several thousand years before our era, the Chaldeans had carved this satirical subject on a decorated plaque, found in the recent excavations at Ur, Abraham's country[16] (Fig. 2).

Fig. 2 The ass musician on a Chaldean plaque.

In the Occident, the donkey-musician primarily represented Absurdity. In the domain of medieval spirituality, absurdity, which darkens men's souls, can be nothing but the action of an agent of hell, who is called the demon of pride or of self-will. The donkey-musician can be seen in the cathedrals of Chartres and of Nantes, in the church of Saint-Sauveur at Nevers, and several others. Sometimes the donkey is replaced by a goat or a pig, but even when the animal is different the symbolic meaning remains the same.

The Christian Middle Ages made the ass the symbol of the stubborn mentality that will not let itself be convinced by the truth. This is why the Germans of Westphalia made it the symbol of St. Thomas, the doubter[17]. Among the Ancients, the myth of Midas corresponded in a certain way with this symbolism of blind obstinacy.

As well as being the symbol for stubbornness and ignorance, the donkey also served in medieval imagery as mount for the demon of sloth. Thus we see him in numerous processions of the personified deadly sins[18].

On the other hand, the red donkey sometimes directly represented the Evil Spirit. In a number of countries, it is still said of an evil and dangerous person that "he is a red donkey." Formerly in Egypt red donkeys were sacrificed to the evil gods Set and Typhon. The whole Near East and India[19] also connects the red ass with evil; and certain occidental legends of sorcery claim that Satan sometimes is incarnated in the body of a red ass. Fortunately, red asses are very rare!

Fig. 3 The stylized Rempham star of the Kabbalah.

In the Kabbalah, the accursed five-branched star Rempham, pointing downward, which Éliphas Lévi says is a symbol of Lucifer, carries between its branches the natural or stylized head of an ass[20] (Fig. 3). This infernal star calls to mind the one pictured in the chapter discussing the symbolism of the buck goat, which carries the goat's head in place of that of the ass[21].

These facts are little known, and taking everything into account, the donkey has not too much to complain of in its treatment by Christian history, which has not failed to recognize either its evangelical functions nor its own special qualities. The only negative connotations are with characteristics with which it was already endowed by the symbolism of times before our era.

NOTES

Title Figure: The ass musician of Aulnay de Sontonge.

1. Cf. Nonnus, *Dionysiaca*, XXXVII.
2. Pausanias, *Voyages historiques*, XXVIII.
3. Cf. A. B. Cook, *Archéologie*, August 1894, p. 122; also Reinach, *Revue archéologique*, T. XXVI, 1895, p. 103.
4. Cf. Glotz, *Civilisation égéenne*, Book IV, p. 271.
5. Ovid, *Fasti*, VI.
6. *Ibid.*
7. See Doré, *Superstitions*, passim.
8. Homer, *The Iliad*, II and VII.
9. Exodus 34:19-20.
10. Judges 5:10. [*Editor's note:* See also Judges 10:4 and 12:13-14.]
11. I Samuel 9 and 10.
12. Zechariah 9:9.
13. Isaiah 1:3.
14. See Part VI, "Scarab," p. 341.
15. Cf. Gust. le Bon, *Les premières civilisations*, p. 336, fig. 196.
16. Cf. L. Abensour, "Une Visite aux fouilles d'Ur," in *Le Miroir du Monde*, T. II, 1931, No. 73, p. 94.
17. De Gubernatis, *Mythologie*, p. 385.
18. Cf. Mâle, *L'Art religieux (1)*, p. 330, fig. 181 and p. 341, fig. 192.
19. See Guénon, "Seth," in *Le Voile d'Isis*, T. XXXVI, No. 142, p. 592.
20. Lévi, *Mystères de la Kabbale*, p. 51.
21. See above, Part II, "The Goat," p. 86, fig. 1.

End Figure: Animal head of a St. Christopher from the Historical Museum in Moscow.

THE DOG

THE DOG RECEIVED little sympathy from the people of the ancient world, and many terrible scriptural texts spoke against it. David described thus his situation with his enemies: "For dogs have compassed me[1]"; and the Church has heard this cry echoed by Christ persecuted by the Jewish priesthood. Solomon's words, "As a dog returneth to his vomit, so a fool returneth to his folly[2]," have been constantly applied by the Church to the worst renegades and backsliders. Jesus himself taught that the children's bread must not be given to the dogs[3], and St. Thomas Aquinas remembered these words when he wrote the *non mittendus canibus* of his *Lauda Sion*[4]. The book of Revelation groups under the title "dogs" those to be chased from the celestial city: "sorcerers, and whoremongers, and murderers, and idolaters, and whosoever loveth and maketh a lie[5]." The ancient Greeks made the dog the emblem, if not the very origin, of the classical philosophy of Cynicism, *kynismos*[6].

Another factor that counted against the unfortunate animal was that the annual periods of greatest heat were suffered under the influence of the stars forming the constellation of Canis Major (July twenty-second to August twenty-third). The ancient world, except for Egypt and Ethiopia, attributed to the period of the dog-days the most disastrous effects. Medicinal remedies lost their efficacy; Hippocrates himself made the statement: "*Sub cane et ante canem difficiles sunt purgationes.*" At such times there was nothing to do but commend the sick to the mercy of the gods, and accordingly the Romans annually sacrificed a red dog at the beginning of the dog-days.

It is strange that the cheetah, which is in many ways similar, should have enjoyed a position in Christian symbolism that it seems should rightly have been reserved for the dog, which is man's particular and devoted friend, defends him and often saves his life[7].

Christian art did render the dog justice in making it symbolize fidelity in all its aspects. In this role it lies at the feet of the effigies of queens and ladies of quality in their burial vaults, and also under the feet of vassal lords and faithful squires[8]; and in St. Peter's Church in Rome, the dog's image accompanies the statue of Fidelity personified.

Since it is also the devoted guardian and defender of the flocks, Christian symbolism has made the dog the emblem of priests of all orders, who are appointed to be caretakers of Christ's human flock. It is thus that the *canes dominici* are shown in the fourteenth-century Spanish chapel in Florence, and on an old reliquary of the Filles de Notre-Dame at Naumur[9].

But never was the dog given the honor of representing Christ himself.

NOTES

1. Psalms 22:16.
2. Proverbs 26:11.
3. St. Mark 7:27.
4. St. Thomas Aquinas, *Roman Breviary*; office of the Holy Sacrament.
5. Revelation 22:15.
6. *Editor's note*: Diogenes, founder of the school of the Cynics, called himself the Hound.
7. *Editor's note*: The Zoroastrians, however, held the dog in great esteem and affection; see the Zendavesta, *The Vendidad*, Chapters XIII and XV.
8. Cf. L. Charbonneau-Lassay, "La Plate-tombe de Jehan de Grimouard, 1532," in *Revue du Bas-Pitou*, 1924, Book IV.
9. Cf. L. Cloquet, *Éléments d'Iconographie chrétienne*, XIII, p. 317.

III

WILD ANIMALS

THE DEER

ONE OF THE symbolic animals that the early Christians adopted with the most certainty as an allegorical image of Christ, and also of his disciple, the Christian, was the stag. Poets and naturalists of ancient times, such as Pliny, Theophrastus, Xenophon, Martial, Lucretius[1], and many others, portrayed the stag as the implacable enemy of snakes, pursuing them relentlessly into their holes. Martial and Plutarch add that with the breath of its nostrils—some say, of its mouth—the stag would drive the snakes from their underground hiding places and devour them, and that in this way its youth was renewed. Reflecting this ancient belief, a Roman marble relief (Fig. 1) from the Naples Museum shows a stag fighting with a snake. The stag has fallen on its knees, but it has succeeded in seizing its enemy's head in its mouth and is crushing it between its teeth.

Fig. 1 Pre-Christian Roman marble from the Naples Museum.

In Afghanistan today there is a species of the deer or goat family that attacks serpents and often eats them. The Persians call these animals "*pausens*[2]." The last Mazdeans living in that region consider the duel between *pausen* and snake as the allegorical image of the triumph of good, or "Ormuzd," over evil, "Ahriman." But since the *pausen* often suffers from gall or kidney stones, it is killed in order to obtain them as potent charms against the bites of snakes and the stings of scorpions.

Medieval manuals are full of accounts of the stag's ingenious methods for forcing his enemy to come out of hiding. *The Armenian Bestiary* tells us: "The stag is the enemy of the serpent. To escape him, the snake hides in the crevice of a rock. But the stag fills up his mouth with water and spits it out into the crack where the reptile is hiding (Fig. 2). If it comes out it is torn to pieces; if it stays hidden it does not escape death, for it is drowned. In the same way, our Lord put to death the demon, the great dragon, both by the celestial waters flowing from his divine wisdom, and by his ineffable virtue. The invisible serpent cannot resist waters of this nature, but perishes at once[3]."

Fig. 2 Stag forcing a reptile to leave its den; miniature from the Divine Bestiary, Bibliothèque de l'Arsenal, Paris.

Thus making the stag the symbol of the triumphant Christ, the Ancients saw the water expelled from its mouth against its adversary as the allegorical counterpart of the Lord's victorious Word. In the liturgies of the ancient mysteries, deerskins were consecrated as a sort of ritual garment of purification that brought the initiate closer and made him more acceptable to the god. In the Greek rites of Dionysus the participants covered themselves with deerskins, and Nonnus portrays the god himself clad in this fashion[4]. In the mysteries of Ceres celebrated at Eleusis, fawns and kids were sacrificed and the participants were draped with the skins of the young victims[5]. In the first century A.D., Pliny seriously advised a sure protection from snakes, to be found by sleeping under a deerskin or by rubbing oneself with the stomach lining of an unborn fawn[6]. And in 1568, Jacques du Fouilloux of Poitiers, in his celebrated book on hunting, also gives a series of cures provided by the deer for all kinds of ailments and injuries, especially from snake venom[7].

Not only can the stag heal others after its death, but it can also in its own lifetime cure itself. According to the Ancients, we are indebted to it for the discovery of dittany, the miraculous herb that cures all wounds. "The wounded deer," says Tertullian, "in order to expel a barbed arrow from its flesh, heals itself by browsing on dittany[8]." The celebrated Greek physician Dioscorides states that in his time dittany was called *Cervi ocellum* (little eye of the deer)[9].

There is a concept in Europe which I think is even older than the tradition of the stag's hatred for the serpent, which relates the stag to the idea, or one might say the cult, of light.

Pre-Mycenaean art quite often shows a stag harnessed to a solar chariot. According to Déchelette, it seems that the idea of the stag sharing this privilege with the horse is also echoed in Greek mythology, which consecrates the stag to Artemis, born with her brother Apollo on the island of Delos and sharing his nature[10].

We also know that the fawn was a special symbol attributed to Apollo, who was himself the god of light; and Pausanius tells of certain statues which depict Apollo carrying a tiny fawn in his hand[11]. Similar statues can be found in the Louvre and the British Museum. One of them is from the sixth century B.C., from a Greek school, another is the hand of a large bronze statue of Apollo found at Tralles (Fig. 3).

In ancient European symbolism, the white stag shared the special importance of the white horse. Deer pictured in the myths of Apollo and Artemis, or later in the miraculous hunts of St. Eustace and St. Hubert, were painted by the early artists in natural tones or in white. "It is a known fact," says Lanoë-Villène, "that the white stag was a symbol which the early Christians attributed to Jesus Christ[12]." In the East the white stag is also very highly honored and one of the hymns of the Rig-Veda compares it with a priest-god[13].

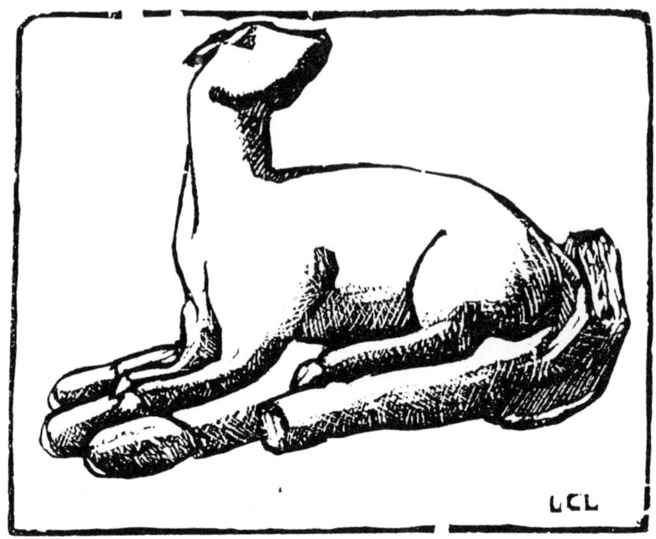

Fig. 3 Apollo's hand holding a fawn; Greek bronze from Tralles.

It seems that another trace of the ancient European traditions that link the stag to the idea of light remained mysteriously hidden among the many medieval documents in which one sees the stag, or simply his head, crowned with a star. For one example, the fifteenth-century tile pavement of the Beaune hospice shows a full face view of a stag's head surmounted by a star, recalling the Orphic Hymn to Dionysus, in which the god is named "Prince of the Mysteries of the Night"; for another, the thirteenth-century seal of Heliot Bertaut bears a stylized stag's head surmounted by the glorifying sign of the sun and moon, which in the Middle Ages was usually reserved for specific images of Christ[14] (Fig. 4). In the "Golden Legend" of the only existing occidental hagiography, several well-known hunting scenes show Christ taking the form of a stag, in order to reveal himself in this manner to chosen souls. The best-known are the hunts of St. Hubert and St. Eustace.

Fig. 4 The seal of Heliot Bertaut.

A very old French tale gives the following account of the second of the two saints: There was a man named Placidus who was a pagan, but all the same a man of virtue, filled with

Fig. 5 The stag of the legendary hunt, from the Abbey of St. Denis; 15th century, now in the Cluny Museum.

kindness for all who suffered misfortune. One day when he and his friends were out hunting, a band of magnificent stags appeared. Soon Placidus left his companions and launched headlong into the pursuit of the biggest and most beautiful stag, which had pulled away from the rest of the band. After a wild chase the stag suddenly leapt to the top of a rock and faced the hunter, saying: "Placidus, why do you not follow me into the heights? I am Christ who loves you and whom you serve without yet knowing it. Your offerings and your spirit of justice please me, and that is why I made myself into a splendid stag, to draw you to me."

"Beautiful Stag, if you are the Christ of such great fame, explain your words and I will believe in you," answered Placidus.

The divine Stag replied, "I am the Christ; I became man and died on the cross; and after three days in the shadow of the tomb I rose to everlasting life. And now I am waiting for you. Come to me, Placidus; I am Christ!" And before the pagan's astonished eyes, the stag grew to immense proportions and soon merged into a dazzling blaze of light, in which appeared a crucified man whose heart and four limbs bled; then, little by little, the rock became bare and stark as it had been before. Placidus went away, abandoned everything, even his given name, and gave himself totally to Christ, who had illumined his soul by means of the miraculous stag.

The same legend, beautifully portrayed in the portal frieze of the royal chapel of the Château d'Ambroise which was sculpted in the late fifteenth century, is attributed to St. Hubert by several other authors of antiquity[15] (Fig. 5).

Since we find ourselves in the domain of the age of chivalry, let us refer to one of the poems of this time about the

Holy Grail. We read that when the three illustrious knights and companions of the Round Table, Galahad, Percival, and Bors, and the maiden She-Who-Cannot-Tell-A-Lie, were seeking their way and prayed for guidance, they saw a stag whiter than the whitest meadow flowers emerge from the woods bordering the path; two lions walked before him and two behind. The knights and the maid followed the magical animal and soon were led into a sanctuary where a priest prepared to say mass. Hardly had he begun when before their wondering eyes the stag changed into a man and seated himself on a richly decorated throne above the altar, while the four lions were also transformed, the first into a winged man, the second into an eagle, the third into a winged lion, and the fourth into a winged bull. When the mass was finished, all four lifted up the throne where the man who had been a stag was seated, and flew away through the stained glass window without breaking a single pane. Then the three knights and their companion realized that the stag and the four lions who had led them there were really the Christ and his four Evangelists[16].

Fig. 6 Part of a Gallic sculpture in the Luxembourg Museum in Paris.

The stag is also a Gallic symbol; in Gallic mythology Cernunnos was the god of abundance[17] (Fig. 6), and as the personification of the divine bestowal of worldly goods he is most often shown in human form crowned with the spreading antlers of a stag.

It should be noted that in certain other European and Asian countries the stag is also connected with the idea of fulfillment and contentment. In Chinese, the character for the stag's name, *lu*, is pronounced like the character for the enjoyment of prosperity, and is the ideogram for this desirable condition[18].

The stag shares with the bull and the ram the honor of representing Jesus Christ in his three-fold capacity of father, leader, and guide watching over the Christian family, which is made up of his spouse the Church, and the faithful, who are their children. In the forest, his behavior in fact confirms this symbolism: as the leader of his herd of does and fawns, he is a fine sight as he stands among the trees, watching and listening, ready to alert his family to the slightest sign of danger.

Among the stranger remedies that ancient medicine borrowed from the stag were several related to human procreation. Even as late as the eighteenth century, a powdered concoction made from the stag's genital organs was still used to increase the generative powers[19]. But it is even better to prolong life than to create it, and throughout the old world the stag was one of the symbols of longevity. Thus, in ancient Europe, Ausonius recounted: "The raven lives for three centuries, but even if she lived three times nine complete centuries, the bronze-hoofed stag would surpass her by three times three of Nestor's lifetimes[20]." In Asia too the stag was a symbol of long life; notably, in China and Japan the god of long life is accompanied by a stag carrying "a branch from the peach tree of longevity (Fig. 7)."

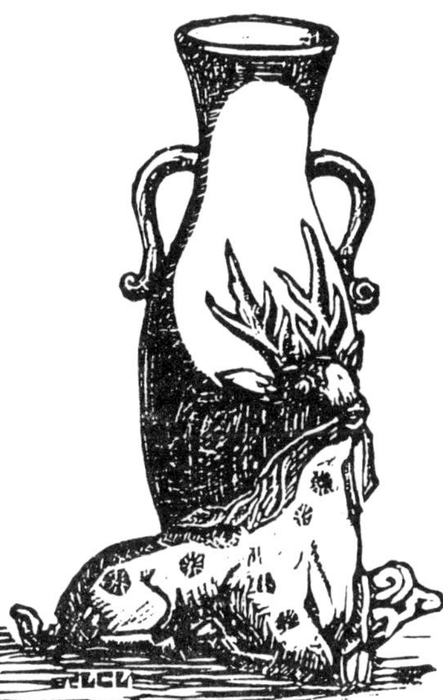

Fig. 7 The stag as the Chinese symbol of longevity: a vase from the Cernuschi collection.

The first words of the 42nd Psalm gave early Christian symbolism the image of the stag as a symbol of the faithful soul aspiring to God: "As the hart panteth after the water brooks, so panteth my soul after thee, O God. My soul thirsteth for God, for the living God." The same text: "*Sicut cervus desiderat ad fontes . . .*" appears on a mosaic in the old baptistry of Salone, mounted above two great stags drinking together from the sacred urn[21].

Fig. 8 The stag and the doe at the four springs of the mystic mountain; from a mosaic at Bir-Ftouha.

Other examples in the works of the early Christian artists portray stags leaning over the waters of the Jordan, where Jesus received his baptism from John, as is shown on a fresco in the Roman catacombs at Pontien[22]. In each of these works from the first five centuries of Christian art it is primarily the thirst for nearness to God through the purification of baptism which is symbolized; and then also the thirst for a closer union through partaking of the Eucharistic blood.

The connections between the symbolic stag and the sacrament of the Eucharist are especially evident in a great many works of art dating from the first centuries of Christianity, such as the expressive mosaics of Bir-Ftouha (Fig. 8) and a pottery lamp found at Tebessa (third to fifth century) on which is depicted a stag placed above the communion chalice[23].

All of these examples convey the quenching of the soul's thirst, which is symbolized by the stag, through the sacrament of the Eucharist, following the symbolism set forth in the psalm of David quoted above.

Many works of art from the first Christian millennium show the stag and the doe, one on each side of the Fountain of Life; others show them drinking from the four living rivers that flow from the hilltop of the triumphant Lamb of God. A wonderful North African mosaic also shows the two con-

Fig. 9 The stag and the doe with the Eucharistic vessel, on a 4th- or 5th-century sarcophagus at Ravenna.

tented animals drinking from the four rivers of the Mount, whose common source is surrounded by a great Eucharistic chalice filled with blood[24]. In Ravenna there is a sarcophagus from the fourth or fifth century on which the stag and the doe drink directly from a huge Eucharistic urn[25] (Fig. 9). On all of these works of art, and many others from the early centuries of Christianity, we are given the most beautiful symbol of conjugal and Christian life ever conceived: a husband and wife drawing comfort from the same source of faith.

NOTES

Title Figure: The Stag bearing Christ's monogram; 3rd- or 4th-century weaving from Akhmim, Egypt.

1. Pliny, *Natural History*, VIII, 50; Theophrastus, *De Causis vegetationis*, Book IV, 10; Xenophon, *Géoponiques*, XIX, 6 [*Editor's note*: Possibly *Oeconomicus*]; Martial, *Epigrams*, XII, 19; Lucretius, *Works*, VI.
2. Cf. M. Karil, "Les Afghans," in *Revue du Monde Catholique*, T. VI (1880), No. 33, p. 401.
3. C. Cahier, "Du bestiaire," in *Nouveaux mélanges archéologiques*, 1874, p. 136.
4. Nonnus, *Dionysiaca*, IX.
5. Aelien, *Variae Historiae*, III, 42.
6. Pliny, *Natural History*, VIII, 50 and XXVIII, 42.
7. Du Fouilloux, *La Vénerie*, XV.
8. Tertullian, *De Poenitentia*, XII, Tr. M. de Genonde, T. II, p. 216.
9. Dioscorides, *De Materia Medica*, Book III, Chapter LXVII.
10. J. Déchelette, "Le culte du Soleil aux temps préhistoriques," in *Revue archéologique*, T. XIII (1909), p. 314.

11. Pausanius, *Voyages Historiques*.
12. Lanoë-Villène, *Le Livre des Symboles*, T. III, p. 70.
13. *Ibid.*, p. 71.
14. See Guillon and Monceaux, *Les carrelages historiés*, I, p. 36.
15. In the Cathedral of Chartres, there is a magnificent thirteenth-century window, dedicated to St. Eustace, which is reproduced by Mâle in *L'Art religieux* (3), p. 324.
16. See Jacques Boulanger, *Le Saint Graal*, XXI, Paris, p. 71.
17. Cf. Reinach, *Guide du Musée de Saint-Germain-en-Laye*, p. 73.
18. Cf. Doré, *Recherches*, Part I, T.II, no. 4, p. 474.
19. *Recueil de recettes de Mme. des Bournais*, eighteenth-century MS.
20. Cf. Doré, *op. et loc. cit.*
21. See Leclercq and Marron, *Dictionnaire*, T. IV, vol. I, col. 106.
22. *Ibid.*, T. II, vol. II, col. 3.301.
23. *Ibid.*, Section LXXXIV, col. 1190, Pl. no. 20.
24. Cf. L. Delattre, *Symboles eucharistiques*. Carthage, pp. 11-18.
25. Cf. Leclercq, *Manuel*, T. II, p. 310.

End Figure: Stags drinking at the sacred fountain; engraved on lazulite; from the Comte de Rochebrune's collection.

THE PANTHER

And other Wildcats, also the Hyena and the Mole

THE PEOPLE OF ancient Egypt greatly admired and were strongly attracted by the very beautiful wild animal called the panther, and endowed this splendid creature with all sorts of unusual and excellent qualities to an exaggerated degree. Their veneration was expressed in the use of the panther's magnificent fur and also the *nebris*, the skin of the panther cub, by the priests in the most sacred rites, and by their masters the pharaohs in the holiest and most solemn events of their royal and priestly lives (Fig. 1). The *nebris* also appears to have been used in the regular liturgy and in the mystery ceremonies. The panther skins placed before Osiris or Anubis were from flawless animals, ritually sacrificed. The skin of the panther cub served too as a garment or wrap for Anubis, god of the dead, thus connecting him with the idea of a second birth.

Fig. 1 Horus robed in panther skin; tomb of Seti I.

In funeral rites, the panther's skin was used as a bed for the deceased and provided "a good burial." Egyptian sacred imagery shows three stylized panther skins attached together: first of all, the amulet *mest*

Fig. 2 The Egyptian amulet mest.

Fig. 3 The Egyptian hieroglyph mes.

(Fig. 2) which was placed in the tombs; and the hieroglyphic sign *mes* (Fig. 3) which means "to be born" or "to bear a child[1]." From these signs we see once again that the panther was an ideogram relating to the appearance of life, and that by extension it became, in certain circumstances, a symbol of strength and of resurrection[2].

It is generally believed that the unshorn pelts of certain wild animals are strongly charged with electrical or magnetic elements. In France, the furs of foxes and several of the small cats are still used to ward off lumbago. To cite only one example, recently the Grands Magasins du Louvre in Paris sold "guaranteed genuine wildcats' skins for use in bandages for the treatment of rheumatism[3]."

On another level, the Egyptians regarded the panther's skin as a powerful source of emanations of a higher kind, and their priests believed in its magical and spiritual effect. The same opinion was held by the ancient priests in Greece, Asia Minor, and from Central Asia to the Far East. In Greek art and mythology it was in turn adopted as a robe for Dionysus or Bacchus, and in certain bronze figurines one sees the graceful animal entwined with ivy or leafy branches of the grapevine dedicated to this god[4] (Fig. 4). Nonnus states that panthers were often harnessed to the chariot of this same god[5]; and here we encounter the most sublime aspect of Dionysus, which made him one of the images of the divine Word among the Greeks, and by means of which certain allegorical comparisons have been made between him and Jesus Christ. A statuette from the Egypto-Hellenic civilization represents "the God of

Fig. 4 The Bacchic panther; Greek figurine in bronze.

the Word" in the form of the child Dionysus bearing wings and crowned with leaves; with one finger he points to his mouth, the instrument of the Word, while in his other hand he carries a horn of plenty filled with grapes[6].

Fig. 5 The panther carrying Astarte; a Phoenician statuette.

The Phoenicians or Sidonians gave the panther to their goddess Astarte to ride (Fig. 5); and as she presided over the human process of procreation and birth, this recalls the Asian role of the panther and also the leopard, in which they were related to the idea of the birth of the world and of the appearance of life there.

The panther is also very frequently connected to the idea of light, and his image often serves to support antique candelabras (Fig. 6); similarly, on the other side of the world, the panther's close relative, the jaguar, appears in ancient Peruvian jewelry as the sacred animal representing the blazing image of the sun.

The ancient symbolism of the panther offered a striking richness of allegory to Christian iconography. By dying and bequeathing his skin to mankind, the ancients believed, the

Fig. 6 Base of a Greek candelabra from the Campana collection.

panther obtained for human beings the gift of holy inspiration and placed them under the sway of celestial influences; just as, according to the mystics, the Savior through his teaching and his death on the cross awakened man to his eternal destiny and sent divine grace down upon him.

Several of the old writers had already attributed to the panther the capacity to give out a scent of such exquisite sweetness that other animals—who, they said, were the only creatures who could perceive it—were irresistibly drawn to it. The Christian authors went even further: they added that among all the animals, only the dragon and the snake, instead of being amorously attracted by the panther's scent, are on the contrary so disturbed by it that they run far away at the first whiff (Fig. 7).

Along with the Ancients, these Christian symbolists regarded the panther, in company with the unicorn and the elephant, as one of the three animals considered to be chaste; hence, the medieval artists harnessed them together to the allegorical chariot of Virginity. This idea recurred up till the eighteenth century, notably on a miniature of Renaissance times which belongs to the Bibliothèque Nationale in Paris[7].

In his twelfth-century *Divine Bestiary*, William of Normandy added the following to his song about the panther's beauty:

In this beast, without any doubt,
There is great and beautiful significance:
And it signifies, without mistake,
Jesus Christ our Savior
Who by his great humility
Took on our carnal nature[8].

Fig. 7 Animals following the panther, and the dragon who flees from it; a 13th-century miniature from a bestiary in the Bibliothèque de l'Arsenal.

The *Armenian Bestiary* from the Middle Ages also says that the female panther sleeps for three days after she has eaten, and then awakens. In the same way, Christ came back to life after three days, having satiated his hunger—that is to say, having achieved his earthly mission. When the panther wakes up she roars with all her force, and from her mouth exhales an odorous breath which makes the other animals come flocking to this intoxicating perfume. "In this same way, Christ, having risen from the dead, made all men near and far aware of a subtle and enticing odor[9]."

Fig. 8 Heraldic panther, from Connaissances nécessaires au Bibliophile *by Rouveyre who mistook it for a griffin.*

As regards the panther and almost everything else, the medieval heraldry of the nobility in our own Western countries coincided with the way of thinking of the bestiaries which had been the sources of heraldry itself; but towards the end of the fifteenth century, the primary meaning of heraldic symbolism changed along with the Christian understanding of it, and the symbol of the panther came to share the same fate reserved till then for the tiger, and to represent implacable ferocity, brutality, and treachery (Fig. 8). One must recognize the fact that in the medieval armorials and bestiaries, the panther and the leopard were often confused with the snow leopard and the tiger, and especially, as we shall see, with the lynx. In fact, in the paintings and sculptures of this period it is often very difficult to tell one of these carnivores from another, since the artists of the time had only an incomplete knowledge of them.

Nearly all the animals which were symbols of Christ in sacred literature and art had also disagreeable characteristics which in other circumstances made them representatives of Satan or of human vices. Here we have the opposite sides of some very beautiful coins. The harmful instincts of human nature which lead to evil were grouped by Christian asceticism into three classes, which are the three concupiscences: concupiscence of the eyes, that of the flesh, and that of worldly pride. The symbolists represented these three tendencies by three animals: the panther, because its spotted coat seems to be covered with eyes, the she-wolf, and the lion, since the former was one of the ancient symbols of immodesty, and the latter of pride. Dante uses this symbolism at the outset of his sublime journey to the three habitations of the dead; the panther is the first to stop him, and is soon joined by the she-wolf and the lion, and the poet is only saved from them by the arrival of Virgil[10].

The symbolic antithesis of the panther in its chief role as image of the Redeemer is the hyena, and in this presentation, the symbolism of Christian times once again relied upon elements from the ancient naturalists. The reference here is to the common hyena of North Africa, the *hyena crocuta*, whose spotted coat is somewhat similar to that of the panther. Pliny specifically places these two animals in opposition to each other. He recounts that in his time it was said that the hyena was the terror of panthers, who would not even try to defend themselves against it. A panther would never attack a man wearing a hyena skin, and "it is an extraordinary thing that when the skin of a hyena is held up in front of that of a panther, the latter's fur falls out[11]." His shadow alone strikes dogs dumb. . . . The truth is that the hyena, although ferocious, is also cowardly.

The old naturalists endowed the hyena, like the panther, with powers of fascination; but woe to those who listen to him: "One hears of marvelous tales; the strangest is that the hyena, roaming around the sheep-pens, imitates human language, and remembering a man's name, calls him outside and devours him[12]." But the most extraordinary fable, still according to Pliny, is that "hyenas are hermaphrodites; they become alternately male and female, and can reproduce without the male[13]."

Everyone, including Aristotle (who did not believe in the hermaphrodite story)[14], agrees in consigning to them the debased behavior of the slut and the scavenger after carrion that makes the hyena disgusting to all; and they also agree in attributing to it a knowledge of magical arts and of disquieting secrets belonging to the dead and to the invisible powers. Pliny says that this animal can also affect people's minds, confusing them in order to attract them to itself[15]. For later Christian symbolists, this notion of the hyena's ability to disguise its voice became the perfect representation of that perfidious tempter, the Devil.

Related to the panther are the cheetah, the leopard, the snow leopard, and the lynx, all middle-sized felines with spotted coats. The cheetah is the least fierce and was formerly

Fig. 9 The hunting cheetah; 10th-century illumination.

compared to Christ, the hunter of souls, because of the docility with which it allows itself to be trained like a hunting dog to pull down other fleet animals upon whom it leaps with remarkable speed and skill. Hunting with cheetahs still takes place in Turkestan and from the shores of the Caspian Sea to the Gobi Desert north of Persia and Afghanistan.

Christian iconography sometimes represents the cheetah in the act of hunting. Dom Leclercq, notably, has reproduced an example found in a concordance of the Gospels from the tenth century[16]. On it we see a hunter setting his cheetah in pursuit of a deer and his doe (Fig. 9). The cheetah can also be recognized in the spotted cat chasing a horned quadruped in the arabesque decor of a pre-Islamic Coptic church, in another example given by the same Dom Leclercq. In the testimonies of art, it is sometimes impossible to distinguish the cheetah from the panther, leopard, or other wild cat; so it should be emphasized here that unless a wild cat is portrayed in the company of its master, the greatest caution must be exercised in identifying it with the cheetah.

In regard to the leopard, Christian symbolism initially propagated an old misconception repeated by Pliny[17], which was that the "leo-pardus," lion-panther, was "engendered by a lion and a panther, as the name seems to indicate[18]." Thus, the animal was sometimes considered to be the emblematic representative of the fruit of illegitimate union. Another allegorical aspect of the leopard's character rests on the illusion which led the Ancients to believe that the animal changes its skin to deceive other animals as well as people. This led to the Christians' choice of the leopard as one of the principal images of the infernal imposter, who with hypocrisy leads human souls astray[19]. By this symbolism the leopard is made the opposite of the cheetah, which represents the Savior pursuing souls in order to save them.

The leopard has earned a reputation for extreme ferocity, and was one of the most feared of the beasts which tore to pieces the Christian martyrs in the amphitheaters of Rome. Records of the martyrdom of St. Marciana of Caesarea show that she was torn apart by a leopard after a lion had spared her[20].

The lynx was designated as "little panther," in his treatise on the hunt by the Greek author Oppien[21], who lived in Cilicia (southeast Asia Minor) during the third century A.D. Along with Oppien, the other classical writers who related the lynx with the panther consecrated it also to Dionysus[22], and attributed most of the same qualities, whether real or fictitious, to both animals. They even created new ones for the lynx, which thus, like Jason's Argonaut Lynceus, acquired the privilege of such piercing eyesight that it could see everything with perfect clarity even through the most opaque substances. Consequently, the lynx became the symbol of Christ's omniscience, described by St. Paul: "Neither is there any creature that is not manifest in his sight; but all things are naked and opened unto the eyes of him with whom we have to do[23]." Finally, thanks to the power of vision accorded to him by the Ancients, the lynx became known as Christ's "Vigilance," like the lion who sleeps with his eyes open, the falcon who was the Egyptian eye of Horus, the crane who keeps watch holding a stone in his raised claw—the illumined vigilance of Christ who watches over his own, and whom nothing escapes (Fig. 10).

Fig. 10 The lynx, from the Hortus Sanitatis.

The Ancients generously attributed to the lynx a keenness of hearing equal to the imagined power of its eyes; it was said to be extremely sensitive to beautiful music, which is why Virgil describes it standing immobile and enraptured by the marvelous songs of Damon and Alphesiboeus[24]. The old world's imagination also endowed with extraordinary properties those conglomerates formed in the lynx's body which they called *lycurium*; the principal virtue of this stone was said to be found in the treatment of mental disturbances, epilepsy, and jaundice. Marbode, Bishop of Rennes, who lived in the twelfth century, reported that the lynx could brush away the traces of its footprints with its tail, so that it could not be followed by people who wished to kill it and take the stone it carried within it[25]. In mineralogy, a type of tourmaline is called "lynx's stone" or "ligurite": it is an aluminum silicate[26].

Very ancient symbolism contrasted the lynx, which sees better than any other living creature, with the mole, who formerly was supposed to have no eyes and to die when exposed to sunlight. Our good friend La Fontaine echoed antiquity's opposition of the mole to the lynx: "We are lynxes toward our fellow men, and moles toward ourselves[27]."

Because of its life hidden in the earth, the Ancients sometimes made the mole the symbol of the earth, as was the snake in other circumstances; like the snake, the mole was thought to know underground secrets. French peasants still say that the mole always knows exactly what time it is, and never pushes the earth from the mouth of its hole except at noon and at six o'clock. The Greeks sacrificed it to Poseidon because they believed the sea god was responsible for the stability of everything built upon the earth; and the mole lives in the upper level of the subsoil on which the foundations of all buildings depend.

Fig. 11 The mole, from an 18th-century woodcut.

Christian symbolism made the mole the sign of the Demon, the Prince of Darkness who plunges the eyes of the soul into wilful obscurity and dwells at the bottom of the abyss, like the mole in the shadows of its subterranean galleries (Fig. 11).

In popular superstitions, the mole plays a variety of roles. In certain parts of the southwest of France, small children wear little bags containing moles' paws, to protect them from convulsions; or the jaws of moles, to prevent intestinal worms, since the moles devour the worms that enter their tunnels.

NOTES

Title Figure: Panther devouring snakes; from the Hortus Sanitatis.

1. Cf. Moret, *Mystères égyptiens*, p. 61, fig. 21.
2. V. Davin, "La Capella Greca..." in *Revue de l'Art chrétien*, T. XXVIII, p. 40.
3. *Catalog*, December 1930.
4. Cf. Reinach, *Repertoire*, T. II, pp. 723-727.
5. Nonnus, *Dionysiaca*, Song X.
6. Cf. Moret, *op. cit.*, II, p. 120.
7. Cf. Barbier de Montault, *Traité d'Iconographie*, T. II, xv, pp. 221 & 235.
8. William of Normandy, *Bestiaire divin*, p. 257.
9. "Bestiaire arménien," tr. by Charles Cahier, S.J., in *Nouveaux Mélanges archéologiques* (1814) pp. 128 et seq.
10. Dante, *The Divine Comedy*, Inferno, I. [*Editor's note:* According to most translators, the first animal to challenge Dante is the leopard.]
11. Pliny, *Natural History*, XXVIII, 27.
12. *Ibid.*, VIII, 44.
13. *Ibid.*, VIII, 30.
14. Aristotle, *De Generationes*, III, 16, and *History of Animals*, VIII, 7, 2.
15. Pliny, *op. cit.*, VIII, 44 and XXVIII, 27.
16. Leclercq and Marron, *Dictionnaire*, fasc. LXIV, col. 1874, fig. 5.503.
17. Pliny, *op. cit.*, Bk. VIII, 17.
18. Vulson de la Colombière, *La Science héroique*, ed. 1669, p. 264.
19. Cf. Louis Cloquet, *Éléments d'Iconographie chrétienne*, XIII, p. 239.
20. Barbier de Montault, *op. cit.*, p. 377.
21. Oppien, *Cynegetica*.
22. Cf. Chompré, *Dictionnaire de la Fable*, p. 250.
23. Hebrews 4:13.
24. Virgil, *Bucolics*, Eclogue VIII.
25. Marbode, *De Ligurio*, XXIV.
26. M. Landin, *Dict. de Minéralogie* p. 237.
27. J. La Fontaine, *Fables*, Bk. I, 7.

End Figure: The cheetah and its prey; a Coptic sculpture prior to the 18th century.

THE WOLF

IN THE ANCIENT traditions of the countries bordering the Baltic and Norwegian Seas, the wolf was always considered to be an animal of light, a sort of solar genie to whom the constellation of the Great Bear was dedicated (Fig. 1). Besides that, the folklore and the lore of the art of hunting of these countries took over certain of the wolf's particular characteristics and habits to enrich their local symbolism[1]. However, this does not prevent the Laplanders in modern times from regarding the wolf as one of the Devil's henchmen and from blessing the bullets they aim at it.

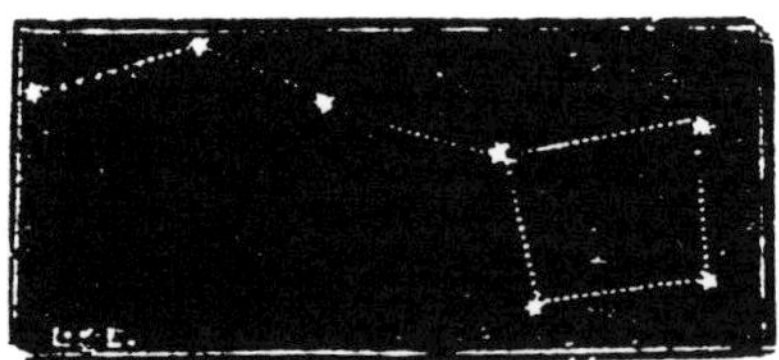

Fig. 1 Constellation of Ursa Major.

Fig. 2 The wolf in a prehistoric cave painting.

Studies of prehistory reveal the wolf together with other representatives of the quaternary age fauna in the most ancient strata that also contain human remains in our South-European countries[2], and wolf's teeth were used in the primitive ornaments of our ancestors, who sometimes decorated the walls of their underground sanctuaries with its image (Fig. 2).

In classical archaeology, we find connections of ideas uniting the most beautiful Olympian god of Greek mythology,

Phoebus Apollo, with the common European wolf, the Greek *lukos*. In the same Greek language, the light of dawn is called *luke*, the light that precedes full daylight. All the mythologists agree that the Greeks received the myth of Phoebus Apollo from the North. Every year, at the end of autumn, it was said, the divine Apollo would leave the temples of Greece and go far away to a mysterious northern country where reigned a perpetual spring and an unceasing light. He would return to Greece in the spring, at the moment when the sun seems to approach the earth. During these annual sojourns in the north country, Phoebus, the personification of the sun, necessarily encountered the two creatures dedicated to him there, the swan and the wolf. Here is a story that explains why the Greeks so often associated the god of light with the wolf, to the point of identifying them with one another:

Apollo, they said, was the son of Zeus and Leto. "Zeus, his father, was the sky from which the light comes to us, and his mother, Leto, personified the night[3]." The sun indeed is born from the night at the hour of dawn[4], and in the shrines of Apollo it was further said that while his mother was pregnant with him, a wolf came to her, and because of this encounter, the vital essence of the solar wolf passed into him. Consequently he received the surname *Lukogenes*, "born of the wolf"; and everywhere under the Hellenic sky the animal was associated with the cult of Phoebus Apollo. In Athens, the land surrounding the temple of Apollo, like the fleece of an animal surrounding its body, was called *Lukeion*, the "Lyceum" or school, meaning "the wolf's skin." It was here that Aristotle taught philosophy.

These and many other similarities between the Sun-god Apollo and the wolf later spread into the whole Mediterranean basin, and it was still remembered in the fifth century of the Christian era when Macrobius wrote that the Ancients represented the sun by the image of the wolf: "The Wolf who is the Sun," he said, and added, "the proof that the sun was given the name *lukos*, wolf, is that Lycopolis, the Theban city, has similar cults of Apollo and the Wolf, in both of which the sun is worshipped[5]."

Apollo-Sun received the posthumous honor of being allegorically identified with Jesus Christ by the western Church of the early centuries, as Dom Leclercq points out. In the fourth century, "the gods gave way to personifications of morality, to allegories. The Christians, by means of their interpretations of the old symbols, gave them a new meaning and baptized some of the most venerable pagan characters; for example, the Sun-god became Christ rising from the earth with the brilliance of the sun[6]."

The image of the wolf appears on certain coins made by Gallic tribes[7]; it was also used as a motif in some unusual statuettes found exclusively in Celtic countries. They show a wolf holding a human being in his mouth, "who seems," as Salomon Reinach justly states, "to be an attribute rather than a prey[8] (Fig. 3)." He makes the very apt addition that the disproportion in size between the animal and the human subject indicates, according to the customs of Celtic art, that this is a divine wolf, a true Wolf-god[9]. Could this enigmatic group have been in distant contact with the old Nordic tradition which has it that the wolf, after having participated in the birth of light, must at the end of time devour the last days?

Fig. 3 The man-eating wolf of Celtic mythology; antique bronze from Oxford.

This union of the symbolic wolf and celestial light extended even into the realm of inanimate things: because of the wolf's glittering eyes which shine in the shadows of the underbrush, the Greek lapidaries gave the name *lycophtalmos*, "wolf's eye" to the most sparkling varieties of agate, as Pliny describes[10]. And the name *lycopodium*, "wolf's-paw," was given to a kind of moss which when reduced to powder produced a very flammable substance still used for fireworks and for theatrical plays of light, and even in the symbolic rites of Masonic initiation.

In certain regions bordering the Baltic Sea, the wolf is still believed to have a power and keenness of sight equal to that which is attributed to the lynx. In the same countries, it was also believed that when wolves come upon amber they stop and sniff it eagerly and for a long time, and in that way enter into contact with celestial forces from which they receive an extraordinary energy whose invisible effects are disseminated around them. The electric air of storms and the appearance of shooting stars and comets were said to affect the wolves and turn them into dangerous adversaries whose strength was increased tenfold by these phenomena, which awakened in them forces of other worlds. The moon's influence also reached them and gave them strange gifts of insight, almost of divination.

In the medieval traditions of the hunt in Europe, although the wolf's symbolic relation to the light is not explicitly spoken of, its penetrating vision and intelligence are highly praised, as well as its stoicism in suffering and death. "Wolves," said du Fouilleux later, "do not complain, as dogs do, when they are killed[11]." All these qualities are linked with the age-old ideas which for northern peoples associated the wolf with the light; and I think that it is in this relationship that one must look for the wolf's connection with the fauna symbolic of Christ.

Nevertheless, for the first Christian symbolists of Rome the wolf had an evil reputation. Its depredations made it feared everywhere; although perhaps not more than the lion, the panther, and the lynx, also predators who feed on what they can find. But the wolf lacks the noble aspect of these animals, and the Latin symbolists, even before the Christian era, built on this fact to make the wolf represent all sorts of vices. In pagan Rome, the female wolf was the symbol for the worst kind of prostitute[12]. Only one escaped the scorn of most of the early Christian writers, and that was the wolf in the Roman legend who suckled the glorious twins Romulus and Remus; the image of this animal symbolized the Empire, or more exactly the power of Rome (Fig. 4). Dante was in accord with all his contemporaries in representing the "concupiscence of the flesh" as a female wolf[13]. The wolf was also made the symbol of other vices: of anger, gluttony, rapacity, and heresy. The Savior himself, in his parable of the Good Shepherd, designated the wolf as the enemy of his spiritual flock[14]. And the evil side of the wolf's character appears again in the dreadful stories of lycanthropy, of transient but repeated transformations of human beings into werewolves. So the image of the wolf, like that of so many symbolic animals, appears by turns in the most luminous and divine aspects and, on the contrary, under the dark shadow of Satan's scepter.

Fig. 4 The Roman she-wolf; a bronze statue in the Capitol in Rome.

NOTES

Title Figure: Wolves from the Hortus Sanitatis.

1. M. du Bellay, Librarian of the Cercle Saint-Hubert of Poitiers.
2. Cf. Déchelette, *Manuel*, T. I, passim.
3. Mario Meunier, *La Légende dorée des dieux et des héros.*
4. In India, the moon is likened to a wolf which devours the night. See Rig-Veda, VII, I: Hymn 2.
5. Macrobius, *Saturnalia*. Bk. I, XVII.
6. Leclercq, *Manuel*, T. II. p. 579.
7. Comte Fr. de Rilly, *Une cachette de monnaies gauloises à Rochefolle*, pp. 2-3, fig. 4.
8. Reinach, "Les carnassiers androphages dans l'art gallo-romain," in *Revue celtique*, T. XXV, pp. 209-224.
9. On the Celtic Wolf-god, see *The Early Christian Monuments of Scotland*, pp. 243-245, figs. 87 & 288.
10. Cf. M. Landin, "Lycophtalme," in *Dictionnaire de Minéralogie*, pp. 231 and 285.
11. J. du Fouilleux, *La Vénerie*, "Chasse du Loup," T. IV (1568).
12. Tertullian, *De pallio*, IV, T. 11, & *Ad nationes*, Bk. II, 10.
13. Dante, *The Divine Comedy*, *Inferno*, Canto 1.
14. St. John 10:11-12.

THE BOAR,
The Bear, and the Hedgehog

IN ALL THE ancient literature the wild boar appears as typical of ferocity, independence, and fearless brutality. In the Hellenic fables, the wild boar of Calydon, which was white and of divine origin, was felled only by the attack of Atalanta and Meleager; the boar of Erymanthus became the living prey of Heracles. In the Celtic countries, the wild boar's reputation was even greater, and of a higher order[1]. The Celtic warriors, and later those of Gaul, adopted it as the military emblem of their fierce tribal independence, and as such it appears on the triumphal arch at Orange (Fig. 1). Even more: the Druids of Ireland and Gaul made the boar an image of intellectual and spiritual strength and supremacy, parallel with the material power and temporal might, both civil and military, which they symbolized by the bear.

Fig. 1 Sacred ensign of a Gallic tribe, first-century B.C.

The presence of the wild boar on Gallic insignia indicates, therefore, that the temporal, military power of warriors bowed before the superiority and sovereignty of the spiritual, priestly authority of the Druids, whose leaders held the title of "Great White Wild Boars." One finds again the symbolism

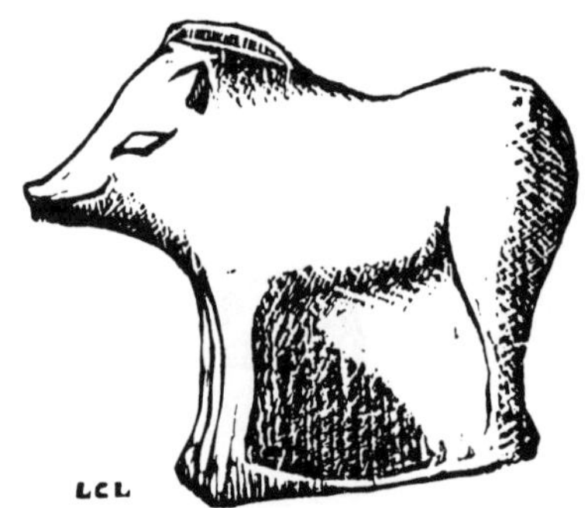

Fig. 2 Gallic wild boar in baked clay, from the Poitiers region.

of the wild boar and the bear, with the same meaning, in the legends of Merlin, the Celtic enchanter, and King Arthur. René Guénon attributes the origin of this symbolism to the far North, and he may very well be right[2]. He has them represent the two polar and solar symbolisms, respectively[3].

The image of the wild boar was very widespread in Gaul; the statue of a Gallic Diana found in the Ardennes sits astride a wild boar[4]. In the nineteenth century two golden boars—probably tokens—were discovered at Vendée in the bank of a pond[5] (Fig. 2); Gallic coins bearing the animal's image are numerous, and on the Luccio coin discovered at Poitou divine rays descend upon it[6] (see Title Figure).

Christianity was severe with the fiery animal which for the Druids has been the emblem of spiritual strength and power. However, during the first four centuries of our era, its image is sometimes found on Christian lamps, where it seemed, according to Dom Leclercq, to symbolize the divine wrath. On one of these it is placed in opposition to a dove, which like the lamb represented Christ's gentleness[7].

Still, the wild boar was sometimes accepted as the image of the just, independent, and courageous man opposing the adversaries of good and the enemies of his soul. In this sense, St. Paulinus, Bishop of Nola, writing in the fifth century to one of his correspondents, compared it with the lamb: "What satisfaction would I not have to find you completely changed: to see that the lion has now the meekness of a young calf; that Jesus Christ inhabits the wild boar, who, conserving all his ferocity towards the world, has become a lamb in regard to God; you are no longer the wild boar of the forest, you have become the wild boar of the harvest."

But the Middle Ages recognized only the wild boar of David, who ravaged the Lord's vineyard[8]. It was regarded as the "evil beast" of the Apocalypse, the Antichrist. It was made the symbol of jealousy and brutality; its mate, the wild sow, was one of the symbols of lust, and in medieval illuminated manuscripts it served as the mount for the personification of anger[9].

What exactly was Dürer's intention when he placed, near the creche where Mary laid down her child, a wild boar and a lion, instead of the traditional ox and donkey?

Another animal that enters into Christian symbolism only from a negative aspect as a "ravager of the Lord's vineyard" is the hedgehog. More in the imagination of the symbolists of long ago than by their real qualities or habits, the sheep and the hedgehog play opposite roles as representatives of Christ and of Satan. Medieval authors, relying on the authority of the ancient Greek and Roman naturalists and on the *Physiologus*, depict the hedgehog as a detestable creature, spiny and mischievous. When it gets into a fruitful vineyard, it chooses the finest vine, climbs it and shakes it until the ripe grapes have fallen on the ground. Then it impales them on its spines and goes off loaded with stolen fruit, to feed its young. Thus, according to Pierre le Picard, William of Normandy, and other thirteenth-century writers, the hedgehog made itself the image of the Evil One as the destroyer of souls and ravisher of spiritual fruits; and William of Normandy advised the Christian to take care lest this demon come to shake his vine or his fruit tree and to rob him of his fruit, that is, the fruit of good works[10].

A miniature from a thirteenth-century bestiary, in the Bibliothèque Nationale in Paris, is a naive image of the devastating hedgehogs, already loaded with stolen fruit, shaking the vine or the berry bush (Fig. 3).

The characteristics of the hedgehog as the allegorical image of Satan, and those of the sheep as the emblem of the Savior, are consequently in complete opposition: the sheep is soft to the touch, the hedgehog harsh and painful; the sheep, as the Eucharistic symbol of its milk, gives of herself to nourish her lambs, and the satanic hedgehog, to feed its young, steals the welfare of others; the sheep is docile and quiet, and the hedgehog on the contrary curls up into a bristling ball as soon as anyone approaches it.

Fig. 3 Hedgehogs shaking the fruit vine, in the Bibliothèque Nationale.

NOTES

Title Figure: Coin of the Gallic chieftain Luccio.

1. See especially: C. Julian, *Gallia et de la Gaule à la France*; Renel, *Les Religions de la Gaule.*
2. Guénon, *Autorité Spirituelle et pouvoir temporel*, p. 20.
3. Guénon, "Le Sanglier et l'Ours," in *Revue des Études Traditionelles*, T. XLI (1936) p. 296.
4. See Renel, *op cit.* p. 251, fig. 21
5. See L. Charbonneau-Lassay, *Les Bijoux d'or et d'argent du Poitou préromain*, p. 18.
6. *Ibid*, p. 19.
7. Leclercq and Marron, *Dictionnaire*, fasc. LXXXIV, col. 1129.
8. Psalms 80:13.
9. Mâle, *L'Art religieux (1)*, p. 330.
10. William of Normandy, *Le Bestiaire divin*, XIII.

THE WEASEL

THE WEASEL IS the smallest European carnivore; it is also the most graceful and one of the most intelligent. It accustoms itself quite easily to man, and develops a singular attachment to the person who takes care of it. Buffon[1] and Mme. Delaistre[2] confirm this, and Christian hagiography agrees with these authors, informing us that the Dominican saint Jordan of Battberg had as his familiar a weasel that was his regular companion; in pictures of him, one always sees the tiny animal at his side or in his hand.

Searching for symbolic images that would convey serious Christian lessons, the early glossarists pointed out that although the weasel is the smallest of the carnivores, yet it can win combats with much bigger animals than itself—so, they said, the weasel is the perfect symbol of a Christian who, no matter how weak in himself, can still triumph over Satan, the most terrifying monster of hell.

Writers of the last pre-Christian centuries imitated, apparently without understanding, an extremely ancient and enigmatic expression which seems to have been current in the whole of the ancient world: "The weasel conceives through the ear and gives birth through the mouth[3]." Plutarch connected this assertion to humanity's earliest times and the very origin of human language. Aristotle[4], Ovid[5], and other ancient naturalists recited the same dictum without understanding it at all, it would seem. This is yet another proof that in the last centuries before the birth of Christ the key had been lost to a host of symbols and enigmas relating to the most ancient metaphysical concepts and religious mysteries.

"The weasel conceives through the ear and gives birth through the mouth"; likewise, the disciple and also the initiate, listening to the word of the master, receives through the ear the seed of wisdom and of inner light which impregnates his spirit; then having thus learned much through attentive listening, the candidate for initiation becomes in his turn a teacher, and through the wise and eloquent speech of his mouth gives birth to disciples who are his spiritual children.

Fig. 1 From a 13th-century bestiary.

The idea of choosing the weasel as the symbol of the perfect disciple is certainly unexpected, and seems incongruous; however, it is understandable if one takes into account that "damoiselle weasel, of long and fluid body[6] (Fig. 1)" was formerly, in some countries, one of the emblems of flexibility, and that flexibility of the mind is the first quality necessary for a disciple to become a perfect disciple. —Let whoever wishes search and find if he can a better resolution to the ancient enigma, that the weasel "conceives through the ear and gives birth through the mouth"; I will adhere to the one I have proposed until there is a better explanation from someone more qualified than myself.

Fig. 2 From the Hortus Sanitatis.

Although the Ancients classified the weasel as an inauspicious animal that one would be better off not to meet on one's path, they did recognize its extreme familial tenderness and care in constantly moving its young so that enemies could not find them, or so that they would be better sheltered. This habitual movement from one place to another explains why certain symbolists made the weasel their allegorical image of inconstancy, but others, looking further and higher, saw in it a symbol of carefulness, vigilance, and active paternal affection (Fig. 2). Given the old symbolists' way of thinking, it did not take much to place the weasel among the fauna symbolic of Jesus Christ: this occurred at the moment when one of them, Brunetto Latini, took upon himself to write: "The weasel often transports its young from place to place so that no one will find them, and if she finds them dead, many people say that she resuscitates them, but how she does this they do not know[7]." So in its own way, the weasel shares the symbolism of revivification with the lion and the pelican.

Fig. 3 The weasel and the basilisk; from Cahier's Bestiaires.

The Ancients were not unaware of the weasel's services in destroying rats, mice, field mice, shrews, and other little ravagers. Phaedrus demonstrates this for us in his fables[8]. Pliny adds that the two European species of weasel wage a vicious war on snakes, and that their spleen is an effective remedy for the bites of venomous animals[9]. I have heard the peasants who live in the swampy countryside around Poitiers say that vipers never remain where weasels have made their holes. Pliny also tells us in two other passages of his great work that the weasel is the most implacable vanquisher (Fig. 3) of that terrifying reptile, the basilisk or cockatrice: "This monster," he says, "as has often been proved for kings wishing to see its corpse, cannot withstand weasels, which lure it into a cave and kill it by the odor they exhale." In another passage he says that the weasel itself will pursue the cockatrice into its lair, where everything nearby is burned by the reptile's breath. Then, with nothing but its odor, the weasel kills it, and dies at the same time[10]. All the ancient Christian symbolists took note of this duel in which the little animal triumphs over the most dangerous of monsters, and kills it by means of its own death. In the works of medieval writers and artists, the weasel became the image of the Savior.

In Christian symbolism, rats and mice which spoil everything are among the emblems of the vices which corrupt the soul[11]. So the weasel, which hunts and destroys rats and mice, was also adopted as the symbol of the one who purifies the world by hunting down the vices that destroy whatever is good. The weasel also sometimes symbolized a means of purification; this is without doubt based on the old legend that said that this animal's scent is enough to purify its dwellings from the presence of filthy reptiles, and also that with this alone it slays the infernal cockatrice.

This idea is in accord with the old peasant superstition that regarded wearing a weasel skin as an effective preventative of poisoning from harmful vapors and infectious diseases. Pliny also says that the weasel's spleen is a very good remedy for snake venom[12]. According to Aristotle, weasels are careful to feed on rue before fighting with snakes, because the reptiles detest the odor of this plant[13]. Rue was one of the plants of the ancient pharmacopoeia used to cure people in the early stages of leprosy, also mange and scurf[14]; but all such skin diseases were constantly taken in the symbolism of Christian spirituality as symbols of sin. The idea of purification emerges from all these diverse elements.

A slightly larger variety of the weasel is the ermine, which changes color with the seasons: in summer it wears a tawny coat with light grey underneath; in winter, it is entirely clothed in snow-white, except for the tip of its tail, which is black. This complete winter white belongs only to northern weasels; in France the animal is greyish and not very handsome[15].

Popular imagination of the past pictured the ermine as an amphibious animal which only visited clear streams, meadows, or mossy, flowering woodlands, and which hated dirt to the point that it would let itself be killed rather than tread on muddy ground and soil its immaculate coat. Seizing on this fiction, medieval heraldry took the ermine as the symbolic image of a man determined to protect the purity of his conscience—an image that is, above all, that of the perfect knight who prefers to undergo any misfortune rather than tarnish his name and his escutcheon by the slightest act contrary to loyalty, fidelity, or knightly honor. It is in this sense particularly that many old and noble families, first and foremost of which were the ancient sovereign dukes of Brittany, adopted or received the ermine as the insignia on their coats of arms (Fig. 4). The Breton dukes displayed it everywhere in their castles and cities with the proud motto: *Potius mori quam foedari*: "Better die than defile myself."

Fig. 4 16th-century sculpture on the facade of the Château d'Azay le Rideau, near Tours.

Thus placed as the perfect sign of the soul's purity, the ermine shares the symbol of the crucifixion with the swan, the dove, the lily, and the snow, embodying the innocence of Christ. Also, the ermine was one of the rare winter symbols of the Resurrection, because, while brown in summer, it then seemed to disappear, only to reappear in all its whiteness with the return of the snowy season.

NOTES

Title Figure: Ermine; early 19th-century tapestry.

1. Buffon, *Histoire Naturelle.*
2. Delaistre, *Histoire des animaux célèbres*, 1657, p. 31.
3. Plutarch, *Isis and Osiris*, LXIV.
4. Aristotle, *History of Animals*, IX.
5. Ovid, *Metamorphoses*, IX, 5.
6. J. La Fontaine, *Fables*, Book III, Fable XVII.
7. Brunetto Latini, *Li Livres dou tresor*, L. I, CLXXXI, "De la Belette."
8. Phaedrus, *Fabulae*, Bks. I & IV.
9. Pliny, *Natural History*, XXIX, 14.
10. *Ibid.*, Bk. VIII.
11. See A. Duchallais, *Le Rat employé comme symbole dans la sculpture*...in *Bibliothèque de l'École des Chartes*, 2nd series, T. III, p. 229 *et seq.*
12. Pliny, *op. cit.*, Bk. XXII, 14.913. Aristotle, *op. cit.*, IX.
13. Aristotle, *op. cit.*, IX.
14. P. Venneuil, *Dictionnaire des Symboles*, p. 160.
15. E. Troussart, "L'Hermine," in *Grande Encyclopédie*, T. V, p. 1187.

End Figure: The ermine of the Dukes of Brittany; 15th-century sculpture of Quimper cathedral, from V. de la Colombière.

THE SNAKE

IN THE GENERAL study of religious or philosophical symbolism of former times, the snake certainly presents the largest and most complex possible subject; however, at present we shall have to limit ourselves to a brief and necessarily incomplete summary of the pre-Christian history of this symbol, probably best known to us in the religious symbolism of Egypt. Primarily it represented the "Great God," threefold and unique, whose power extends from heaven to earth (Fig. 1). A serpent-goddess healed diverse human ailments[1]; another was represented by a magic ring with a snake's head[2]; and the goddess of the North, Wadjit, was also represented by a snake[3]. Of another order from the great and unique God, the souls of those secondary gods, who were simply the

Fig. 1 Hieroglyph of the Great God, in the temple of Seti I.

deified souls of the ancestors, chose the bodies of snakes for their terrestrial abode[4]: "The souls of all the gods reside in the serpents," says a text from the tomb of Seti I.

Many of the big Egyptian cities looked upon snakes as their protectors. The sacred uraeus, the asp Haje, was the protector of the pharaoh, winding itself around his crown and defending his forehead (Fig. 2).

Fig. 2 The double crown of the pharaohs, encircled by the uraeus.

The common practice in ancient magic of accepting only two cold-blooded creatures, the snake and the scarab beetle, as sacrificial victims, seems surely to have originated in Egypt[5].

From the most ancient times the Africans have dedicated many different cults to the serpent. The Dinkas in central Africa believe that the spirits of their deceased ancestors have been transformed into certain snakes who are supernatural beings living in this world. The same belief existed in a slightly different form in ancient Egypt. The missionaries in Dahomey complain of the preponderant place given to snakes in the religions and fetichism of the natives, and the reverential fear with which they honor them: they prostrate themselves before the reptiles as if they were intelligent and dangerous deities whom they dread rather than love[6].

The old religions of Assyria, Elam, Chaldea, Susa, and Media and in our times those of India, China, and Japan all present us with the serpent either as a god or as a good or an evil spirit. Both Brahmanism and Buddhism had and still have their more or less divine snakes, beneficent or otherwise, such as the one vanquished by Indra, whose victory was sung in one of the hymns of the Rig-Veda[7].

Greece also had its mysterious and celestial serpents: the nearest to the divine was that of Zagreus-Dionysus; the most infernal was the Python of Apollo. In the well-known legend, Dionysus, son of Demeter the Earth-Mother, also called

Zagreus, was cut up by the Titans into pieces of which one, the heart, was found by Athena. The heart then came back to life and gave birth to a new Zagreus[8], who was symbolized by a horned serpent also called Zagreus. In the mystery ceremonies of Dionysus-Sabazius, a golden serpent—ordinarily a harmless grass snake—was put inside the top of the garment worn by the candidate for initiation; it was pulled out through the bottom of the robe[9] during a chanting of these enigmatic verses: "The Bull is the father of the Dragon, and the Dragon is the father of the Bull." This was connected to high questions of the transformation of soul and spirit[10] as was also the well-known formula, "A serpent never becomes a flying dragon until it has devoured another serpent."

The snake's annual shedding of its skin was also the Ancients' symbolic image for the ascending transformations of the human being; and certain Christian mystics referred to this symbolism in saying that, like the snake who sheds his unwanted husk, the believer must cast off the "old man" in order to begin a new life.

The serpent, representing the spirit of good, of life, and of happiness, born like Zagreus from Demeter, the Earth-Mother, leaves her breast and climbs up the staff of Aesculapius, the god of medicine; it thus maintains the role of guardian deity, for it is a symbol of renewal and of the restoration of life.

The Druids, who according to Strabo figured among the wisest men of the ancient world, concealed in the symbol of the serpent some of the highest concepts of their mysterious teaching. They apparently adopted the mode of thought of the rest of their world, which saw in the snake, born of the Earth-Mother from whom it comes forth renewed each springtime, the image of life. Coming from the earth, the snake was considered the knower of all its secrets, and this is why the oldest legends made it, like the dragon, the guardian of all sorts of hidden riches: the treasures of metals, of medical cures, and of magic. Gallic statuary and iconography very often show us the druidic serpent endowed with the horned head of a ram. We find this representation on the Gallic altars of Mavilly in the Côte d'Or[11] and Montluçon[12] (Fig. 3). Gods holding the ram-headed snake in their hands have been discovered at Montluçon, Épinal, the Hôtel-Dieu in Paris, Vignory, etc.

Fig. 3 The ram-headed snake on the Gallic altar at Montluçon.

The relationship which the Ancients believed to exist between the Celts, the Thracians, and the Illyrians would seemingly allow a correlation between the horned reptiles of the Gallic Druids and Zagreus, the horned serpent of the Orphic mysteries of Thrace and Greece[13].

For the Ancients the snake was also one of the emblems of light[14]. From Phoenicia to Chaldea, the old traditions associated the serpent with the flash of lightning snaking across the sky; and this is why the reptile was also the symbol of fire in these same countries[15]. The art of these regions recognized two luminous serpents, one crowned with rays (Sol), and the other with a crescent (Luna), the two torches of day and night; represented together next to three stars, they formed the symbolic image of five planets which in Chaldea, according to Diodorus Siculus, were considered to be the five regents of the heavens and governors of the worlds[16].

In Egypt, the asp Haje, the sacred uraeus of the pharaohs, was one of the solar emblems; for the Greeks of heroic times the rainbow was allegorically represented by three blue serpents. From Homer we learn that this symbol appeared on Agamemnon's armor, alluding to the rainbow, the arch of Iris: "and as a memorable sign to humans traced by Zeus in the heavens[17]."

The book of Genesis recounts the disobedience of Adam and Eve to the orders of their Creator, and the divine curse that fell as punishment upon the human race and the serpent kingdom[18]. The Mosaic story leaves no possibility of mistake as to the snake's part in this drama; he is definitely the seducer, the tempter, the deceiver, and the very incarnation of

Fig. 4 Enlarged from a Babylonian cylinder in the British Museum.

the Spirit of Evil. The oldest picture we have of this passage of the Bible is found engraved on a Babylonian cylinder that is now in the British Museum in London. On it we see a tree, a stylized palm bearing two clusters of fruit; on either side at the foot of the tree are seated a man and a woman, their hands outstretched towards the forbidden fruit; behind the woman the Snake stands upright on its tail (Fig. 4). Basing his opinion on the evidence of some very important documents, Mr. Broussac of the Cairo Institute judges that the date of this cylinder is later than the account given by Moses, and is an echo of it translated in the Babylonian style[19].

Early Christian artists frequently portrayed this biblical scene of the fall, and to characterize it they often transposed the snake's head into a human face, sometimes the face of a young man smiling at Eve,

Fig. 5 From the Hortus Sanitatis.

as we may see in the Roman catacomb of St. Agnes; but even more frequently the snake has the face of a woman (Fig. 5). A large number of artistic works from the early Christian centuries in which the temptation of Eden was represented undoubtedly drew their inspiration from even older picturings of Jason and the sorceress Medea. As Dom Leclercq says, the placement of the subjects "on either side of the tree around which the serpent is entwined is too obvious a reminder of the scene imagined by the early Christians to illustrate the biblical story for us not to see the resemblance between the two compositions[20]."

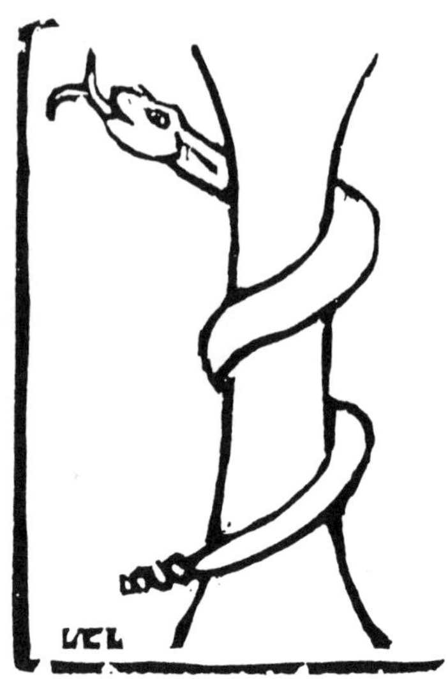

Fig. 6 Pre-Columbian sculpture at Chichen Itza, Yucatan.

In all the heterodox sects, as it was in pre-Christian antiquity, the serpent in its divine aspect is commonly represented as ascending, either winding itself around the staff of Aesculapius or that of his daughter Hygeia, or else around a tree trunk, as we see on certain Christian tombs from the early centuries[21]. When it is in a descending position it nearly always represents the principle of evil, and for the Christians,

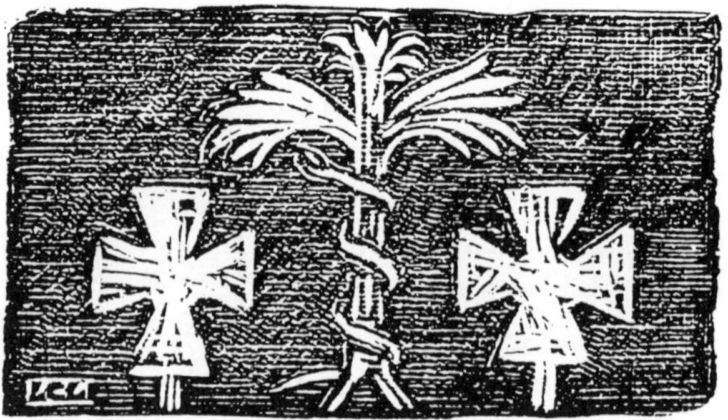

Fig. 7 The serpent around the Tree of Life; Merovingian sculpture in the church at Pouille in Vendée.

Satan. It is remarkable to find this same symbol of the reptile and the tree in America, at Chichen Itza in Yucatan[22] (Fig. 6), just as one also sees it in a Gallic-French sculpture, wound around the Tree of Life, this time in a definitely Christian context, between two altar or processional crosses[23] (Fig. 7).

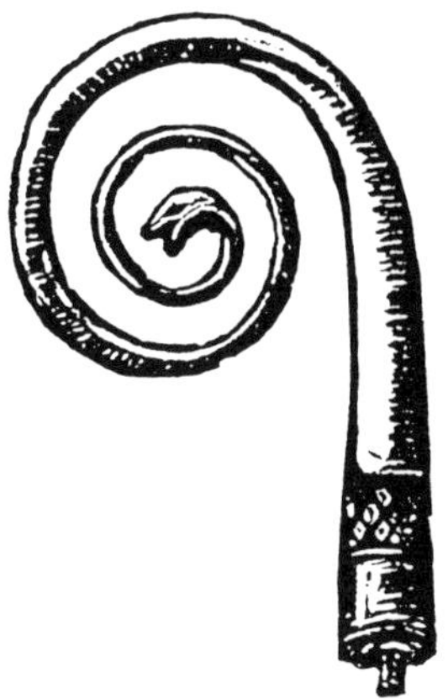

Fig. 8 The abbot's crozier from Airvault, Deux-Sèvres.

A brief mention here of Voodoo, the Votan of the Antilles, a venerable grass snake that gave its name to a Black sect in Haiti, of whom a large number practice the Christian religion. They nevertheless regard the snake Voodoo as a sort of second-class divinity who holds his great and sacred power from Christ. The warm blood of victims sacrificed to the reptile is drunk by the adepts in secret ceremonies[24].

Fig. 9 The lamb, the serpent, and the dove; enameled copper crozier in the Soissons Museum.

It is important not to forget the double aspect, good and evil, of the serpent in the symbolism of the Church. "Even in Christian iconography," wrote Guénon, "the serpent is sometimes a symbol of Christ[25]." This is indeed true, and a huge book could easily be written on the religious and profane roles of the snake in the Church's first seven centuries. During the second part of the Middle Ages, especially from the eleventh to the fourteenth centuries, the pastoral staffs or croziers of many bishops and abbots ended in a spiral terminating in a serpent's head. Such is the case with the crozier of St. Hannon, preserved at Siegbert[26]; likewise, that of Gilles the Archbishop of Tyre, preserved at Samur[27]; that of a certain abbot of Airvault at Poitiers[28], and many others (Fig. 8). In each of these cases, according to Canon Auber, the serpent almost always represents the Savior, especially when it holds the cross between its teeth, or carries the head of a lamb[29].

In the Gospel, Jesus advised his followers to be "wise as serpents, and harmless as doves[30]." Here, once again, Christian symbolism goes hand in hand with older ideas which had made the serpent the ideograph of wisdom. For the ancient Egyptians, the snake represented divine wisdom. On several of the more famous croziers we may also see a dove perched on the serpent's head or even taking refuge in its mouth (Fig. 9).

In its role as the seducer, the agent of evil and provoker of sin in the story of Genesis, the serpent was the image of Satan. In the French provinces, some of the country folk also see the very image of the demon, or I might say an agent of the demon, in the snakes which they say sometimes get into the stables and stealthily milk the cows, goats, and ewes, and thereby make them sterile.

The bestiaries of the Middle Ages ordinarily consign the snake to the maleficent role of tempter under the name of viper or asp. In the common language, "viper's tongue" was the expression which described that of slanderers, hypocrites, traitors, and liars. Because the tip of certain snakes' tongues ends in a fork, the artists exaggerated the natural form and made the point into a dart, an arrow, or a javelin. Like these weapons, an evil word also strikes and wounds, and sometimes kills.

In our own ancient tradition the serpent's tongue had another, more benevolent role: in certain regions of Europe its name was given to the fossil teeth of sharks which in other places were called "wolf teeth." These pseudo-snakes' teeth, mounted in a setting of precious metal, were supposed to reveal the presence of poisons which might have been added to food or drink, into which they were plunged in order to "test" them; hence the name "testing stones" by which they were sometimes known.

It would be interesting to rediscover the origin of this practice. While the snake's venom always symbolized the works of Satan, we have seen, on the other hand, that this same snake was also one of the emblems of Christ the Savior. The stone called "serpent's tongue," which revealed and unmasked the presence of poison and thus protected the user from death, could well have been, in the beginning of its history, not so far as one might think from the subject occupying us in this book.

A frequently used symbol shows the snake bending its head, as if to drink, over an amphora or chalice (Fig. 10). It seems certain that when this image was conceived, the snake was regarded not as drawing life from the vessel, but as calling forth this life in itself. It must be remembered that for the Ancients the serpent was connected "above all to the very idea of life[31]," and that on the other hand, in the same time and place, the amphora was the hieratic and mysterious image of the pregnant woman, and the cup, that of femininity itself. Knowing only the first and more exoteric of these interpretations, which seems to show the snake drinking in life and health, artists of modern times have linked the snake drinking from the cup with medicine and medicinal illustrations. On the other hand, we will see later that the drinking vessel was and still remains one of the symbols consecrated to Christ; and this allows us to see, in the image of the serpent and the chalice, the earth, or its king, drawing vitality from Christ as the eternal principle and reservoir of life. This is the interpretation we may give it when we see it, as we still frequently may in Provence on the old stational crosses or those along the roadsides or at crossroads.

Fig. 10 Serpent drinking from the chalice; Loudun, 19th century.

In the Middle Ages, artist-initiates sometimes disguised the serpent in this symbol with the appearance of a capital G; we

Fig. 11 Medieval seal from Lady Londesborough's collection.

Fig. 12 The Hebrew samech *and its reverse.*

see it thus on a seal in Lady Londesborough's collection, attributed to the thirteenth century (Fig. 11). It is more than probable that this letter G was chosen here because it is the same shape as the Hebrew *samekh* reversed (Fig. 12); for in the ancient Kabbalah the *samekh* represented the snake[32]. Perhaps it is a chance coincidence that the G on this seal simulates the silhouette of Zagreus, the horned serpent of the Greeks. It is also possible that the letter G was the initial of the seal's first owner; in which case there would be an overlapping of meanings in the same symbol, as very often happens.

Especially during the last half of the eighteenth century and the first half of the nineteenth, in France, the motif of the drinking serpent was often placed on cemetery crosses and funeral monuments (Fig. 13). And in this case the serpent is a symbolic evocation of Death; because it brings death with its venomous bite, and because like human cadavers it lives un-

Fig. 13 Serpent drinking from vase; sculpture on an 18th-century cross in Avignon.

derground, in the "kingdom of the dead." Thus before our eyes rises the striking image of Death drinking from the divine vessel of life, from Christ, the kernel of survival, of the eternal life which he promised: *Ego sum resurrectio et vita: qui credit in me, etiam si mortuus fuerit vivet*: "I am the resurrection, and the life: he that believeth in me, though he were dead, yet shall he live[33]."

NOTES

Title Figure: From the 15th-century Arca Mystica *by Richard de Saint-Victor.*

1. Cf. Maspéro, *Bibliothèque égyptologique*, T. II, pp. 405-7.
2. Cf. Virey, *Religion de l'ancienne Égypte*, p. 230.
3. *Ibid.*, p. 112.
4. *Ibid.*, pp. 40-45.
5. Cf. Thirion, "La Magie en théorie et en pratique" in *Revue Int. des Sociétés Secrètes*, T. XXI, 1932, p. 161.
6. For the serpent cult in Dahomey, see A. Demaison, *Les Rois de Dahomey*, Illustration, T. 92, no. 4.756, April 1934.
7. See de Gubernatis, *Mythologie*, T.I, 84.
8. See Mario Meunier, *La Légende dorée des dieux et des héros*, p. 206.
9. Cf. F. Lenormant, "Sabasius," in *Revue archéologique*, 2nd series, T. XXVIII, 1874, p. 305.
10. See Clement of Alexandria, *Stromates*, II; Nonnus, *Dionysiaca*, V & VI.
11. Renel, *Les Religions de la Gaule avant le Christianisme*, p. 245.
12. Alexandre Bertrand, "L'Autel des Saintes et les Triades gauloises," in *Revue archéologique*, 2d series, T. XL, 1880, p. 15.
13. See Reinach, in *Revue Archéologique*, 1891, I, pp. 1-6; and 1897, II, pp. 313-326; also Zagreus, *Le serpent connu*, *loc. cit.*, 1899, p. 216.
14. See P. le Cour, *À la recherche d'un monde perdu*, pp. 43, 90, etc.
15. Cf. Ch. Vellay, "Le Culte d'Adonis Thammouz" in *L'Orient antique*, 2d part, I, p. 81.
16. Cf. E. Soldi, "Les Cylindres babyloniens," in *Revue archéologique*, 2nd series, T. XXVIII, 1874, p. 152.
17. Homer, The *Iliad*, XI.
18. Genesis 3.
19. Hipp. Broussac, "Le Serpent de la Génèse" in *La Nature*, no. 2848, January 1931, p. 6.
20. Leclercq and Marron, *Dictionnaire*, T. I, vol. II, col. 2705.
21. Cf. A. Boulanger, *Orphée*, p. 144.
22. Le Cour, *op. cit.*, p. 38.
23. See J. Salvini, Departmental Archivist of Vienne, *Une sculpture mérovingienne a Pouille* (Vienne).

24. *Editor's note*: Commonly the serpent is called *Damballah*, and *voodoo* is a more generic term.
25. *La Voile d'Isis*, T. XXXVI, No. 142, p. 589.
26. Cf. Ch. Cahier, S.J., "Ivoires sculptés," in *Nouveaux Mélanges archéologiques*, 1874, p. 27.
27. Cf. Bodin, *Recherches historiques sur l'Anjou*, T. II, plate III.
28. Cf. Barbier de Montault, *Bulletin des Antiquaires de l'Ouest*, 1882.
29. Cf. Auber, *Histoire et Théorie du Symbolisme religieux*, T. III, p. 38l.
30. St. Matthew 10:16.
31. Guénon, "Seth," in *La Voile d'Isis*, T. XXXV, 1931, no. 142, p. 590.
32. Cf. Papus, *Traité élémentaire de Kabbale*, p. 292.
33. St. John 11:25.

End Figure: The winged serpent in a temple in Yucatán, Mexico.

THE FROG AND THE TOAD

THE FROG—HERE is another humble member of God's family whose name many Westerners will be surprised to see among those whom the reverence of the first Christian centuries linked with the personal symbolism of the Lord Jesus Christ. Nevertheless there are few whose Christlike significance is more explicitly attested in ancient art, and very few indeed who can boast of so long a past history in the symbolism of the human race in general. In the ancient world, two varieties of frog found favor with the symbolists: the green frog of the swamps (the *rana esculenta* of Linnaeus) is the more familiar. It is essentially aquatic and hardly ever comes out of the water except to warm itself in the sun. It is this creature that in the lovely warm twilights of summer utters the strange sounds that Aristophanes expressed for his countrymen with the well-known onomatopeia "bre-ke-ke-kex, koax, koax[1]!" The other is the russet frog of the woods (*rana temporaria*, according to Linnaeus), common in the woods and copses of France, which does not enter the water except to lay its eggs in February, and rarely returns to it. More mysterious in its habits than its aquatic cousin, it was regarded as a small omen of good fortune in the popular traditions of the past; it shared the good will of simple folk with the European tree-frog, the *hila viridis*, as it was said that both brought with them a bit of good luck. As the russet frog rarely approaches human beings, in many country areas it was considered a favorable omen to come across it, and it was not harmed. It is to this frog in particular that the thinkers and mystics of earlier times gave symbolic meanings.

The prehistorians have discovered a number of times the bones of the frog with those of the most ancient humans. Usually there seems to be no recognizable significance in this, but not always, since quite recently at Vieil-Auzay in Vendée, a scientist, Dr. M. G. Guérin, found that the skeletons of a necropolis dating from the Neolithic era, well before metal was used in France, were buried with a frog's foot in the hand. And one finds again in this same region the same funerary rite in burials two thousand years later[2].

In Egypt, several thousand years before our era, the frog was one of the symbols of the general fecundity of nature; and the most serious zoological studies authorize this symbolism, as several times a year the frog lays some ten thousand eggs at a time[3]. A text from the epoch of the Ramses pharaohs shows the frog as the hieroglyph for the renewal of life, and others connect it with the ideas of birth, of creation, and of resurrection. As in several other very old symbols, the resurrectional character is partly based on the fact that the frog disappears during the winter season and returns with the renewal of plant life. This may explain the presence of the allegorical frog in the hand of the Nile god, whose fertilizing waters "renew the face of the land of Egypt." It is this meaning that must be connected with the little stone or ceramic frogs which were used as seals and were placed in the tombs. These amulets express belief in the idea of resurrection and of the renewal of life beyond death.

The Egyptian priests also used the frog to express divine descent; this is proved by the presence of the frog in reproductions of scenes of the birth of pharaohs, who were supposed to be born of their mothers and the supreme god Amon. It must have been intended to show reverence to the royal figures in this parthenogenesis, this virgin birth which was attributed to all the great mythic figures of the Mediterranean region from about the seventh century before the Christian era: Attis, Orpheus, Adonis, Dionysus, Tammuz—and then to Buddha, all of whom were said to have been born of a virgin divinely impregnated. The Egyptian priests, whose knowledge was so astonishingly extensive, may have known that the frog's egg is capable of giving birth to a normal, living creature even if it is not fertilized by the male, on condition that it is lightly pricked in the water by a fine, hard point such as that of a thorn[4]. The work of our contemporary biologists, notably Loeb and Bataillon, has incontestably demonstrated this fact, and who can say with certainty that the learned ones of Egypt did not also know it?

The Egyptian idea of fecundity is also linked with the role of Heqet, the frog-headed goddess who holds the "key of life" in her hands and who is called in one text "she who causes to give birth[5]." Her function was perpetually to conceive and give birth to "the Egg of the World" which is perpetually being shaped and molded by the male god Khnum; she is thus the goddess of birth and of rebirth[6] (Fig. 1).

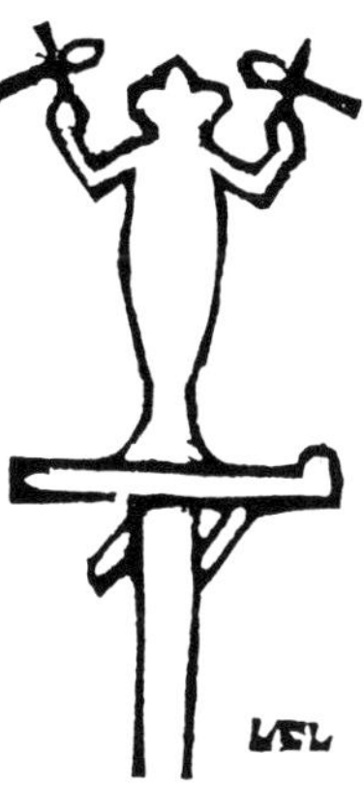

Fig. 1 Heqet in a sculpture at Luxor.

Is it because the frog represents the goddess Heqet that in consequence it expresses the same idea that she does in the language of the hieroglyphs? According to Maspéro, it does not itself directly express the idea of resurrection, which is indeed the goddess Heqet's role[7]; but it does however imply this idea because of its reappearance in the spring after its winter's absence. Heqet, with her frog's head, can be seen at Deir-el-Bahri, in the depiction of the union of the god Amon-Ra with queen Ahmes, the mother of Hatshepsut[8].

In the funerary treasure of princess Knumit, a lapis lazuli frog was found next to the mummy; it had garnet eyes set in gold[9], and this detail immediately brings to mind the russet frog of our woodlands whose sclera, or outer rims of the eyeball, are golden in color. Other frogs made of jasper, of lapis, and of carnelian, also from Egyptian burials, make up a part of the important Passalacqua collection[10]. Also, Salomon Reinach has acquainted us with the frogs of Egypto-Grecian art in bronze and agate in the museums of Berlin and the Louvre[11], and still others coming from Cairo, Berne, Austria, etc.[12]

Chaldea, too, brought the frog into its symbolic bestiary, but we do not know to what extent the idea it represents coincides with that of the Egyptians; the Babylonian seal cylinder which Delaporte brought to public notice, on which the frog is depicted, does not give us the key to the mystery, as it is difficult to identify clearly the personages appearing with it[13].

The little tree-frog of France, like the fabled frog of Japan[14] is said to make itself invisible whenever it pleases, and that notion comes from its real capacity to change color in accordance with its surroundings, which often baffles its enemies[15].

But who will tell us the exact meaning of the metal frogs in the museum of Saint-Germain-en-Laye, which come from burials in Colombia earlier by many centuries than Christopher Columbus' exploration in 1492? A tomb of the same date and locality has revealed a frog cast in gold, thirteen centimeters long and six centimeters high[16]; its size and weight show it is not a jewel, so it can only be a symbol, probably a talisman, connected according to all appearances with the idea of rebirth or of fecundity even in death.

The Africans of the Chari basin also revere stone or metal frogs which they use as amulets.

It is interesting to underline here the equality of symbolic interest in the frog in the ancient and the new worlds, before the Christian era (Fig. 2).

Fig. 2 Pottery frog, from Deux-Sèvres.

I have said before that nothing is

more variable than the scale of dignity or sympathy that human beings have established for animals in different parts of the world; and we see that the first Christians in Egypt did not hesitate to use the frog as a sign of the Resurrection, and even to take it as an allegorical image of Christ. "We have dedicated a special study to the frog," says Dom Leclercq[17], "and this ungraceful creature itself has been elevated to the dignity of a symbol of the Resurrection. From this example one might be tempted to think that there is no animal, even among the most repulsive, that does not have a special meaning for someone." Thus the first Christian symbolists in Egypt found it natural to keep among their numerous symbols of resurrection the old one of Heqet, the goddess of the renewing of the life principle, and to connect it with Christ himself.

Edmond le Blant has suggested that "among the batrachians, the transformation of a rudimentary animal into a complete one might have offered an image of the Resurrection[18]." It is an indisputable fact that for the Ancients, the process: egg, caterpillar, chrysalis, then the butterfly; or egg, larva, chrysalis, then the bee or the dragonfly, were natural images of the successive transformations by which they believed human souls had to pass before they attained the definitive state of blessedness. So one should not be surprised at the number of Christian lamps of baked clay coming from Luxor, from Edfu, Helicanus, old Cairo, etc., bearing the image of the symbolic frog. They can be seen in the Louvre, the British Museum, and the museums of Berlin, Leiden, and other places (Fig. 3). The two lamps of the ancient Cabinet de France and the one in the museum of Turin are especially revealing. One of those in the Louvre, and another in the Turin museum, show the frog with the cross on its back, and the inscription *ego eimi anastasis*: "I am the resurrection" (Fig. 3).

Fig. 3 Egyptian lamp from the Greppo collection.

The Gospel tells us Christ thus designated himself[19].

There are many other Christian lamps bearing the image of the frog, and all these are from before the sixth century. Three centuries earlier, the Gnostics admitted the frog among their symbolic animals, and it can be seen on the leaf of a lead booklet where it represents the renewing principle beside a serpent symbol of the Agathodaimon, the divine spirit of good[20]; or perhaps the image of death confronting that of the principle of revivification? On a carved stone of Gnostic origin, also, the frog appears between the fish, which is certainly 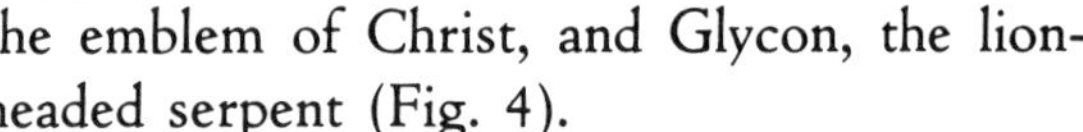 the emblem of Christ, and Glycon, the lion-headed serpent (Fig. 4).

Fig. 4 Gnostic intaglio on carnelian.

Although the Egyptians' reverence for the frog is evidenced by all the symbolic characteristics they conferred upon it, the Hebrews, on the contrary, placed it among the unclean beasts; indeed, it was the instrument of the second plague which the Lord visited upon the Egyptians in Moses' day[21]. And this repulsion felt by the Hebrews seemed to be reflected in the book of Revelation, where we read: "I saw three unclean spirits like frogs come out of the mouth of the dragon, and out of the mouth of the beast, and out of the mouth of the false prophet. For they are the spirits of devils, working miracles[22]." And this was echoed in the *Clavis* attributed to the pseudo St. Melito (which seems in fact to be of the eighth century), with the pitiless and unjust verdict: "The frog is the demon." Msgr. Barbier de Montault is right in saying that here the symbolic meaning of the toad has been mistaken for that of the frog[23]. Because of the similarity of shape of the toad and the frog, the former was long ago taken, at least indirectly, as the antithesis of the latter. Although the frog does not necessarily inspire disgust, the toad on the contrary is everywhere the object of general revulsion, as much because of its pitiable gait as it drags itself along as on account of its warty skin, which exudes at times a disgusting, poisonous slime. This unfortunate aspect has made people so unjust to the poor creature as to forget that it is one of their most useful friends and co-workers in the garden, where it feeds on nocturnal worms[24].

In Christian symbolism, the toad has been used to represent the sin of lust in its filthiest aspects. In the Middle Ages, sculptors, painters, and engravers show it along with the serpent and lizards devouring the sexual organs of naked sinners, or suckling greedily at breasts swollen with lust; we see this in many Romanesque churches, for example at Montmorillon in Vienne, Saint Cernin of Toulouse, at Saint-Jouin-de-Marnes in Deux Sèvres, at Sainte-Croix of Bordeaux, at Moissac and in many other places[25].

One of hell's punishments for the sin of greed was represented as the toad being eaten by the damned. In addition, in the symbolism of the vices, the toad was the emblem of jealousy, which explains why Edmond Rostand, in his *Chantecler*, made it the image of the basest envy. But the usual role of the toad is to represent the Devil (Fig. 5): on the twelfth-century portal of the church of Saint-Léger de Montbrillais, in Vienne, the toad emerges from the mouth of one possessed by a demon which a priest is exorcizing. At Foussais, in Vendée, on one of the roof vaults of the portal, also of the

Fig. 5 Toad issuing from the mouth of a demon; 14th-century miniature, taken from Barbier de Montault's Traité.

Fig. 6 The mermaid and the toad, on the doorway of a Romanesque church at Foussais.

twelfth century, the toad is placed next to the mermaid, another symbol of the demon of lust (Fig. 6).

This symbolic connection of the toad with the Evil Spirit was formerly made throughout the whole ancient world; even today, in Annam, the buffalo-toad, which in the eerie twilight gives out a sinister sort of bark, is supposed sometimes to be the embodiment of Macui, the Spirit of Evil. In Europe, dried and made into a powder which was dispensed by the pharmacists of times past, it has always been part of the equipment of rustic witchcraft and of that debased sorcery which still makes use of evil philters, such as that containing the pus scraped from the toad's back, of which a greater quantity is obtained by rubbing the animal with salt.

The poor toad is useful in the general economy of creation and deserves better treatment from humans whom it helps, in its own way, quite as much as do the swallow and the woodcock. But I know of only one case in which the credulity of earlier days has endowed the toad with a beneficent aspect,

Fig. 7 Extracting the toadstone, from the Hortus Sanitatis.

and this only by means of an illusion which often brought about its death. The Middle Ages inherited from previous centuries the belief that there might sometimes exist in the head of very old toads a marvelous stone, which developed after the creature's death. In France, these stones of imaginary origin were called *crapaudines*, toadstones, and they played an important role in traditional customs up to the very threshold of our present times. They were still sold for a good price in 1634, as bezoars, or poison antidotes[26]. The Greeks called this fabulous stone *batrachites*, and the Latins, *bora* (Fig. 7).

Superstitions are generally the distorted reflections of religious ideas, or of symbols whose meanings have deviated in the course of too prolonged a pilgrimage on time's road; who can tell us what thought was at the origin of that strange, mistaken belief of past centuries in the toadstone, although the toad itself was an object of general repulsion? Is it simply the result of human stupidity? Like the ocean pearl, the toadstone was supposed to discover any poison that had found its treacherous way into the wine, and to annul its mortal effects—a faculty which reminded our forefathers, imbued as they were with the Christian beliefs, of the one who said of his disciples: "They shall take up serpents; and if they drink any deadly thing it shall not hurt them[27]."

NOTES

Title Figure: Fetish toad in copper; Bergeonneau collection.

1. Aristophanes, *The Frogs*.
2. M. G. Guérin, "La Station néolithique des Châteliers du Vieil-Auzay," in *Revue du Bas-Pitou*, 1930, Book III.
3. G. R. de Noter, *La Grenouille et son élevage*, I.
4. Cf. Charles Nordmann, *L'Au-delà*, p. 115.
5. See Moret, *Du caractère religieux*, pp. 51-53.
6. Cf. Leclercq and Marron, *Dictionnaire*, fasc. 62-3, col. 1810. [*Editor's note* (J.A. West): It is worth noting that the frog is the highest life form that undergoes metamorphosis.]
7. See Maspéro, in *Revue critique*, 1879, T. I, p. 199. [*Editor's note* (J.A. West): Perhaps a distinction should be made here between the ideas of *resurrection* and *reincarnation* and *metamorphosis*, which though complementary are separate.

Schwaller de Lubicz speaks of the "Way of Osiris" in connection with cycles of renewal, or reincarnation, and of the "Way of Horus": the attainment of divinity within a single lifetime, which became the doctrine of resurrection and the central theme of Christianity.]

8. See Moret, *Rois et Dieux*, pp. 19 and 21, fig. 21.
9. Cf. de Morgan, *Revue archéologique*, 3rd series, T. XXVI, p. 261.
10. Passalacqua, *Collection des Antiquités découvertes en Égypte par J. Passalacqua*, Paris 1826, p. 14.
11. Reinach, *Répertoire*, T. II, Vol. II, p. 778, and V, 856.
12. *Ibid.*, *op. cit.*, T. V, p. 550.
13. See L. Delaporte, "Catalog des Cylindres orientaux," in *Annales du Musée Guimet*, 1909, p. 60 and plate V, #80.
14. Cf. M. Devox, "Le Shintoisme," in *Revue de l'Histoire des Religions*, 1904, p. 342.
15. Cf. J. Trousset, *Nouveau Dictionnaire encylopédique*, T.V, p. 10, 1st col.
16. See J. B. in *Aréthuse*, fasc. XX, 1928, p. 29.
17. Leclercq, *op. cit.*, fasc. 84, col. 1117, 17.
18. Le Blant, *Les Sarcophages chrétiens de la Gaule*, p. 109, #123. See also note 7, *Editor's note*.
19. St. John 11:25.
20. See Leclercq, *op. cit.*, T. II, Vol. I, fig. 1398.
21. Exodus 8:2-14.
22. Revelation 16:13-14.
23. Barbier de Montault, *Traité d'Iconographie*, T. II, p. 191.
24. See Jean Rostand, *La Vie des Crapauds*.
25. See especially A. de Caumont, *Abécédaire archéologique*, I, p. 59; also Mâle, *L'Art religieux* (2), p. 21, fig. 17 and p. 375, fig. 217.
26. See Boccone, *Observations naturelles*, 1674, p. 257.
27. St. Mark 16:18.

End Figure: Symbolic frog on the pommel of a 16th-century dagger.

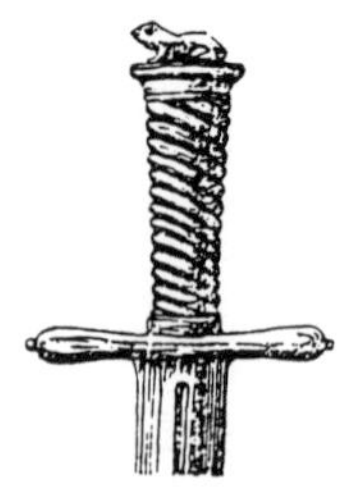

THE SALAMANDER

SALAMANDERS ARE AMPHIBIOUS, lizard-like reptiles of many colors—red, black, light yellow, orange, and violet—and in spite of having a bad reputation, they are inoffensive creatures, and useful because they destroy a considerable quantity of harmful insects and their larvae. There are several species of salamander, some of which, Cuvier tells us, reach an enormous size. The kind which interested the symbologists is the spotted salamander which is common in Europe and which is about twenty centimeters long. Its body is covered with small, bulbous protuberances which, when the creature is in pain or danger, secrete an abundant yellowish-white mucous substance; if the animal were placed on live coals, this could postpone for a brief moment its being burned up, but certainly is not a guarantee of that immunity to fire which at the end of the thirteenth century the salamander was still believed to have, in spite of the contrary opinion of Albertus Magnus.

There are few animals upon whom the Greek and Roman naturalists have lavished more fantasies and fictions than the salamander. Pliny relates in all seriousness that "it is so cold that it puts out fire by its touch, as ice does." He adds that its spittle "would make all the hair drop off the body of any human being it touches[1]." Aristotle and especially Aelian[2] also exaggerated the salamander's marvelous properties; and after them, the authors of the bestiaries and other medieval works on symbolism stated that the harmless beast fatally poisoned the water of the wells and fountains that it entered, and that it even spoiled the fruit of the trees it climbed[3]; others added that its presence alone was enough to change the character of liquids in food and drink, that it was itself neither male nor female[4], or was both at once, etc. Brunetto Latini affirmed that not only can fire do it no damage but that its very nature extinguishes fire[5].

In addition, the Middle Ages attributed to the salamander the power of working with different materials in the middle of burning braziers and thereby transmitting unique qualities of incomparable efficacy to what was worked on. Thus we read in Eschenbach's *Parzival*: "This tunic had been made in the midst of flames by ingenious serpents called salamanders. . . .[6]" The "tunic" spoken of here is a coat of mail or of steel plates.

Fig. 1 Fire personified holding the salamander, in the Saint-Omer Museum.

In the sixteenth century, the grave and frequently ingenuous Ambroise Paré, however, had lost faith in the salamander's invulnerability, and expressed the matter thus: "Mattioli says that the salamander, thrown into the midst of a great fire, is suddenly consumed; it is a great folly to hold to the belief that fire cannot consume it and that it can live on fire as the chameleon lives on air[7]."

But relying on ancient fictions, our forefathers often made the salamander the emblem of fire, and of "the spirit of fire." Fire personified on the base of a twelfth-century cross, in the museum at Saint-Omer, holds the symbolic reptile in his hand[8] (Fig. 1). The alchemists made it the sign of the work of calcination (Fig. 2), and this, according to the neo-occultists, would be what it represents esoterically, under the exoteric aspect of Justice, on the portal of Judgment in the cathedral of Paris (Fig. 3). Cloquet says of the medieval identification of the salamander with fire, that "It is the king of this element and as a consequence of this royalty, the image of Jesus Christ[9]."

Fig. 2 The salamander curled like the ouroboros, from a Greek alchemical manuscript in the Bibliothèque Nationale in Paris.

The salamander also represented impartiality: because the ancient legends say that it could live in the midst of flames by "maintaining the good fire and extinguishing the evil." This is what François I made his symbolic salamander express, by surrounding it with the legend: *Nutrisco et exstinguo*: "I nourish and I extinguish"—I nourish the good fire and extinguish the evil[10] (Fig. 4).

Fig. 3 The salamander in the flames, on the 13th-century doorway of Judgment of Nôtre Dame de Paris.

Thus the judge must be impartial and sustain the innocent and punish the guilty with perfect integrity.

Chastity and virginity also claim the salamander as emblem because they pass through the midst of the passions flaming around them without being burned. A sixteenth-century miniature, now in the Bibliothèque Nationale in Paris, depicts the salamander as representing the virginity that passes through the most hotly

Fig. 4 Heraldic salamander of Francis I; window decoration at the Château of Azay-le-Rideau in Touraine; 16th century.

burning seductions of this world, and by the same token, the Savior, and also his mother whom the Church calls the Immaculate. Like the salamander in the flames, the Mother and Son pass through the sinful human realm without acquiring the slightest shadow of stain. Thus the salamander is seen in the ornamentation of cathedrals as an attribute of these virtues; and if in certain cases the condition of the carvings is such as to make it unsure whether it is the salamander or the phoenix that is represented, much more probably it is the salamander that should be recognized[11].

With the same idea of miraculous resistance to fire, William of Normandy makes the salamander the image of the three young Hebrews who emerged unhurt from the fiery furnace of Babylon[12]. Mystical conceptualization at the end of the Middle Ages, basing itself on all these stories and on the uses to which they had been put by the writers of the tenth to the fourteenth centuries, naturally applied certain aspects of this symbolism to Christ. Msgr. Barbier de Montault suggests that the fire represented by the salamander is one of the attributes of the Savior, who said: "I am come to send fire on the earth; and what will I, if it be already kindled[13]?" We have already heard the statement of the iconographer Cloquet, that the Middle Ages made the salamander the image of

Christ because of his kingship over fire. As the three young Hebrews emerged alive and joyful from the Babylonian furnace, Christ also after descending into the fires of hell came through them victoriously. Here the salamander is joined with the hydra of the Nile in the symbolic representation of the descent into hell of the Apostle's Creed. Isaiah also had prophesied in terms which the medieval symbolists adopted[14]: *Si transieris per ignem, non combureris, flamma non exuret te*: "When thou walkest through the fire, thou shalt not be burned; neither shall the flame kindle upon thee[15]."

The science of heraldry, often a very faithful echo of the themes of the symbolists, maintained the salamander's character as emblem of purity and integrity in every aspect. Heraldry also made it express "constancy in adversity," because it endures the fire where no other living creature can dwell with impunity. The salamander of chivalry manifested the power to keep beyond the reach of all evildoing, injustice, dishonesty, cowardice, or anything else that might besmirch an escutcheon.

NOTES

Title Figure: Symbolic salamander on the escutcheon of the Salamandris of Sienna; one of its exoteric meanings was that of impossible trials.

1. Pliny, *Natural History*, Book X and LXXXVI.
2. Aelian, *History of Animals*, Book II, 31.
3. Cf. William of Normandy, *Le Bestiaire divin*, XXXIII, "De La Salamandre."
4. Cf. Vincent de Beauvais, *Speculum naturale*, Book XX and XLIII.
5. Brunetto Latini, *Li Livres dou Trésor*, Bk. I. CXLVI.
6. Wolfram von Eschenbach, *Parzival*, XV.
7. Paré, *Oeuvres*, Book XXI, "Des Venins."
8. Cf. Barbier de Montault, *Traité d'Iconographie*, T. 1, p. 122 and Plate VIII, #86.
9. L. Cloquet, *Éléments d'Iconographie chrétienne*, p. 353.
10. Cf. Henri Clouzot, in *Bulletin de la Societé des Antiquaires de France*, 1908, p. 193.
11. Cf. Mâle, *L'Art religieux* (3), p. 147.
12. William of Normandy, *op. and loc. cit.*; Daniel 3.
13. St. Luke 12:49.
14. Cf. *Le Bestiaire divin de Guillaume clerc de Normandie*, p. 176, Hippeau ed.
15. Isaiah 43:2.

THE CROCODILE

THE TWELFTH- AND thirteenth-century artists who illustrated the not very well documented tales of their contemporaries represented the symbolic crocodile more as a heavy pachyderm than as a big lizard several meters long. The bestiaries called it "cocodrille" and even "cockatrice"; this last name, as we have said, is still given in certain parts of France to the egg from which the basilisk is supposed to hatch. In ancient Egypt, the crocodile was the terror of those who lived along the banks of the Nile, and magical spells were recited for protection from it. Plutarch informs us that it was the symbol of Typhon-Set and his son Maka, who personified evil[1], which explains why the monuments show the crocodile beneath the feet of Horus. However, some tribes honored it as a god, under the name Sebek— doubtless a carry-over from a totemic or heraldic role that it had played among their remote ancestors[2] (Fig. 1). The cult of the crocodile still exists today here and there in the Sudan and southern Nigeria, especially at Ibadan, Nigeria's chief city, where in a little lake in the center of the town dwells an enormous saurian, revered by the inhabitants, which is said to have lived there for a hundred and fifty years.

Christian symbolism never showed any sympathy for this

Fig. 1 The Typhonian crocodile; late old Egyptian sculpture.

evilly disposed creature, and made it the personification of hell itself, doubtless because of the immense size of its gullet which engulfs the small animals and fish on which it feeds. The artists in stained glass, the illuminators, and the first wood-engravers before the Renaissance often depicted the entrance to hell as the gaping maw of a dragonlike monster in which the demons roasted the condemned souls; and the dragon is nothing else but the crocodile endowed with wings.

In opposition to the crocodile, Christian symbolism placed a very dangerous enemy: the hydra of the Nile, which it made one of the symbols of Christ, the conqueror of hell. Now, ever since the Greeks created the fable in which Hercules vanquished the hydra of Lerna, a horrible reptile whose seven heads grew back as fast as they were cut off, the mere name of this monster was enough to terrify and repel, and the hydra joined the company of the accursed beasts of the day. How could the early symbolists make of this creature, under this very name, a symbol of the Redeemer? The only possible answer is in the astonishing stories told by the old Greek and Roman naturalists about the crocodile, of which they seemed to know very little.

The Bestiary of Pierre le Picard describes the Nile hydra as a long, slender reptile, or rather as a sort of small, water-dwelling dragon. It is possible that after all, the Nile hydra's prototype was the varan, a big lizard which lives on riverbanks in Africa, from the French Sudan to the banks of the Nile[3], but who in reality has to let the powerful crocodiles alone. This hypothesis is supported by the fact that the varan is considered a sacred animal from the borders of Egyptian Nubia to the Saharan region of Timbuktu. Benhazera says that the Touareg had and still have a cult dedicated to the varan, which the Arabs call *ouran* and the Touareg, *ar'uta*. The animal is never killed or eaten by the nobility among these people.

"The varan, which has been known since the earliest antiquity, was depicted on Egyptian monuments. Herodotus called it 'the terrestrial crocodile,' although it is more closely related to the lizard than to the crocodile. . . .[4]"

In any case, here is what William of Normandy, writing at the end of the twelfth century in the language of an older day, tells us about the hydra: "The hydra is a very wise animal and knows well how to do harm to the cockatrice. The cockatrice is this proud beast who lives in the river Nile. It is twenty cubits long, it has four feet armed with claws, and sharp and pointed teeth. If it meets a man, it kills him, but then remains inconsolable the rest of its life[5]. The hydra who has mortal hatred for the cockatrice sees it asleep in the sun with jaws agape[6], it rolls in the mud and when it is well coated with slime, heads straight into the cockatrice's mouth, enters its belly, tears out its entrails and emerges by piercing its enemy's flank. The latter dies, for there is no cure for such wounds[7]."

Here we hear again a legend told of the mongoose smearing itself with clay to attack the asp—a fable which both Aristotle and Pliny have included in their celebrated works[8].

Fig. 2 From a 13th-century bestiary in the Bibliothèque Nationale.

Pierre le Picard tells the story a little differently: he says that when the cocodrille sees the hydra, it launches itself at its enemy and swallows it alive; but the hydra then tears out the huge creature's entrails and breaks out through its belly, wounding it mortally[9] (Fig. 2).

Neither William of Normandy nor Pierre le Picard troubled themselves, any more than did the ancient author of the *Physiologus*, to find out whether their accounts were true or fantastic. The only thing that was important to them was to find an image of Christ's triumph over hell and death, so as to have a symbol to which St. Paul's saying could be applied: "Death is swallowed up in victory. O death, where is thy sting[10]?" William of Normandy concludes thus[11]:

"The cockatrice signifies death and hell, do not doubt my

Fig. 3 13th-century illumination in a manuscript book.

word; thus, as the hydra kills it, so did our Lord Jesus Christ who covered his divinity with human flesh (as the hydra covers itself with clay), entered hell to deliver his friends, and could say with the prophet: 'O grave, I will be thy destruction[12].'' Pierre le Picard, for his part, says much the same.

This then was the symbolism of the relation of the hydra with Christ, the theory of which was well established at the time of the Capetian kings.

In the realm of iconography, the decoration of the altar of Narbonne which is in the Louvre, and is attributed to the hand of the fourteenth-century Jehan d'Orléans, depicts Jesus with the cross in his hand, standing in the opening of the enormous, flaming maw of a saurian—the cocodrille of the bestiaries—and out of it drawing forth Adam, the first of the righteous ones[13]. An illumination taken from a thirteenth-century manuscript gives an even better image of Christ, who seems to come forth like the hydra from the flank of a winged crocodile[14] (Fig. 3). The victorious battle of the hydra against the crocodile is thus the illustration of the Descent into Hell spoken of in the Apostle's Creed, which in the Middle Ages was so often interpreted by more theatrical and more complicated compositions[15].

NOTES

Title Figure: Roman coin from Nîmes from the author's collection.

1. Plutarch, *Isis and Osiris.*
2. Cf. Virey, *Religion de l'ancienne Égypte*, pp. 184-5, 218, etc.
3. Cf. L. Henrique, *Les Colonies françaises (Afrique)*, T. V, p. 235.
4. Maurice Benhazera, "Les anciennes Croyances du Touareg du Nord," in *Atlantis*, T. VI, 1933, p. 133.
5. Perhaps this is the source of the proverbial "crocodile's tears."
6. The *Physiologus*, and later the medieval bestiaries deriving from it, enlarged these old fantasies even more by saying that the crocodile is the only animal whose throat faces heavenward, since its nostrils, eyes and ears are open in the bottom of its head!
7. William of Normandy, *op. cit.*, "De Ydru," pp. 134 and 244.
8. Pliny, *Natural History*, Book VIII, 36; and Aristotle, *History of Animals*, book IX, chapter 7, 4.
9. Cf. Ch. Cahier, "Bestiaires," in *Mélanges archéologiques*, T. III, p. 212.
10. I Corinthians 15:54-5.
11. William of Normandy, *op. cit., loc. cit.*
12. Hosea, XIII, 14.
13. See Mâle, *L'Art religieux* (1), p. 11, fig. 8.
14. From the private collection of the author.
15. See especially the works of Grimouard de Saint-Laurent, Msgr. Barbier de Montault, and Émile Mâle.

End Figure: From an illustrated 13th-century bestiary in the Bibliothèque de l'Arsenal in Paris.

IV

BIRDS

THE VULTURE

THE LAMMERGEIER, OR sheep vulture, is the largest bird of prey in the Old World; its wingspread at full extent reaches nearly three meters. This bird is found especially in the countries bordering the eastern Mediterranean and the Black and Caspian Seas, in the Caucasus, the Ural mountains, and western Asia from India as far as Siberia. It has the nature of both the eagle and the vulture, but its formidable beak is larger and harder than that of either.

The lammergeier was the sacred bird of the Scythians, who inhabited the southeastern part of Russian Europe; perhaps it is this bird that is so often represented on Syrian tombs in Roman times, instead of the eagle as has generally been supposed. At the beginning of our era, the Goths, who occupied southern Scythia, adopted the lammergeier as one of their national emblems and placed it in the front rank of their symbolic fauna. We know nothing about the meanings attached to the huge raptor by these two barbarian races, but we can well imagine that among other things, they saw in it the symbol at least of strength, if not courage, since the lammergeier's attack is terribly fiery and powerful.

In any case, in their migrations toward the west through the valleys of the Danube, the Adige, and the Po, and through northern Italy, the Goths left behind examples of the crude but brilliant and extraordinarily stylized art of their goldsmiths, which the Franks adopted after the collapse of the Roman empire. Thus the image of the lammergeier (doubtless often confused by the Romans and the Gallo-Franks with that of the eagle) was spread through the West mostly in the forms of clasps, buckles, and other ornaments; and it is the lammergeier again that must be recognized in the bird which some people still call "parrot" because of the exaggeratedly hooked beak that the Gothic artisans gave it as if with the intention of marking the difference between it and the falcon or the kestrel. We can recognize Christian handiwork in several of these bird-shaped ornaments (Fig. 1). It seems certain that after their conversion to Christianity, the Goths transferred to their national bird all or part of the symbolic connotations that Western Christian symbolism then attached to the eagle[1].

Fig. 1 Gold clasp from San Merino.

Other members of the vulture family occupied a high place in the symbolic thought of the Egyptians. The vulture accompanied the pharaohs in the role of protector in the depictions of their battles and their victories. On the royal tombs or in the decorations of the temples, the bird usually held the divine seals in its talons, and this was its highest honor; we see it thus, for instance, above the effigies of Seti I and of Ramses II, in the temple of Beit el Wali in Nubia[2] (Fig. 2).

Fig. 2 The vulture as protector of Ramses II, from the temple of Beit el Wali.

Connected in a certain way, like several other creatures, with the question of the origin of human life, the vulture was the emblem of maternity in the iconography of the learned men of Egypt[3] (Fig. 3). For the same reason, it stood for parental self-sacrifice, for the Egyptians attributed to it the generous impulse to wound itself, in times of hardship, so that its flowing blood could nourish its young[4]. In the West, toward the beginning of the sixteenth century, this fable was transferred to the pelican, which according to the ancient symbolists and the authors of the bestiaries brings its chicks back to life, not by feeding them with its blood, but by pouring it over them. When we come to consider the symbolic pelican, we will see that the reason it became a Eucharistic emblem was because of the transference made to it of the fable, which in ancient times belonged only to the vulture, of nourishing its starving children with its own blood.

Throughout the Near East, the vulture was recognized as a beneficent purifier, fulfilling the same role as the ibis which in this aspect was undoubtedly one of the emblems of Christ. In the parts of western Asia where the bodies of the dead were exposed to the elements and to the birds of the heavens, the vulture was formerly venerated as the active agent in delivering them from their decayed flesh—and doubtless it still performs the same office there in the solitude of the funeral "towers of silence."

In ancient Europe, the Greek and Roman naturalists, echoed by Pliny, represented the vulture as being one of the most powerful enemies of dangerous snakes. "The mere odor of its feathers," he tells us, "chases the reptiles away, and whoever carries with him a vulture's heart is safe from their attacks and from those of all venomous creatures[5]." The Ancients also believed that the vulture's head contained another powerful talisman, the *quadratus* stone which brings perpetual felicity. A learned friend of mine is convinced that it was on account of these things and in general of its honorable reputation from the past that the first Christian sects—Theban,

Fig. 3 The vulture as symbol of maternity in ancient Egypt.

Coptic, Ethiopian, and those from the valleys of the Euphrates and the Caspian regions—were persuaded to bring the pharaonic vulture into their religious symbolism, if only on the basis of popular folklore. This is quite possibly the case, for in all these places, especially North Africa from the Red Sea to Morocco, the vulture has always aroused lively sympathy. Every year the neighborhood of Constantine, in Algeria, celebrates the "Feast of the Vultures." A banquet of choice meats is placed at the threshold of the venerated Marabout Sidi M'eids' tomb, from which the sated vultures arise and fly away in the evening, carrying toward the saint the prayers and petitions of his followers[6].

It is true that the Christian East in its early centuries sometimes saw in the vulture an allegorical image of the purifier of the world and the vanquisher of the infernal serpent, as it did in the ibis and the stork whose habits are as disgusting as the vulture's own; however, our Western symbolism credited the bird with only one of its supposed virtues: the highly illusory one of the *quadratus* stone mentioned by Pliny. About 1490, Joannes de Cuba reminded his contemporaries that the *quadratus*, *quadros*, or *quarridos* stone is "sometimes found in the vulture's head." And after extolling the rare virtues of this miraculous talisman, he shows a man breaking the head of a submissive vulture to get possession of the precious stone[7] (Fig. 4).

Religious thought has drawn the following moral from this fantasy: just as the person who wishes to possess the stone of happiness has to break the vulture's skull, it is necessary to break "the head" of our vices, represented by the vulture—that is, our inclination toward our "besetting sin"—in order to find rest for the conscience and quietness for the soul, which provide the first and indispensable condition for happiness.

Aside from this, our medieval symbolists made the vulture the sign of the demon of gluttony, on account of the rotting

Fig. 4 Looking for the quadratus stone; from the Hortus Sanitatis.

flesh and filthy creatures that this bird avidly devours[8].

For others, the mythological vulture, which ceaselessly tears the continually renewed liver of Prometheus chained to his rock, is Satan plundering the soul chained to its vice. "It represents human sin," says Godard[9], and its constant punishment in a life that is forever renewed.

The heraldry of the nobility made the powerful but cowardly vulture, which sometimes when overfed lets itself be killed with a stick, the antithesis of the royal and noble eagle which is always alert and valiant. It was the emblem of cowardice and of low habits, to be scorned by all high-minded people.

NOTES

Title Figure: The Egyptian goddess Nekhbet in the form of a vulture; from a 5th-dynasty bas-relief.

1. See above, Part 1, "The Eagle."
2. Cf. Gustave le Bon, *Les premières Civilisations*, p. 173, fig. 102.

3. Cf. Paul Rouais, *Histoire des Beaux-Arts*, p. 31.
4. See van Drival, *Grammaire comparée des langues bibliques*, Part 2, XVI, p. 115.
5. Pliny, *Natural History*, XXIX, 24.
6. Cf. Dr. Rochon-Duvigneaud, *La Protection des Vautours*, p. 7. Also Henri Rabinii, *La Fête des Vautours*.
7. See Joannes de Cuba, *Hortus Sanitatis*, Part 2, CVI.
8. Cf. Barbier de Montault, *Traité d'Iconographie chrétienne*, T. I, p. 134.
9. A. Godard, *Le Messianisme*, p. 186.

End Figure: Clasps found in Austria, Italy and the Isle of Wight.

THE FALCON

THE DIURNAL BIRDS of prey trained to serve man in hunting were divided in European falconry into two groups, called by some "noble" and "ignoble"[1]. The former included the gyrfalcon, the peregrine, the lanner and saker falcons, the kestrel, the merlin, and the hobby. Among the second were the goshawk, the kite, and the sparrow hawk. Of all these, the ancient cults, arts, and literature seem to have retained for symbolic purposes almost exclusively several of the falcons, including the kestrel, the hobby, and the sparrow hawk (Fig. 1). These birds, even when captured as adults, become relatively tame; while I write these lines, one of them, cured long since of a gunshot wound, sits motionless and free within reach of my hand, and allows itself to be stroked, which is the extreme limit of condescension on the part of a raptor.

Fig. 1 Enameled insignia of the falconer at the court of the duchy of Boulogne; from the Rochebrune collection.

Pliny wrote: "The ringdoves have a particular attachment to the kestrel, because it defends them against the sparrow hawk which flees at the sight of it or at the sound of its voice." He distinguishes here between two species of raptor although most ancient authors grouped all the small birds of prey indifferently under the name of falcon or kestrel[2].

All the European manuals of falconry are full of praises for the falcon, and the one written by the emperor Frederick II, in the thirteenth century, which Albertus Magnus included in his own works[3], is not the least curious of these.

In order to speak of the falcon as they did, and to represent it in painting and sculpture in postures so characteristic that they imply a deep knowledge and keen observation of its habits, the ancient Egyptians must have lived habitually in the company of this bird, whether in the falcon house or in the hunt itself, for the art of falconry is extremely old. A protohistoric artwork from Armenia, dating from the Iron Age, shows a hunting falcon, leashed[4] (Fig. 2), and Pliny speaks of falcons and kestrels trained for the hunt.

Fig. 2 Prehistoric Armenian art showing the leashed falcon.

As early as the first dynasty, thirty-five hundred years before Christ, the pharaoh Djer, successor of the great Menes, took the title of Falcon-King. The noble bird was already what it has always been, the protector of the royal person, and at the same time one of the most revered images of the Divinity. A little later, at the time of the great empire of Memphis, the formidable Chephren, builder of the highest of the pyramids, established a cult for the falcon which he proclaimed everywhere and which his successors and their subjects maintained until the disappearance of the Egyptian religion.

As we have already seen, in the religious concepts of ancient Egypt, the splendid image of God was the triple aspect of the Sun: the actual sun, incarnated on earth in the pharaoh; and Ptah, who represents above all the divine fatherhood, and is the architect and protector of all things. A second trinity appears, as we said in speaking of Man in the Tetramorph[5], in Ptah himself, the father god and king of all, Horus, the heart of divinity, its intelligence and goodness, and Thoth, the Word. Certainly this is an oversimplification of the complex theogony of the Egyptian religion, for the purpose of defining the meaning of Horus, the heart of God, who was from the beginning represented by the symbol of the falcon: Horus, whose nature gives the Egyptian religion the special character, universally recognized today[6], which sets it apart from other ancient religions, as one of benevolence and of generosity. All the Baals and the gods of Chaldea, Babylonia, and the other great nations were terrifying gods, and for the Hebrews, Jehovah was presented above all in the aspect of a severe master demanding justice.

Very special qualities have brought the falcon, especially the one that in England is called the hobby, the honor of incarnating the great and moving myth of the god Horus in Egyptian sacred art. One of these is that in spite of the fierce pride that characterizes the bird, it approaches more closely the dwellings of human beings than the other raptors, and even deigns to share a house with them if it is built high enough. The priests saw that while the other birds of prey sought out lonely cliffs and forests, these falcons alit and made their nests in the summits of palaces and temples; and they said that Horus also, the heart and essence of the loving-kindness of the divine Being, bends down closer to us than do the other gods.

Fig. 3 The falcon, heart of Horus, on the pharaoh Chephren's standard.

As far back as the fourth millennium before the Christian era, this symbolism was in general use and the falcon was shown everywhere. Crowned with the double tiara of the pharaohs, it stands on the royal banner of Chephren above the hieroglyphic inscription: *Heru ousir haiti*, "Horus whose power is his heart[7]." The Egyptian hieroglyph for heart is the vase (Fig. 3). And when the same powerful monarch Chephren ordered the impressive statue which represents him today in the Cairo museum to be carved in very hard stone, the artist represented the bird of Horus, the falcon god, covering the pharaoh's nape with his body. A number

Fig. 4 The pharaoh Chephren and the divine Falcon; basalt statue in the Cairo Museum, approximately 2700 B.C.

of Egyptologists explain this as the sign of Horus' protection of the royal person; this is certainly true, but I believe there is another meaning also, which has been spoken of earlier[8]. The divine falcon is shown here in the act of fecundating the thought of the pharaoh, who is the earthly agent of the divinity (Fig. 4). The divine nature is thus infused into him and animates his intelligence. Chephren, by the action of the Horus-Falcon, "heart of the only God," becomes the son of God. He will be able to invoke "his father Amon" on his monuments, and to present himself to his subjects as the inspired one, the absolutely infallible interpreter of the divine will[9].

Inscriptions on monuments confirm this theory, and their texts have allowed Egyptologists to write of the pharaoh: "The king is Horus by right, direct successor to the falcon-headed god; king, god, standard of excellence, he is the master of all humanity among whom he acts according to his will with the infallibility that is his birthright[10]."

This same symbol of the falcon placed on the pharaoh's nape is found again, according to Rougemont, in the hieratic iconography of the kings of Assyria[11]. Probably this came through the contact of their realm with neighboring Syrian possessions in Egypt.

Like all the great gods of Egypt, Horus is the personification of one aspect of the one and only God: he is the prolific father, and his images often show him holding the Key of Life (Fig. 5), or crowned with the lotus, the flower of life[12]. In Egyptian iconography, the falcon represents not only the god Horus but also the god Ra, and even Khonsu, the son of Amon and the goddess Mut, whom the Thebans, in particular, also depicted with a falcon's head. When this bird stands for Horus, it wears on its head the double crown of the pharaohs

(Fig. 6), and when it stands for Ra, its head carries a disk formed by the uraeus curved into a circle (Fig. 7). And the god Ra, in the aspect of the Falcon, is saluted thus on a pottery fragment found in Cairo:

Thou awakest in beauty, magnificent Falcon of the morning,
Who openest the eyes . . .
Carrier of light, destroyer of darkness,
Glorious, multicolored,
Who createst the light with thy divine eyes;
The earth is blind when thou goest.
Magnificent Sun, radiating brilliance,
Great Falcon with speckled plumage
Thou that traversest the skies with thy swift flight,
Splendid light of dazzling whiteness . . .

It is probable that the falcons often found in the minor statuary of ancient times are also connected with sun-worship, and in Assyria as in Egypt, the falcon was the protector of the country's rulers.

In spite of the falcon's violent habits, the relation which the Egyptians found between it and the heart of God and of humanity connected it with the symbolism of love. This idea,

Fig. 5 The falcon and the Key of Life; a Theban sculpture from the author's collection.

Fig. 6 The Falcon Horus at the entrance to the temple of Horus at Edfu; stone statue twice as tall as a man.

Fig. 7 The Falcon Ra, from le Bon, Les Premières Civilisations.

though rarely expressed, nevertheless persisted through the centuries, at least to medieval times; for the Tuscan poet Francisco da Barberino (1264-1348) described love as having the feet of the falcon[13].

One of the most alert and watchful of the raptors, the very essence of this bird's character seems to be an anxiety that imposes a constant, vigilant attention; and for that reason, the vigilance of Horus, the loving heart of Divinity, found in the falcon a truly appropiate symbol (Fig. 8). The author of *The Imitation of Christ* wrote: "Love waketh much and sleepeth little, and sleeping, sleepeth not[14]." The ancient naturalists affirmed that the falcon, like the lion, slept without closing its eyes. The only thing I can say on this subject is that I have tried many times during the night hours to surprise my tame falcons with their eyes closed, and I have never succeeded. It has even been said that the bird has no eyelids, which is not so, for in death, the lids close by themselves over the bird's eyes; but what is sure is that this bird's sleep is extraordinarily light.

Fig. 8 Horus with a falcon's head, wearing the double crown and the panther skin and holding the Key of Life.

The eye of Horus was often shown by itself, quite separate from the god's person or the falcon's shape, in the hieroglyphs or the decor of Egyptain art, in the form of a highly stylized bird's eye (Fig. 9), an ideogram charged with meaning and evoking not only the vigilance of Horus but every good thing coming from the Divinity for the life and happiness of mankind. His look purified the flesh of the dead as it consumed it, and it was believed that each year he brought new fire down to the world. Philippe Virey has drawn a very striking connection between this many thousand-year-old Egyptian ceremony of the new fire and our Christian rituals on Holy Saturday, considered by the Church to be rites of renewal[15].

In Egyptain art, when the symbolic falcon wears a human head on its bird body, it is one of the representations of the human soul; and the bird's nature admirably serves the role. Just as the soul must try to find the heights and not linger on the low levels of material things, so the falcon when it is free in the open air seeks the high places, the rocky summits or the tops of buildings, and enclosed in the falcon house or its master's room, it will always perch on the highest point possible.

Fig. 9 The hieroglyphic eye of Horus.

Since for the Egyptian the supreme god was the Sun, whether in the aspect of Amon, Ra, or Aten, the highest sacred act is the union of the soul with him. Behold the falcon when after a few dark days the sun comes out and it receives the first touch of its rays: deliberately and at once, its eyes, round as the sun itself, turn to gaze at it and though they stare at and through the fiery disk they are not dazzled[16]; its chest expands and lifts, its feathers fluff out. Even more frequently, it exposes its nape to the warm touch of the sunlight; then its wings spread and beat in a kind of cadence, and its whole body throbs in rhythm; one senses that the bird gives itself completely to the ascendancy of the sun. Young birds are especially expressive in a bath of sunlight. The theologians and mystics of ancient Egypt could not have found a better emblem to depict the holiest souls and the intensity of their meditations: "Hail, ye two divine hawks who are perched upon your resting places, and who hearken unto the things which are said," says the *Book of the Dead*[17], and this, says Lanoë-Villène, "seems to relate to the souls of the holy

Fig. 10 Mummified falcon, from the collection of M. le Comte Fr. de Rilly.

teachers of divine knowledge[18]."

All this explains the funerary honors the Egyptians paid to the sacred falcons which they mummified carefully after their death before sending them to Buto to be buried, as Herodotus describes (Fig. 10).

There is no ancient text that I know of that supports our certainty that the early Christians in Egypt made the falcon a symbol of Christ. On the other hand, the evidence of the inscriptions proves that they certainly made an allegorical assimilation between Jesus and Horus, the son of Amon and Isis[19]. According to Dolger[20], André Boulanger mentions a jewel engraved with the image of the god Horus and the designation: "CHRISTOS[21]"; and in that inexhaustible treasure-house of our past, the *Dictionnaire d'Archéologie chrétienne*, Dom Leclercq reproduces a painting of the Christian catacomb of Karmuz, in Egypt, which represents Jesus trampling under his feet the lion and the dragon, according to David's saying[22]; and he compares this work of art with an Alexandrian stele in the museum of Gizeh which shows the god Horus trampling underfoot the Typhonian crocodiles[23].

There was an advanced Christian school in Alexandria in the third century known as the Didasculum[24], which strove to harmonize with Christianity everything in Egypt's religious past that could be accepted by the new religion; and it was understood here that wherever the falcon appeared in the old monuments of Egypt are falcons, and not eagles. The eagle was very rarely employed as a symbol in ancient Egypt, but after the introduction of Christianity it appeared a little more frequently, in connection with the prophecies of Ezekiel and in representations of the Evangelists. Aside from these two cases its use was so exceptional that in the fifth-century church of Baouit, where it was pictured holding the Key of Life in its talons, the artist found it expedient to write at one side: AETOC: "This is an eagle."

In Egypt's past, the falcon was not only the emblem of the human soul but also that of resurrection, like the eagle. It seemed indeed that the Christian religion had given to the falcon of Horus all the eagle's chief mystical and allegorical meanings, even while conserving its pre-Christian connotations as the "symbol of life, of continuity, perhaps of eternity[25]." It was easy to make this transfer. As we have seen, the eagle represented Christ's triumph; and in ancient Egypt, the falcon took part in all the triumphs of the pharaohs, the sons of Amon. Among the Ancients, the eagle was above all others the solar bird; in Egypt, this was the falcon. Among the Greeks and Romans, the eagle was the emblem of resurrection; and the eye of Horus' falcon purified the dead and prepared them for a new life. For the Christians, because of its hatred for reptiles, the eagle was the sign of Christ the warrior against evil, and we have taken note of the Alexandrian stele showing Horus crushing the crocodile beneath his feet. Other parallels can be drawn, and we can be certain that at least in Christian Egypt, the falcon was one of the symbols for Christ.

It might also be noted that in western Asia, this bird appeared in very ancient times as the destroyer of evil spirits: "the falcon slays the evil demons with iron talons," and the Rig-Veda says that the god Indra often takes on the falcon's form[26].

Like the bird of paradise, the falcon was placed by a certain form of symbolism at the service of the third person of the Trinity. At the beginning of the sixteenth century, the mystical society *L'Estoile Internelle*, in which later was incorporated the *Fraternité des Chevaliers du divin Paraclet* (Brotherhood of the Knights of the Holy Paraclete), invoked the Holy Spirit in the guise of the dove to ask for the gifts of piety, fear of God, wisdom, and counsel; and behind the symbol of the falcon, to implore him for the gifts of knowledge, intelligence

Fig. 11 The Holy Spirit in the image of the falcon; 16th-century bas-relief from the church of Notre Dame of Croaz-Batz.

and strength[27].

A superb altar-piece corresponding with this symbolic theme is found in the church of Notre Dame of Croaz-Batz, in Roscoff, Finisterre. It is composed of seven sculptures in alabaster, the Annunciation, the Nativity, the Flagellation, the Descent from the Cross, the Resurrection, the Ascension, and Pentecost. On the first and last of these sculptures the Holy Spirit is represented by a bird: in the Annunciation, by a dove; in Pentecost, by a falcon soaring above a hearth of flames directed downward, above the Virgin and the Apostles (Fig. 11).

In heraldry, there was a figure called "flight," composed of a pair of wings joined together without a body. Some heraldists, especially after the Renaissance, took these to be eagles'

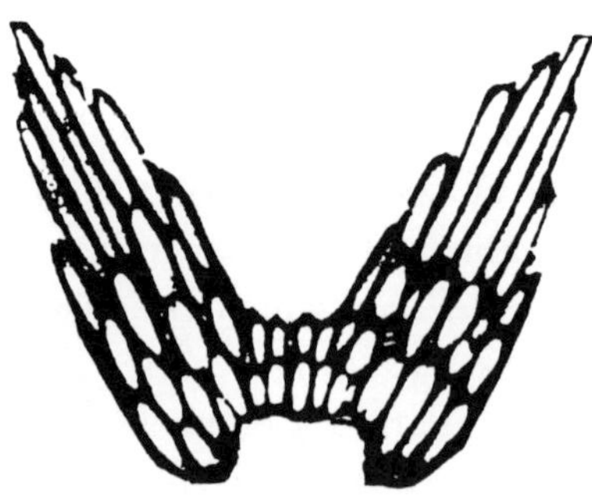

Fig. 12 The heraldic image of flight.

wings, others said they were those of the falcon which was much more common and familiar than the eagle and unquestionably one of the best-known birds to the creators of the heraldry of the nobility. In that noble science, the "flight" represented the chosen soul enamored of a high ideal, which has thrown off the domination of matter and dwells in the luminous heights. In religious heraldry, the "flight" was the symbol of the spiritual being, and above all others, the Holy Spirit, the Paraclete.

The hermetists who used the symbol with the same connotation showed it descending from the sky; that is, with the wing points above (Fig. 12). The "flight" which goes up toward heaven, with the wing points downward, more clearly depicts spirits that strive upwards while still attached to bodies, showing the highest aspirations of our souls.

Fig. 13 The double-bitted axe, from a painting on an old vase.

In the same little-known places which I have just mentioned, a similarity was drawn between the heraldic spiritual "flight" and the holy symbol of the ancient world, consecrated to the fire cult, of the double-bitted axe, called by the Romans the *Bipennis*, the "axe with two wings" (Fig. 13). The name, as well as a certain similitude of shape, is an indication of the connection of these ideas. Furthermore the fact that the "two-winged" axe is an ancient symbol of fire brings it into closer relationship with the divine Spirit which on the day of Pentecost showed itself in the form of tongues of flame.

In the same way that the falcon was taken to symbolize the Holy Ghost by the fraternity of *l'Estoile Internelle* at the end of the medieval period, the same bird was also the chosen emblem of certain associations and companies of workers in roof construction. These workmen found falcons and their nests in the high roofs of towers and cathedrals, and the very pose of the bird at the moment of flight took the exact shape of the roofers' hammer; which explains the drawings of the hammer and the bird next to each other found on the walls of the fifteenth-century chateau of Montsoreau in Anjou (Figs. 14). This reminds us that the Ancients often found hidden meanings in the positions and shapes of animals and birds. Tertullian says: "Cattle and wild beasts pray in their way, and so also the bird which lifts itself toward the sky makes the shape of a cross with its wings spread as a man does when he prays and extends his arms[28]."

Although as we have seen the falcon was allotted an exceptional number of noble roles in the Christian past, in general the raptors were more often taken by the teachers of the Church as images of demons who ravish the souls of men: the writings of St. Thomas of Villeneuve and St. Alphonse de Liguori[29], in these later centuries, testify to this. To those well acquainted with the Middle Ages and the great favor in which falconry was held, however, it seems that this ugly role was confined more or less to the raptors called "ignoble." In the symbolism of the epoch, the sparrow hawk was the figure of Envy[30]. In a thirteenth-century stained glass window in the cathedral of Bourges, a raptor devours a heart (Fig. 15), in spite of statements by Pliny[31] and Aristotle[32] that falcons and

Fig. 14 The falcon and the roofers' hammer; graffiti at Montsoreau.

Fig. 15 The infernal raptor from the Cathedral of Bourges.

sparrow hawks never eat the hearts of their victims. Perhaps it is the demon of Envy that should be seen in the Bourges raptor, which tears the heart of anyone it possesses.

NOTES

Title Figure: Egyptian funerary stele; the falcon between alpha *and* omega *here represents Christ.*

1. Cf. M. de Boissoudan, *Le Falconnier parfait*, 1745, pp. 8-10 (MS property of Antiquaires de l'Ouest). Also J. Trousset, *Nouveau Dictionnaire encyclopédique*, T. I, p. 351 and T. IV, p. 68.
2. Pliny, *Natural History*, Book X, 10 and 52.
3. Albertus Magnus, *Opera Omnia* ("De animalibus"), Borgnet edition, T. XI, p. 453. Also *De Falconibus, Asturibus et Accepitribus.*
4. Morgan, *L'Humanité préhistorique*, p. 173.
5. See above, Part I, "The Man," p. 42.
6. Cf. Major Russo, "L'Atlantide et le Maroc," in *Atlantis*, T. II, # 12; November 1928, p. 28.
7. Cf. Maspéro, *Histoire ancienne*, T. I, p. 262.
8. See above, Part I, "The Man," p. 42-43.
9. For the mystical connections between the pharaoh and the falcon, see Alexandre Moret, *Mystères égyptiens*, especially pp. 157-172.
10. Marcel Zahar, "Les Caractères de l'Art égyptien," in *L'Art vivant*, T. V, # 18, January 1929, p. 72.
11. Taken from Argos, in *Le Voile d'Isis*, T. XXXV, 1930, #123, p. 135.
12. Reinach, *Répertoire*, T. II, vol. II, p. 175, # 7.
13. Da Barberino, in *Documenti d'Amore*.
14. Thomas à Kempis, *The Imitation of Christ*, Book III, Chapter 5.
15. Virey, *Religion de l'ancienne Égypte*, p. 299.

16. Aelian, *De Nat. Anim.* XX, 16; (third century): "These birds, with the eagles, are the only ones who can look easily and without hurt at the sun's rays. Without closing their eyes, they raise themselves very high and the divine flame does them no harm."
17. *The Book of the Dead*, Chapter LXVI.
18. Lanoë-Villène, *Le Livre des Symboles*, T. IV, p. 98.
19. *Editor's Note*: Horus is generally considered the son of Osiris.
20. Dolger, *Ichtus*, T. II, p. 256, plate 36.
21. Cf. Boulanger, *Orphée*, p. 148.
22. Psalm 91:13.
23. Leclercq and Marron, *Dictionnaire*, T. I, vol. I, col. 1138, fig. 285 and 286.
24. See Part VII, "The Sphinx," p. 455; also *Regnabit*, T. XV, Sept.-Oct. 1928, p. 141.
25. Cf. Robert Chauvelot, *Atlantis*, supplement to # 26, p. 2.
26. Cf. A. de Gubernatis, *Mythologie zoologique*, T. II, p. 141.
27. *Fraternité des Chevaliers du divin Paraclet*, 16th century MS in *Arch. de L'Estoile Internelle.*
28. Tertullian, *De Oratione*, XXIX.
29. Alphonse de Liguori, *Le Pouvoir de Marie*, Marne edition, 1907, p. 95.
30. Cf. de Saint-Laurent, *Guide*, T. III, p. 476; also A. Martin, *Mélanges d'Archéologie*, T. I, II, p. 29.
31. Pliny, *Natural History*, Book X, Chapter X.
32. Aristotle, *History of Animals*, Book IX, Chapter XXIV.

End Figure: Gold falcon holding the divine seals.

THE OWL

THE RAPTORS WHO fly by day have often enjoyed a favorable reputation in ancient symbolism—the goshawk, the merlin, the gyrfalcon, not to mention the eagle, are noble birds; but the sinister, nocturnal flyers, especially owls, are "birds of ill-omen." Only one kind of night-flying raptor inspires a certain sympathy, at least in some French provinces: this is the little *chouette-chevêche* or *chevêchette*, the pygmy owl[1], the size of a quail, which is very common in France, and whose call in the darkness is not at all frightening. Of its own accord, it accompanies the late traveler along the country roads, and often makes its nest and raises its young on the roofs of dwellings.

The country people divide the nocturnal raptors in two categories: the *chouettes*, which have smooth heads without any crests of any kind, and the *hiboux* whose heads have two tufts of feathers like horns or ears. This classification, which depends only on the bird's exterior appearance, corresponds to the way of thinking in ancient times in which owls were unpopular except for the little *chouettes*, which were very numerous in Athens and all of Greece and were looked upon with great favor there as well in the rest of the ancient world.

It seems that the symbolism of the owl, like that of the swan, comes to us from the early people in the far North. And as in that region and that far-off time the swan symbolized the birth of daylight, the owl would on the other hand symbolize the mystery of the shadows of night. This is the significance which the Lapps and other northern races still recognize in the handsome *chouette*-owls of their country which they look upon as the white spirits of the night, for the plumage of these birds, except for a few streaks of very pale rust color, is almost as snowy as that of the swan[2] (Fig. 1). In some parts of Scandinavia, this bird is made the emblem of moonlight.

Fig. 1 The white owl of the North.

The symbolism of the owl seems to have followed the same route as that of the swan, down from the Pole toward southern Europe. We find the oldest religious and talismanic images in the provinces of European and Asiatic Russia which extend along the chain of the Ural mountains, as far as Hellenic Asia Minor, and into Africa, via Egypt (Figs. 2 and 3).

In Greece in Mycenaean times, the most ancient representations of the goddess Pallas Athena, the Latin Minerva, show her with a woman's body and the face of an owl[3]. Several variations of this Aegean idol, of the same date, have been found in Abyssinia, with the peculiarity that the personage represented sometimes has no mouth[4].

Fig. 2 & 3 Protohistoric bronze owls from Russia.

Returning to Greece, we find Athena's bird represented on a number of coins of the Golden Age, which were called by the name of the bird they pictured, *glaus* (Fig. 4). Everywhere in the old world they were signs of Athenian prosperity; "to send owls to Athens" was a common saying in Rome to indicate unnecessary generosity[5].

Fig. 4 Archaic Athenian coin.

The symbolism of the owl was used for Minerva by the Latins just as it was for Athena among the Greeks, in spite of Ovid's translation of a later legend telling of Nyctimenus' penitential transformation into an owl[6].

We might add here the words of Johannes Lydus: "Athena was called *Glaucopis* because she shared the nature of fire; and the owl, her sacred bird, stays awake all night to signify the human soul which is never lazy, always in movement by its very nature, which is immortal[7]."

In the bird that sees clearly in the dark when all others are blind, and when it is hunted has the good sense and the caution to remain hidden all day, the Greeks saw a symbol in which were united the three qualities of wisdom, knowledge, and prudence. For this reason they connected it with Athena, the chaste goddess of wisdom, who issued from the head of the supreme god. "The owl's eye shines in the darkness like the glory of the wise man in the midst of the foolish crowd," says an old text.

Some people have claimed that eating the eggs of the owl makes a person temperate and well-balanced; this seems to be an echo of what Pliny says of the beliefs current in his day, according to which the eggs of the nocturnal flyers mixed with wine were a cure for drunkenness.

In Asia, also, the owl was always a venerated symbol. In explanation of this, the Kalmuck Tartars of Mongolia tell that their great emperor Genghis Khan (1162-1227), pursued by his enemies, was saved by the presence of an owl perched on the thicket where he lay hidden. In the seventeenth century, the French heraldist Vulson de la Colombière repeated this legend; but it does not explain the origin of the veneration in which the bird was held long before the time of the Tartar hero[8].

In spite of some disagreeable connotations, in the main the owl was still regarded in medieval times from the point of view of the Ancients. Especially in the monasteries, where all day long the bird keeps to its place on the wall or in the hollow tree, it was taken as the sign of meditation. In the lamaseries and hermitages of Tibet, it is also taken as the image of the disciple who performs his period of "retreat" from the world, isolated from all others, during which he works inwardly to attain the mastery of his spirit over his body. Symbolizing this ancient practice of meditation, the owl, according to Lanoë-Villène, became "the symbol of the light of the Holy Spirit illuminating the dark soul of the unbeliever[9]." The owl, especially the *chouette*, also had the honor of being likened to Christ. Eustathius, archbishop of Thessalonica in the twelfth century, expressing the view of his time, said that the owl's clear vision in the darkest night was due to a luminous force in its eyes which could dissolve the shadows. In the same way, the mystics said, Christ by the power of his divinity always and everywhere sees all, and no mystery exists for him.

Fig. 5 The symbolic chouette *owl; 12th-century sculpture from the interior of a church at Bouchet, Vienne.*

Another aspect of this connection was brought by applying David's words in the psalm to the Savior abandoned by his friends in his Passion: "I am like an owl of the desert[10]."

The bestiaries, less daring, were at somewhat of a loss in comparing Christ with the nocturnal raptor. Here is how the twelfth-century *Armenian Bestiary* studied by Father Charles Cahier extricates itself from the difficulty: "It is said that the nocturnal bird loves the night more than the day. And our Lord loves us who are in darkness and who dwell in the shadow of death. But it will be said: the night bird is unclean under the Law, how can it be compared to Christ? And I will show you the passage from the Apostle where it is said: 'Him, who knew no sin, he hath made sin for us, that we might be made the justice of God in him[11].'"

In the decorative art of the Middle Ages, it is sometimes difficult to distinguish whether the image of the lone owl is intended to represent the student of holy scripture or the forsaken Christ (Fig. 5). Often the milieu is a help: in a cloister, for instance, or on the outside of a church, especially if the bird is perched on a book or a scroll, it is usually the meditative student. Inside the church, it is clearly a symbol of the Savior when there is a cross drawn on its breast or head[12], and it may very well represent him if it is on the gospel rather than the epistle side. This latter is so for the following curious reason: the hatred for Jews of the medieval Christians classified them with other outcast groups, such as sorcerers and practitioners of black magic, whom the owl symbolized in its evil sense, as a bird of darkness. It was said that as the Jews were blind to the light of the gospel, in the same way the owl closes its eyes to the light of day. Since it is on the epistle side of the church that lessons from the Old Testament, the Hebrew Bible, were read in the Catholic liturgy, images of the owl are more frequently seen on that side of the church[13].

It was quite natural that in popular symbolism, Satan, "the prince of darkness," should be represented by the owl, the bird of night, especially the barn owl, the ghostly "diabolic bird" that we see on ancient amulets with which evil spirits were evoked. The owl was also the emblem of the demon of avarice[14], and symbolists have contrasted its lunar character with the solar one of the eagle and the falcon[15].

NOTES

Title Figure: The owl on the "evil eye"; mosaic in a Roman basilica.

1. *Editor's note*: Probably the saw-whet owl (*aegolius acadica acadica*) is the closest New World species.
2. Cf. *L'Aventure*, V, July 1927.
3. Schliemann, *Mycènes*, I, "Fouilles à Thirinthe," p. 64, fig. II and p. 74.
4. Cf. Edm. Pothar, "Les découvertes d'un Français en Abyssinie," in *L'Illustration*, April 1927, p. 381.
5. Cicero, *Letters*, CXLIV, "To Glaucus."
6. See Ovid, *Metamorphoses*, Bk. II, fable VIII and IX; Bk. V, Fig. VIII. [*Editor's note:* The *chouette* was called *nyctimenus* as well as *glaucos*.]
7. Lydus, *De Mensibus*, IV, 54.
8. See de la Colombière, *La Science héroique*, p. 372, #104.

9. Lanoë-Villène, *Le Livre des Symboles*, T. IV, p. 67.
10. Psalms 102:6.
11. II Corinthians 5:21 (Douay-Rheims version). See also Cahier, *Nouveaux Mélanges archéologiques*, 1874, p. 122.
12. Cf. Abbé J. Corblet, "Vocabulaire des Symboles" in *Revue de l'art chrétien*, T. XVI, p. 461.
13. See Cahier, *op. cit.* (in note 11 above), p. 142.
14. Cf. Grimouard de Saint-Laurent, *Guide*, T. III, p. 476.
15. Cf. Guénon, *Regnabit*, January 1927, p. 160.

End Figure: The chouette-chevêche. *Heraldic symbol of clear-sightedness and wisdom, on the coat-of-arms of the Hevrat family.*

THE SWALLOW

THE SWALLOW HAS always and everywhere been one of mankind's favorite birds. Among the ancient Egyptians, numerous local legends cluster around it[1]. The texts of the Great Pyramids and the *Book of the Dead* testify to the existence of a swallow goddess; a high official of the fifth dynasty, who was a priest of the double axe, was at the same time her priest[2]. This cult lasted until the end of the sixth dynasty when it disappeared from the official liturgy; but from the earliest to the latest times, the most advanced religious teachings and arts made the swallow the image of the human soul, which it was said assumed the swallow's shape in the course of its transformations[3]. This explains why the bird is so frequently represented on mummy cases (Fig. 1) and in tombs (Fig. 2), connecting the idea of resurrection and the freedom of the spirit separated from the body with the soul of the one who has died.

Fig. 1 The swallow-soul on a fragment of a mummy case.

The swallow also entered the touching myth of Isis, who was said to have taken the form of a swallow to go to Byblos to bewail the death of Osiris[4].

Fig. 2 The swallow-soul on the tomb of Ramses IV.

In Babylonia, the swallow's image was consecrated to the goddess Aruru-Ninmakh[5], and seems also to have symbolized the idea of liberation into a life after death.

In some of the most beautiful of the Egyptian sacred texts the smoke of incense, which has been the symbol of prayer ever since those far times, is compared to the swallow. And because of its flight that lifts it toward the sky and also because of the soft, earnest twittering of its call, the Ancients of classical times also made the swallow, called *chelidon* by the Greeks, the image of prayer. In Greece[6], the urgent, supplicating chant with which the poor begged for alms was called *chelidonisma*; it was a kind of hurried and confused psalmody which tried to imitate the swallow's twittering, *chelidoniso*. For the Greeks this graceful bird also symbolized that discriminating moral taste which makes a person avoid bad company; for it was said that the swallows shunned Thebes in Boeotia because it had weakly allowed itself to be taken twice, and also Bizia because of the crimes of Tereus, whom the terrible Procne punished so severely before she herself was changed into a swallow[7].

The swallow's return in the spring after its winter's absence, not only to the region but to the very nest which it built in preceding nesting seasons, was for the Ancients, as it is today in many places, one of the most natural representations of the idea of resurrection. The wind which blew at the moment of the swallows' return, the softest and sweetest of all the breezes that move under the skies of Greece, was called by the Greeks the "chelidonian wind[8]."

It is not only the regularity of the annual reappearance that has given the swallow its symbolic character; this is also supported by a mistaken belief, which lasted for centuries, that, as Aristotle and the Ancients claimed, the swallows of the northern countries bury themselves in the winter in piles of leaves or in the crumbling wood of hollow trees, or even in the silt of rivers, whence they emerge in spring as from a tomb[9]. Painstaking research by eighteenth-century naturalists caused these notions to be placed in the category of fables[10]. But all in all, it is easily comprehensible that the former Christian symbolists made use of the swallow since an early period to depict the triumph of the Redeemer at Easter. A very ancient Armenian legend tells that on Good Friday evening, all the swallows of Judea and Galilee gather around Jesus' tomb, and as Easter dawns they fly swiftly away in pairs to all of the countries of the world to carry the startling news: "The Lord is risen indeed: alleluia[11]!" Today, the swallow still enacts the role of the herald of Christ's rebirth; and in several parts of France, the country folk consider it a favorable sign if they see the newly-arrived birds between the two triumphal feasts of Palm Sunday and Easter.

The whole ancient world took the swallow to be a bird of light. Pliny says that it makes use of a plant with golden sap, named in its honor *chelidoine*, the celandine poppy[12] (Fig. 3), to cure the eyes of its young or others of its kind. This flower, which is very common in Île-de-France, was a popular motif among the sculptors of the great Gothic cathedrals during the thirteenth and fourteenth centuries; and perhaps it was because of this that the swallow became one of the Middle Ages' emblems for architecture[13]. In any case, we find the celandine poppy, "swallow flower," in the decoration of the cathedrals of Paris, Rheims, Amiens, Beauvais, Chartres, and Bourges[14], as well in a number of less important churches.

Fig. 3 The celandine poppy of France and its cruciform flower.

Pliny recommends the use of swallow's blood as an ingredient in eye lotions for human use, and Celsus and others, indeed the whole body of Greek and Roman medical opinion, were in agreement[15]. Popular tradition also echoed these beliefs; in Biscay it was claimed that anyone who killed swallows needlessly would go blind in old age, if indeed that person lived to grow old[16]. It was believed moreover that in every swallow's body there was a marvelous stone that would not only improve or restore sight but that possessed many other virtues as well. It could be red, black, or white. The archbishop of Rennes, Marbode, who wrote during the reign of King Philippe Auguste of France (twelfth century), states that the red chelidonian stone cured lunacy, mania, and declining health, and helped to develop eloquence; the black stone promoted success for one's projects and the water in which it was soaked strengthened the vision[17].

Relying on such ancient fantasies, the bestiaries, which were the unquestioned manuals of medieval symbolism, and the works derived from them, stated that when the young swallows showed a premature urge to escape from the nest to go out and see the world, the parent bird itself destroyed their eyes before leaving them, but on returning, according to a bestiary quoted by Father Cahier, "it makes its little ones see clearly. No one knows how it does this, nor with what means[18] (Fig. 4)"; perhaps, as Tertullian says, this miracle was wrought by the application of the celandine poppy[19].

Fig. 4 The swallow and its young; illumination of a 13th-century bestiary in the Bibliothèque de l'Arsenal.

The medieval bestiaries also declare that the swallow here symbolizes the Redeemer who gives, takes away, and gives back the light of the soul and of the intelligence to the human being according to his merits or to the needs of his spiritual welfare.

I might add that if the first Christian symbolists were not disturbed by the biblical story of old Tobias' misfortune in their view of the swallow as a bird of light with curative powers, it was because the Bible expressly states that the old man's blindness was brought about by the swallows' *excrement*, something the birds rejected as so foreign to their nature that it could not be assimilated[20].

In some parts of the Mediterranean coast, the swallow has been made a symbol of hope and is then shown head downwards. This symbolism rests chiefly on the fact that when this

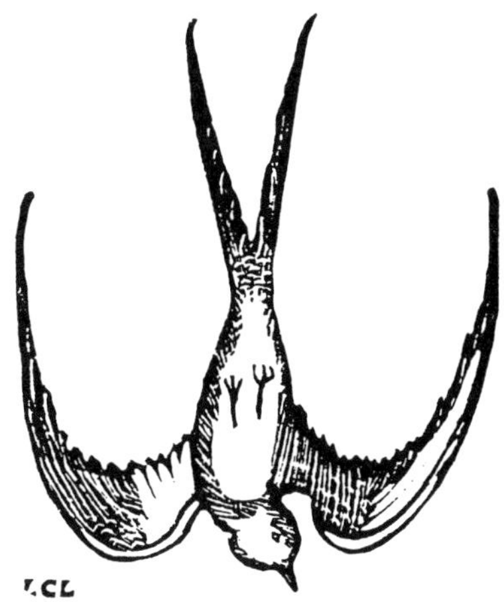

Fig. 5 The swallow in the position symbolizing hope.

bird drops down to earth from the sky, its curved wings and long tail feathers give it the shape of the anchor which from the time of the catacombs has symbolized the theological virtue of hope[21] which also comes down from heaven into the heart of the Christian (Fig. 5). In several provinces in France this same idea gave the celandine poppy, the "swallow flower," the connotation of "awaiting a joy that is soon to come[22]."

The seventeenth century also made the swallow the symbol of the Lord, who withdraws from the soul when it darkens and becomes cold, and who returns to it when it regains its ardor. In the same way, the swallow leaves a region invaded by cold and fog, and returns in the warmth and sunlight of spring[23]. On the other hand, its annual departure and return, and the astonishing instinct that brings it back exactly to its family nest, have connected it with the parable of the Prodigal Son, and the allegorical image of the sinner who departs from Christian life and practice, but returns at last to the Church.

Since the ancient naturalists, who provided so much material to the early Christian symbolists, related the swallow with the cure of epilepsy, Pliny suggested that an excellent remedy for this illness was to eat young swallows taken from the nest; and as a preventive amulet, he recommended a small stone, also taken from the bird's nest, different from the chelidonian stone[24]. Epilepsy, madness, convulsions, eclampsia, hysteria, and other illnesses of the same sort were generally ascribed to the influence of evil spirits, so it was quite natural that a symbolic connection should be made between the bird thought to cure these attacks and Christ who in his earthly journeys cast out evil spirits. The swallow's continual aerial pursuit of insects strengthened still more its image as the enemy of demons, for flies and gnats were commonly taken as representatives of maleficent spirits even before the coming of Christianity[25], in which the fly symbolized equally the demons and Satan. One translation, though apparently faulty, still is given of the name of Beelzebub (the Baal of the city Zebub)[26] as "king or lord of the flies." We shall speak of this again in connection with the symbolism of the bee[27].

In certain parts of France, swallows' nests are still considered to protect the houses on which they are built; I have heard peasants in Vendée say that a swallow's nest, even in winter, frightens off the demons of the night. In several provinces, the nest is commonly accepted as the ideogram for a human family dwelling so well endowed with warmth and concord that it is the place to which the family members always return, as does the swallow. Those who wilfully tear down a nest risk being themselves made to fall victim later to the *grand mal* of epilepsy[28].

A complete reversal of what has just been said about the swallow's pursuit of insects is that in the last three hundred years, various symbolists have taken the swallow as the image of Satan the ravisher of souls, which he pursues as relentlessly as the swallow pursues the gnats. I know of only one other symbolic theme, that of the spider, in which the fly and the gnat symbolize human souls; their usual role is to represent the spirits of hell.

Some others have also tarnished the swallow's image by making it represent various human weaknesses: inconstancy, because when it is flying it seems never to stop anywhere, and also because every year it leaves the country where it was born; impurity, because it touches the ground only to gather mud, and builds out of mud the place where it dwells[29].

The heraldists of the nobility after the Renaissance were also severe with the swallow: "The swallow," said the best-known of them all, "represents the flatterer, and the false friend, because in winter it goes away and leaves us[30]." Others, however, have made it the symbol of prudence.

NOTES

1. Cf. Hip. Boussac, "L'Hirondelle dans les mythes égyptiens." in *Cosmos*, December 1905.
2. Cf. Percy Newberry, *A Bird Cult of the Old Kingdoms*.
3. See E. Guimet, "Les Âmes égyptiennes," in *Revue de l'Histoire des Religions*, 1913, p. 4.
4. Plutarch, *Isis and Osiris*, 16. See also Amélineau, *Essai sur le Gnosticisme égyptien*, p. 142.
5. F. Steinmetzer, *Beitrage der assyriologie*, VIII, 2, 1910, pp. 1-38.
6. Lefébure, "La vertu du sacrifice funéraire," III, in *Sphinx*, T. VII, pp. 83 and 209, and VIII, pp. 1 and 51.
7. Pliny, *Natural History*, Book X, 34.
8. Nonnus, *Dionysiaca*, Ch. XI.
9. Olaus Magnus, *Histoire des Nations Septentrionales*. Cf. *Les Oeuvres complètes de Buffon*, 1835, T. IX, III, p. 25.
10. See Buffon, *Histoire naturelle*, 1769, T. XXI, pp. 236 and 271.
11. *Roman Catholic Breviary*, Office of Easter matins.
12. Pliny, *op. cit.*, VIII, and XXV, 50.
13. Cf. L. Cloquet, *Éléments d'Iconographie chrétienne*, p. 328.
14. Cf. Émile Lamblin, *La Flore des grandes Cathédrales*, passim.
15. Celsus, *De Medicina*, Book VI, ch. 6, 39; see also H. de Villefosse and H. Thédenat, "Note sur quelques cachets d'oculistes romains," in *Bulletin monumental*, 1882, p. 709.
16. Dr. Pommerol, "Folklore d'Auvergne," in *Revue des Traditions populaires*, T. XII, p. 444.
17. Cf. Marbode, *Poème*, *Le Lapidaire*, XVII, *De Chelonidio*.
18. Charles Cahier, "Bestiaires," in *Mélanges archéologiques*, T. II, p. 145.
19. Tertullian, *De poenitentia*, XII.
20. Tobias 2:11—Douay-Rheims version. [*Editor's note:* The KJV (*Apocrypha*) cites the sparrow, not the swallow, as the bird whose dung blinded Tobias; Tobit 2:10.]
21. Cf. Cloquet, *op. cit.*, p. 243.
22. Cf. P. Verneuil, *Dictionnaire des Symboles, emblèmes et attributs*, p. 38.
23. *Emblèmes et devises chrétiennes*, Chavance edition, 1717, p. 181.
24. Pliny, *op. cit.*, Book XXX, 12 and 27.

25. Chompré, *Dictionnaire de la Fable*, p. 275.
26. See J. Halévy, *Comptes rendus de l'Académie des Inscriptions*, March 4, 1892.
27. See below, Part VI, "The Bee and The Fly," pp. 330-331.
28. Information from Arthur Bouneault (Deux-Sèvres and Vendée).
29. Cloquet, *op. cit.*, pp. 328 and 351.
30. Vulson de la Colombière, *La Science héroique*, 1669, p. 372.

THE NIGHTINGALE

IN GREEK MYTHOLOGY the nightingale is the reincarnation of Philomela, the sister of Procne, the swallow, who took a terrible revenge on the cruel Tereus who had betrayed them both. The transformed Philomela withdrew into the shade of the woods where she sang in the summer nights whenever these tragic memories assailed her. This sorrowful theme from the Greek fable did not exert as strong an influence as some others did on Christian symbolism, however, for the nightingale very early became for the Christians one of the emblems of joy—that joy that ever since the soul-testing days of the Roman persecution was the outstanding characteristic of the Christian spirit[1] and which medieval spirituality called "The holy joy of the children of God." There can be no doubt that the nightingale was one of the birds uppermost in the thought of the artists who decorated the subterranean sanctuaries of Rome, during the first four Christian centuries, where so many small birds flutter among the painted flowers and garlands.

The medieval bestiaries, by whatever name they call the nightingale—Oussegnol, Rousegnol, Roussigneul, Noussigneux—also make it the symbol of the holy joy which fills the righteous soul. In the thirteenth century, Pierre le Picard wrote of it: "This is a small bird which the *Physiologus* tells us prefers beautiful gardens and forests where it sings all night, but louder when the dawn approaches; and at sunrise it shows great joy in itself and its song. And it is the image of the holy soul which in the nighttime of this life awaits our Lord, the true Sun of Righteousness, and when it feels that he has come into its heart, it experiences such joy that it cannot keep silence[2] (Fig. 1)."

Although there is no mention in this medieval text of the ancient interpretations by which the nightingale was made one of the symbols of Christ, the divine Word, it is no less certain that the early mystics, tracing the stream back to its source, saw the incarnate Christ as "the author of our joy." Moreover, symbolists before and after Pierre le Picard often saw in the night chant of the nightingale an image of the divine Word that made itself heard well before Christian times by the mouth of the Hebrew prophets and of the inspired ones among the Gentiles[3].

Fig. 1 The joyous nightingale; manuscript illumination from the 13th-century bestiary of Pierre le Picard.

In the same epoch in which le Picard wrote, St. Bonaventure celebrated the nightingale in these terms: "I have read of this bird that at the approach of death, it rests in a tree, and at daybreak, lifting its head, its whole body expands in beautiful song. Its sweetest notes are those that herald the dawn, but when the sun shoots forth its first rays, the bird's voice lifts up at once louder and sweeter, and it sings without pause or rest. At the third hour it seems to exceed all measure: its joy exalts itself higher and higher, its breast seems about to break with its exertion; the sound of its voice mounts with ever-growing force; it is consumed with ardor. But when at midday the sun sends forth its hottest rays, the bird's fragile body gives way under the excess of its singing. Its voice fades out in its still-opening beak, its body throbs with a supreme effort, and at the ninth hour it gives up its last breath.

"My son, I wish thy soul to become this Philomena who

lives and dies in its song of love. May life appear to thee only as a day of waiting, whose hours are marked by the blessings of God, before the eternal tomorrow of the marriage of the Lamb[4]."

This last song of the nightingale is like an echo of that of the swan, whose symbolism is almost exactly the same.

NOTES

Title Figure: The nightingale on the bronze signet of Martin Segneul, 14th-15th century.

1. See Leclercq and Marron, *Dictionnaire*, T. III, col. 1286.
2. Pierre le Picard, in Charles Cahier, "Bestiaires," in *Mélanges archéologiques*, T. II, p. 159.
3. See André Godard, *La Pieté antique et Le Messianisme*, passim.
4. St. Bonaventure, *Philomène*, Tr. by R. Zeller, *Chroniques du royaume de Dieu*, p. 112.

THE LARK

IN THE NEAR EAST, the lark of our meadows and wheat fields, *alauda arvensis*, the skylark, was the subject of a legend even older than the literature of Greece, which we find reflected in the works of Theocritus, Aristophanes, Aesop, and several other writers. According to this story, the lark was the first created being on earth, and since entering this life it has enclosed—literally "buried"—its father and creator inside its head: whence the crest it carries so gracefully[1].

The Greeks called the lark *korydallis*, from *korys* which means "crest," and which was also the word for the crested war-helmet. We shall see later how this crest connected the bird who wore it with the symbolism of Christ. In France the crested lark was called *cochevis*.

In the very ancient mythologies of some northern regions, the lark was considered to be very closely related with the "Spirit of the Wheat," who was thought to bestow the same mysterious influence on both graceful bird and nourishing plant. After the introduction of Christianity in these same regions, the "Spirit of the Wheat" was more or less identified with Christ, who according to the testimony of St. John, said of himself: "I am the living bread which came down from heaven[2]." All of this symbolism comes from the lark's predilection for its favorite dwelling place:

> The lark makes its nest
> In the unripe wheat . . .[3]

To the farm laborer, the lark is a daily sight as it skims over the sown fields or the neighboring meadows, and starts up from the green wheat to rise like an arrow straight toward heaven, seeming to penetrate the blue sky so high that the human eye can no longer see it; and this has given rise in the countryman's mind to a very simple and expressive symbolism. First of all, the lark seems to him the image of prayer, which is a lifting up of the human soul toward God; because when the bird reaches the dizzy heights it soars there for a time singing with all its strength. In France the peasants of the western provinces call their little children to show them the bird and tell them that it is praying up there to the Christ Child for the children and the sowers of the wheat. The lark is also a symbol of joy and of freedom in our countryside.

Fig. 1 The crested lark of France devouring a harvest beetle.

An anonymous seventeenth-century writer, among many others but more aptly than most, took the lark as a symbol for the Savior saying to his disciples before his Ascension: "I go to my Father, and there I shall pray for you." Then the holy text says that "while they beheld, he was taken up: and a cloud received him out of their sight[4]." St. Gregory seemed to be referring to this symbolic ascensional characteristic of the lark when he wrote: "It is right that the Lord should be called a bird, because his body was lifted up into the air[5]."

Although not specifically a worm-eater, the lark must nevertheless be classed among the active destroyers of larvae, small worms and caterpillars; it is a special enemy of the harmful harvest beetle (Fig. 1). Plutarch says that formerly larks were held in great honor on the island of Lemnos because they devoured the eggs of the locust[6], the big destructive grasshopper which Christian symbolism, taking its authority from the Bible[7], uses as an emblem for Satan.

The water-lark or sea-lark is found everywhere on the shores of the English Channel and the North Sea, and even on the most desolate rocky islets off the coast of Brittany. This bird, the *anthus obscurus* of the ornithologists, nests on the ground, and is very similar in size and color to the skylark, which it also resembles in the way it springs up toward the sky, lingers there for a few moments and then drops down again almost vertically[8]. The sea-lark is a great favorite with sailors and with the people who live on the shores of the Channel, but I do not know if they have made it a part of their religious tradition, to which its habits lend themselves equally with those of our beloved skylark.

NOTES

1. See Clermont-Ganneau, *Comptes rendus de l'Académie des Inscriptions*, 1906, meeting of Nov. 9.
2. St. John 6:51.
3. La Fontaine, *Fables*, Bk. IV, 22.
4. Acts 1:9.
5. St. Gregory, *Homilies*, XXIX.
6. Plutarch, *Isis and Osiris.*
7. Exodus 10:12-15 and Revelation 9:3-10.
8. Cf. Mme. Feuillée-Billot, *La Réserve ornithologique des Sept-Îles, en Perros-Guirec (Côtes du Nord)*, p. 36.

THE DOVE AND THE RAVEN

The Sparrow and the Crow

BECAUSE OF ITS mild and peaceful habits, its attachment to its mate, even its color and its song, the dove, from the beginning of ancient humanity's use of symbols, has been taken as the ideogram of peace, purity, simplicity, patience in suffering, and conjugal fidelity. Horapollo believed that doves put to death any of their kind that commit adultery[1], and the Ancients insisted that this bird had no gall bladder, and consequently knew no malice.

The oldest evidences of the cult of the dove are found in the island of Crete and in the ancient Hittite empire in Asia Minor, and are even earlier than any traces there of the use of metal (Fig. 1). The scholar Gustave Glotz writes: "We find baked clay models of doves dating from the Neolithic era and continuing almost to the end of the pre-Hellenic period. Before becoming symbolic votive offerings, these little figures were actually idols to whom sacrifices were offered of stone-martens, which are enemies of birds. In those times, the dove was a strong enough symbol to serve as a talisman for the dead[2]."

Fig. 1 The divine dove of Crete on the sacred columns; pottery from Knossos.

In this Cretan world, at the time of the beautiful middle-

Mycenaean art, the dove, like the fleur-de-lis, was shown everywhere, and later, the great goddess of Cnossos would wear it on her head as the very emanation of her divine nature. Among the Hittites, the supreme goddess Astarte also was crowned with a dove made of, or plated with, gold, as a sign of divinity[3]. In Phoenicia also, the dove was also the bird of the great goddess of love, Atargatis, who is the equivalent of the Hittites' Astarte. Lucian says that a golden dove, which seems to have more or less explicitly represented the spirit of the divinity on earth, was paraded twice a year on the coasts of Syria[4], and the inhabitants were forbidden to eat the flesh of Atargatis' bird[5].

Diodorus Siculus, recounting the death of the famous queen Semiramis, who called herself the daughter of Atargatis, describes how "she suddenly disappeared; some people claimed that she was changed into a dove and flew away in the middle of a flock of these birds that had been seen swooping down over her palace at the moment of her death[6]." The very name of Semiramis, Diodorus also says, means "dove" in the language of the Assyrians, who were the Syrians' neighbors[7].

Witness to the fact that this cult of the dove extended east from Syria to Babylonia and Susiana is a big dove-image made of lapis lazuli, found by Jacques de Morgan during his excavations at Susa[8]. It can be observed also in the old cults of Persia and India[9]. Among the Philistines the dove was the tutelary bird of the city of Ascalon, and the goddess of that city also carried it as a divine emblem. The name Pleiades, "doves," was given to the priestesses of Zeus[10], and Ovid recounts the metamorphosis into doves of the daughters of Anius, king of Delos[11]. This bird was especially dedicated to the goddess Aphrodite, among the Greeks, and to Venus by the Romans. In the Greek archipelago and in greater Greece, the human soul was sometimes pictured as a dove with a human head, a little like the androcephalous swallow of the Egyptians which was also an image of the soul. Here doubtless we find the explanation for the little doves in various Sicilian tombs; they appear also sometimes in Gallic and Gallo-Roman burial places (Fig. 2).

Of all the symbols from the earliest times that the Christian church adopted, the dove was perhaps the one most frequently shown on the walls of the catacombs in Rome and elsewhere, on the tombs of martyrs and saints in the first Christian buildings, on ritual vessels and lamps, and in all the liturgical art. It represents especially the Holy Spirit and Jesus Christ, often also the faithful, and later it became one of the emblems

Fig. 2 Bronze dove in a Gallo-Roman tomb at Ponant, Vienne.

Fig. 3 The dove of the Ark; fragment of a Roman epitaph from the time of the catacombs.

of the Virgin Mary. It always indicated divine peace and the Christian virtues of purity, gentleness, simplicity, and resignation. One of its first roles in Christian art was to call to mind the biblical story of Noah's ark.

Everyone knows from childhood the part played by the dove in the Flood story and how by means of the olive branch it announced to Noah the abating of the waters and of the tide of God's anger (Fig. 3). This quite naturally led Jews and Christians, first of all, to the idea of the olive branch as a sign of peace, and of the dove as its symbolic herald. In Christian representations of this event, the ark became the symbol of the Church, and Noah that of the Christian soul to whom the Christ-Dove brings peace, depicted by the branch. A Roman epitaph shows a ship carrying two jars or amphoras, and perched on the high stern, the dove of Christ brings his peace. Nothing in this case evokes the memory of the deluge or of Noah. The ship is the Church; and it is well worth while to remember that although the amphora, on account of its shape, in ancient times represented the pregnant woman[12], in Christian symbolism it was also one of the signs for the Reservation of the Sacrament of the Eucharist, because it was used to hold wine (Fig. 4).

Fig. 4 The dove and the ship; Roman engraving from early Christian times.

On the ancient monuments, the dove appears with the branch, symbolizing the obtaining of Christ's peace by the soul whose suffering of martyrdom or practice of the Christian virtues has merited peace through victory; for often in Christian iconography the olive branch has the same triumphal meaning as the palm.

The white pigeon or dove was chosen by almost all the Christian artists to represent the Holy Spirit. The sacred texts which were most influential in this choice were certainly the passages from the Gospels that recount Jesus' baptism in the waters of Jordan by John the Baptist. The other St. John speaks thus of the Baptizer:

"And John bare record, saying, I saw the Spirit descending from heaven like a dove, and it abode upon him. And I knew him not: but he that sent me to baptize with water, the same said unto me, Upon whom thou shalt see the Spirit descending, and remaining on him, the same is he which baptizeth with the Holy Ghost. And I saw, and bare record that this is the Son of God[13]."

Thus, from the beginning of Christian times, the dove appeared in decorative art as the accepted emblem of the Holy Spirit. The first representations of Christ's baptism naturally portrayed it above the Savior's head, and shortly after Constantine's Peace, the mosaic workers who decorated the great arch of the Basilica of St. Mary-the-Greater, in Rome, placed above Mary's head the image of the dove descending from heaven at the moment of the Annunciation.

Sometimes seven doves with halos, gathered around the figure of Christ, represent the seven perfect gifts of the Holy Spirit which Jesus promised his apostles he would send them after his death: "But the Comforter, which is the Holy Ghost, whom the Father will send in my name, he shall teach you all things[14]." The seven doves are also to be seen around the Virgin Mother who was "the living tabernacle of incarnate wisdom" and "filled with the gifts of the Holy Spirit." There are examples of these representations of the seven doves surrounding both Christ and Mary in the stained glass windows of the thirteenth and fourteenth centuries at Chartres, Mans, Saint-Denis, Freiburg im Breisgau, etc.[15]

Although the dove was used less frequently to symbolize the Savior than to represent the Holy Spirit and the faithful soul, it was nevertheless numbered among the personal emblems of Christ since the earliest days of Christianity. In the second century, this symbol was accepted by the Church, if we can believe Tertullian's testimony; writing at the same time that the Carthaginian potters were producing ritual lamps decorated with the symbolic dove, he said: "The dove usually represents Jesus Christ[16]." Often, too, the dove appeared in the first Christian art between two fishes[17] who unquestionably stood for the faithful; and it is customary to find between them a personal emblem of Christ, towards which they are moving. The same idea is given by an earthenware dish in the Nardoni collection, on which two doves adore another, larger dove placed above the shortened monogram of the holy name *XPistos*[18] (Fig. 5).

Fig. 5 The three doves, from the Nordoni collection; 4th or 5th century.

On picturings of the "mystical deer hunts" of the Merovingian dioceses of western France, the dove soars above the deer, the emblem of the soul, which is pursued by dogs—

representing the passions—and which runs from them at full gallop toward the cross. On one example (Fig. 6) of these "hunts" found at Nantes and at Rezé (in the region of the lower Loire), the dove is carrying inner peace to the harried soul and above it is shown a cross lying along the length of its body[19]. Here, the dove is Christ bringing the help of his divine grace.

Fig. 6 The dove and the deer hunt; Nantes, 6th or 7th century.

As the bird dedicated to the goddess Venus, the symbol of human love to the people of ancient times, the dove has kept this same character as the bird of love in the most advanced Christian symbolism. So perhaps we must recognize in the mutual caresses of the doves, on the frescoes of the catacombs, a more subtle expression of the same symbolic meaning indicated in those depictions of Eros kissing Psyche, by which we believe that early Christian art allegorized Christ's love for the loving and faithful soul[20].

The symbolism of love and that of fire have been closely linked since ancient times, and I might mention in passing the presence of the dove on many Christian lamps of the early centuries[21]. But I think it should be remembered that the mysticism of the Middle Ages emphasized the connections between, on one hand, the love of God and of Christ for humanity, and on the other, the new fire which the priest lights and hallows in the liturgical office of Holy Saturday; and it seems that an old legend says that in the church's early days, there was a miraculous dove which brought the new fire to the principal church in Jerusalem, every Easter Eve. In this role, the dove is the messenger bringing to the earth both spiritual light and the fire of divine love.

Some medieval mystics took the white dove as the image of the essence of the Deity, without distinction of Person, at the same time one and threefold. This was however an infrequent usage and very little known in our times. But there are images of doves placed sometimes in the midst of a nimbus, crowned with a triangle of rays, or perhaps framed by a triangle, which are more often seen in the religious art of the Mediterranean than elsewhere. These seem to relate more to this concept and to be less an emblem of the Holy Spirit than of the Trinity.

Sometimes, though rarely, the dove has allegorically taken the place of the Virgin Mary because of the connections that the *Song of Songs* makes between this bird and the Bride chosen over all other women; and also because it symbolizes perfect purity, on account of which the dove presents a satisfying picture of her whom the Church calls the Immaculate. In this role, the dove was nearly always shown in a way whose significance could not be mistaken. But certain hermetic groups of the Middle Ages accepted a complete correspondence between the Person of the Holy Spirit and that of the Virgin Mary. This view was based on a particular interpretation of this passage from Genesis: "God created man in his own image, in the image of God created he him; male and female created he them[22]." This was taken to mean that there must then exist in God a masculine and a feminine principle; and since the divine feminine cannot be either Father or Son, it can only be the Spirit. So it was thought that the Holy Spirit was actually incarnated in Mary's body at the moment of the Annunciation. From the beginning of Christianity, this concept of the femininity of the Holy Spirit[23] and the Virgin as one of its earthly manifestations was found in certain Gnostic sects; and this theme is explicitly stated in the apocryphal *Gospel to the Hebrews*. Speaking of Jesus' temptation in the desert, this ancient work gives as Christ's words: "... my Mother, who is the Holy Spirit, lifted me by my hair and took me from the desert to the high mountain Tabor[24]." This concept, which was adopted by the Albigenses and which some heterodox groups in Italy also accepted, still has adherents today who call the Holy Spirit "*Madona divinita*."

In fact, some doves of these times that represent the Holy

Fig. 7 16th-century painted wooden panel from Fontevrault.

Spirit are stylized in such an exaggerated manner that the bird has lost its natural shape and assumed one that strangely resembles the initial letter of Mary's name. This is the case with a dove painted on a small wooden panel from the presbytery of Fontevrault (Maine-et-Loire), of the sixteenth century (Fig. 7). There are some medieval representations of the dove in stained glass windows that are similar in type[25].

The art which followed Constantine's Peace often represented the Apostles by twelve doves; on one of the flat sides of the altar of St. Victor of Marseilles, the doves fly six by six toward the Constantinian monogram of Christ[26]. St. Paulinus of Nola relates that in his episcopal city there was a cross surrounded by twelve doves which signified the Apostles[27], and on a large mosaic of St. Clement in Rome, upon a cross bearing the body of Jesus are scattered twelve doves whose meaning is instantly clear[28].

As we have seen, the dove very often represents the faithful Christian soul. The sense of orientation, of knowing which direction to take, that best qualifies the pigeon over all other creatures to be a messenger for human beings, was applied by the masters of Catholic spirituality to the symbolism of souls.

They said that in the same way that doves find the way back to their dovecote, no matter how far away they may have been taken from it, Christians must keep the sense of direction that guides them back to their dovecote, which is the Church.

In its aspect as emblem of chastity, the dove was contrasted in medieval symbolism to the sparrow. We see, for instance, Chastity personified by a young woman mounted on a unicorn, and holding in her hand sometimes a flower, sometimes a dove; and on the contrary, Lewdness rides on a goat and carries a sparrow on her shoulder or in her hand. We see the idea thus depicted at the end of the fifteenth century, in the *Livre d'Heures* of Marguerite d'Orléans, countess of Angoulème; the painter, thought to be Simon Marmion, painted an ardent youth astride a white she-goat, holding the sparrow in his hand, and written beneath, one word: Lewdness (Fig. 8). Later, during the sixteenth century, Goltzius, in an engraving of Lewdness, made it feminine, accompanied by a buck goat, and in her hand the lustful sparrow whose excesses of mating have earned it this role in symbolism. Well before our era, the Greeks and Romans had established the sparrow's lascivious reputation[29].

Fig. 8 The sparrow, emblem of lust; 15th century.

But the humble sparrow, with no exact name, has also played its small part in the official symbolism of Christ. The custom of keeping small birds in cages must be as old as the world: the Greeks and Romans, and many others before them, like us, constructed elegant prisons for them of wicker and of metal, and the first Christian artists who decorated the catacombs often depicted birds in cages, or escaping from them. In this latter case, the symbolic sparrow certainly represented the human soul delivered by death from the bondages of life, mounting joyfully to heaven.

The sparrow has also been made the hieroglyph of Christ, deserted on the Mount of Olives just before his Passion, when all of his disciples had gone away except three who were nearby, but asleep. The Church describes this moment of anguished loneliness by the words of the psalm: *Vigilari et factus sum sicut passer solitarius in tecto*: "I watch, and am as a sparrow alone upon the house top[30]." The monastic heraldic bearings of Dom Granet, Cistercian abbot of Sénanques (1898), carry this symbol of the Bird-Christ alone upon a roof top, with the device: *Sicut passer solitarius in tecto* (Fig. 9).

Fig. 9 Coat-of-arms of Dom Grasset, Abbé of Sénanque.

Once, at least, sparrows represented the Apostles: several apocryphal books of early Christian times relate that one day the child Jesus, playing near Joseph's workshop, made twelve little birds out of clay; he breathed on them and they came to life and flew off. Mystics have seen in these twelve clay sparrows the image of the twelve Apostles whom Jesus chose among his many followers and whom the breath of the Holy Spirit, at Pentecost, made into new men[31].

The best-known antithesis to the dove is the raven, due to the biblical story of the Flood[32] and also to its color and its character. Many ancient Christian works of art show the dove arriving at the Ark and the raven flying away. Dom Leclercq gives several examples of such testimony from the first Christian centuries[33], and the illustrated bibles since the sixteenth century, like the numerous illuminated medieval manuscripts, almost always show the flight of the raven, which did not return to the Ark. In devotional literature, the raven represents the devil himself[34]. Teachers of Christian spirituality, such as St. Augustine[35], interpreted its cry by the onomatopoetic "*Cras, cras!*"—*cras* being a Latin word which means "tomorrow." Because of this croaking sound, the bird is taken as exemplifying the careless sinner who postpones his conversion always to the next day. Other teachers have made the raven the image of the pagan, the faithless, the renegade, or the shameless person, because it feeds on unclean foods[36].

On the other hand, Benedictine symbolism, supported by the *Golden Legend*, has made the raven the special emblem of St. Benedict and of his monks, since the dove represents his sister, St. Scholastica, and the Benedictine nuns; every coin has its good side.

All the corvine family, not only ravens and crows but also the rooks and jackdaws common in Europe, must unquestionably be classed among the most intelligent of birds, and probably that is why the Ancients connected them with rites of divination. In Germany, the worshipers of Wotan-Odin dedicated the raven to their god, and two of these birds, one named *Hugin*, which means "thought," and the other *Munin*, "memory," accompanied him everywhere and made everything in the world known to him[37]. And among all of the corvines, crows are the most intelligent and the most sociable.

Fig. 10 Crow on the coat-of-arms of the Hunyadi of Hungary; sculpture from the château of Vajdahunyad, 15th century.

The Greeks and the Romans took the crow as the sign of longevity: Aristophanes claimed that it lived five times as long as the human being [38], Horace spoke of "the century-old crow which announces rain[39]"; and Ausonius affirmed that this bird "goes on living three times three ages[40]." Exaggerated as these statements are, it is a fact that the crow is hardy and long-lived (Fig. 10).

At one time the Greeks and Romans considered the raven a bird of good omen, and the crow as one of evil[41]. Quite on the contrary, however, Herodotus tells that one day two black doves flew away from Thebes, in Egypt, one going toward Libya and the other toward Greece, where it stopped at Dodona, in Epirus. There, this black dove, in human language, commanded the people of Dodona to build a temple where great Zeus would deliver his oracles. In these black birds Herodotus sees two swarthy Egyptian priestesses. However, the worship of Zeus did not have any place in the Theban region of the Nile Valley, and some commentators think that crows must be understood instead of black doves.

It is not surprising that Christian symbolism in Asia Minor and the Near East sometimes gave the crow the same meaning as that given in the west to the dove and the turtledove, in regard to the reciprocal love and fidelity between Christ and the Church. Others praise above all another of the crow's qualities, its maternal love and devotion.

The crow also depicts the Virgin Mary, in whom the Church recognizes the Beloved of the *Song of Songs*, which sings to the virgins of Israel: "I am black, but comely, O ye daughters of Jerusalem, as the tents of Kedar, as the curtains of Solomon. Look not upon me, because I am black, because the sun hath looked upon me...[42]"; and by this "sun," say the old mystics, must be understood the sun of love which sets holy souls afire and burns away even the smallest stain. The Latin liturgy has sanctified this symbolism in applying the antiphon *Nigra sum sed formosa* (I am black but comely) in the most solemn prayers[43]. Formerly the mystics applied these same words also to the Church, as is proved by this passage from *La Queste del Saint Graal*, of the thirteenth century: *Par le noir oisel... doit entendre sainte Eglise qui dist: Je suis noire mes ie suis belle: sachez que mielz volt ma nerte que autrui blancheur ne fel*: "By the black bird... must be understood Holy Church which says: I am black but I am beautiful: know that my blackness is of more worth than the whiteness of any other[44]."

In certain French provinces, the jackdaw is called "the Nun," because its favorite nesting place is in clock towers, where it is awakened every morning, like the nuns, by the bells ringing for the morning office[45].

White crows, formerly greatly venerated, exist only as isolated cases of albinism; but the fowlers of ancient times tried to bring about this phenomenon by soaking the baby birds in a special liquid, before their feathers appeared. Usually the chicks died from these premature immersions.

The crow has no mystical significance in heraldry, and on medieval coats of arms it usually represents someone of the black or brown race, a Moor or a Saracen[46].

NOTES

Title Figure: The dove on the cross in a representation of the Etoimacia, *the preparation for the last judgment. From a mosaic in a church at Nicea.*

1. Horapollo, *Hieroglyphica*, Bk. II, p. 30.
2. Glotz, *Civilisation égéenne*. Bk. III, p. 277.
3. A. H. Sayce, *Les Hétéens*, p. 113.
4. Lucian, *De Syria Dea*, 31-33.
5. *Ibid.* p. 21. Glonneau edition.
6. Diodorus Siculus, *Library of History*, Bk. II, Ch. XX.
7. *Ibid.*, Bk. II, 54. See also Fr. Lenormant, *La Légende de Semiramis.*
8. Now in the Musée du Louvre, Salle de la Colonnade.
9. Cf. Lanoë-Villène, *Le Livre des Symboles*, IV, p. 251.
10. Homer, *The Iliad*, XI, and Pausanias, *Description of Greece.*
11. Ovid, *Metamorphoses*, XIII, 4.
12. See L. Charbonneau-Lassay, "Le Sphinx," in *Regnabit*, Sept-Oct. 1928. Vol. XV, p. 139 and fig. VI.
13. St. John 1:32-34; see also St. Matthew 3:16, St. Mark 1:10, St. Luke 3:22.
14. St. John 14:26.
15. Cf. Mâle, *L'Art religieux (3)*, passim, also Cloquet, *Éléments d'Iconographie chrétienne*, p. 103.
16. Tertullian, *Adv. Valentinianos*, II.
17. Cf. Leclercq and Marron, *Dictionnaire*, Vol. V, I, 67.
18. Cf. *Bulletin d'Archéologie chrétienne*, 1893, p. 136, Pl.X, no. 2.
19. See Parenteau, *Catalogue raisonnée de l'Exposition des Beaux-Arts*, 1872, Pl. XI, no. 3; and *Inventaire archéologique*, p. 44, pl. XXI.
20. Among the Romans, the diviners, seeking to know the omens in affairs of the heart, consulted the still-palpitating lung of a just-sacrificed dove. Cf. Juvenal, *Satire*, VI, 550.
21. Lamps were even made in the shape of the dove. See a lamp of this kind in Fortunio Licetti, *De antig. lucern.*, Book VI, 50.
22. Genesis 1:27.
23. Cf. A. Godard, *La Messianisme*, p. 102.
24. Cf. Origen, *In Joan.*, II, 12.
25. See Cloquet, *op. cit.* in note 15 above, p. 103.

26. Engraving from Grimouard de Saint-Laurent, *Guide*, Vol. II, p. 67.
27. St. Paulinus of Nola, *Epistle* XXXII, in Migne, *Patrol. lat.*, LXI, 336.
28. See Bottari, *Sculture e pitture di Roma*, L. 118.
29. See H. Roux, *Herculaneum et Pompeii*, Vol. VIII, p. 215.
30. Psalms 102: 7.
31. See *Infancy Gospel of Thomas*, Latin text, IV; also M.R. James, *The Apocryphal New Testament.*
32. Genesis 8:8.
33. Leclercq, *op. cit.*, Vol. III, Book II, col. 2912.
34. St. Eucher, *Liber formularum*, V.; Dom Pitra, in *Spicilège de Solesmes*, T. II, p. 80, 12.
35. St. Augustine, *In Johannis Evangelium*, VI, 2.
36. See Leclercq, *op et loc. cit.*
37. Cf. Tonnelat, "Mythologie Germanique," in *Mythologie générale de Guirand*, p. 226-7, Paris-Larousse, s.d. (1935).
38. Aristophanes, *The Birds*, VI; and Horapollo, *op. cit.*, II, 40.
39. Horace, *Odes*, Bk. III, to Aelius Lamiae.
40. Ausonius, *Idylls*, XI.
41. Phaedrus, *Fables*, Book III, fable 18.
42. Song of Solomon 1:5-6.
43. Roman breviary, *Office of the Blessed Virgin Mary*, before vespers, II.
44. *La Queste del Sainte Graal*, Edit. Albert Pamphilet, p. 185.
45. Cf. P. Covil, *Encyclopédie*, Vol. 1, p. 497.
46. De la Colombière, *La Science héroique*, 1669 ed., p. 368, No. 89.

End Figure: Coat-of-arms of the Cozquerou family.

THE SWAN

THE SYMBOLIC SWAN, immaculately robed in pure white, comes to us from those northern countries that are nearly always blanketed in snow. A study of the oldest signs of human presence in these upper European regions shows that the swan was the first bird to appear in their developing symbolism.

Who were the people who lived then under the magnificent sky of those harsh lands? They had no sooner begun to add tools of copper and bronze to their already skilfully worked utensils of stone when the swan made its appearance everywhere in their decoration, as the graceful expression of their belief in a luminous superior being, the master of the world and the father of their race.

The prehistoric archeology of the ancient peoples of Finland, Scandinavia, and Denmark provides numerous examples in bronze of the solar boat or chariot, both ends of which are in the form of a swan's neck and head. This indicates that for those races the swan had the significance that Apollo would later hold for the classical countries as the image and personification of the Sun-god, of his radiant splendor and the gifts of heat, light, fruitfulness, and joy which he sends to the world from on high. This is why their artists harnessed the swan not only to the boat[1] or chariot, but also to the solar wheel; and in that connection it becomes a symbol very like that of the sun horse[2].

It seems most probable that this pure and noble prehistoric

symbol was handed down in very early times from the northern regions to central and southern Europe, since from the Bronze Age onwards, it is found in Hibernia, Germania, southeast Gaul, and Lombardy. A fragment of a belt tip discovered in Liguria, mentioned by Déchelette, which seems very clearly to belong to the same remote epoch, shows us the swan in front of the solar wheel[3] (Fig. 1); one would say it was Scandinavian work.

Fig. 1 The swan and the solar wheel; bronze belt tip from Liguria.

We find also the astral swan in Greece; but who will say by what unknown routes it came also to be the symbol of the sun in the Veda of ancient India[4], or how it arrived at the designation there of the conveyance of Brahma[5]?

I will add here that it has been claimed by serious writers that symbolic characteristics very similar to those which the northern peoples attributed to the swan were connected equally with the duck, especially the white duck.

Greek mythology, inherited by the Romans, brought the swan into a number of its stories whose original meaning is hidden from our eyes, no doubt by the changes and additions brought by the centuries which have passed since they were first written down. Various personages appear under the name and form of the noble white bird: Cycnus of Tenedos, the son of Poseidon (the Romans' Neptune), whom Achilles found was invulnerable to any weapon and whom he could vanquish only by strangling him, and whom the gods turned into a swan; another Cycnus, the son of Ares (Mars to the Romans), whom Heracles conquered and slew, but whose father brought back to life in the form of a swan; then Cycnus, the king of Liguria, who so loved his cousin Phaethon, Apollo's son, and wept so much at his death, that the god of light changed him into a swan and placed him among the stars[6].

In all these poetic fantasies about the changing into swans

of various men named Cycnus, there is one thing to remember: that they all relate to a kind of resurrection hidden behind the image of a miraculous transformation.

The Greeks, who sometimes harnessed the swan to the chariots of Dionysus[7] and of Aphrodite, connected it above all with Apollo: their legends tell how at the moment of his birth in Delos, the infant god leapt into the midst of a flock of swans who sang a melodious hymn of praise for his coming. The bards said that every year, in the autumn, the Sun-god Apollo went back to the far North where behind a barrier of ice reigned a perpetual spring, bathed in the still light of a silvery sun. And the god of beauty dwelt there among the swans, who brought him back to the palm groves of Delos in a golden chariot as soon as the oleanders budded there and the first flowers began.

The same poets sang of the marvelous maternity of Leda. From the heights of Olympus, Zeus-Jupiter loved the grace and beauty of this young princess of Etolia, and in the shape of a glorious swan, the king of the gods came down to her while she slept in the shade at the foot of Mount Taygetus. As she awoke, she heard the divine bird saying: "Leda, do not be afraid; I am the king of heaven, and I wish you to be the illustrious mother of my twin sons, who will live like the sun and the moon, one giving place to the other. They will be named Castor and Pollux, and they will become gods whose

Fig. 2 Eros, Leda, and the Swan; Coptic Christian sculpture from Upper Egypt.

benevolence will soften the harshness of death for human beings[8]." Nine months later, Leda produced a miraculous egg from which emerged two children exactly alike: "From their birth, the same star sparkled over their heads; later they rode the same white courser, and bore in their hands the same javelin[9] (Fig. 2)."

What fragment of truth is hidden in these astonishing stories? We might remember here that several of the most thoughtful of our present-day mythologists look on all these stories of impossible adulteries and rapes among the ancient gods as manifestations (perhaps too realistic for our taste) of an imperishable belief, anchored by the earliest traditions in the soul of our race, in the possibility of a bodily union between humanity and divinity descending from heaven.

It certainly seems, however, that in the last pre-Christian centuries, whether or not the "key" was still retained by some initiates, there no longer existed a general understanding of the meanings behind most of the ancient myths, and so for most people the stories of lovely Leda and the swan were no more than charming fables of sensual games. But if we place ourselves strictly within the boundaries of art, we have to recognize that marvelously lovely images were drawn from this theme by the classical artists, in sculptures, carvings, and especially in the engravings cut in semiprecious stones.

As for the egg from which the Dioscuri, Castor and Pollux, were so strangely born, its symbolism is connected with that of the fossil sea-urchin which we shall study later on; here we shall simply note that the swan's egg, like that of the snake, was considered in ancient times as being related with the Egg of the World, and consequently mysterious. The Dioscuri's origin from it would, it seems, have caused them to be looked on as swan men[10].

It is not surprising that in Christianity's first centuries depictions of the fables of Zeus the Swan and Leda were rare in the decorative art of the West; there were some notable ones, however, and as Father Le Cour has written, "It must in any case be observed that Leda's adventure was not looked upon as a carnal act by certain churchmen[11]."

"Leda's adventure" was however quite widely used as a sculptural motif among the Christian communities of the Upper Nile, and it would be extremely interesting to know what was the thought behind this singular choice for the decoration of churches in what could only have been a purely ornamental function. It is quite possible of course that it was simply the fact of the fecundation of a virgin by the swan god, seen as a sort of prefiguration of Mary "overshadowed" by the Holy Spirit: "The Holy Ghost shall come upon thee, and the power of the Highest shall overshadow thee[12]." Was it the same thought that prompted the pope to have the image of Leda beside her swan reproduced on the great door of St. Peter's in Rome?

Fig. 3 The "Cygne de la Croix" on an old French commercial sign.

We find the swan by itself on some Christian lamps: Dom Leclercq cites eight ornamented with birds which he classifies as "Swans or Pelicans," of which some are clearly swans[13].

It seems that in former times a link that is now obscure for us connected the swan with the cross of Christ, at least in the western provinces of France. In the fifteenth century, Gilles de Laval, baron of Retz (the Bluebeard of Perrault's tales), who was a companion of Joan of Arc, carried on his coat of arms the heraldic cross of the Laval family; on his seal the shield bearing the cross is held by two swans, and the crest of the helmet is a swan. In the seventeenth century, during the reign of Louis XIII, the hostelry of the "Swan of the Cross[14]," where Laubardemont lodged[15], had on its signboard a white swan marked with a cross. Paul Reboux has emphasized that "there still exist commercial houses having as their trademark a swan whose neck is twisted around a cross, and with the legend *Au Cygne de la*

Croix[16] (Fig. 3). It has been suggested to me that these cross-bearing swans could be considered as images of Christ carrying the Rood. This may perhaps sometimes be the case, but there is not the slightest proof of it, although they bring to mind much of the symbolism connected with Christ, and must be something more than a play on words.

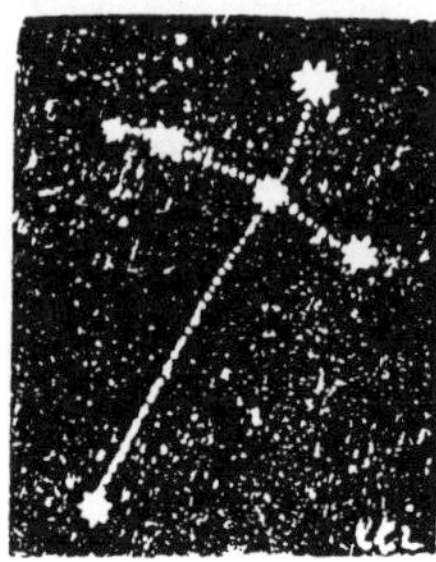

Fig. 4 An aspect of the constellation of the Swan on the Milky Way, in November, from Paris.

It should also be remembered here that the constellation known as "The Swan" is "formed principally of six stars, of which five form a great, slightly crooked cross, lying in the Milky Way[17] (Fig. 4)."

Jesus the son of Mary was probably not the first Christ with whom the Scandinavian people connected the swan. Well before the belated conversion of the Nordic races to true Christianity, there existed among them a beneficent deity whom they called Balder, who was the king of true, pure love and of beauty in all its aspects. The first incursions of Northerners into the countries to the south, providing contacts with the last of the Gallo-Romans or with the Gallo-Franks, may well have given them a certain acquaintance, however vague, with Christian doctrines, long before their ninth-century invasions of the French and British coasts; for it is really astonishing to see how deeply the Balder myth bears the Christian stamp, to the point that he was called the "White Christ." From the more southern countries, then, according to Per Skansen, "the belief in the White Christ, strange, pure, appealing, would spread through the whole of the North: and Balder, god of beauty, justice, innocence, and love, whose precepts were admired by all but followed by none, is formed on the pattern of the Son of Man himself[18]." The swan in its total whiteness could not fail to be connected with this White Christ, who evokes the idea of the true Christ in his transfiguration, when he showed himself "exceeding white as snow[19]."

Because of its liking for clear water, and its white plumage—more absolutely white than that of the dove, the ibis, or any other bird—the swan, in the northern countries which were unaware and so untroubled by the classical southern story of Leda, became one of the emblems of chastity, of the perfect purity whose sole archetype in Christian thought was Jesus Christ.

With the swan and the dove, then, we have the emblems of two kinds of chastity: one active and austere, the other more gentle and more feeling; for example, monastic and conjugal chastity: "One like the swan and the other like the dove," as Victor Hugo says[20]. With this symbolic meaning, the legend of St. Brigitte, queen of Sweden, tells us that the great wild swans of the northern seas, drawn to her by the perfume of her virtue, came to alight on the frozen pond of Kildare to be caressed by her saintly hands.

We are not speaking here of the big *cygnus ferus* of Lapland and Siberia as much as of the wild *cygnus olor*, which is the only variety whose young are born absolutely white; those of the others are first gray—as indeed are even those of *cygnus olor* when domesticated in Europe.

Fig. 5 15th-century sculpture from the Château de Belleau, Calvados.

It would seem to be the precept of purity, the purity necessary to approach the Eucharistic "sacrament of love," that we have to understand when we look at the medieval sculptures showing, in different ways, two swans drinking from the chalice (Fig. 5). And because among the Ancients it was always, like the dove, the symbol of love, the swan was also an emblem of the ideal and perfect love, filled with the "candor" (Latin, "whiteness") which its plumage evokes.

There is a legend—only a legend, but how ancient, and how suggestive!—that when it becomes aware that death is about to release it from its ties with the earth, the swan sings a beautiful song of liberation, with the light of another life shining before its eyes. Callimachus, Theocritus, Euripides, Lucretius, Ovid, Propertius, Aristotle, and other Greek and Roman writers have celebrated that lovely melody of the death-song of the swan so convincingly as to cause our older French writers to say that "swans have even been observed dying in the midst of their music and the singing of their funeral songs[21]." Pliny, however, had warned that this belief was erroneous, but what he said did not prevent Bruno Latini, at the end of the thirteenth century, from explaining that the swan is advised of death's approach by one of the feathers on its head which enters its brain, "and thus it perceives its death, and thereupon begins to sing so sweetly that it is marvelous to hear, and thus singing it ends its life[22]."

The ideal, imagined beauty of this pre-death song has provided the mystics with elements of comparison, not only in speaking of the joyful death of saints, but also in celebrating the sublimity of the most touching words which Christ ever spoke and which St. John recorded as the true testament of his Master[23]. They were spoken a few hours before his death and immediately after celebrating the Eucharistic Supper. We cannot blame those who have dared to compare this divine song of love and sacrifice with the swan's song of the ancient poets.

Still other connections have been made: in the North, stories were told of wild swans coming of their own accord and letting themselves be captured by the harpist who played so excellently as to charm them. This provides the allegory of Christ, divine swan of heaven, coming to the one whose prayer reaches a sufficient intensity; since the time of King David the psalmist, the harp has been the symbol of such fervent prayer, which is essentially a call from the soul to its Savior. A beautiful thirteenth-century miniature, from the Bibliothèque de l'Arsenal, reproduced by Father Charles

Fig. 6 The swan and the harpist; 13th-century miniature.

Cahier, gives a naive image of the swan yielding to the spell of the harp[24] (Fig. 6). The same learned Jesuit says further, quoting the literal text of a thirteenth-century bestiary from Picardy, "It is a true melody to hear, when the Swan attunes itself with the harp to sing[25]."

There is a Greek legend according to which the swans assemble in the "royal isle" of Basileia, and there alone are able to harmonize together the songs that each one of them can sing only at the moment of death. This legend was taken as an allegory of the gospel passage where Jesus tells his disciples that he will always be present among them when several are gathered in his name[26].

It is rather a strange coincidence that in the folkore of several northern and European countries, camomile was called "swan weed." The flower of this plant, like the field daisy, has a yellow center with white petals radiating out from it; this image is very frequently used in the ancient sacred art of the North, and also of Media, Susa, and Babylonia, and considered a symbol of the divine Word and its radiating expansion through the world.

Like the peacock, the swan has also found its place among the emblems of Christ guiding to heaven the souls he has saved. Here also is simply a continuation into Christian times of a symbolic characteristic connected with the swan in earlier centuries. Two successive phases must be recognized in this symbolism of the "Way of Salvation": first, the crossing of "the sea of this world" by the faithful soul, then its ascension toward "the kingdom of heaven." When it symbolizes the first of these journeys, the swan shares the role of the dolphin which we shall come to later; we shall see that the dolphin is sometimes represented in the earliest Christian art carrying on

Fig. 7 The swan and the ship; Roman lamp from Carthage.

its back the boat which stands for the Church. The swan does not carry it above the waves but draws it over their surface toward the haven of safety and peace.

Half a Roman lamp of Christian manufacture, found in Carthage, shows us a swan pulling a boat in which there are three passengers under a sort of canopy held up by the central mast[27] (Fig. 7).

In the Middle Ages, especially in Germany, the Low Countries, and the north of France, the poets and artists of chivalry took over this theme for works of romance and heroism, and the swan became the noble bird par excellence. In the thirteenth century, Wolfram von Eschenbach produced the poem of Lohengrin, celebrating the hero's deliverance of the princess of Brabant with the help of a miraculous swan who guided his boat to her. This was a theme for the troubadours, but the mystics saw in it something more than the image of the pilot-swan and the knight charged with doing "God's deeds" on earth. An anonymous manuscript, *The Order of the Noble Knights of the Swan*[28], dating from the time of Louis XIII, contained these words, following an account of Lohengrin's adventure: "Thus Our Lord, the true Swan of God, descended from heaven to earth for our salvation, and led the Church his bride over the sea of this world (Fig. 8)."

The second journey, the ascension of the soul toward heaven, was envisaged as having two different, successive stages: first, Christ inspiring his follower by his grace, thus lifting and maintaining his thoughts above the common level of earthly life; then, with the coming of death the liberator, who breaks the soul's bodily bonds, Christ draws it to heaven and receives it there to establish it in everlasting peace.

For this ascension of the soul carried by Christ to the heavenly kingdom, symbolists found an allegorical image in classical myth. Camarina, we are told, like Amphitrite and several other nymphs, was the daughter of Oceanus[29]. Her home was in Sicily, on the cool shores of a blossoming marsh whose waters nourished the most beautiful fishes and the most colorful waterbirds, and there the nymph passed her days happily. But the gods summoned her to come to them, and a large, beautiful swan approached her, lifted her gently and took flight toward the empyrean. Soon afterwards, a city was founded near the marsh which she had loved, and the nymph, now a divinity, protected it. But there came a time when the inhabitants of the city disobeyed the oracle and drained the marsh beloved by their protectress; after that, their enemies entered by this new approach and sacked their city[30]. During its golden days, before it became ungrateful, the city of Camarina struck superb coins, imitating Grecian art, and representing the nymph seated gracefully on the back of the swan which carries her toward the skies over the calm waters of her marsh.

Antiquity also recognized in the swan one of the enemies of the redoubtable serpent, and this above all, it seems, opened

Fig. 8 The swan leading its ship to the Knight of the Swan; 13th-century miniature from the Bibliothèque de l'Arsenal.

the door in central and southern Europe for its admittance among the symbolic fauna of Christ. It is certain moreover that the swan feeds freely on the little eels and young snakes of the marshes, and we often find it represented in their company on the jewelry of the Bronze Age. A handsome gold pendant found at Aegina in the Greek archipelago represents the Sun-god in his boat, attacked by snakes, and to defend him two swans hold them off at a safe distance[31] (Fig. 9).

Fig. 9 Prehistoric gold pendant from Aegina.

In French heraldry, the swan is often the sign for courage allied with beauty. Aristotle said of it that "it is not afraid to do battle with the eagle, and often is the conqueror[32]." Often also on heraldic escutcheons the swan is the symbol of clean living and of purity of conscience.

The Middle Ages had still another symbol which brought forth very beautiful ornamentation in heraldry and which has two different interpretations. It is composed of two swans facing each other, with their necks intertwined. The heraldry of the nobility made of this the ideogram of tender and faithful affection, for the swan, although it knows how to fight, also knows like the dove how to express love, and again like the dove, it is monogamous. The attitude of the cloister, however, was more severe than that of chivalry, and Vincent de Beauvais, who wrote at the time of St. Louis of France, states expressly that "two swans with necks entwined are the symbol of lascivious games and caresses[33]." But if this had been their only significance, they would not have been so widely exhibited on the escutcheons of noble and worthy families, such as the Darots of Poitou, for example, whose blazon shows the swans holding the nuptial ring in their beaks

Fig. 10 Armorial bearings of the Darots of Poitou from an 18th-century bookplate.

(Fig. 10); this carrying of the wedding ring clears the symbol of all suspicion of anything unworthy.

However, because the Romans harnessed the swan to Venus' boat, as the dove was harnessed to her aerial chariot, and also because of the role it apparently played in the myth of Leda, the first Christian symbolists did sometimes use the swan as the emblem of lust, and the artists of the Middle Ages and the Renaissance often did the same, forgetting that the golden Aphrodite of the Greeks, mounted on her swan, inspired in men the pure love of divinity. The symbolists of Christianized Rome also let themselves be swayed by the habit of the famous and wealthy Roman courtesans of anointing themselves with swan's grease, which according to Pliny enhanced their beauty by preventing or even erasing wrinkles[34]. Taken thus in its negative aspect, in complete opposition to the mystical sense we have spoken of as the bird of purest love, the swan becomes the symbol of those who are full of hidden vices but who adorn themselves with the outward appearance of pure souls: the "whited sepulchres" of which Christ speaks[35].

In the thirteenth century, Walter Map wrote in accordance with this: *Par blanc oisel qui avoit semblance de cisne doit on entendre l'anemi, et si voi dirai comment li cisnes est blanc par dehors et noirs par dedenz, ce est li ypocrites*: "By a white bird resembling the swan must be understood the enemy, and if I tell you how the swan is white without and black within, thus is the hypocrite[36]."

Like the eagle, the heron, the stork, and the crane, who are usually preeminent symbols of Christ, but who also occasionally represent Satan, the ravisher of souls, the swan sometimes appears on ancient works of art with a fish in its beak. Here without doubt the swan is the impure demon who has snatched a Christian soul from the pure waters of a chaste life, and will devour it without mercy. I reproduce here, following Father Cahier, an imposing medieval swan holding in its beak the unfortunate fish[37] (Fig. 11).

Fig. 11 The swan symbolizing Satan; a 13th-century miniature.

If my information is correct, the black swan, the *chenopis atrata* of the naturalists, would not have been known to the West until a comparatively late date, probably not before the sixteenth-century discovery by Europeans of the big islands of the Oceanian archipelago to which it was native. In any case, the symbol for traitor and for Satan which was made of this bird, simply on account of its color, seems of fairly recent history. Artists of the last centuries have placed it in opposition to the white swan which in this juxtaposition stands for the virtue of loyalty or for Christ himself.

NOTES

Title Figure: The swan on a Eucharistic embroidery from Brageac.

1. See de Morgan, *L'Humanité préhistorique*, p. 266, and Déchelette, *Manuel*, T. II, Part I, pp. 426-453.
2. Cf. Déchelette, "Les origines de la Drachme et de l'Obole," in *Revue numismatique*, 1911, pp. 28-9.
3. *Idem.*, "Le Culte du Soleil aux temps préhistoriques," in *Revue archéologique*, 4th series, T. XIII, 1909, p. 349.
4. Maury, *Religion de la Grèce*, T. I, p. 147, note 6; also P. Decharme, *Mythologie de la Grèce antique*, p.104.
5. Guénon, *Man and His Becoming According to the Vedānta*, Chapter V, p. 56, note 2.
6. Ovid, *Metamorphoses*, Book II; also Mario Meunier, *La Légende dorée des Dieux et des Héros*, 1925, p.118; and Chompré, *Dictionnaire de la Fable*, 1786, p.122, etc.
7. Cf. Malet and Isaac, *L'Orient et la Grèce*, p. 210, engraving.
8. Cf. Meunier, *op. cit.* in note 6 above, p. 32.
9. On the seal of the Order of the Knights Templar is an engraving of two horsemen mounted on the same horse. Cf. Fr. Eygun, *Sigillographie du Poitou*, p. 443, and plate LXVII.

10. Cf. Reinach, in *Comptes rendues de l'Académie des Inscriptions*, meeting of Feb. 15, 1901; and *Revue archéologique*, 3d series, T. XL, 1902, p. 382, note.
11. Le Cour, "Le Cygne," in *Atlantis*, #35, May 1931, p. 118.
12. St. Luke 1:35.
13. See R. P. Delattre, "Lampes chrétiennes de Carthage," in *Revue de l'Art chrétien*, 1890, and *Symboles eucharistiques*, pp. 66 and 92. Also Leclercq and Marron, *Dictionnaire*, fasc. 84.
14. *Editor's note*: French, "Cygne de la Croix," Swan of the Cross, is a pun for "Signe de la Croix," sign of the cross.
15. See Dr. Legué, *Urbain Grandier*, and Aubin, *The Devils of Loudun*.
16. Reboux, "Les Enseignes-rébus," in *Figaro artistique illustré*, T. VIII, March 1931, p. 27.
17. *Annuaire du Bureau de Longitudes* for the year 1921, p. 361.
18. Skansen, *Mélanges de Litterat. Philolog. et Hist.*, Poitiers, 1934, p.198.
19. St. Mark 9:3.
20. Hugo, *L'Aurore*.
21. Buffon, *Histoire naturelle*, 1769, T. XXXVI, p. 41.
22. Latini, *Li Livres dou Tresor*, "Dou Cygne," Book I, CLXIII.
23. St. John chs. 14-17.
24. Cahier, "Bestiaires," in *Mélanges archéologiques*, T. II, Plate XXII, A-Z.
25. *Ibid.*, T. III, p. 233.
26. St. Matthew 18:20.
27. See P. Monceaux, "Abraxas et poignée de lampe de Carthage," in *Bulletin de la Societé des Antiquaires de France*, T. LXVI, 1906, p. 323. Also Leclercq, *op. cit.*, T. III, Vol. II, col. 3212.
28. The reference is to *The Order of the Swan*, founded in the fifteenth century by Frederick II, elector of Brandenburg; the knights had to distinguish themselves by personal works of charity. This order was reorganized in 1843 by the king of Prussia.
29. Pindar, *Works*, V, 24.
30. Chompré, *op. cit.*, p.88.
31. See Déchelette, "Le Culte solaire aux temps préhistoriques," in *Revue archéologique*, 4th series, T. XIII and XIV, 1909.
32. Aristotle, *History of Animals*, IX, II.
33. De Beauvais, *Speculum majus*, XVI, 50.
34. Pliny, *Natural History*, XXX, 10.
35. St. Matthew 23:27.
36. *La Queste del Saint Graal*, Edit. Albert Pamphilet, p.185.
37. Cahier, *op. cit.*, *loc. cit.*

End Figure: 13th-century seal of Jacques Bonneau.

THE PELICAN

THE PELICAN, LIKE the swan, is a big web-footed bird, sometimes as much as a meter in length. On the water, it has all the grace and elegance of the swan; it is white, ringed with salmon pink[1], but its drooping wings and the huge pouch sagging under its extremely long beak make it, in regard to beauty, no more than the swan's poor relation.

The European pelican, which entered Christian symbolism as an emblem of Christ, was called *pelekos* by the Greeks, from *pelekus*, axe, because the opening of its enormous beak, widening out in the shape of a fan, recalls the ancient axe head when the bird drops from the sky onto the fish swimming near the water's surface, on which it chiefly feeds. The ancient Greeks also called it the *onokrotos*, because they thought its strange cry, *krotos*, resembled the braying of *onos*, the ass.

A very old legend says that sometimes the young pelicans are hatched in such a feeble state as to be almost lifeless; or else that the parent bird on returning to the nest finds them killed by a snake; or it may happen that the chicks are quite lively, but that they treat the father bird shamefully, striking him in the face with their wings and beaks, so that he, justly enraged, kills them on the spot. But however the young ones come to their death, after three days their father, seeing them dead, is touched to the heart; he cries aloud with grief and bending over their bodies he tears his breast with his beak so that his blood pours over them. Under this warm shower very soon the dead baby birds begin to stir and come back to life, beating their wings joyfully and burrowing into their father's downy feathers (Fig. 1).

In the second century of our era, the Christian author of the *Physiologus* picked up the fable of the pelican reanimating its young, and in the following century the Carthaginian potters represented the scene among the symbols of the Redeemer with which they ornamented Christian lamps[2]. In fact, it was this meaning that Christian symbolism gave it from the beginning: like the pelican's young, the human race is dead to the life of the spirit, and soiled moreover by its sins. The Savior poured his blood over humanity, purifying it by his sacrifice, and gave it back true life. This is what all the medieval bestiaries expressed with varying degrees of felicity:

De son bec perce son coste	He pierces his side with his beak
Tant qu'il en a del sanc oste	So that the blood flows;
De cel sanc qui d'ilec est fors	From the blood which issues from him
Lors ramaine la vie et cors	He brings life back into the bodies
A ses poucins, n'en doutez mie	Of his chicks, be in no doubt of it;
Et en tel sens les vivifie.	And in this way he gives them life[3] (Fig. 2).

Fig. 1 The pelican wounding itself on the right side; 13th-century drawing in the Bibliothèque Nationale.

Fig. 2 The pelican reviving its young on a 13th-century sculpture in the Strasbourg cathedral.

Fig. 3 The pelican on the top of the cross, 15th century; in the Louvre.

Neither this text nor scarcely any other of the period says that the symbolic bird *nourishes* its little ones with its blood (since they are *already dead* when it is shed upon them) but that it purifies them of sin and brings them back to life. This was the way the fable was understood by all the great mystics of the time—Vincent de Beauvais, Albertus Magnus, and St. Thomas Aquinas, among others[4].

During the last three centuries of the Middle Ages, artists very often represented the pelican and its brood on the top of the cross[5], usually above the heading I.N.R.I. (Fig. 3); sometimes they even gave the tree of deliverance an extra branch whose foliage surrounds the nest. I have at hand some thirty of these images, all of which show the pelican wounding itself in the center or on the right side of the breast; the bird thus represents the simultaneously purifying and vivifying qualities of the blood which Christ poured out upon the world. It would seem that Dante had in mind this image of the pelican placed above the crucified Christ when he wrote of St. John:

> This is he, this, who on the breast reclined
> Even of our Pelican; 'tis he who bore
> The great charge from the Cross to him consigned[6].

In the ancient art of the Church, the mystic pelican is shown more often from the side than facing to the front; but in both cases, it strikes itself with its beak on the right side, or, infrequently, in the center, but never on the left. If this latter does occur in very rare instances, it is because of an error on the part of the engraver, who failed to reverse his model as he must to get a correct imprint. In the same way, the old representations of the crucified Christ show the lance-wound on the right side of his body; also from the fifteenth century on, the images of Christ's bleeding heart show it pierced on the right side. This iconographic rule was strictly observed until the fifteenth century. It goes back to the text describing a vision of Ezekiel's, repeated in the Roman Catholic liturgy as an Easter anthem: *Vidi aquam* ... "Behold . . . the waters came down from under the right side of the house . . . . And it shall come to pass, that everything that liveth, which moveth, whithersoever the rivers shall come, shall live[7]." This text is sung before solemn masses and observances, while holy water is sprinkled to purify the congregation.

From the close of the sixteenth century, a lack of understanding of the authentic Catholic symbolism caused waverings in the strict rule prevalent until then that the pelican was always shown striking its breast from the right or center, never from the left. Later, during the eighteenth century, Freemasonry adopted and revived a number of ancient symbols, almost all Christian ones, retaining their already sacred meanings. The pelican was one of these, and it kept for the Masons two of the roles the Church had given it, those of representing the Redeemer and the virtue of charity (Fig. 4). Here is part of a dialog on the meaning which the Masonic initiate into the secret order of the Rose-Cross should find in the wounded bird:

Fig. 4 The Masonic pelican at the foot of a cross bearing the rose and the compass; 19th-century wood carving.

> The Wisest One asks the Most Respectable candidate:
> "Do you know the Pelican?"
> "Yes, Wisest One."
> "What does it mean?"
> "It is the symbol for us of the Redeemer of the World and of perfect humanity[8]."

Since then, the pelican has expressed this meaning everywhere among Masons who have firmly attached to it the iconographic characteristic of wounding itself *always* on the left side of the breast, and of having its neck bent *always* to this side, opposite to the traditional pelican in Catholic iconography; and this representation began to become generally accepted, even in the churches. This came about in the following way: At the end of the eighteenth and beginning of the nineteenth centuries, Compagnonnage[9] was at its height. Workmen of all trades and crafts went from town to town, working for a certain time in each, in order to perfect their skills; those affiliated with Compagnonnage were almost sure of finding work and assistance on arriving in a new place of any size. The Compagnons were numerous and Freemasonry soon took charge of the institution; although it does not seem to have been its founder, it gave the Compagnons secret signs by which to recognize each other, and part of their own insignia, including the pelican as well as the triangle, the trowel, the square, the compass, and the acacia. In fact, Compagnonnage became a sort of workingman's third-order of philosophic Freemasonry, and for some, an antechamber to the Lodge.

By means of Compagnonnage, Masonry entered all the industries, all the factories, all the workshops, and this facilitated the substitution of the left-sided pelican for the traditional representation of Christian art. And because Christian artists as well as those who should guide them have abandoned the study of the true and traditional principles of Christian symbolism, sadly enough we see daily all sorts of anomalies. In a number of churches the Masonic pelican dominates the altar; it is seen on canopies, doors, on the vestments of priests, everywhere. But we should remember the words of Prof. Hippeau, quoted before[10], that symbolic images are not arbitrary, and that they "constitute a kind of artistic orthodoxy" from which we depart at our peril[11].

It was in the sense of total purification that the old alchemists thought of the pelican when they designated under the name of "pelican's blood" the state of elements destined for the Great Work, after an initial purification[12]. A legacy of their work remains in an instrument used in modern chemistry which bears the name "pelican," a kind of one-piece alembic with two spouts from a tubular neck.

But in the course of time, another idea became associated with the primary ones of purification, redemption, and resurrection which Christian symbolism had related to the pelican, and this later association has since become predominant: the idea that has made this bird the emblem of Christ's love for human souls, exemplified in the gift of his blood in the Eucharist. In the twelfth century, Hugh of St. Victor, after telling the fable of the pelican, expressed himself thus: "We have struck our God in the face, we have denied him. And yet he gave up his Son to be tortured; the soldier's lance pierced his side from which issued the water and the blood which have given us our redemption. The water is the grace of baptism, and the blood, the Chalice he has given us to drink of for the remission of our sins[13]."

Since the crown of love, or charity, is to give oneself, the pelican provides an excellent example of this kind of heroism. A number of fifteenth- and sixteenth-century miniatures showed the pelican above an image personifying Charity[14]. It seems to express maternal love when it accompanies images of the Virgin Mary, and in clerical heraldry it speaks of the devotion of fatherly love among those who have charge of souls. In civil heraldry it also stands for paternal love extending into personal sacrifice. Musset refers to this in speaking of the pelican:

Slow-footed, climbing a high rock,
Sheltering his brood with drooping wing,
Melancholy fisherman, he gazes at the sky!
The blood flows in long streams from his open breast . . . [15]

The Ancients had long ago attributed to Musset's "melancholy fisherman" a native sadness that caused it to seek deserts and desolate places. David lamented to God, "I am like a pelican of the wilderness[16]" —a cry of anguish that was later applied by mystical writers to Christ in two circumstances of his life: when he withdrew into the wilderness for forty days, and particularly when he was abandoned by his followers in the Garden of Gethsemane at the time of his arrest. A pelican, accompanied by David's text, expresses this on a medieval stained glass window in the Cathedral of Bourges[17]. This aspect of the pelican is found on a number of works of art of the past, but above all in literary imagery.

In our Western, Christian symbolism, there was complete opposition between the pelican and the monstrous creature called the vampire. The former pours out its own blood and thereby gives life to those who have lost it; the vampire sucks blood from its victims through a wound that it inflicts, and causes their death. The former corresponds to the *Jesu auctor vitae* of the liturgic text, the other represents the "Devastator," the "Prince of Darkness." In the old legends and superstitions of France and England, and above all in those of Germany, central Europe, and the region of the Danube, vampires were thought to be the spirits of the wicked dead, who come out by night from the tombs of rotting corpses and suck the blood of the living as they sleep, after wounding them in the left vein of the neck; they kill their victims quickly by draining them of blood and sometimes even decapitating them. Medieval art shows us these nocturnal evildoers either in the form of a horrifying demon or of an enormous bat. There are in fact types of blood-sucking or vampire bats in the Americas, which are actually not dangerous to human beings. But the beliefs of eastern Europe which linked

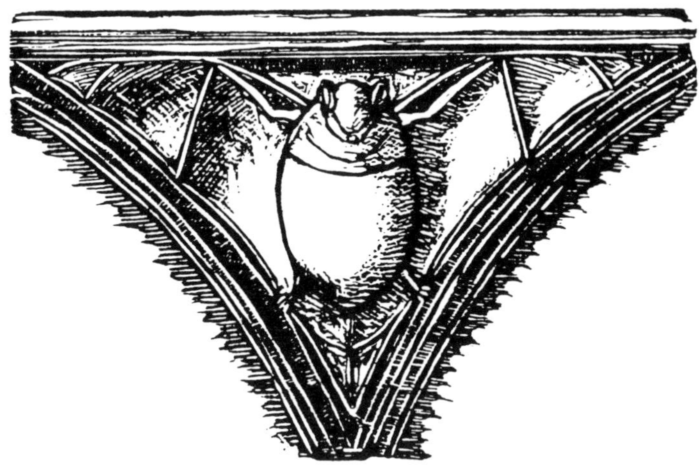

Fig. 5 The vampire bat, on the back of a choir stall in the Poitiers cathedral; 13th century.

the bat with maleficent nocturnal spirits are of very ancient origin, as the *nykteris* had an evil reputation among the Greeks, and Pliny reports that in his time they were nailed upside down to the doors of houses to chase away noxious spirits and magical spells of ill omen[18]. In some backward areas in France to this day, bats that can be caught are thrown into the fire, in spite of their services as insect eaters.

The huge bat of the thirteenth-century choir stalls in St. Peter's Cathedral in Poitiers (Fig. 5) must refer to the idea of vampires, since Origen had designated the bat as the symbol of the heretic because it hides during the daylight hours, and because it shares the characteristics of both bird and mammal. In France, in any case, the heraldry of the nobility took the bat as the symbol of heresy. Medieval art sometimes gave bat wings to the mermaid; she can be seen thus on a fifteenth-century cornice in the ancient church of Saint-Germain in Poitiers. She then becomes the image of Asmodeus, the demon of lust, who drains the fluids from the human being that are the life of the body, and dries up the fountain of grace that is the life of the soul.

NOTES

Title Figure: The Pelican reviving its young, from a woodcut in the Hortus Sanitatis.

1. *Editor's note*: This is the European variety. In other countries there are other species and colorations.
2. Cf. L. Delattre, *Carthage, Symboles eucharistiques*, p. 91.
3. William of Normandy, *Le Bestiaire divin.* Hippeau ed., pp. 207-210.
4. Albertus Magnus, *Opera*, T. XII, *De animalibus*, p. 524; ibid., *Des vertus des Herves, Pierres, Bestes et Oyseaux*, Book III. St. Thomas Aquinas, Hymn, *Adoro te.*
5. See de Saint-Laurent, *Guide*, T. II, pp. 354, 365, 375 and Book XIX; T. IV, p. 524.
6. Dante, *The Divine Comedy* : *Paradiso*, canto XXV. [Laurence Binyon trans.]
7. Ezekiel 47:1, 9.
8. *Receuil précieux de la Maçonnerie Adhonhiramite*, by a *chevalier* of all the Masonic orders, 5.807, p. 31.
9. *Editor's note*: The workmen's guild of Les Compagnons du Devoir, which is still in existence in France.
10. See Introduction, p. X.
11. *Bestiaire divin*, Hippeau ed., p. 34, note.
12. Cf. *Le Triomphe Hermétique de la pierre philosophale*, Desbordes edition, 1704, p. 129.
13. See *Bestiaire divin*, Hippeau ed., Introduction, p. 95.
14. Cf. de Saint-Laurent, *op. cit.*, p. 445.
15. Alfred de Musset, *Poésies diverses*—"La nuit de mai"—Charpentier edition, Paris, 1846, p. 340.
16. Psalms 102:6.
17. Cf. de Saint-Laurent, *op. cit.*, T. II, p. 283.
18. Pliny, *Natural History*, Bk. XXIX, 26.

End Figure: The purifying Pelican, on a ceramic water pitcher of Oyron; 16th century.

WADING BIRDS

THE FAMILY OF wading birds includes a number of species, among them the sacred ibis of the Egyptians, the stork, the crane, the heron, and the marabou. Although they played different roles in different places, a symbolism common to them all was that of good struggling with evil, and so later of Christ combating the Evil Spirit and his agents—no doubt because all these birds are formidable enemies of snakes and of a host of small animals and reptiles that are destructive or disagreeable. Many of the waders also are connected with the idea of wisdom and of guidance.

In Egypt the ibis was the symbol of Thoth, who represented the action of the divine Word. In the Creation by the supreme god Amon-Ra-Ptah, the theologians distinguished between "the part played by the creative thought which they called the *heart*, and that of the instrument of creation, the *tongue*[1]." The divine heart, seat of eternal thought and intelligence, was called Horus, the falcon-headed god, and this holy tongue which actualized the sacred concepts by its speech was named Thoth, the god with the head of an ibis. Returning from Egypt, Plato wrote that in this country there was a god who had been worshipped since the earliest times, to whom the ibis was sacred. He added that this god, who was named Thoth, was the inventor of numbers, mathematics, astronomy, writing, and the game of chess, and had commanded the first pharaohs to spread the knowledge of these things among their people[2]. It is because of this, Plutarch says, that the first character of the Egyptian alphabet has the form of an ibis[3].

In Greece, the heron was one of Athena's messengers, and so partook of the quality of wisdom connected with Minerva-Athena. Lanoë-Villène is probably right in saying that this bird "must certainly have been taken in ancient times as one of the symbols of sacred science[4]." The religious ideas of the ancient Toltecs of Mexico related the white heron to the action on earth of divine knowledge, and, in consequence, to what René Guénon says of the ancient *Tula* of the Mexicans, which owes its origin to the Toltecs: Tula is "the high point of the world," the *Thule* of the Greeks. On Mexican monuments the ideogram for Tula is the heron[5].

In certain Asiatic regions, the marabou or adjutant stork is still thought to have a strange power of introspection into the human being which enables it to see clearly the state of each person's conscience. Very ancient traditions connect this bird, like the ibis and the heron, with divine wisdom; Guénon wrote: "Wisdom is nearly always identified with the divine Word, and as the marabou was a symbol of wisdom, it must by the same token represent the Word[6]."

Hesiod tells us that storks announce the propitious moment for sowing crops, and the flight and cries of this bird, migrator par excellence, were carefully observed by ancient ornithology: in the Roman empire, soothsaying and augury derived omens and warnings of all kinds from them[7].

The ibis was believed to be the means of helping the soul to attain the eternal dwelling place of the divinity. According to the religious poetry of Egypt, it was on the wing of Thoth the Ibis that the gods who visited the earth were borne back to heaven, and this was also the sure and holy vehicle which carried the souls of the just to their eternal joy[8]. In Bengal, it is believed that the marabou stork carries within itself the soul of a holy Brahmin[9]: in like manner, the Indians of North America say that herons contain the souls of wise men who have returned to the earth on mysterious pilgrimages.

We know very little about the symbolism of animals among

the Druids, but such writers as Diodorus Siculus, Strabo, Pliny, and various others have testified to the knowledge attained by their high priesthood, whose members, directly or indirectly, controlled practically all the phases of life among the Gauls. The symbolism expressed on Gallic coinage of that era, toward the beginning of the second century B.C., certainly could not have escaped their influence. On some of the oldest gold coins of the Gallic tribes, we find the symbol of the stork, most frequently placed on the back of a large animal, such as a horse or a bull. In these images Charles Renel sees these birds as spirits who direct the big animals; "sometimes the bird even holds the horse's bridle in its claws, and at others its feet clutch the mane[10]." Certainly in these cases the birds occupy exactly the same place in which we find winged spirits with human bodies on other Gallic gold coins—those of what is now Poitou, for instance[11], which inspired the coinage of Philip of Macedon. A Gallo-Roman altar found near the foundations of Notre Dame in Paris shows a bull with a crane perched on its head and two others on its back (Fig. 1). Ingenious hypotheses have been offered, but no absolutely satisfactory explanation of this puzzle, nor of a somewhat similar one in an altar at Trèves[12].

Fig. 1 The bull with three cranes, on a Gallo-Roman altar in the Cluny Museum.

The Egyptians saw in the ibis, as also in the marabou, a "world purifier," because it consumed carrion and other unhealthy substances. On the other hand, it would not touch water that was not perfectly pure. Plutarch wrote: "The Egyptian priests who are the most scrupulous in observing their rites, in order to purify themselves, take water from which the ibis has drunk, for it never drinks water if it is unhealthy or unclean and will not even approach it[13]."

Aelian tells us that the Egyptian religion dedicated the ibis to the moon, and that this bird takes the same number of days to hatch its eggs as the moon to complete the cycle of her phases[14]. This is possibly true, but the real reason for the connection is that Thoth was the god who ruled the moon[15] and was often represented with the lunar disk and crescent on his head (Fig. 2). Another concept of Egyptian religious thought connected the sacred ibis with Osiris, and made of it one of the emblems of resurrection of which the moon with its waning, disappearance, and rebirth is, like Osiris, a notable example.

Fig. 2 Thoth with the ibis' head crowned with the lunar disk and crescent; in the temple of Ramses II at Antinoe.

René Guénon is right in affirming that the ibis, the heron, and the stork play the same symbolic role and that all three were considered, and remain, emblems of Christ[16]. The gray heron, with the penitential color of its plumage, had a particular character of melancholy in the eyes of former symbolists. Pliny had stated that this bird when oppressed by misfortune weeps tears of blood, and this connected it in their minds with the moment of Christ's agony in Gethsemane when "his sweat was as it were great drops of blood falling down to the ground[17]." The heron's preference for solitary places has also made of it one of Christian symbolism's rare living examples of silence, a silence which is precious because it leads the human being from reflection to wisdom. Medieval artists, especially the heraldists, represented this idea by showing the heron standing and holding in its beak a stone that keeps it from uttering a sound[18]. This stone was called by the Ancients *leuc-*

Fig. 3 Battle of the cranes and the pygmies; from a woodcut in the Hortus Sanitatis.

Fig. 4 The crane fighting a snake; from a vase found at Hadrian's villa at Tivoli, now in the Cluny Museum.

ochryse (white crystal), a gem of a pale golden color, traversed by white lines, which was believed to help the person who carried it to acquire wisdom.

The symbolism of the struggle between good and evil shared by all these birds took the form in ancient times of a fabled war between the cranes and a race of pygmies coming from the region near the Nile's sources[19], who invaded Egypt mounted on partridges and goats (Aristotle says, on pygmy horses), and ravaged the countryside. The cranes, handsome big birds and friends of mankind, opposed them, exterminating many and putting the rest to flight, pursuing them up to the walls of their city which Pliny calls Gerania (Fig. 3) (from the Greek name for the crane, *geranos*, *geranion*).

The crane was a sacred bird in the Euphrates valley at the time of Babylon's splendor, and also in Susa and Media. As these birds are willing to live in a semi-domestic state, they could be observed easily and the attitudes they assumed in their singular dances were taken as portents, since they were regarded as results of an almost divine inner state. As we know, all the various kinds of cranes perform a sort of dance at one time or another, sometimes with infinite grace and seriousness, so that our forefathers were led to give the bird's name to foreign ballerinas; later, the name passed to women of light morals. In China and Japan today, stage entertainers train these birds to perform even more complicated dances[20].

Old popular traditions in Europe dedicated to the crane the little wild geranium which grows in rocky places and has five-petalled blooms of a lively rose-red. It is the prototype and forerunner of all our garden geraniums, and is named for the crane, *geranos*, because the shape of the seed pod represents quite well the bird's beak which is so terrible to reptiles[21] (Fig. 4). This is probably why in some western regions the wild geranium is called "devil-chaser."

Fig. 5 Asiatic symbol of longevity: the crane standing on the turtle; Cochin China bronze candlestick.

Both crane and stork, mounted on the back of a turtle, were taken as symbols of longevity (Fig. 5). The Orientals allow the crane up to a thousand years of life, a claim which remains to be proved. Among the Greeks and Romans, the stork was also taken as the symbol of piety, filial gratitude, and of conjugal and maternal love.

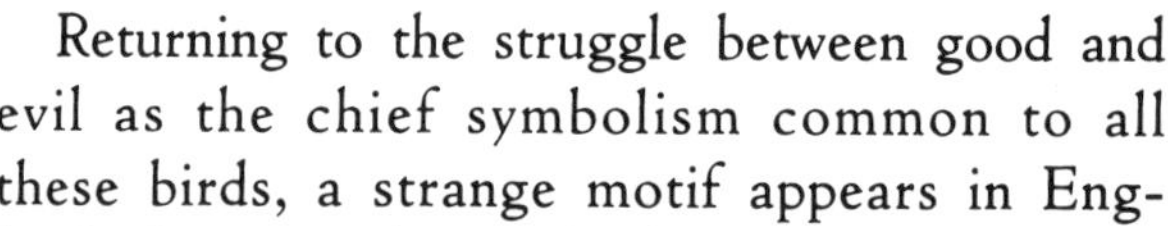

Returning to the struggle between good and evil as the chief symbolism common to all these birds, a strange motif appears in England, for example on the base of twin columns on the porch of the church at Monkwearmouth, near Durham, which dates from the ninth century[22]. Two heads on the long necks of wading birds seem to sharpen their beaks reciprocally, one against the other, above the figure of two intertwined serpents (Fig. 6). This singular image seems to connect solely with the struggle between good and evil, a struggle waged here not directly by Christ but by his followers. That at least is the exoteric meaning of the Monkwearmouth sculpture, but I would not be surprised if there were not a more esoteric significance hidden beneath this representation of the two serpents on the one hand, and the two birds on the other. Looking at the twined serpents, what has to be noted is that their heads, stretching away from each other, form a very spread out V, an accursed figure in

Fig. 6 Sculpture on the door of the church at Monkwearmouth, Durham.

black magic. They are shown here exactly in the position of other entwined snakes which are presented in conditions which leave no doubt whatever of their satanic character—for example, on the elements of the sacrilegious Eucharist of Wintras, of which Éliphas Lévi has commented: "... instead of approaching each other in two parallel semicircles, the heads and the tails went outwards, and there was no intermediate line representing the caduceus. Above the serpents' heads was visible the fatal V, the Typhonian fork, the character of hell[23]." The wading birds of Monkwearmouth can only be the adversaries of the accursed serpents. Perhaps better-informed English symbolists could give the exact meaning of this strange symbol.

NOTES

Title Figure: The sacred ibis of Egypt.

1. Moret, *Mystères égyptiens*, p. 122.
2. Plato, *Phaedrus*.
3. Plutarch, *Quaestiones Conviviales*. LX, 3.
4. Lanoë-Villène, *Le Livre des Symboles*, IV, p. 143.
5. Guénon, *Le Roi du Monde*, ch. X. [Editor's note (J.A. West): The stork's annual return to its nest made it the symbol of *reincarnation* which our author sometimes seems to confuse with *resurrection*. See above, Part III, "The Frog," note 7, Editor's note.]
6. Guénon, note mss. January 20, 1932.
7. Hesiod, *Works and Days*.
8. Cf. Moret, "Du Sacrifice en Égypte," in *Revue de l'Histoire des Religions*, 1908, p. 97. Also, Lefébure, *Sphinx*, VIII, p. 16.
9. Cf. T. Trousset, *Nouveau Dictionnaire encyclopédique*, T. III, p. 745.
10. Renel, *Les Religions de la Gaule avant le Christianisme*, p. 207.
11. See Lecointre-Dupont, *Essais sur les Monnaies du Poitou*, p. 6; A. de Bartholémy, "Étude sur les Monnaies gauloises (etc.)" in *Mémoire de la Soc. des Antiquaires de l'Ouest*, vol. XXXVII, p. 493. Also G. Chauvet, *Petites Notes charentaises*, p. 25, etc.
12. Cf. Reinach, *Catalogue du Musée de Saint-Germain-en-Laye*, p. 35. See also d'Arbois de Jubainville in *Revue Celtique*, T. XXIX, pp. 245-250.
13. Plutarch, *Isis and Osiris*, LXXV. [Editor's note (J.A. West): The ibis, endlessly searching for its food in the mud, also symbolizes the element of "search" in acquiring wisdom.]
14. Aelian, *On the Nature of Animals*, II, 35, 38; X, 29.
15. Cf. Virey, *La Religion de l'ancienne Égypte*, p. 142.

16. Guénon, *op. cit.*, p. 114, note.
17. St. Luke 22:44.
18. Barbier de Montault, *Traité d'Iconographie chrétienne*, T. I, p. 201.
19. Aristotle, *History of Animals*, Book VIII, 14.
20. Cf. "Grue de Mandchourie," in *Magasin pittoresque*, T. XXVIII, 1860, p. 289.
21. Cf. Jacques Peyrot, "L'Herbe à Robert," in *Le Matin*, May 15, 1933.
22. Cf. Leclercq and Marron, *Dictionnaire*, T. II, Vol. I, col. 1200, fig. 1559 & col. 1224, fig. 1695.
23. Lévi, *The Key to the Mysteries*.

End Figure: The triumphant crane on a Japanese porcelain in the Jacquemart collection.

THE OSTRICH

IN VARIOUS PARTS of the ancient world, the ostrich was taken as the symbol of stupidity, because of the mistaken idea that it thinks that by hiding its head in bushes or in the sand, it can make itself invisible to pursuers. In some other parts it represented gluttony, because it was thought that it would eat iron (Fig. 1). Nevertheless, it was also known in many places in more flattering aspects. In Nubia, Arabia, Persia, Sumeria, Mesopotamia, Assyria, and Asia Minor, the learned scholars and teachers looked upon the ostrich as one of the birds most favored by various astral influences and as possessing in itself elements of the divine. The Greeks and Romans regarded the ostrich as receiving in particular the emanations of the planet Saturn, and of another star designated in the old texts by the name of *Virgil*[1]. Elsewhere, in western Asia, in the most ancient centers of Brahmanism, where urine is considered a holy thing, the ostrich is revered because it is the only bird that has the faculty of urinating.

The ostrich lays the perfect egg, the largest and most beautiful of all eggs; and in the mind of the Ancients, part of the effluences from the stars which the bird receives must be contained in it. And as we shall see, in medieval times this incomparable egg became one of the liturgical symbols of Christ.

Fig. 1 Symbol of gluttony; the ostrich eating iron. Wood carving of the 17th century.

The old naturalists have told that the ostrich, which they say with some exaggeration lays twenty-four eggs[2], begins to lay them in June, the month in which the star called Virgil appears in the sky. The eggs are laid on a mound of sand which the sun heats, and left there to hatch. But when the moment comes for the chicks to emerge into the free air of the desert, the ostrich, warned by its star, returns to the eggs and hatches them with a single ardent look which summons them to life.

The medieval symbolists claimed that the ostrich chicks would never see the light if the parent birds did not soften the excessively hard shells of their eggs by coating them first with honey, and then moistening them with their own blood[3]. One sees at once what meaning the symbolists of that time could draw from this fable, nor did they fail to do so: "When the blood touched it, the shell broke and the young bird escaped swiftly; thus Christ broke the stone before the door of the sepulcher and flew up to heaven to sit on his Father's right hand[4]." Others explain it like this: The honey is the blessed image of Christ's doctrine, and the ostrich's blood is that of the blood of the Redeemer; Christ gave us first his teaching, then his blood, and by that double gift he liberated humanity, his children, from the fetters of the "law of fear" and from the shadow of ancient idolatries.

In the spiritual beliefs of present-day Coptic monks, the heat of the sun that hatches the eggs of the ostrich is looked upon as the symbol of God's grace which brings virtue to blossom in the soul of the faithful, especially that of the monk. From another aspect, the ostrich itself, which always moves straight ahead without ever turning, also represents the monk who must always go straight forward toward perfection, never looking back at the past and the worldly things he has left behind.

Evidently the biblical severity in regard to the ostrich, which blames it for abandoning its eggs and being "hardened against its young ones[5]," did not impress the old Christian symbolists very deeply, since they made it represent the return to God of the wandering soul, and also the symbol of that virtue in which almost all the others are implicit, that of impartiality.

NOTES

1. Cf. Barbier de Montault, *op. cit.*, T. I, p. 115. [*Editor's note*: The Pleiades, a group of stars in the constellation Taurus, were also known as *Vergiliae*.]
2. Aelian, *On the Nature of Animals*, XIV, 14.
3. See next chapter, "The Egg."
4. William of Normandy, *Le Bestiaire divin*, Hippeau ed., p. 167. Also Didron, *Annales archéologiques*, T. XI, Book V, p. 259; and Cloquet, *Éléments d'Iconographie chrétienne*, p. 308.
5. Job 39:16.

THE EGG

FROM THE DAYS of the most primitive human societies, the egg has figured as an important religious emblem and as the ideogram of the starting point, the initial germ of life. Primitive people knew instinctively what was later formulated by the learned biologist Harvey in his famous aphorism: *Omne vivum ex ovo*, "Every living thing comes from an egg"; that is to say, from a seed enclosed in some kind of envelope[1].

From Egypt's earliest dynasties, the egg was connected with the idea of the beginning of everything and the very essence of living beings. In ancient Crete, in the Mycenaean epoch and during the last two thousand years before our era, the symbolic eggs of large birds such as the ostrich, sumptuously mounted like cups, were placed in the tombs of the wealthy. Recent excavations made at Ur in Chaldea—the birthplace of Abraham—have unearthed the tomb of Queen Sub-Ad, of the fourth millennium before our era. Among the precious objects in the tomb was an ostrich egg, mounted like a cup on a tripod of fine gold; it is ornamented with plaques of mother-of-pearl and incrustations of red stones and lapis lazuli (Fig. 1). A copy of this ostrich egg[2] in gold was found in the same tomb.

I do not know whether a symbolic meaning should be attributed to the egg shells which are sometimes found in the burial places of independent Gaul. The ones I have found there[3] accompany the bones of animals, which show that a "viaticum" for the future life was put in with the human remains. The Gallo-Romans continued the ancient custom of placing eggs in tombs not only as provisions for the long journey, but also perhaps as a symbol of the life principle, of survival, in the very heart of death; also, to fulfill certain more or less traditional magical practices. That is why in this epoch whole owl's eggs were sometimes placed near human remains, for instance at the Quenouillière in Angoumois[4]. At Seurre, in Bourgogne, an egg made of white clay placed in the same way may well have had the same significance[5], as well as a symbolic egg found in a tomb at Blois[6].

Macrobius tells us that in the Greco-Roman mysteries of Liber Pater, the egg "was so greatly venerated because of its oval, almost spherical, shape which has no opening of any

Fig. 1 Ostrich egg mounted as a cup; ½ actual size. From the tomb of Sub-Ad, queen of Ur.

kind, and because it contains life in itself[7]." And we might remember here the crystal egg worn around the neck by the great Druids in more or less this same period of time, which has been thought to represent among other things their claim to see into the future[8].

The Romans, doubtless following the example of the Etruscans, ascribed to the egg a mysterious power of purification, and also—perhaps springing from the same idea—that of driving away evil spirits of the air from human dwellings. In the sixteenth century Cornelius Agrippa of Metterheim wrote that in the past the egg was used in purification ceremonies, and from this came the title "lustral eggs," and these verses of Ovid: "Let an old woman be called who shall bless bed and bedchamber, having sulphur and eggs in her trembling hand[9]." I have never discovered any trace of this ancient meaning in any popular custom in France[10]. But another concept, more oriental and Greek than Roman, makes the egg—or, more exactly, the ovoid shape whose natural model is the egg—one of the symbols of linear, regular, perfect beauty; and all the ancient arts have favored the use of the ovate form in ornamental work. Following the custom in ancient Egypt, the Near East very frequently gave the egg shape to its lamps of baked clay, and in its first centuries Christian art followed the same usage. In the New World, since time immemorial the Sioux Indians of North America have believed that storms are enclosed in the invisible eggs which a small bird-divinity, the Thunder Bird, lays in a sacred place, where they go with offerings of tobacco leaves[11].

The egg, like the seed—which is the egg of the plant—contains a promise: that of a new life which will soon emerge and which nature has a right to expect from the very fact of the egg's existence. So it is quite understandable that the egg was very early taken as a symbol of hope, and Christianity, taking this idea to a higher level, made this feeling one of the three theological virtues. St. Augustine wrote: *Restat spes quae quantium mihi videtur, ovo comparatur. Spes enim nondum pervenit ad rem; et ovum est aliquid, sed nondum est pullus*: "There remains hope, which in my opinion can be compared to the egg. For hope has not reached its goal; likewise the egg is something, but it is not yet the chicken[12]." This is certainly what is also meant by the inscription encircling a little sixteenth-century ivory egg hanging from a ring of silver filigree, which reads: *Post tenebras spero lucem*: "After the darkness, I hope for light" (Fig. 2). And this brings us to the best-known Christian symbolism of the egg, which expresses the highest of all hopes: for a rebirth into a blessed life beyond death. This explains the presence in Rome of marble eggs the size of hens' eggs in the tombs of martyrs[13], and often in the catacombs natural eggshells[14]. I myself have found the hen's egg in two Christian burials from the period of the Franks (sixth or seventh century) at Saint-Marceau (Deux-Sèvres) in 1900 and at Sammarçolles (Vienne) in 1904. There is no doubt that in all these cases the egg represents the idea of rebirth in the very bosom of death[15].

Fig. 2 16th-century symbolic egg in ivory; de Fontaine's collection.

It is not surprising that the people of ancient times considered the most beautiful type of the egg to be that of the ostrich, not only on account of its size but also the perfection of its shape. In addition, what the naturalists had to say about the method of its incubation was enough to assure its place as the truest symbol of the hoped-for resurrection. In the time of King Philippe-Auguste, William of Normandy, echoing the voices of the past, wrote that the ostrich lays its eggs in the month of June, at the moment when the "Virgil Star" appears in the sky; caring for nothing except its star, the bird buries its eggs in the desert sand and forgets them, but the sun warms them through the sand and the chicks hatch without the help of their mother[16]. However, the *Physiologus* says that the ostrich calls its little ones to life, hatching them with one

Fig. 3 Symbolic eggs at the feet of Christ in the Burgos Cathedral; 15th or 16th century.

look at the moment that the Virgil star announces that the time has come[17].

An inventory of the Bayeux cathedral, established in the fifteenth century, mentions an ostrich egg[18] that is placed on the altar on certain holy days (Easter and perhaps Christmas). These eggs were sometimes hung in front of altars, like those that are seen in the *turbehs* of mosques and even today over tombs, where again they represent the idea of resurrection. In the Middle Ages merchants set up their stalls near the entrance pillars of Notre Dame in Paris and sold to those who came to worship such things as candles, coconuts, ostrich eggs, etc.[19] These latter were offered in the church like candles. There are still today ostrich eggs in almost all Coptic churches, and in one of the great cathedrals of Spain, in Burgos, very large eggs are hung at the feet of the crucified Christ (Fig. 3).

In certain cathedrals, it used to be the custom to place an ostrich egg with the Eucharist in the ritual of the "Tomb" on Maundy Thursday, and on Easter Day it was solemnly taken away at the singing of the "Invitation" at matins: "The Lord is risen indeed: alleluia!" It is quite clear that in this liturgical custom, the egg became the direct representation of the body of Jesus Christ, entombed and then raised again.

An inventory of the fifteenth century of the treasures of the cathedral of Angers gives this interesting detail: "There are two ostrich eggs in a large reliquary hung on silver chains. On Easter Day, the two eggs must be placed on the altar of St. René. . ."[20], the saint born twice: *Re-né*, the saint brought back to life like the Savior; for in fact St. René of Angers, who died young, was miraculously revivified[21].

In the Middle Ages, several of the big churches had ostrich eggs set up more or less richly as cups, some of which were reliquaries[22], and others simply formed decorated cups; I do not know to what use these latter were put. Possibly they were related to the idea of purification which the ancient world attached to them and were used to hold holy water. This is only an hypothesis.

In connection with the allegory of the Resurrection, on Holy Saturday the medieval Church blessed the eggs which would be eaten by the faithful the next day, before any other food was taken; and this custom still exists in Rome. On Holy Saturday the priests "go to the houses of the families of their respective parishes to bless the rooms, the marriage bed, and the Easter eggs[23]."

The Romanians, Serbs, and Greeks still use Easter eggs which are blessed and painted red[24]; those to be given to important personages are often elaborately decorated. This recalls the eggs offered by the Saracens to the Crusaders near Damiette, when they released them from their prisons, which

Joinville speaks of: "For the honor of our persons, they have had the shells painted in diverse colors[25] (Fig. 4)."

In Burgundy it is still the custom today to gather with great care the eggs laid on Good Friday in order to eat them on Easter Day, because of the legendary virtues with which old traditions have endowed them. In the west of France, as well as many other places in the world, Easter eggs are still tinted in various colors and pastries are prepared with layers of chopped meat and hard cooked eggs cut in circles. These popular customs and many others share the same symbolism and commemorate in their way Christ's Resurrection.

The simultaneous blessing of the bedroom, the marriage bed, and the Easter eggs by the Roman priests seems to bring together the idea of resurrection with that of the propagation of life through Christian marriage. Other customs could be connected with this, for instance one that was still observed in the nineteenth century by the young girls of the island of Ushant when they wished to marry, and found it difficult because so many of the young men of the island were away at sea: on Easter day they took eggs to the church, placed them in front of the altar during mass to be blessed, and then very carefully carried them away again[26].

In contrast to the eggs which call to mind earthly life, or

Fig. 4 Romanian Easter egg, colored purple, yellow, and white.

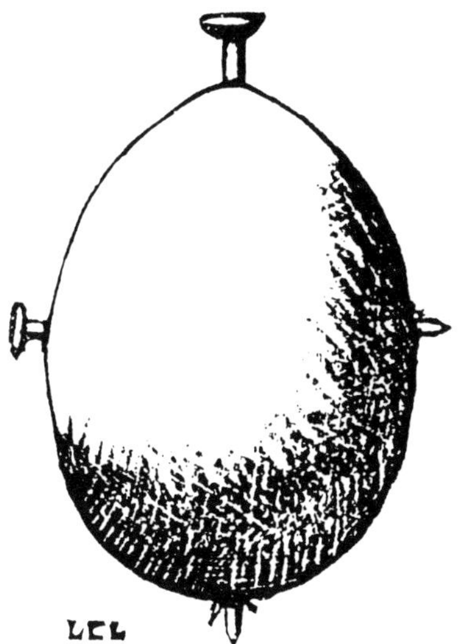

Fig. 5 Hen's egg, hardboiled and pierced with two nails after the performance of rites of witchcraft, in order to bring about an abortion.

the revivified Person of the Savior, we could place the accursed eggs which European tradition attributed to demonism. In speaking of the basilisk I have already mentioned that legendary egg that the whole medieval period took seriously, whose shell, if we are to take the word of Vincent de Beauvais[27], is so hard as to be practically unbreakable, and which is sired by an old cock begotten in hell. The basilisk comes out of this egg. The country people have given this infernal product a very close relative. Everyone who has lived in the country has seen the little elongated eggs that are found in the farmyards at the beginning or end of a hen's laying season, which contain only the egg white, without yolk or germinal disk. They are the result simply of an insufficiency in the hen of the matter that constitutes the egg; but in many country districts they are still attributed to roosters, or to "serpents" impregnated by roosters. These little eggs, considered as evil objects possibly containing the germ of the basilisk, were formerly thrown into a fire which was then put out with holy water (Vendée, Deux-Sèvres), so as to protect the farmhouse from the evil effects that they might cause. They are used in low forms of witchcraft, and are called by different names depending on the province: cocatrie, cockatrice eggs, eggs of the basilisk-cock, of the "Jau-vermine," the "coco-diable" or the "coq-au-diable," etc.[28] And when a hen is unlucky enough to imitate the cock's crow at the moment when one of these eggs appears, it is mercilessly put to death as the herald of some misfortune.

There are also eggs dedicated to maleficent purposes in rites of magic or sorcery, such as the owls' eggs placed in ancient tombs, with or without the corpses of the birds themselves[29], and the eggs of snakes or toads which the country sorcerers use in working their miserable spells (Fig. 5).

The mysterious "Egg of the World" of the Chaldeans, the Egyptians, the Thracians, and the Greeks, which was represented by the fossil sea-urchin among the Druids, will be spoken of in Part V.

NOTES

1. See Déchelette, *Manuel*, T. I, pp. 345-365.
2. Cf. L. Abensour, *Une Visite aux fouilles d'Ur.*
3. Excavations of Châtelliers-Châteaumur and of Pouzages, Vendée, 1898-1901.
4. Gustav Chouret, "Une Tombe Gallo-romaine à incinération à la Quenouillière (Charente)," in *Bulletin de la Societé des Antiquaires de l'Ouest*, 1925, 3d series, T. VII, p. 164.
5. Abbé Clément, in *Mémoire de la Societé Éduenne*, 1881, 2d series, T. X.
6. L. Grognard, *Bulletin de l'Association française pour l'avancement des Sciences*, 1886, I, p. 276.
7. Macrobius, Book VII, 16.
8. Cf. Auriger, "Le Culte d'Isis en Gaule," in *Le Voile d'Isis*, T. XXXVII, #147, p. 174.
9. Cornelius Agrippa, *De oculta philosophia*, Book III, Chapter LVII.
10. Pliny treats at length the beliefs of his time concerning the various properties of hens' eggs and their shells: *Natural History*, LXXIX, 12 and 13.
11. George Catlin, *Life Among the Indians*. [*Editor's note*: There are now many more accurate sources of information on the customs and symbology of the Sioux and other Native Americans.]
12. St. Augustine, *Sermon CV*, 8.
13. Cf. Boldetti, *Observations sur les cimetières des martyrs etc.*, p. 519.
14. Cf. Raoul Rochette, *Mémoire de l'Académie des Inscriptions*, T. XIII, p. 181.

15. The placing of eggs with the dead by the ancient Egyptians seems to come from a similar idea; cf. J. Capart, *Les Débuts de l'Art en Égypte*, p. 40.
16. William of Normandy, *Le Bestiaire divin*, XXX, "De l'Ostrice," pp. 165 & 272.
17. For further fables about the ostrich, see Vincent de Beauvais, *Miroir historial*, Book XVI, c. 230; Hugh of St. Victor, *De claustro animae, c. XXIII*; Hesychius, *Ad Plinium*, Book X, l; etc. See also preceding chapter, "The Ostrich."
18. Cf. Charles Bazin, *Bulletin monumental*, T. X, 1844, p. 330.
19. Cf. J. Moura and P. Louvet, *Notre Dame de Paris, centre de vie.*
20. Didron, *Annales archéologiques*, T. XI, 1891, p. 259.
21. *Ibid.*, also *Le Bestiaire divin*, p. 167.
22. Cf. Abbé J. Corblet, *Revue de l'Art Chrétien*, T. XVIII, p. 354.
23. Barbier de Montault, *L'année liturgique à Rome*, p. 160.
24. S. Petrides, *Dictionnaire d'Archéologie chrétienne*, Vol. I, col. 905.
25. Joinville, *L'Histoire et Cronique du très chrestien roy St. Louis II* etc., E. de Marvel ed., dedicated to Francis I; folio LXXXV.
26. Cf. André Lavignon, *Les Filles de la Pluie*, p. 45.
27. De Beauvais, *Spec. Nat.*, Book XX.
28. In the medieval bestiaries, the cockatrice is a kind of dragon of which the crocodile is the prototype.
29. See Abbé F. Baudry, *Les Puits funéraires gallo-romaines du Bernard (Vendée)*, pp. 67, 247, 315. Also Gustav Chouret, *op. et loc. cit.*

WINGS AND FEATHERS

EVERYWHERE IN ANCIENT times birds' wings were used as ideograms to express glory, beauty, sublimity, exaltation, favor or help from on high that was hoped for or received, and aspiration toward spiritual or philosophical heights. In the spiritual or religious sense, "flight" was the picture of the soul enamored of its highest ideal, appearing in this image as freed from matter insofar as existence on this earth permits, like the two wings of the "flight" which have rid themselves of the weight of the bird's body[1] (Fig. 1). Thus unburdened, it mounts ever upward and finally soars in a luminous region of serenity. This is why mysticism makes the "flight" the symbol of prayer and contemplation.

Fig. 1 Painted wooden panel from the Château of Puy-de-Fou in Véndee.

In the sixth century, the pope St. Gregory the Great presented thus the symbolic role of the wings of the four mysterious animals of the Tetramorph: "An ingenious and penetrating description shows us these four animals which the prophet's spirit foresaw in the future: each had four faces, each had four wings. What can the face mean but knowledge; and what the wings, if not flight? It is by the face that each person is known, and by the wings that birds lift themselves into the air. The face then refers to faith, the wing to contemplation, for by faith the almighty God knows us. By contemplation, which raises us above ourselves, we lift ourselves as it were into the air[2]."

During the Middle Ages, sculptors and painters sometimes endowed with wings the human images representing all the virtues, especially those of hope, charity, truth and truthfulness, evangelical poverty, and penitence[3].

But there are accursed wings which beat against the sides of the infernal animals, vampires, basilisks, dragons, and sometimes mermaids. In the fantastic picturings of such animals these wings are not formed of feathers, but of a naked membrane, whose appearance makes their evil character more evident. In Christian symbolism, wings of skin are connected with the idea of the perversion of the intellectual faculties, and of the uses to which these are put by those who study for evil purposes; for by such work—as with all mental exercise—they raise themselves above the ordinary level of humanity; not to those high regions of deep peace, but to those of the storm, to descend again scattering over the earth the seeds of confusion, trouble, discord, and perversity. These are the wings that Christian art sometimes gives to Death[4] (Fig. 2) and often to Satan. Sometimes demons are depicted as bats[5].

Fig. 2 The accursed wings: Death the destroyer (14th century).

In general, birds' wings provided the large feathers that had often a sacred connotation. In the iconography of Egypt, the ostrich feather was the hieroglyph of the goddess Maat, who was the personification of truth, sincerity, and justice, cosmic equilibrium, hence *law*, and accordingly expressed these same

Fig. 3 Hieroglyph of the goddess Maat, from an Egyptian painting.

ideas. This is why the judges, assessors for Osiris, at the tribunal of the dead, sometimes wore a feather on their heads like Maat herself. The disembodied soul also sometimes wore the feather as a sign of sincerity and the rectitude of its actions during life. In the theological concepts of Egypt, Maat was the daughter of the sun, and through this birthright, not the goddess of light but the light itself, coming directly from the divine sun and showing everything in its absolute reality and truth. This is why her emblem was an ostrich feather, pure white like a spotless ray of light (Fig. 3).

From the other side of the world, since time immemorial the big feathers of raptors rather than of ostriches have always been regarded as the symbolic representations of the rays of the radiant sun, and the Incas of South America crowned their heads with them[6].

Fig. 4 17th-century armorial bearings of the "Corporation of writers and school teachers" of Brest.

Among the Greeks and Romans, the birds' largest feathers, the quills, symbolized speed, because they came from the wings of swift birds and because they equipped arrows for flight[7]. Since the time of the Caesars, this same big feather, the *penna*, sharpened like the old reed pen, served for writing. Although this use of it did not become general until about the fifth century, it was practiced already from the beginning of the second century, as we know from the iconography of the columns of Trajan and Anthony. The Word of God is known to us not only by speech but also by what has been written, and this Word transmitted in writing has been represented by various symbolic objects, especially the Evangelistary which contains the four narratives of the life of Christ. This latter is symbolized not by an open book, but by the *scrinium* containing four scrolls. To this must be added the stylus of metal or bone that was used to write on wax tablets, the reed pen or its bronze copy, and the sharpened quill of goose, swan, or peacock that was used for writing with ink. Christian iconography very soon put the reed pen and the quill in the hands of writers of sacred texts, evangelistic letter-writers, teachers, and all those whose writings made them venerated by the Church. After the medieval period, the quill became the typical symbol of the written word and those who served it, and the professional emblem of all writers and scribes (Fig. 4).

NOTES

Title Figure: The flight symbol on the coat-of-arms of the de Verdilhac family.

1. See above, "The Falcon," pp. 204-205.
2. St. Gregory the Great, *Homiliarum in Ezechielem prophetam libri*, Homily III, Bk. 1.
3. Cf. de Saint-Laurent, *Guide*, T. III, passim and Plate XX.
4. Ibid., *loc. cit.* p. 321, fig. 41; see also his *Manuel*, p. 268, fig. 98.
5. Poitiers Cathedral. Also see above, "The Pelican," p. 264.
6. Cf. G. Bouchet, *Cosmogonie humaine*, p. 466. [*Editor's note:* See also the use of feathers among the Aztecs and the Indian tribes of North America.]
7. A. Rich, *Dictionnaire*, Cheruel tr., p. 546.

End Figure: The heart lifting itself up toward God; an 18th-century image of piety.

V

SEA CREATURES

THE FISH

IT IS AN unquestionable fact that some two thousand years before our era, the cult of the fish, as the image of divinity and hence identified with divinity itself, was established in Turan in Asia Minor, in India and the Far East, in Chaldea, Babylonia, Media, Susiana, Mesopotamia, Assyria, Persia, Syro-Phoenicia, the Aegean region, Egypt, Libya, and Numidia; and crossing the ocean, we find its image again, beautifully sculptured or carved, in the oldest monuments of Mexico, as for instance Palenque. In the northernmost parts of Europe, the water spirit, pictured at first in the form of a fish, little by little was endowed with human intellectual faculties and became the dual being, half man and half fish, such as the god Dagon of the Philistines and the Phoenicians who is spoken of in the Bible[1].

In all the early civilizations of the old world of Europe and Asia, the fish was considered as the sign of human and animal fecundity; on one hand, because of the incredible number of eggs that it carries—sometimes hundreds of thousands, according to the naturalists[2]—and on the other hand, because of the ancient belief that life originated in the depths of the sea. "In Sumerian thought," says Delaporte, "all that has life comes from the watery principle[3]."

In these same parts of western Asia, for many centuries before the Christian era, sacred art chose and retained various other symbols besides the fish to represent this fecundity, notably the cones of the cedar and the pine; and with the fish was identified the god Oannes, who as the Nordic water spirit was turned by the artists into a fish-man. He was regarded as the Lord of the world and of all the lives it harbors, and as the mediator between earth and sky[4]. Recent researches have all confirmed what the Babylonian historian Berossus had already said in the third century before our era[5].

Fig. 1 The god Oannes; sculpture from Calach.

Cylindrical seals from the above-mentioned regions, with which our European museums are bountifully provided, often show Oannes or Anu, whether in the guise of a fish placed on an altar or perhaps swimming, or in the hybrid form between fish and human. In certain aspects he approximates the Logos of the Greeks, the eternal Word. To celebrate his cult, the priests dressed themselves and the images of the god in a cloak shaped like the split body of a fish whose head crowned that of its wearer like a miter or a helmet. An Oannes in this dress is pictured on one of the doors of the Calach palace (Fig. 1). Among the Phoenicians and Philistines, Oannes took the name of Dagon, whose origin seems to be Assyrian[6] and which "expresses simultaneously the idea of the fish and of wheat[7]," thus recalling the origin of life and its maintenance on earth (Fig. 2). His temples of Gaza and of Azotus, or Ashdod, are often mentioned in the Bible, and it was to the latter that the Philistines conveyed the Ark of the Covenant after their victory over Israel at Aphek[8].

Fig. 2 The god Dagon; bas-relief from Khorsabad.

We again find Oannes-Dagon, the man-fish, under the name of Baal-Itan, on coins of the city of Itanos in Crete, which were struck during the time when the island was under

Phoenician influence[9]. Like Poseidon, Baal-Itan carries a trident.

Oannes, on the north and east of the Euphrates, and Dagon, on the west and south, were regarded as symbols of male fertility, both human and animal. Their female counterparts were Ishtar of Chaldea, and Astoreth or Atargatis of Syro-Phoenicia, who were sometimes represented as naked but chaste women and sometimes as half woman, half fish—like the mermaids of a later date, whose artistic prototype they seem to have been.

It is difficult to imagine the extraordinary magnificence in which the Eastern peoples clothed these cults. About two hundred years before the Christian era, the Greek Lucian wrote that the statue of Atargatis-Derceto in her temple at Hierapolis was covered with gold and dazzling jewels of all colors, brought from Egypt, Ethiopia, Armenia, Phoenicia, Media, and Babylonia[10]. In the sacred fish pond adjoining her temple, the fish raised in her honor were themselves venerated and came to eat out of the priests' hands when they were called. They wore corselets made of gold, and rich jewels sparkled in their gills, fins, and sometimes in their lips[11].

These sacred fishponds are found in Asia to this day: at Saravane, in Indo-Chinese Laos, the Buddhist library is built on pilings over a pond "where the sacred fish swarm[12]." It might be remembered that the fish is the Hindu *Matsya*, the first avatar of Vishnu, at once the revealer and the savior[13].

Fig. 3 The Chaldean god Ea, on Melishipak's boundary stone.

Chaldean mythology gives us a relative of Oannes, the god Ea, whose body was formed of the forequarters of an antelope and the lower part of a fish. Ea, "lord of Apsu," was the Chaldean god of wisdom, a powerful wisdom in accordance with the horns that crowned his head: he is seen thus on king Melishipak's boundary-stone, carved about twelve hundred years before Christ, which is now in the Louvre[14] (Fig. 3).

In the Egyptian Sudan, rites springing from fetishism are still practised which connect the fish and the male sex organ; while in Laos, where sacred fish are kept, young girls wear around their necks, between gold and silver fish, metal ornaments in the shape of the female organs. This same custom can be found in some regions of China and several of the Pacific islands.

The old Chaldeo-Syrian myths of Oannes, Anu, or Dagon may well have lent themselves to adoption by the early Christians as a symbol of the Savior. We should remember that the Apostle Peter, when he left Jerusalem, established his first episcopal see in Antioch, in Syria, in the heart of Oannes' kingdom, and a connection might well have been made between Christ and the Syrian fish-god. And then one day it happened that a Christian, thought to be an Alexandrian Greek[15], perceived that by taking each letter of the Greek word ΙΧΘΥC, *ichtus*, "fish," as the initial of a word, a phrase could be obtained which read IHCOYC XPICTOC ΘΗΟΝ ΥΙΟC CΩTHP, "Jesus Christ, God's son, Savior." This acrostic was a great success in Rome, and from there spread to all the areas of Christendom where necessarily "the discipline of secrecy" was in force; the fish's shape or its name were drawn or written everywhere, their meaning a mystery which only Christians could understand. When Constantine was converted to Christianity and made peace with the Church, he placed a sign on the imperial standard which was composed of an X and a P superimposed—the first letters of the Greek word XPICTOC, Christ (Fig. 4), and it was sometimes shown supported by the divine Fish[16].

Fig. 4 The Ichtus and the XP initials of Christ; on a Phoenician tomb at Cannes.

Under Constantine's successors, the old Roman empire weakened and its frontiers were invaded everywhere by its barbarian neighbors. The Goths, partially converted to the Christian faith, brought with them an art that was rude and earthy, but full of life and rich with brilliant colors. And it was the merging of these new forms, little by little, with the old artistic traditions that brought forth, several centuries later, the marvelous French medieval art which remains the purest and richest expression of the Christian spirit and of its thought.

Here again, from the end of the fifth century, we find the image of the sacred fish, brought by the Goths from the shores of the Black Sea, coming into favor once more throughout the valley of the Danube, Liguria, Emilia, and Gaul where it was especially popular. From there it entered Ireland where it became a dominant symbol[17] even as its use in Rome diminished.

Fig. 5 Al-Khizr, "The Holy One." From a painting in A.K. Coomaraswamy's collection in Boston.

In western Asia, Moslem or Hindu symbolic art shows the Saint, Al-Khizr or Kawaja-Khizr, with the figure of an aged man dressed in a green coat, carried on top of the water by a fish, which thus conveys him over the river of life[18] (Fig. 5).

I must at least make mention here of a strange trinitary symbol: three fishes exactly alike which are united in that their three heads form only one. It is a very ancient symbol that the Middle Ages preserved apparently without connecting it with the idea that would allow and explain the attribution of the fish symbol, usually reserved for the Son, to the Father and the Holy Ghost. I reproduce this symbol here, taken from a twelfth century keystone in the Benedictine Abbey of Luxeuil (Fig. 6). Under the name of *Trinacria*, the heraldry of the nobility preserved this figure on rare coats-of-arms such as that of Die Hunder, of Franconia[19]. Gevaert's recent treatise on heraldry recognizes it as one of the symbols of the

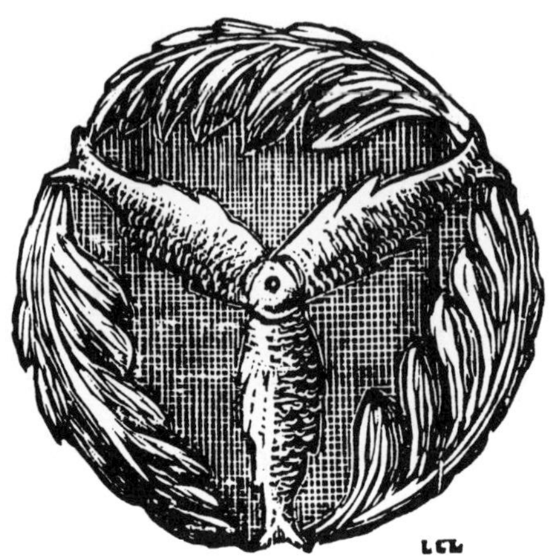

Fig. 6 The Trinacria on a keystone on the Benedictine Abbey of Luxeuil, Haute-Saône; from a sketch by M. le baron Pidoux de la Madière.

Holy Trinity[20]. It seems to affirm the identity of the divine nature, common to all three Persons by the similarity of the three fishes, as the unity of their substance is attested by the single head which makes all three into one being. Like the Swastika, the Trinacria is a figure with an imagined central pivot which essentially expresses the turning movement which animates everything, which engages everything, and which is at the point of origin of all life. And in this sense, the Trinacria symbolizes the continual creative action of the three divine Persons that is expressed by the holy Word of whom St. John says that "All things were made by him; and without him was not any thing made that was made[21]."

The first Christians called themselves "sons of the celestial Ichtus," the Great Fish which they must follow and imitate in everything: "We, small fish," wrote Tertullian in the second century, "like our Fish, Jesus Christ, swim in the (baptismal) water, and we can be saved only by remaining in it[22]." And in the following century, St. Cyprian expressed himself thus: "It is in the water that we are reborn, in the likeness of Christ, our Master, the Fish." The artists who were contemporaries of these two doctors of the church illustrated this allegory in a thousand ways; one of the most beautiful examples is the great mosaic medallion in the catacomb of Hadrumetum, at Susa, in Tunisia; it shows the Christ-Fish, lying on the anchor, the hermetic image of the cross of Calvary, and all around it, smaller fish, representing the faithful, swim peacefully among the seaweeds.

Long before the birth of Christ, some Asian cults celebrated the mysteries of the divine fish, with special rites, in which the fish is sacrificed and solemnly consumed as food. This cult is attested by monuments in Syria, Mesopotamia, Assyria, and Chaldea. A bas-relief of Nimrod placed beneath the Ilu image, the symbol of Assyria's chief god, shows the sacrificed fish placed at the foot of the altar, under the lunar crescent and the star of Ishtar, goddess of love and fertility. On one side is Oannes, or a priest identified with him, and on the other a winged personage—perhaps the sacrificer, as behind him we see an unsheathed sword. And on a carved stone now in the British Museum (Fig. 7), we see the fish laid on the altar, again with the star and crescent moon above. Seated on either side for the ritual meal are a man whose head seems to be in contact with the symbol of Ilu, and a woman who like the man opposite her lifts a bowl to her lips. A third personage, holding an indefinable object, seems to be taking part in the ceremony.

Fig. 7 Assyrian ritual meal; from a carved cylinder in the British Museum.

And in both these carvings[23], even if there is no relation with the subject we are discussing, we cannot help noting the seven mysterious globes.

Ceremonies analogous to those of Egypt, Assyria, and Chaldea in which the ritual consumption of the fish was the essential act, were practiced also in Asia Minor and, it is believed, in Cyprus. All had the same intention: the intimate union of the purified human being with the divinity, by the ingestion of the flesh of the sacred fish—as if it were an actual participation in its nature and qualities. The Roman conquests and the Pax Romana spread the knowledge of the fish-god's liturgies through the whole immense empire of the Caesars, as it did those of Athys and Mithra also, on the eve of the appearance of the Eucharist as the hearth of spiritual life in the new religion of Christianity.

Salomon Reinach says: "Surely no reasonable person will try to find the origin of Christianity in the sacrificial cult of the fish, but this cult did exist in Syria well before Christianity, and it is an historical certainty that we find it again there as we find survivals of two other zoomorphic cults, those of the dove and the lamb[24]." The possibility remains that these last echoes of the sacrificial rites of the symbolic fish and of the cults of Oannes, Dagon, and Ea had some influence on the choice of the fish as the symbol of the Redeemer and of the Eucharist.

Fig. 8 The fish carrying the eucharistic bread-basket. Painting in a 3rd-century Roman catacomb.

Because of this eucharistic significance, the first Christian artists depicted the fish in numerous, very clear ways. Sometimes above the chalice or on the altar, it seems to offer itself to the believer on the frescoes of the catacombs; it swims holding on its back the basket full of consecrated bread, or sometimes it has in its mouth the bread or the grape; on other occasions it waits on a platter, between the chalice and the wafer, to be distributed like them as food (Fig. 8). The banquet scenes are numerous in the paintings in the Roman catacombs, and the presence of the symbolic fish is very probably an allusion to the meal that Jesus shared after his Resurrection with seven of his disciples who were fishing on the shores of Lake Tiberias. When they approached, St. John says, they saw on the shore a fish placed over live coals with bread beside it, and Jesus said to them: "Come and dine," and he took the bread and gave it to them, and the fish also[25]. It seems certain that this gospel text contributed greatly to the eucharistic significance given the fish, for this episode of the seven favored disciples was the most popular of all the mystic banquets in early Christian art.

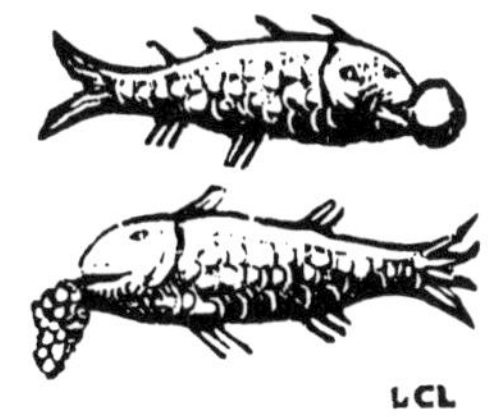
Fig. 9 Eucharistic fish from the catacomb of St. Calistus in Rome.

There are two fishes in the Roman catacomb of St. Calistus, one of which carries in its mouth the eucharistic bread, and the other the grape (Fig. 9). Sometimes the bread carried thus by a fish is contrasted with the fatal fruit of Eden, which has the same globular shape. On a bronze lamp, a dolphin carries the "living bread" and a griffin, symbolizing the Evil Spirit, holds in its beak the cursed fruit. It is the duel between Christ, the "New Adam," and the infernal spirit who caused the old Adam to sin, a duel symbolized by the opposition of the bread of life and the apple of death. "This interpretation," says Dom Leclercq, "is certainly beyond doubt[26]."

Fig. 10 Clasp in the museum at Nantes, from the Parenteau collection.

It seems to be the same symbolism on a bronze buckle in the Parenteau collection, which was found at Angers and which goes back to Gothic art. A dolphin holds a globular object in its mouth; its body turns back on itself in a serpent shape, terminating in a head that also holds a globule (Fig. 10).

Fig. 11 Angels battling with Leviathan; from a 13th-century illumination.

Like nearly all the chief symbols for Christ, in Christian symbolism the fish sometimes stood for the Evil Angel, Satan. It is chiefly the Book of Job, designating the monstrous king of the sea as Leviathan, who "maketh the deep to boil like a pot[27]," that has inspired the fish images that are often seen in medieval stained glass. On the other hand, in the Bibliothèque Nationale in Paris, we see angels with swords attacking the infernal fish (Fig. 11), accom-

Fig. 12 The "Devil of the Sea," from the works of Ambroise Paré.

plishing in God's place and in his name the prophecy of Isaiah: "In that day, the Lord with his sore and great and strong sword shall punish leviathan the piercing serpent, even leviathan that crooked serpent, and he shall slay the dragon that is in the sea[28] (Fig. 12)."

NOTES

Title Figure: Fish engraved on bone from the art of the Magdalenian epoch.

1. Judges 16:23 and *passim.*
2. Cf. Milne-Edwards, *Zoologie*, p. 488.
3. L. Delaporte, "Les Cylindres orientaux de la collection de Luynes," in *Aréthuse*, XII, 1926, p. 87.
4. See M.C. in *Le Voile d'Isis*, T. XXXIV. 1929, p. 153. Also Grasset-Dorcet, "Cypris et Paphos," in *Gazette des Beaux Arts*, 1868, p. 333.
5. Berossus: see the Leipzig edition, 1925, *passim.*
6. Cf. J. Menant, *Le Mythe de Dagon.*
7. Charles Lenormant, *Commentaire sur le Cratyle*, p. 125.
8. I Kings 4:5 (Douay-Rheims version), I Samuel 4:5 (KJV).
9. Cf. Mionnet, "Descriptions des medailles antiques," in suppl. T. II, p. 285, and Guillaume Rey, "Note sur un bronze phoenicien," in *Revue archéologique*, 2d series, T. X, p. 217.
10. Lucian, *De Syria Dea*, XXII.
11. *Ibid.*, XLV.

12. Alix Aymé, *Une Française au Laos*, 1932.
13. Guénon, "À propos du Poisson," in *Regnabit*, Feb. 1927, p. 218.
14. See M. Pezard, *Catalogue des Antiquités de la Susiane*, in the Louvre Museum, 1926, pp. 50 & 51.
15. Cf. Didron, *Histoire de Dieu*.
16. Cf. Leclercq, "Le Musée chrétien de la Chapelle de Saint-Germain-en-Laye," in *Revue archéologique*, 4th series, T. II, 1903, p. 291.
17. Leclercq and Marron, *Dictionnaire*, T. II, Vol. II, col. 21942.
18. Cf. Ananda Coomaraswamy, "Kawaja-Khadir et la Fontaine de Vie," in *Études Traditionelles*, T. XLIII, 1938; no. 224-225, p. 304.
19. Cf. de la Colombière, *La Science héroique*, p. 330 & Pl. 24.
20. Gevaert, *L'Héraldique*, p. 36.
21. St. John 1:3.
22. Tertullian, *De Baptismo*.
23. Cf. J. Menant, *Glyptique orientale*; also A. de Longpérier, in *Bulletin archéologique de l'Athaeneum français*, 1855, p. 100 and 1856, p. 96.
24. Reinach, *Cultes, Mythes et Religions*.
25. St. John 21:9-13.
26. Leclercq and Marron, *Dictionnaire*, T. IV, vol. 1, col. 293.
27. Job 41:31.
28. Isaiah 27:1.

End Figure: Lead seal from Tyre.

THE DOLPHIN

AMONG VARIOUS OTHER kinds of sea creatures, it was notably the dolphin that was taken as the emblem of Christ; but in pre-Christian times its use as a symbol was not as widespread as that of the anonymous fish. The use of the dolphin's image began and developed on the northeast shores of the Mediterranean and around the Black Sea, especially in Asia Minor, Greece, and Italy. Navigators of these countries regarded the dolphin as an animal of good omen and a benevolent traveling companion; it came to be called "the sailor's friend." Marvelous qualities of intelligence, almost of divination, of physical skill and of devotion were attributed to it, as well as wonderful feats of life-saving. The legend of Arion is well known—the gifted lyre player who was thrown overboard by his jealous companions and received by the dolphins who carried him safe and sound to the coast of Lycaonia[1]. It is said that the fishermen and sailors of those times considered it a crime against the laws of friendship to keep any dolphins that by chance became entangled in their nets, and carefully freed them and let them go[2].

This respect for the friendly sea animal explains the thousands of pre-Christian images of it on all sorts of monuments and art objects. But in primitive Christian art, in Rome at least, although the image of the fish in its generalized form had long been common in the iconography of the Savior, the dolphin did not appear till the end of the second century or the beginning of the third, when it began to be used to specify Christ the guide, or Christ the friend (Fig. 1); and it is in the role of friend and savior, guide of souls, that we see it presented, not only as the rescuer of the shipwrecked, but as the kindly and sure conductor of ships to harbor in sudden storms and darkness. The mystics found here the very image of Christ coming to the rescue of the soul especially in the dark hours of life and the shadows of death. Perhaps it was in this connection that Christianity accepted the relation of the dolphin with the cult of light, which was affirmed by a very ancient symbolism whose origin seems to be lost, but which the Ancients thought came from the mysterious regions of the North[3].

Fig. 1 Dolphin stamped on an amphora from the Greek island of Thasos.

We have seen the monster-fish of the Bible, Leviathan, emblem of Satan, attacked by angels; here we shall see the octopus, taken as the image of the prince of hell, attacked by Christ himself. The octopus, with its long, supple tentacles which like snakes paralyze and strangle its prey, presents an image really suggestive of Satan and his work of death. On a tomb of the Romanesque period in Aix-en-Provence, two dolphins are depicted, one devouring a fish, the other an octopus; perhaps this is only an allusion to the dolphin's voracity, for these animals fabled to be so full of gentleness and goodwill are in fact "the most carnivorous and cruel of all the family of cetaceans to which they belong[4]." But on the agate pastoral ring of Bishop Adhémar d'Angoulème (Fig. 2), whose episcopacy was in the eleventh century, there is carved the image of a dolphin twined around the trident, a symbol of Christ on the cross. Between its clenched jaws the divine Fish crushes the head of the octopus. I think there can be no doubt that this is the victory of Christ over Satan.

Fig. 2 Ring belonging to Bishop Adhémar of Angoulème.

Here the dolphin's symbolism joins that of the eagle, the

lion, the deer, the ibis, the stork, and other creatures that Christian iconography presents as victorious enemies of the serpent; and Dom Leclercq cites an example, taken from Rossi, of an antique seal embellished with a dolphin devouring a serpent[5].

Since the Renaissance, the symbolic dolphin appears rather rarely in religious art, except in ecclesiastical heraldry which has presented it several times in the course of the last two centuries[6].

NOTES

Title Figure: The dolphin on the cruciform lance; illumination in a 15th-century book.

1. Cf. Ovid and the Greek Athenaeus, XIII, 30. Aristotle assures us that the dolphin's speed is unimaginable; he goes so far as to say that it can leap over the largest ships: *History of Animals*, Book IX, ch. XXXVI.
2. Cf. Demoustier, *Lettres à Émilie sur la Mythologie*, LXXV.
3. Guénon, in *Regnabit*, Feb. 1927, p. 219.
4. Cuvier, *Regne animal*, T. I, p. 257.
5. Leclercq and Marron, *Dictionnaire*, col. 200.
6. Cf. d'Arlot de Saint-Saud, *Armorial des Prelats français au XIXe siècle*, p. 209.

End Figure: Graphite rubbing of graffiti in the Abbey of La Boissière d'Anjou; 13th or 14th century.

THE SEA URCHIN

IN THE TWELFTH century in the castles of France, the shells of fossilized sea urchins brought back from Palestine by the Crusaders were reverently collected. Special qualities were attributed to them and they were called "Stones of Judea[1]." Those better-informed in hermetism saw in the sea urchin the symbolic image of the earth's northern hemisphere, the only region known by the Ancients—the lines of dots descending from the top over the whole of the shell's surface were taken as meridians coming down from the pole, and the base represented the equator; two shells placed bottom to bottom thus formed a model of the whole terrestrial globe. More commonly, the sea urchin, whether living or fossilized, was looked upon as the symbol of rebirth after death. It is probably in this context that ancient Freemasonry took the theme of the sea urchin as "emblem of death and resurrection," as reformulated by René Guénon from one of the oldest Masonic books[2].

In France as in other western countries the fossil sea urchin is still the subject of widely differing superstitions. In the south, low forms of sorcery have taken possession of it, and in England it is still "one of the fetishes of white magic[3]" when considered as "the snake's egg." At Chamalières, in Auvergne, for instance, it is still regarded and venerated as a bringer of good luck.

An old legend from the north of France says that when the Virgin was baking bread in Nazareth, the child Jesus amused himself by shaping the dough into little rolls which he decorated with dots and gave to his playmates. Those that remained he multiplied to an infinite number and the angels carried them away to scatter in the countries where later the priests of Christ would change his own body into bread.

It may have been in Gaul, or a little further east, that the idea arose of the fossil sea urchin as a symbol of the "Egg of the World," as the Ancients called it, the *ovum anguinum* (snake's egg) of the Druids. "I have had the opportunity of seeing one of these (serpent's) eggs," wrote Pliny; "it was the shape and size of a small apple; its surface, cartilaginous and pitted with holes, resembled a polypary[4]." This could only be a sea urchin[5].

Nineteenth-century archeology was not mistaken in equating the sea urchin shells found in several pre-Christian Gallic burials with the *ovum anguinum* of the Druids, symbolizing the Egg of the World, thus the life of the world and its renewal. The sea urchin appears in some pre-Roman tombs in very special circumstances. In 1899 I myself with some companions dug up a tomb in Deux-Sèvres, still partly surrounded by a circular mound twenty meters across, which contained nothing but a little stone enclosure with a sea urchin in its center (Fig. 1). And there are other instances: A Breton tomb excavated by M. du Chatellier contained nothing but a fossil sea urchin, like a Neolithic tomb in Charente-Inférieure, and others; in one case the shell was accompanied by two beautiful bronze bracelets. It is generally thought that these funeral mounds empty of any occupant are cenotaphs commemorating the dead whose bodies could not be found.

Fig. 1 Symbolic sea urchin from the tomb of Poiron at Saint-Amand-sur-Sèvre in Deux-Sèvres. Actual size.

Some scholars claim that well before the Druidic period,

people of the Neolithic age or their immediate successors symbolically depicted the serpent and the egg by the alignment of menhirs such as those of Avebury in England and of Carnac in French Brittany. Their cromlechs or sacred circles of stones, symbolizing the Egg of the World, would thus delineate "the constellation of the Dragon, the Mount of Saint Michael representing the pole of the heavenly equator[6]." If this theory were accepted it would lend authority to the claims of other lithic sites in France, Scotland, and even North Africa to be seen as symbols of the Egg of the World.

It seems probable that the first idea of this symbolic egg arose in the countries where human beings first learned exact notions of the great astronomical laws—Chaldea, Susiana, Bactriana . . . Long before our era the pattern of many of the stars' paths was known there, and the Zodiac had been created. At its origin, the Egg of the World would only have been the space defined by the elliptical movement of the earth's rotation around the sun[7], and thus the compass of the vivifying action of the sun on our planet.

As it passed farther from its source, this first idea of the World Egg was soon wrapped in a cloud of fantastic interpretations which have often made it unrecognizable; but in spite of this, it can be found even today in the far corners of the earth. The Buddhist priests say that before time began, the world was enclosed in a mysterious egg which floated on the surface of the waters, and when it broke open, the world emerged from the night of nothingness. In the ancient cosmography of Japan, Chaos was represented by the lunar Bull who broke with his horn the golden egg from which the world emerged[8]. The Hindu Egg of the World, the *Brahmānda*, was contained in the primordial waters and hatched by the mysterious swan who was the vehicle of Brahma, the golden Embryo[9]. The orientalist René Guénon says that it is by the operation of the universal spirit, *Atma*, that the celestial ray of the uncreated germ is projected which will act upon the potential Universe, the *Brahmānda* or World Egg[10]. Some orientalists connect the black-and-white symbol of the *yin-yang* with the emergence of the World Egg from primordial chaos, when, in the words of Genesis, day and night were separated[11].

The Mazdeans of Persia also knew of a divine egg, connected with the creative action of Ahura Mazda; and in the iconography of the ancient Assyrians, the Egg of the World, appearing more often in a globular than an oval form, was attached to the idea of the propagation of life within the bounds of the sun's action, as it was also with the Syro-Phoenicians. For the Egyptians, the concept of the World Egg represented their idea of the entry of life into the created world, and they also gave it the globular form (Fig. 2). Creation of the Egg was sometimes attributed to Ptah, the father of life, and sometimes to Khnum, who was also said to give birth to the Egg through his mouth, which according to Guénon connects it with the symbolism of the Word[12]. Also, it is the function of Heqet, the frog-headed goddess, symbol of the embryonic state[13], who holds in her hand the key of life, the Ankh, "to give birth perpetually to the Egg of the World, which the male god Khnum perpetually fashions and shapes. She is the goddess of birth and rebirth[14] (Fig. 3)."

All this symbolism of the egg as the principle of life and so

Fig. 2
The Egyptian Egg of the World upheld by two sacred uraeus, each carrying the Key of Life.

Fig. 3
The Egg of the World on Egyptian monuments.

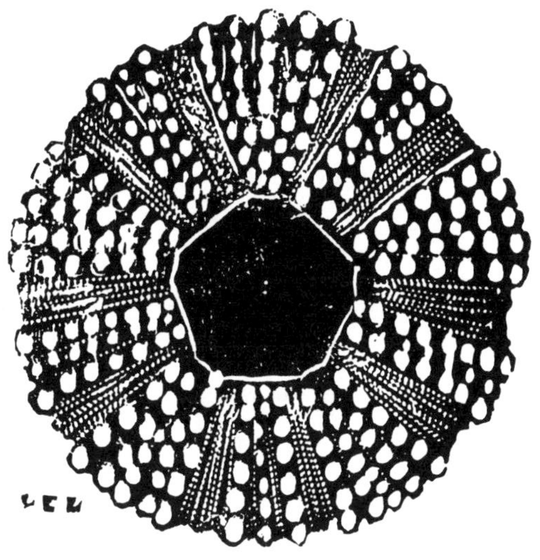

Fig. 4 Underside of sea urchin, showing the pentagonal mouth.

also of resurrection and the future life, and moreover of its production by the Word of the divinity—whether of the creator god or of his serpent[15]—brings us back to the symbolism of Christianity. The Mediterranean Albigenses of the twelfth century, affiliated with Manichaeism, who preserved the Christian symbols of the fish, the vase, and the dove, saw also in the living sea urchin an emblem of the Word made man: the body unseen within the shell showed the hidden divinity of Christ, the shell his human covering, and the long spines which cover the whole, like arrows all pointing outwards, signify the spreading of his word throughout the world. In the living sea urchin, the large pentagonal opening on the bottom of the shell corresponds to a mouth, placed at the creature's center (Fig. 4). It is equipped with five sharp teeth and is proportionally larger than that of nearly any other animal.

Perhaps the great attention given by Catharist symbolism to the pentagonal shape manifested by the lines on the surface of the sea urchin's shell as well as by the mouth opening might be a distant reflection, an obscure survival of Celtic ideas. In any case it evokes strangely the starry pentagon of Pythagoras, the most mysterious symbol of his teaching, the "Pentagram." It may be too bold to suggest that Pythagoras might have lent his Pentagram to the Druidic interpretation of the sacred *ovum anguinum* of the Gauls, with which he must assuredly have been acquainted.

Jar representing the sea urchin from Saint-Michel-Mont-Mercure in Vendée; Gallo-Roman period.

NOTES

Title Figure: Sea urchin carved as human face, from the Abbéville area. Pre-Roman.

1. Cf. Landin, *Dictionnaire de Minéralogie*, p. 334.
2. Guénon, letter to the author, July 12, 1925.
3. Cf. J. Gregorson Campbell, *Witchcraft and Second Sight in the Highlands*, Glasgow, 1902; pp. 84-88.
4. Pliny, *Natural History*. [*Editor's note*: A polypary is the base of a colony of polyps.]
5. Cf. Reinach, *Zagreus*, p. 217.
6. Th. Basilide, "La Pierre," in *Le Voile d'Isis*, T. XXXIX, 1934, no. 171, p. 99.
7. G. Bouchet, *Cosmogonie humaine*, p. 29.
8. *Ibid*., p. 78.
9. See Guénon, *Man and his Becoming According to the Vedānta*, pp. 56 & 101.
10. *Idem*, *Symbolism of the Cross*, ch. XXIV, p. 106.
11. Genesis 1:4-6.

12. Guénon, "Seth," in *Le Voile d'Isis*, T. XXXII, 1931, #142, p. 589.
13. Cf. Virey, *Religions de l'ancienne Égypte*, p. 291.
14. Leclercq and Marron, *Dictionnaire*, fasc. LXII, col. 1810.
15. See Moret, *Mystères*, II, *Le Mystère du Verbe Créateur*, pp. 105-139.

End Figure: The radiating spines of the sea urchin.

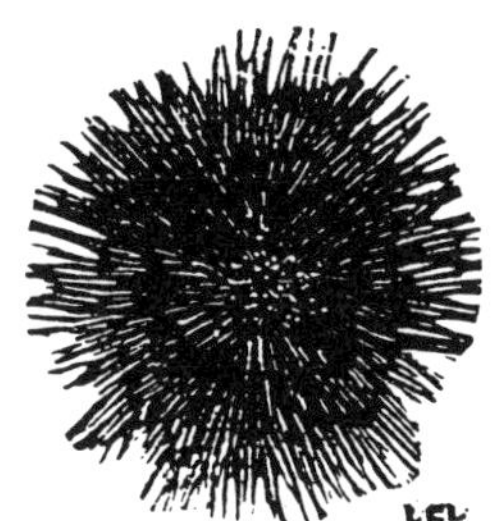

VI

INSECTS

THE BEE AND THE FLY

SINCE THE WORLD was young, human beings everywhere have looked upon the honeybee as one of God's gifts; in every language, poets have sung praise for its wisdom, its activity, its consummate industry. The oldest testimony we have of the relationship between the human being and the bee is painted on the wall of a prehistoric cave in Spain, the "Cueva de la Araña." This painting probably dates from the Magdalenian epoch, the earliest era of human life. It shows two people hunting for honey who, with the help of three supporting ropes, are robbing a swarm of bees on the face of a sheer cliff[1] (Fig. 1). Long after this, in the oldest hieroglyphs in Egypt, a honeybee appears in an essentially symbolic form, designating the pharaoh, who is represented by the double image of bee and reed, giving the meaning of: "Lord of Upper and Lower Egypt" (Fig. 2). A funerary hymn to the pharaoh Senwosret (Usertsen or Sesostris) III is expressed like this: "You have married the reed to the bee," which means that he ruled over the two lands of Egypt.

Fig. 1 Prehistoric painting in the Cueva de la Araña.

Fig. 2 Pharaonic bee from the stele of Amenenhet III in the Egyptian gallery of the Musée Guimet.

In this same civilization, the bee symbolized the human soul; as we shall see a little later on, it is found again with this meaning in tombs as the sign of humanity's hope, and of the soul's survival after death. This is probably also the idea behind the design of an Egyptian necklace made of gold beads, now belonging to the Museum of St. Germain[2].

The oldest Egyptian symbolists were able to make such good use of the bee's qualities because their contemporaries were the first civilized people to practice beekeeping in a methodical way. In the upper valley of the Nile, hives placed on boats floated down the river to lower Egypt, thus taking advantage of a succession of blossomings[3]. There is an immense distance between such well-arranged conditions and the occasional, chance scavenging of wild honey.

In Crete, the supreme god, born of the Earth Mother (Demeter-Ceres), was said to have been brought up in a cave by a Cretan princess on Amaltheia's milk and the honey of the queen bee Melissa; a coin from Praisos bears on one side the head of Demeter and on the other is a honeybee, the goddess Melissa[4] (Greek *meli*, honey). The cult of the honeybee spread very quickly from Crete through the Aegean islands and mainland Greece[5], and its traces can be seen in the archeological remains of the cities of Eleusis, Corinth, Miletus, Samothrace, and especially Ephesus and several other large Hellenic towns[6]. Even today, the honeybee is venerated with more or less superstition in the islands of Thasos and Athos and in Chalcidice, whose honeys are worthy of the poetic reputation of the honey of Hymettus; "bee-weed," the sweet-smelling melissa plant, is abundant in these regions.

At Eleusis and at Ephesus, the priestesses who in former times celebrated the ancient mysteries were called *Melissai*, "the Honeybees," and certain initiates who had obtained an unquestioned degree of purity were given the same name. The bee was thought to be endowed with divine gifts of astonishing and mysterious powers, and this belief was taught to the candidates for initiation in the inner circles of Samothrace, another religious center where the bee was revered[7].

Doubtless it is in connection with the liturgical and initiatic role played in the religious celebrations in Greece by the bee and its honey and wax that it enters as chief decorative motif into such pieces of jewelry as the metal bee-clasps mentioned by Reinach[8] (Fig. 3) that were found in excavations at Ephesus by English archeologists, and which recall the golden cicadas which fastened the hair of the devotees of Hera in the temple of Samos[9].

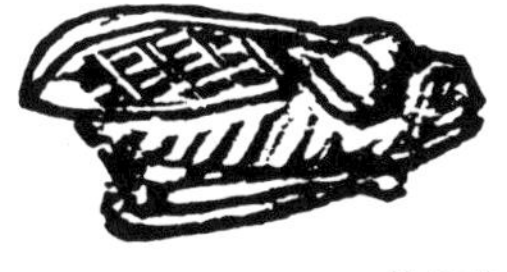

Fig. 3 Ephesian bee clasp, taken from Reinach, Répertoire.

At Camirus, at Miletus, at Delos, Thera, and Melos, plaquettes of gold have been found representing the Melissa goddess whose human torso is similar to that of Diana, the Persian Artemis, and whose lower body is that of a bee. The connection between the insect and the Latin Diana recalls not only the bee coins of Ephesus but also the passage in the Acts of the Apostles which describes St. Paul's visit to that city and the reverent regard there for the cult of "the great Diana of the Ephesians[10]."

This same regard extended from Lebanon to the extreme limits of Assyria, Medea, Susiana, and Babylonia. Only the Hebrews, although they valued honey very highly, took exception to the insect that produced it. From the Caucasus to modern Hungary, numerous barbaric examples of jewelry in the form of the bee from the first centuries of our era prove that it was venerated in all these regions[11].

Among the Romans, who were so strongly influenced by Greek ideas, honeybees were also greatly valued, and Virgil honored them with a beautiful song which is a veritable manual of ancient apiculture and at the same time a tribute of sincere admiration[12], although his contemporaries and compatriots sometimes regarded bees and the passage of their swarms as presages of ill fortune[13]. Among the Gauls also, the hard-working insect played an important part in their most ancient customs; hydromel, or honey water, (the basis of mead before it ferments), was their celebratory drink, and honeyed wine their stimulant. The bee also took part in the metaphysical symbolism of the Druids.

Even today, this symbolism is a living fact in Asia and also among the western Catholics. The Mazdeans maintain the early Persian belief that honey was a component part of the heavenly soma which intoxicated the divine beings, and among the Hindus, Krishna and Vishnu were likened to active honeybees; the latter is sometimes represented by the figure of a bee poised on a lotus leaf, and Krishna wears a blue bee on his forehead[14].

As I have said, the presence of bee symbols in ancient tombs seems to be related to the idea of the soul's survival after death. Even today, popular tradition in France, like that of all the Ancients, places the honeybee among the springtime signs of the Resurrection and sometimes associates it also with bereavements in the family. Bee symbols were found in the funerary treasure of Queen Ah-hotep I, which was taken to the museum at Gizeh.

Probably the same meaning should be recognized in the bee symbols found in the barbaric burials of the Gauls, whether Christian or not. In the tomb of the Frankish king Childeric, who died in 481, there were several hundred images of honeybees, made of garnets set in gold (Fig. 4). Tombs of approximately the same date in the districts of Aisne, Somme, and Lyons contained similar jewels.

Honey was also related to the human hope of another life that would be eternally happy, and was offered whenever possible to the spirits of the dead. The old historians Herodotus and Strabo inform us that in Assyria, the bodies of important people were buried in honey after having been coated with

Fig. 4 Bees made of garnets set in gold, from the tomb of Childeric at Tournai.

wax. This recalls the fable of Glaucus, the son of Minos and Pasiphaë, who after falling dead into a vat of honey came to life again when his lips touched this miraculous substance[15]. (The intervention of Aesculapius and his serpent which is sometimes applied to this tale is thought to be a later addition.)

From all these facts, modern archeologists are obliged to conclude, with Cook and Reinach, that among the Ancients the bee certainly represented the soul's survival "and another, limitless existence[16]."

Christian symbolism, following that of the Ancients, accepted the bee as one of the emblems of resurrection and immortality. The reason for this was the same as with the butterfly, the swallow in the West, and the frog in Egypt. The honeybee disappears during the winter season and reappears in spring; and since for ancient symbolism, as we have already noted, a season lasts for three months, these three symbolic months are translated as the three days during which the body of Christ was hidden in the tomb, after which it reappeared as does the bee after its three months in the darkness of the hive. And this is exactly how our country people in France think of it to this day[17].

The Bulletin of the Grand Lodge of Iowa, after several successive articles on the subject, came to the conclusion that the symbolic ideas of order, industry, and charity still associated with the honeybee are of fairly recent origin, and that in the past it was above all the emblem of resurrection and immortality[18].

Long before Plato uttered his inspired praise of the divine Word, the sacred Logos, the honeybee was in all likelihood already the emblem of human eloquence and the power that it can exert upon mankind. The Greeks, charmed by the magic of the spoken word and the sound of the human voice, compared their greatest orators and singers to the bees who by the work of their mouths produce delicious and strengthening honey; and also another honey, spoken of by Xenophon, Horace, and Pliny[19], which after a moment begins to trouble the hearer's thought and to keep it in confusion. Pertaining to the first of these two kinds of honey, that is, to wise and virtuous eloquence, are the fables telling how the bees of Thrace died all at once at the moment when the heart of the inspired singer Orpheus ceased to beat; also how the bees of Hymettus put drops of honey on the lips of the child Plato as he slept, and fed with their finest nectar the baby who was the future poet Pindar[20]. This legend was later transposed in *The Golden Legend* to apply to one of the most eloquent of the Christian pontiffs, St. Ambrose, the illustrious bishop of Milan: as a sleeping baby, it was said, the bees came to him and one by one entered his mouth and from there shot skyward like arrows. Seeing this, his father cried, "Blessed be the Lord! My son shall be holy before him and great in the company of men[21]." Among the Hebrews, the bee was related to the idea of language because of its name, *dbure*, and the Hebraic root *dbr* which means word or speech[22]. In the Orient, the Hindus dedicated the bee to the cult of the divine Word, Bhagavat, represented as within a white tent, robed in yellow and girdled with a rope of sweet-smelling flowers which the bees are busily plundering[23].

Virgil declared that "in bees there is a particle of the divine intelligence[24]." These words and others with which Virgil paid homage to the bee have supported a number of symbolists in their comparisons between the ceaseless spiritual activity of Christ in his church and the vivifying role of the mother bee in the hive. The comparison is made even more telling by the fact that Virgil, like Aristotle[25] and all the other ancient writers, never speaks of the "queen" bee but of the "king of the bees[26]," recognizing that the entire swarm owes its existence to her, that she is the center of their attention, and that the order and peace of the hive are her work.

By the very fact that she protects the hive, and that in it she finds the necessary conditions for her life-work of caring for the brood-comb and producing honey, the hive has been taken as the apt ideogram of a community life that is wisely ruled, peaceful, and fruitful, under the governance of one single head. The pre-Christian centuries understood this analogy, especially in Greece where, as for instance at Delphi and Ephesus, the priests and priestesses were called "bees" and their community was known as *hyron*, the hive. In medieval France, for the same reason, some big monasteries took a name derived from the life of the bees (French *abeilles*), such as the Cistercian *abbey* of Melleray, at the Meilleraie-de-Bretagne, in the diocese of Nantes, whose armorial bearings are still "of azure with a silver hive, accompanied by three bees of the same[27] (Fig. 5)."

Fig. 5 Coat-of-arms of the Abbey of Notre Dame de Melleray.

The Church, also, whose head is the pope, has been allegorically likened to the hive: within its shelter, the care and the authority of the supreme pontiff must preserve the sacred teaching which is symbolized by honey, and set forth the discipline which gives each one his place in the Christian society.

In the same way that it represents the spiritual sense of the monastery and of the Church, quite naturally it also represents the human family; and by extension, the ancient symbolists and all their successors have taken it as the natural representation of nations and powers[28] where, as in the hive, there is one sole chief of state in command and responsible for its welfare, like the pope in the Church's government and the emperor or king in a monarchic state. From this single head, as from the queen bee, derives the social life and order which constitutes the nation's prosperity. In this symbolic sense, heraldry has made bees represent the subjects who owe their sovereign the same obedience that is rendered to the queen mother in the hive[29]. In this traditional mode, honeybees and their hive symbolize the social virtues that make nations great: respect for authority, submission to law, honest hard work, economy, and justice. This is undoubtedly what is meant to be expressed by the bee harvesting a flower on one of the most beautiful modern Italian coins, from the reign of Victor Emmanuel III. The thirteenth-century writer Thomas de Cantimpré, inspired by Albertus Magnus[30], compared the hive with the Christian city[31].

The bees' life in the hive, and their wonderful relations with their queen and with each other, have naturally come to represent wisdom, order, and agreement; their industry and the valor with which they defend their hive and their honey have made them perfect symbols of activity, courage, and self-sacrifice. The ancient authors saw in them also the representation of justice, and in this were followed by the medieval symbolists, who at the same time made them emblems of Christ as judge[32]. In the profane sense, in medieval heraldry the life of the bee represented forethought, because their summer's work ensures provisions for the winter[33]. But the virtue exemplified most particularly by the bee is that of chastity. Virgil has sung more beautifully than any other ancient writer of the pure life of the bees "who do not abandon themselves to love nor weaken themselves with pleasures, and know not either the union of the sexes nor the labor of giving birth[34]." Plutarch goes further and assures us that bees become angry if a man approaches them directly from a woman's bed[35], and will aim their stings at libertines[36]. These statements at least show what a reputation for chastity the honeybee held in ancient thought. In medieval heraldry of the nobility, it was taken as the image of moral purity: Vulson de la Colombière, echoing in 1669 the old French heraldists, said of the bees that "they denote chastity and virginity, from which it comes that their wax is offered to God as something very pure[37]."

Whence comes the strange belief that certain bee-swarms, instead of emerging from an overpopulated hive, are born from the rotting bodies of animals sacrificed to the divinity? It is a very old notion and seems to be connected with the ancient Egyptian mysteries. With every appearance of probability, Alexandre Moret relates to the rites of Isis one which is said to consist in bringing about the spontaneous formation of bees in the skin of a sacrificed bull; and he sees in this a sign of resurrection symbolized by the flight of the new swarm[38]. This corresponds to what I have said before about the pre-Christian origins of the role formerly attributed to the honeybee as an emblem of resurrection. For others, this image is simply that of the initiate who, wholly dedicated to the pursuit of duty and goodness, produces thereby for himself and for others fruitful virtues which will go on exerting their beneficent action after his death.

Virgil describes the process, in his time, in Egypt near Canopus, of the sacrifice of a two-year-old bull which was to give birth to the sacred swarm: it was killed, he said, by successive blows, without the letting of blood; then it was enclosed in a little roofed building just big enough to hold it. This little temple had four windows open to the four winds. The victim's body was laid on planks of aromatic wood. "Soon the flesh of the animal's body begins to heat and to ferment, and surprisingly, a cloud of insects is seen to emerge from it, first crawling, then vibrating their wings, then growing gradually strong enough to launch into the air, and finally taking flight with a great noise like a heavy summer rain, or like the hail of arrows let loose by the Parthian as a signal of war[39]."

This bloodless sacrifice of the bull was made in the spring "before the coming of the swallows," Virgil says, "before the meadows are adorned with new flowers." Again, the bees born of this death belong to the symbolism of the soul's survival after death.

The ancient Jews were suspicious of honey because of these practices which the Syrians and other neighbors must have copied from the Egyptians. The Alexandrian Philo Judaeus, a contemporary of Jesus Christ, wrote that according to the law "the Eucharistic bread must be without leavening and without honey, not wishing that either substance be brought to the altar: the honey perhaps because the bee that makes it is a filthy creature, said to be engendered in the rotting flesh of cattle, as wasps and bumblebees are from the bodies of horses. . . .[40]"

The Bible does not say that the bees of the swarm that Samson found in the lion's carcass were formed in its body, nor does it call impure the honey he gathered from it and which he presents as a symbol of sweetness and comfort born from strength: "Out of the eater came forth meat, and out of the strong came forth sweetness[41]."

Moret says that the idea that souls sometimes took the form of bees and emerged through the skin of the dead being was familiar to the Egyptians, and Rudolf Steiner praises the Greek concept which compares the soul to a bee: "like the bee which leaves the hive and gathers the nectar of flowers to make it into honey, the soul coming forth from God enters the world and gathers the nectar to take it back to the spirit's home[42]." Four centuries before Steiner, St. Francis de Sales also compared souls to bees during their earthly sojourn, alluding to Samson's lion[43]. *La Vigne mystique*, attributed to St. Bernard, the twelfth century "doctor with the honeyed tongue," says that bees "are an image of souls which can and know how to lift themselves on the wings of contemplation."

From one century to another, Christian spirituality has seen in the bee the allegorical image of the person who works in every worldly season to gather merits for another life, as the bee during the summer collects the honey that will nourish the colony during the winter.

In the popular traditions of several European countries, there are legends which say that the souls of dead family members that have not yet found grace before God sometimes come to take shelter in the hives belonging to their descendants; this doubtless is why "the countryman of Vendée still associates the hive with deaths in his family[44]." In certain undeveloped countries, the bee is simply the good spirit which protects the human being's existence. Among the Eskimos, for example, a live bee is rolled over the bare shoulders of a woman about to have a child, in order to ease the birth. This bee fetish is carefully saved and given later to the child as a powerful amulet to protect its life[45].

In spite of what certain authors have written, the dipterous insect which one sometimes sees represented in connection with sorcery or directly with demonism is *not* the bee, nor is it the wasp or the bumblebee, but the fly: not, to be more precise, the bothersome little house fly, but the blowfly, which includes several different species. With its deplorable reputation in the symbolism of the Ancients, in that of Christianity the blowfly has always been regarded as the antithesis of the honeybee. The bee hardly ever alights except on the blooming cups of flowers, and lives continually in a perfumed atmosphere; it uses only the purest nectar and pollen for its nourishment and for making its honey and wax. Its brood-comb is born and grows in sweet-smelling compartments; everything about it is pure, beautiful, and admirable. The blowfly, on the contrary, crawls about on dung and lives habitually among the most nauseating smells; it spoils clean things with the deposit of its eggs, and feeds on poisonous substances fermented in rotting flesh; its larvae hatch and develop in corruption; everything about it is filthy and repulsive. The Middle

Fig. 6 18th-century hermetic image of Asmodeus, the demon of impurity.

Ages made it the symbol of the base instincts in that class of people that can be called "the scum of the earth" which lives in shame, and in ascetic symbolism it is the image of carnal desires. Throughout the Christian era it has been considered one of the emblems of lewdness. Popular heraldry in its turn adopted it to represent "importunity and effrontery," because it alights with equal impudence "on a king's brow and on the bosom of a queen[46]."

Ancient demonology has always placed a blowfly, symbolizing a demon, near the ear of a Christian who is undergoing temptation. Two infernal entities (who in fact are the same), Asmodeus and Beelzebub, have been represented by the symbolic fly: Beelzebub, who is called in the Gospel "the prince of devils," and which demonology designates with the name "lord of the flies"; Asmodeus whom the Talmud also names "the prince of devils," and whom demonology terms "the spirit of impurity."

Even in glacial regions, flies represent evil spirits: "The Lapps claim that their sorcerers keep 'miraculous flies,' that is, malevolent spirits[47]."

The copy of a drawing in a sixteenth- or seventeenth-century manuscript, among the papers of the Abbé Leriche, the author of several works on diabolic possession, symbolizes Asmodeus by the skull of a goat; the animal's horns end in darts which, if one can rely on the language of asceticism, must represent the "prickings of the flesh"; between the horns is the fly of carnal desires[48] (Fig. 6).

Beelzebub appears in the Gospels in the scene where the Pharisees accuse Jesus of being possessed by this demon: he casts out devils, they say, through the prince of devils[49]. The name Beelzebub has been translated as "Lord of the Flies," and as such, under the name Myode, he was honored in pre-Christian Rome and invoked against the attacks of flies of all kinds.

The commonly accepted translation of the name Beelzebub as "Lord of the Flies" is not, however, indisputably correct. In his study of Arad-Hiba, the governor of Jerusalem, M. J. Halévy, has shown that according to the evidence of tablets found at Tel el-Amarna, there existed in Palestine an ancient village called Zebub; Beelzebub, or Baal-Zebub, might be the local god, the Baal, or Bel, of the town of Zebub[50].

But the popular association "Lord of the Flies" persisted in numerous tales of diabolic possession. In 1630, at Limoges, it is said that after the hanging of a sorcerer, there emerged from his body "a demon in the form of a huge green fly ... that passed whistling over the gallows drawing a long trail of smoke behind it[51]." In 1663, during her trial as a witch, Catherine Ebermann was constantly harassed by flies[52] and her judges came to the conclusion that she was being visited by "her Beelzebub," the king of the flies[53].

Gnats and the common small fly have always been taken as signs of something valueless and without duration. Human life, even if it attains the centenary, is ephemeral in the context of the infinity of time, and is often represented by the image of a fly which lives only for a single season or perhaps a single day, and is swept out of existence by a trifle. Between the two infinities of the past and the future, human life is only a moment and the soul is an eagle which ought not to waste its energy in futile things. "The eagle does not catch flies," says an heraldic device: *Aquila non capit muscas*[54].

NOTES

Title Figure: The Roman hive in Virgil's time.

1. See Comte Fr. de Rilly, *Gazette Apicole*, T. XXIX, 1928, #287, p. 222.
2. Salomon Reinach, *Catalogue du Musée de Saint-Germain-en-Laye*, p. 177, B. 2.

3. *Gazette Apicole*, *loc. cit.* (note 1), #217, p. 233.
4. See Glotz, *Civilisation égéenne*, Book III, Ch. II, p. 291.
5. Cf. Antoine Diogène, *Oeuvres*, Book XIII.
6. See E. Neustadt, *De Jove Cretico*, III.
7. Cf. Strabo, *Geogr.*, x, 3.
8. Reinach, *Répertoire*, T. IV, p. 550, #8.
9. Cf. Athenaeus, *Deipnosophistae*, C. XIII.
10. Acts 19:24-34.
11. Baron T. de Baye, "Bijoux barbares en forme de mouches," in *Bulletin et Mem. des Antiquaires de France*, 1853, pp. 137, 139.
12. Virgil, *Georgics*, Book IV.
13. See Titus Livy, *Historia romana*, XXI, 48 and XXII, 1. Also Plutarch, *Parallel Lives*, "Brutus," 44-58.
14. Cf. de Gubernatis, *Mythologie zoologique*, T. II; also G. Lanoë-Villène, *Le Livre des Symboles*, T. I, p. 11.
15. Lanoë-Villène, *op. cit.*, T. I, p. 13.
16. *Ibid.*, *loc. cit.*; also Reinach, *Revue archéologique*, 3d series, T. XXVI, 1895, p. 213.
17. Cf. Leo Dessaivre, "Essai de Mythologie locale," in *Bulletin de la Société des Sciences, Lettres et Arts de Deux-Sèvres*, 1880.
18. Fasc. February-March 1930.
19. Xenophon, *Anabasis*, IV, 5; Horace, *Ars poetica*, XXXVII, 3; Pliny, *Natural History*, XXI, 13.
20. Aelian, *Historia divina*, XXI, 45.
21. See the biographies of St. Ambrose; also A. David, "Rome au quatrième siècle" in *Le Foyer*, T. XII, p. 77.
22. Cf. Fred. Portal, *Les Symboles des Égyptiens*, 1840, p. 56.
23. *Bag. Pura*, III, 15.
24. Virgil, *op. et loc. cit.*
25. Aristotle, *History of Animals*, Bk. IX, Ch. XXVIII.
26. Virgil, *op. et loc. cit.*
27. Cf. d'Arlot de Saint-Saud, *Armorial des Prelats français du XIXe siècle*, p. 336.
28. See Lanoë-Villène, *op. cit.*, T. I, p. 17.
29. De la Colombière, *La Science héroique*, p. 376.
30. Cf. Albert Garreau, *Saint Albert le Grand*, p. 25
31. De Cantimpré, *Bonum universale de Apileus*, Colvenerius, Douai, 1627.
32. Cf. *Revue de l'Art chrétien*, 1887, p. 167.
33. De la Colombière, *op. cit.*, p. 326.
34. Virgil, *op. et loc. cit.*
35. Plutarch, *Precept. conjug.*, XLIV.
36. *Idem, Caus. nat.*, XXXVI.
37. De la Colombière, *op. cit.*, p. 376.
38. Moret, *Rois et dieux*, p. 100.
39. Virgil, *op. et loc. cit.*
40. *Oeuvres de Philon Juif*, French tr. 1588, p. 341.
41. Judges 14:8-14.

42. Rudolf Steiner, *Le Mystère chrétien* (introduction), Perrin edition, p. 38.
43. François de Sales, *Traicté de l'Amour de Dieu*, 1617, p. 1078.
44. André Godard, *La Piété antique*, p. 285.
45. Knud Rasmussen, *Du Groenland au Pacifique*, p. 189.
46. De la Colombière, *op. et loc. cit.*
47. Edm. Demâitre, "Une visite à un Mmaïd ou grand Sorcier lapon," in *Excelsior*, Sept. 23, 1931.
48. See above, Part II, "The Goat," Fig. 2, an image of the same kind and from the same source.
49. St. Matthew 12:22-30; St. Mark 3:20-30.
50. Cf. *Comptes rendus de l'Académie des Inscriptions*, meeting of March 4, 1892. [*Editor's note:* Still another reading of *Zebub* translates it as *devil*, which would give *Bel-Zebub* the strange and comprehensive meaning of *God-Devil.*]
51. According to Robert du Dorat: see Dom Fonteneau, *Recueils manuscrits de la Bibliothèque de Poitiers*, T. XXI, # 603.
52. See J. Diffenbach, *De la Sorcellerie en Allemagne avant et après la Reforme*, p. 96.
53. Cf. Fred Delacroix, *Les Procès en Sorcellerie au XVIIe siècle*, p. 77.
54. Andigné, Anjou, et Poitou, *D'argent à trois aiglettes au vol abaissé de gueules.* V. R. Pétiet, *Armorial Poitevin*, p. 7.

End Figure: 18th-century medal showing the bee and flower.

THE SCARAB AND THE SCORPION

THE SACRED SCARAB of the Egyptians is at the head of an important family of insects among the numerous species of the coleoptera. Beetles are squat, awkward creatures without any claim to elegance. The kind venerated by the Egyptians (*scarabeus sacer, Ateuchus Aegyptorium*) is big and dark-colored with metallic glints; the body is divided in three parts—head, corselet, and abdomen which is protected by two solid, horny wing-sheaths covering the delicate wings. These insects live in dung which they consume, and their bodies secrete an oily substance that prevents filth from sticking to them. In spring, they mould a ball of ordure in which they place their eggs, in which the larvae find nourishment from the moment of birth. "The scarab," says Horapollo, "buries its ball in the earth where it remains hidden for twenty-eight days, a period of time equal to that of a lunar cycle, during which its offspring come to life. On the twenty-ninth day, which the insect knows because it is the conjunction of the Moon with the Sun, and the birthday of the world, it opens the ball and throws it into the water, and the young beetles come out of it[1] (Fig. 1)."

Fig. 1 The scarab pushing its ball backwards; from Fabre, La Vie des Insectes, *in* Souvenirs Entomologistes.

This ball, which among the Egyptians represented "the Egg

of the World," is not perfectly round: the end is elongated, so that it is slightly pear-shaped. The hatching chamber is in the pointed end, where the larva, just out of the egg, first begins to move. This beetle inhabits all the regions surrounding the Mediterranean, even Provence, but it is especially numerous in the hot countries of the Near East, where it grows to its greatest size.

Since the days of the oldest dynasties, the scarab was connected with the symbolism of the rising sun[2]. Brugsch says that when it is shown in flight, it symbolizes the sun in its course[3] (Fig. 2). In this position it was also the emblem of the swift, vivifying, and intelligent ray of the sun, the *spiritus et mens*, *logos* or *ratio* of the Ancients, that is, the breath of life, the soul, the understanding, the inspired word, reason. It is then represented with spread wings passing underneath the wing-sheaths; its front legs hold the solar disk and the hind legs the ball of dung containing the eggs of its offspring, or

Fig. 2 The scarab lifting the sun above the solar bark; painting on a mummy case (actual size).

Fig. 3 Scarab from the tomb of Ramses IV, from Lefébure.

perhaps the "divine seal" (Figs. 3, 4, and 5), or the "key of life."

The black insect and the radiant sun have one thing in common: both are purifiers. The former demolishes foul and noxious ordure, the other dries it up and gets rid of it with the heat of its rays. The Egyptians considered both to be instruments of the divinity and were grateful, transforming the actual triviality of the little beetle's beneficent action into pure glory; they placed it in surroundings of perpetual light by giving the scarab the "Star of the Morning"—the Venus of our modern astronomy[4], according to Maspéro—as its companion by night, and the sun by day.

Pushing this hearth of light in front of him, the scarab appears on the walls of gigantic monuments and on many inscriptions of the most varied kinds, like a veritable light-bearer holding the torch of the world above its head. It is the illuminator and at the same time the purifier, and also the vivifier, because its ball of filth is a receptacle of life, so that the Egyptian symbolists saw in it an image of the mysterious Egg

Fig. 4 Scarab holding the solar disk and the divine seal.

Fig. 5 Scarab holding the solar disk, and behind it its egg-ball, symbolizing the Egg of the World. From a painting on wood, from Alexandria.

of the World, the life-principle itself. In their hieroglyphic language the scarab at rest is the ideograph of existence; its name, *kpr* (*kheper, khepra*) is translated by the infinitive *to be*[5]. Kheper or Khepra is Being, Existence, "which is a perpetual becoming[6]." That is why in the Egypto-Hellenistic epoch, the god Khepra was connected with the symbolism of the fecund Aphrodite, the Mother Goddess.

Sometimes the scarab pushes before him not the solar disk but the Egg of the World (Fig. 6), characterized by the life that emanates from it and which itself is sometimes represented by the image of the ankh or "key of life." The symbolic insect, thus linked with the idea of the universal life principle, was attributed to the god Kheper or Khepra, whose head was shaped like the scarab or who carried above his head the image of the insect of the same name. "It thus symbolized the transformations that ceaselessly renew life in the world, as every morning a new sun replaces the sun of the day before[7]." Khepra—whose name is the name of the scarab—is an image of the One God. An Egyptian hymn which chants the mysterious names of the immanent God expresses it thus: "Khepra is an image, Ra is an image; He himself created himself in millions of ways. He remains forever in all things, the Unique Living One in whom all things live[8]."

Fig. 6 The scarab within the solar disk, upheld by the falcon of Horus, on a shaft of Tutankhamon's chariot.

The contemplatives and wise men of the most ancient times in Egypt made a veritable microcosm of the scarab in flight. When shown in this way, its wings are separated in three parts covered successively with scales, with hair, and with feathers (Figs. 3 and 6), symbolizing fish, animals, and birds: ocean, earth, and air—the whole universe! These three zones of the scarab's wings, in another order of ideas, also represented three planes of ascending levels: the material plane, the psychic, and the divine.

Symbolizing the transformations through which life on earth is maintained and perpetuated, among the Egyptians the scarab or *khepra* also symbolized those that lead the human soul beyond death to the fulfilment of their destiny. So it is one of the images of survival and of "becoming"; the very word *khepra* means "to become" and "to be transformed[9]." On the ceiling of the subterranean burial chamber of the pharaoh Seti I, facing the place of the sarcophagus, an enormous scarab rolls the ball of the sun, and on each side of it are depicted the hieroglyphs: Resurrection—Eternity[10]. The scarab keeps this same double meaning of resurrection and eternity when it refers to the myth of Ptah, the god of everlasting life, "primordial father of fathers, older than the sun[11]," as can be seen at Memphis where the solar insect crowns the image of Ptah whose feet crush the crocodile, the symbol of darkness and of evil[12].

The symbol of resurrection which gives new life to beings, and of eternity which ensures the possibility of life everlasting, the scarab was also the symbol of the human heart which the Egyptians regarded as the seat of the knowledge of conscience. Since this knowledge implies responsibility for one's actions, it follows that transformation and the soul's future life are dependent on the human heart facing the tribunal of Osiris, he who weighs souls and whose judgment determines their fate for all eternity. Consequently, in the process of mummification of the dead, a scarab of molded glass or of common stone for the middle class, or of gemstone for those of rank, was placed inside the chest in the central region of the heart, and the hierophant who consecrated the symbol recited a formula over it: "My heart which comes to me from my mother, my heart necessary for my existence on earth, do not rise up against me, do not testify against me[13]." All the Egyptian sacred literature consistently joins the human heart

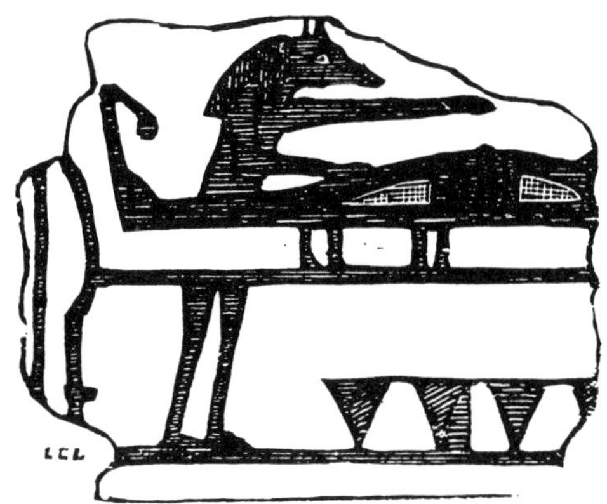

Fig. 7 An Egyptian priest representing Anubis performs the Osirian rites on a mummy. Painted on wood, from the de Rilly collection.

with the two sacred symbols of the scarab and the vase.

An Egyptian painting shows a priest who wears the head of Anubis practicing the Osirian rites over the chest of a mummy in which the scarab has just been placed (Fig. 7).

This sacred insect also represents the myth of Horus, the heart of the Divinity of which Thoth is the Tongue or Word: "Horus, the Heart; that is, the spirit which animates, and Thoth, the Word, instrument of creation[14]."

Thus representing Horus, it sometimes happened that the scarab was shown with a human face[15]. Sometimes also the symbolic falcon of Horus carried on its head the image of the scarab within the solar disk itself (Fig. 6). The beetle, carrying the Egg of the World, "hath set his tabernacle in the sun[16]" and as is also said elsewhere, "O Lord my God, thou hast put on praise and beauty, and art clothed with light as with a garment[17]."

Veneration for the symbolic scarab survived the disappearance of the Egyptian pharaonic religion. It persisted for some time in the same way in Phoenicia, Cyprus, Asia Minor, and even in the Mediterranean regions of central and western Europe. South of Egypt, even after the introduction of Christianity, the scarab continued to hold its place in the popular superstitions among the Copts and the Abyssinians, and progressively down the length of the equatorial coasts; we even find it once more in the eighteenth century among the Kaffirs and the Hottentots who revered the rose-chafer beetle, with its golden glints, more religiously even than the moon itself, which was nevertheless considered the divine protectress and the dispenser of rain and fruitfulness[18].

Fig. 8 Three ladybirds; 18th-century ornamental motif.

There are simple country traditions concerning several members of the beetle family who live close to us in Europe. Two of these are the rosebug and the ladybird. The rosebug in the popular belief brings good fortune to anyone who finds it during the week of Corpus Christi, especially when it is found in the roses cut for the festival processions. The ladybird—of which we know over a hundred varieties of different colors: orange spotted with black, black with white, yellow with purple, etc.—is called by the country people in France God's Creature or Jesus' Creature[19]. It used to be said that it drives away evil spirits and reverses the effects of malefic enchantments, perhaps because its larva is an active aphid-killer who wages efficient war on noxious plant lice on the stems of young plants (Fig. 8).

In ancient Europe, especially in the regions east of Italy, the scarab was one of only two cold-blooded creatures accepted in magic as a sacrificial victim; the other was the snake.

The first Christians of Egypt considered the myths of Greece and Rome, and of Syria and Persia, as accursed, but not the old gods of their own ancestors, seeing in Horus a sort of prefiguration of Christ, and in the ibis the symbol of his role as purifier of the world. These Christians, who recognized Christ in the images of the sphinx, the phoenix, the falcon, or the eagle, must certainly have given consideration to the scarab whom their forefathers had revered in the triple role of purifier, illuminator, and vivifier. I do not know, however, of a single orthodox text that could sustain this very probable hypothesis; but it is a different matter with the Gnostics. It is well known that they borrowed a great deal from ancient Egypt, and at the foremost Christian school in Alexandria, a Gnostic text, written in Greek, says the following in the course of an invocation:

"Fire has overtaken the greatest idols, and heaven has been swallowed up, knowing nothing of the circle of the holy Scarab called *phorei*; the scarab with wings, the Lord who dwells in the midst of heaven, has had his head pulled off, has been torn in pieces; his greatest and most glorious powers have been destroyed, and after being taken prisoner, the master of heaven has been put to death[20]."

Under these intentionally enigmatic, mystery-veiled terms, it seems clear that "the holy Scarab" here designates Jesus Christ who for the Gnostics was identified with the young Horus seated on the sacred lotus of ancient Egypt.

On a Gnostic scarab of carnelian which belonged to Canon Davin of Versailles, the line of separation between the wing-sheaths of the beetle and the connection with the corselet, which naturally represent the Greek letter *tau*, T, are so emphasized that it is the obvious intention to underline this symbolic form which is one of the primitive images of the Christian cross. The underside of the scarab carries an open hand marked with a five-pointed star and accompanied by a crescent, a palm branch, and a sign that somewhat resembles the crooked staff carried by the augur in pagan Rome (Fig. 9).

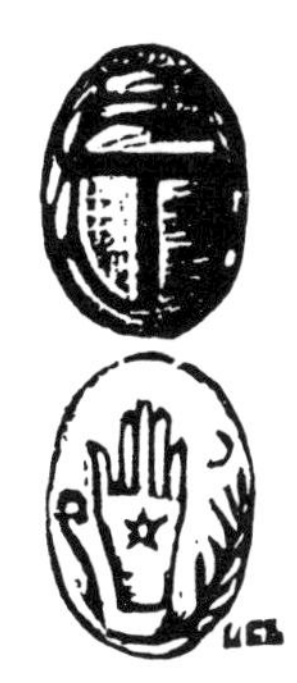

Fig. 9
Gnostic scarab, the back in relief, the underside engraved.

The image of the scarab, related to the myths of Ptah and Horus, is one of the ideograms for good; on the same monuments, Horus, symbol of the principle of good, struggling against the destructive evil principle, tramples the scorpion under his feet together with the crocodile and the serpent[21]; evidently the scorpion here is one of the signs for evil.

For the ancient symbolists, many characteristics place the scorpion and the scarab in opposition. In the symbolic iconography of ancient Egypt, the scarab carries the solar disk which is the source of life; its hind legs hold the ball which contains its eggs and symbolizes the Egg of the World, the divine principle of universal life. The scorpion, on the contrary, holds its victim in the claws of its front legs so as to devour it, and carries behind it its poison gland and dart, reservoir and instrument of death.

Fig. 10
The scorpion on the Egyptian zodiac of Denderah.

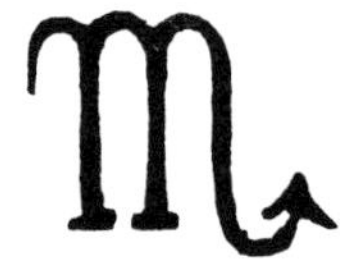

Fig. 11
The astrological sign of the constellation Scorpio.

The scorpion's sting is very painful and sometimes fatal. Appolodorus assures us that the poison is white and that the sting, often mortal for women, is always so for virgins[22].

In the most ancient zodiacs the scorpion is the sign ruling the two neighboring halves of the months of October and November; according to an author of former times, this is because its sting is more terrible at that moment than at any other time (Figs. 10 and 11). Because of the dread inspired by its sting, the scorpion's name was given to one of the most efficacious of the ancient machines of war, which hurled sharp steel javelins for a considerable distance[23]. Polybius tells how Archimedes made use of this engine of death in the defense of Syracuse in the year 212 before our era[24].

Christian symbolism has retained the scorpion's former place as the specific emblem of evil[25], although David did not mention it, along with the asp, the basilisk, the lion, and the dragon, as one of those put under the feet of the Messiah[26].

The old astrology, whose roots extend much farther back than our era, made the scorpion the ruler of the human genital organs, and claimed that the astral influence of the zodiacal sign Scorpio on those whom it touched led to fornication; this was also believed in early Christian times[27]. From the beginning, Christian symbolism made the scorpion and its poison the sign of heresy and its ravages. At the end of the second century, Tertullian authenticated this meaning then he wrote *Scorpiace*, which he began with a description of the terrible insect and its method of attack. Christian art in every epoch has maintained the scorpion's image as the representation of heresy. In the Middle Ages it was often personified as a woman pouring scorpions and reptiles of every kind from a horn of plenty[28]. In the heraldry of the nobility of the same period, at least in France and up until today, the scorpion stood for "impostors, slanderers, and traitors whose tongues are full of venom[29]."

In a different order of ideas, the Middle Ages made the scorpion one of the attributes of dialectic[30], "because it does not easily let itself be captured[31]." A fresco in the cathedral at Puy-en-Velay shows us Dialectic teaching Aristotle. She holds a lizard in her right hand (as does a similar statue at Chartres) "because it is sly, and in the left hand a scorpion, from which she has nothing to fear as she is invulnerable[32]."

Fig. 12 The scorpion on a medieval zodiac, from Austria; 15th century.

On several medieval works the scorpion is shown as it were with a double life, a double malevolence, with its tail ending in a second head, that of a reptile ready to strike. This is shown by several images of the fifteenth century *Grant Kalendrier et Compost des Bergiers* (*Shepherd's Kalender*), and the one I reproduce here (Fig. 12).

NOTES

1. Horapollo, translated by J.H. Fabre, *La Vie des Insectes*, p. 52.
2. See Mario Menier's French translation of Plutarch's *Isis and Osiris*, p. 48, note.
3. Brugsch, *Religion und Mythologie der alten Aegypter*, pp. 213 and 249.
4. Cf. Maspéro, "Les Hypogées royaux de Thèbes," in *Revue de l'Histoire des Religions*, (1888) p. 310.
5. Cf. Steinilber-Oberlin, *Les Hiéroglyphes*, p. 23.
6. E. Amélineau, "La Cosmogonie de Thales et les Docteurs de l'Égypte," in *Revue de l'Histoire des Religions* (1910) p. 32.
7. Virey, *Religion de l'ancienne Égypte*, p. 146.
8. *Ibid.*, p. 196. Also, Hilbert, *Hilbert Lectures*, p. 233.
9. Virey, *op. cit.*, p. 228.
10. Cf. Myriam Harry, "La Vallée des Rois," in *L'Illustration*, (March 22, 1924) p. 256.
11. Virey, *op. cit.*, p. 170.
12. See P. Rouais, *Histoire des Beaux Arts*, p. 26, and Gustav le Bon, *Les premières Civilisations*, p. 271.
13. Virey, *op. cit.*, p. 213.
14. Moret, *Mystères égyptiens*, p. 126.
15. Grasset-Dorcet, "Cypris et Paphos" in *Gazette des Beaux Arts*, October 1868, p. 337.
16. Psalms 18:6, Douay-Rheims version.
17. Psalms 103:1-2, Douay-Rheims version.
18. See F. Kolbe, *Description du Cap de Bonne Espérance*, (1741), p. 180.
19. For such titles connecting the ladybird with Jesus Christ or with the Virgin Mary in other European countries, see de Gubernatis, *Mythologie zoologique*, T. II, p. 225.
20. Cf. Leclercq and Marron, *Dictionnaire*, T. I, vol. I, col. 1069.
21. Virey, *op. cit.*, pp. 218-219.
22. Pliny, *Natural History*, Book XI, XXX.
23. See Vitruvius, *De Architectura*, X, 1; Vegetius, *Rei Militaris Instituta*, IV, 22.
24. Polybius, *History*, Bk. IV.
25. Cf. L. Cloquet, *Éléments d'Iconographie chrétienne*, p. 337.
26. Psalms 90:13, Douay-Rheims version.
27. See *Le grant Kalendrier et compost des Bergiers*, 1480, folio NC iij.
28. Barbier de Montault, *Traité d'Iconographie*, T. II, p. 445.
29. De la Colombière, *La Science héroique*, (1669), p. 314, #11.
30. Cf. P. Verneuil, *Dictionnaire des Symboles*, p. 165.
31. Barbier de Montault, *op. cit.*, T. I, p. 306.
32. *Ibid.*, Pl. XVII, Fig. 174.

THE CATERPILLAR AND THE BUTTERFLY

THE CATERPILLAR DOES not share with other kinds of worms the simple and immediate method of metamorphosis by which they emerge transformed into beautiful little beings directly from the matter on which they fed from the first day of their existence. The caterpillar, when cool weather comes and the plants that have nourished it during the summer wither and disappear, finds a shelter and installs itself there. It contracts the multiple rings of its body, pulls in its feet, and unreels from the invisible spinneret that opens on top of its head an imperceptible silken thread which it slowly and carefully wraps around itself; then it exudes a liquid which is soaked up by the silk of the cocoon, and very soon the whole length of its body is encased in an impermeable covering. It gradually disappears from view inside a rigid case: the cocoon has become a veritable coffin.

In the surrounding darkness and peace, a mysterious sleep comes upon the caterpillar—a fruitful sleep, in which its wormlike aspect melts into another shape: the head is transformed and provided with antennae; the body divides itself, and all the rings that composed it become a sort of corselet from which grow wings and a long abdomen which is the only part of the new insect that is reminiscent of the worm. But all this is still wrinkled and shrunken, the wings stuck to the body and indeterminate; for the former caterpillar has become what is as yet only the chrysalis, until the first flight, under the warmth of the sun's rays in the free air, makes it into the butterfly.

It was by pondering the mysteries of the cocoon that our forefathers established the analogies which have made the caterpillar a symbol of Christ. All worms, destined to undergo a metamorphosis, are his emblems, but the transformation of the caterpillar, more than that of any other larva, figures in Christian symbolism as the representation of the broken body of Jesus transformed into the glorious body which emerged from the darkness of the tomb. The fifth century pontifical decree of Pope Gelasius I declared that Christ was a worm, not because he was humbled, and humbled himself, but "because he was resurrected": "*Vermis quia resurrexit*[1]."

The caterpillar, representing at the same time the body of Christ and that of the Christian, was often depicted in early Christian art in conditions which leave no doubt about the symbolic intention of the artist. An example is a Roman funerary stone, which carries the inscription: *QVAE VIXIT ANI ...In XPisto Quiescas?* Below these words are traced Christ's monogram and a caterpillar[2]. M. de Longpérier referred to this inscription when he called attention some time ago to the large bronze caterpillars inlaid with molten glass found in Ireland[3]. They are about ten centimeters long and seem to be contemporary with Merovingian French art (sixth to ninth centuries). A very beautiful ring made of fine gold, in the Montpellier museum, has a setting ornamented with the symbolic fish, and on each side of the setting a caterpillar in relief: the Fish-Christ, the *Ichtus*, and the double emblem of his and mankind's resurrection[4] (Fig. 1).

Fig. 1
Merovingian gold ring, 6th or 7th century. Montpellier Museum.

In several regions, the caterpillar's chrysalis, enclosed in the darkness and silence of its cocoon, has been taken as the im-

Fig. 2 A golden disk from one of the royal tombs at Mycenae; about 10th or 9th century B.C.

age of the human being that has separated itself from the agitation, noise, and anxiety of ordinary life to transform its inner state into a more perfect one. Some Asiatic ascetics of the Himalayas even today live in almost inaccessible caves and subsist on a minimum of food, sometimes for years[5], in order to expose their souls more directly to the light of the Compassionate One, and thereby they become great gurus; they compare themselves to the huge butterflies that inhabit the marvelous valleys of the Indus and the Ganges. Mystical language made frequent mention of this analogy between the soul that works for its own transformation in the retirement of the cloister, and the ugly insect that becomes beautiful in the retirement of its cocoon.

The analogy between the dead person and the caterpillar in its chrysalis state arose spontaneously in ancient Egyptian thought. Their mummified dead, wrapped in endless strips of cloth soaked in bitumen and balsams, were like the chrysalis in its silken sheath. The thought of the Greeks followed the same lines[6] in placing gold butterflies in the tombs to symbolize the reawakening to a new life, implied by the butterfly's flight. For all of them, the human body was only the envelope, the container of the soul, which escaped through the gate of death just as the chrysalis breaks through the cocoon and

Fig. 3 *The butterfly-soul; modern ornament in silver and enamel.*

comes out, becoming a butterfly only on the first unfolding of its wings in the freedom of space.

In the royal tombs of the Mycenaeans, contemporaries of Priam, Schliemann found impressive butterflies engraved on great golden disks[7] (Fig. 2), and even on the pans of a small pair of symbolic scales[8] which recall those used by Zeus, according to Homer, to weigh the fates of long sleep and of death to which Hector would be destined[9]. "The butterfly here," Schliemann says, "is, as it is in later Greek art, the emblem of the immortality of the human being[10]."

This interpretation remained unchanged from the time of the Mycenaean civilization to that of Posidonius of Apameus, in the second century before Christ; and what is certainly referred to here is a soul from a level higher than our nature, for the Pythagorean school affirmed "that the soul comes from God and not from nature, and consequently is pre-existent to the body in which it is incarnated; from which it draws the conclusion that once it is separated from the body, it will escape from pain and no longer be subject to death[11]." The butterfly emerges from its cocoon and flies joyfully and gracefully away in the exact image for the Ancients of "the soul rid of its carnal covering (Figs. 3 and 4). These butterflies, pursued by Eros in the Pythagorean basilica of the Porta Maggiore, are souls overcome by divine love and filled with its delight[12]."

Fig. 4 *The soul in the form of a human butterfly, showing Greek influence.*

The Greek language uses one and the same word for the human soul and the butterfly: *Psyche*. And for ancient Christian symbolism, the dove-winged Eros in amorous pursuit of the butterfly Psyche, the human soul, was one of those prophetic symbols that the Church adopted unchanged and transferred to Christ. In the times of the catacombs, the Roman pontiffs countenanced without hesitation the inclusion of the fable of Eros and Psyche on the sacred decoration of the underground sanctuaries. In one chamber of the catacomb of Domitilius, there are three symbolic paintings that show Eros, ardent love, and Psyche, the sought-for soul[13]. In the catacombs of St. Peter and St. Marcellinus, Eros naked and Psyche clothed exchange ardent caresses and embraces; doves' wings are attached to the shoulders of Eros-Christ, and Psyche's carry the wings of the butterfly[14].

Thus all the records of art concur in making the butterfly the emblem of the soul that has escaped from the flesh by the gateway of death and been lifted above the earthly plane by divine love. Some ancient authors used the term "flying souls" in speaking of the butterfly[15].

Fig. 5 The Cleopatra butterfly, ⅔ life size.

In the countrysides of our western French provinces, there is one butterfly that is particularly attached to the symbolism of the resurrected Christ: this is the "Cleopatra" of the naturalists, which is bright yellow and very elegantly shaped and is the first of all to come forth in the sunlight of March or April (Fig. 5). In certain regions it is called the "Easter Jesus," because its appearance more or less coincides with Eastertide and because it is the first of the butterflies to emerge from its cocoon as from the tomb.

But the symbolism of the butterfly has its unfavorable side as well. Because it goes from one flower to another without settling for long on any, it has become the image of inconstancy; and the night-flying moths, in the words of St. Francis de Sales, "seeing a flame, go to it and fly around it seeking to know if it is as sweet as it is beautiful, and continue until they are lost; so also does the young heart with the flames of desire[16]."

Among the nocturnal butterflies or moths there is one

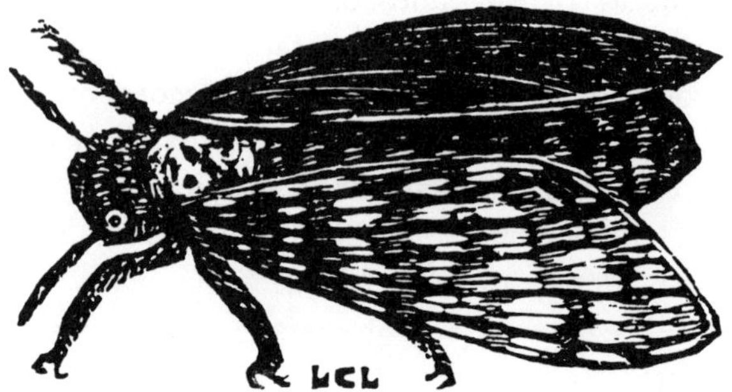

Fig. 6 The Atropos or Death's-head moth, slightly less than life size.

called the Death's-head, which for Christians represents Satan. Naturalists call it the *sphinx atropos* (Fig. 6), after one of the three Fates of Greece, she whose merciless scissors cut the thread of human life. The death's-head sphinx, which in France sometimes attains seven centimeters in length and thirteen in wingspread, has a light yellow marking just above its dark thorax that resembles a skull. This ominous sign and the stridulent sound that it sometimes makes while flying in the night have made, and continue to make, this moth regarded as a bearer of infernal influences and a messenger of death[17].

NOTES

Title Figure: Enameled medal, of the late medieval period, from the de Rochebrune collection.

1. Leclercq and Marron, *Dictionnaire*, T. VI, Vol. 1, col. 744; also G. Hoffet in *Regnabit*, 1927, p. 195.
2. Cf. Oderici, S.J., *Dissertationes et admonestationes in aliquot ineditas veterum inscriptiones*, 1765, p. 254, 291.
3. Adrien de Longpérier, "Fibules irlandaises," in *Bulletin de la Société des Antiquaires de France*, 1859, p. 150.
4. See M. Deloche, *Les Anneaux Sigillaires*, p. 289, #CCLV.
5. See J. Marques-Rivière, *A l'ombre des Monastères tibetains*, 1929, and *Vers Benares, la Ville Sainte*, 1930. Paris, Attinger.
6. Cf. Schliemann, *Mycènes*, pp. 245, 247.
7. *Ibid.*
8. *Ibid.*, p. 277.
9. Homer, *The Iliad*, XXII.

10. See also *Comptes rendus de l'Académie des Inscriptions*, meeting of Feb. 2, 1883.
11. Carcopino, *Basilique*, p. 185.
12. *Ibid.*, p. 104.
13. See Dom P. Guéranger, *Ste. Cecile et la Société romaine*, p. 147.
14. See Leclercq, *Manuel*, T. I, p. 148.
15. Cf. Hesychius, *Lexicon*, Vbo *Phalle*: from Roux, *Herculaneum et Pompei*, T. VIII, p. 215.
16. Saint Francis de Sales, *Introduction à la Vie dévote*, 1608.
17. See "Le Sphinx, tête de mort" in *Magasin pittoresque*, 1833, T. I, p. 244.

End Figure: The noxious vineyard sphinx moth.

THE ICHNEUMON WASP & THE GRASSHOPPER

THE MONGOOSE, A little meat-eating quadruped that attacks reptiles and above all, at least in the Nile valley, devours the eggs of the dreaded crocodile, was called *ichneumon* by the Greeks of Egypt, and in the early days of Christianity it became an emblem of Christ as the adversary and destroyer of evil. Equally the Greeks of Europe applied the name *ichneumon* to a kind of wasp which also renders valuable service to mankind[1]. There are myriads of these ichneumon wasps in all of the countries bordering the Black Sea, the Euxine Sea of the Ancients (Fig. 1). These countries are infested during the summer by hordes of ravaging grasshoppers whose depredations are a veritable plague, and the wasps attack them; clinging to their backs, they grip them with their feet so that they cannot fly and plunge their sharp stings between the grasshopper's head and body. The Ancients, and up till quite recently the entomologists also, believed that the grasshopper thus stung died almost immediately after receiving the egg that the wasp then placed in its body, and which hatched soon after. Encyclopedias at the end of the last century gave the same information. But in fact, the grasshopper is only paralyzed by the sting, and it is in this semi-catalyptic state that it receives the wasp's egg, which has thus during the hatching process a supply of fresh, still living food. Needless to say, the victim dies as it is devoured from within, but it is not killed outright, even when it is small enough to be dragged into the wasp's subterranean nest. This practice has gained the ichneumon the nickname of "grave-digger wasp."

Among the victims of the ichneumon wasp, for which in particular the ancients gave it grateful credit, is the big spider the Greeks call phalanga, similar to the tarantula and very much feared[2]. With equal frequency, this wasp places its eggs in the bodies of caterpillars or harmful worms.

The coinage of the ancient Greeks, which often carried the image of animals and of insects less useful to humanity, never represented the ichneumon wasp—a surprising neglect among the Greeks who often depicted the bee on their coins. It seems that it was not until the Christian Middle Ages were well advanced that for the first time acknowledgment was made of the good offices of the ichneumon wasp, and it was accepted by symbologists as one of the creatures emblematic of the Savior, being recognized, like the mongoose, as the invincible enemy of evil and all its works.

Fig. 1
The Near-Eastern wasp.

The grasshopper, chief victim of the ichneumon wasp, has always been an image of devastation and death among the nations it afflicts, and in the scriptures, from Moses to St. John the Evangelist, it is represented among the earth's scourges. In Exodus, when Moses struck the Egyptians with the ten plagues that liberated Israel, the eighth of these ordeals was a great cloud of grasshopper locusts that stripped the soil of Egypt of every green thing, and pursued the Egyptians into their houses[3]. And in the terrifying visions of the Apocalypse, when the great angel had cried three times: Woe to the earth! the fifth of the heavenly trumpets announced the coming plague. Then from the bottomless pit, in the midst of the whirling smoke, issued an incalculable number of grasshoppers, as venomous as scorpions, commanded to torture the people of the

Fig. 2 Grasshopper from the bottomless pit; from Éliphas Lévi.

earth... "And the shapes of the locusts were like unto horses prepared unto battle; and on their heads were as it were crowns like gold, and their faces were as the faces of men. And they had hair as the hair of women, and their teeth were as the teeth of lions. And they had breastplates, as it were breastplates of iron; and the sound of their wings was as the sound of chariots of many horses running to battle. And they had tails like unto scorpions, and there were stings in their tails; and their power was to hurt men five months[4]."

An example of kabbalistic iconography given by Éliphas Lévi shows fantastic insects evidently inspired by this passage in the Apocalypse[5] (Fig. 2), and there are several other examples alluded to by Grimouard de Saint-Laurent[6]. I remember that one of them shows the grasshopper clothed in the cuirass of a knight and helmeted with the bassinet, engraved with a crown of flowers, that was in use at the end of the fourteenth century. When in the twelfth century the Benedictine monks decorated the church of their magnificent abbey at Vézelay, their sculptors carved in the stone capital of a pillar the image of a grasshopper with a human head, next to another of Satan's emblems, the basilisk, completing its "demonic significance[7]."

Fig. 3 Cricket of southern Europe; average size.

In the course of time, the grasshopper also became for Christian symbolists the image of the heretic, and of any propagator of error, of discord, or of rebellion who sought to devastate the field so generously sown by the divine Sower (Fig. 3).

NOTES

Title Figure: The French wasp (Sphex sabulosa).

1. See "La Guêpe ichneumon et la Sauterelle" in *Magasin pittoresque*, Book 34, p. 268.
2. Pliny, *Natural History*, Book X, XCV.
3. Exodus 10:1-19.
4. Revelation 9:1-10.
5. Lévi, *Les Mystères de la Kabbale*, p. 153.
6. See de Saint-Laurent, *Guide*, T. IV, p. 475.
7. Cf. Barbier de Montault, *Traité d'Iconographie chrétienne*, T. II, p. 181.

THE MANTIS AND THE SPIDER

THAT SINGULAR LITTLE creature, the mantis, measures five or six centimeters in length, and varies in color, mostly through every shade of green, according to differences not only in species but in location. Here we are speaking only of the praying mantis, the *mantis religiosa* of Linnaeus, which inhabits the whole Mediterranean basin and several of the winegrowing regions of western France, as for instance Poitou and Anjou[1].

The mantis' body is provided with a long corselet to which are attached two large arms. When it is still, the praying mantis folds these arms in the gesture of supplication that has given it its names: in Provence, it is called *lou prego Dio*, "the one who prays to God[2]," and elsewhere, the "praying mantis," the "devotee" (Fig. 1), and also for reasons which we shall find later, "the guide."

The customs of the mantis are atrociously cruel. It feeds only on living things, and the female devours the head of the male during their sexual union, and lets go her hold on him only to push away a corpse. This cruelty, which is common to a number of insects, was probably unknown to the Greeks who greatly honored the mantis: they attributed to it strange divinatory powers, *manteia*, from

Fig. 1 Mantis in its praying posture; from Fabre.

which came the name they gave it of *mantis*, the seer, the inspired, the prophet. They said that on first sight of a traveler, this little creature divined the goal of his journey and the dangers awaiting him on the way, and indicated to him with a clear gesture the direction to take to avoid them (Fig. 2).

Another, also very ancient, idea made the mantis the symbol of the ease with which human thought adapts itself to its surroundings. M. Beule says: "The praying mantis is a graceful insect which as soon as it is approached folds its forelegs, joins them together and seems to ask for mercy; in Attica it is observable how it takes on the color of the ground it inhabits, and is green in verdant areas, gray on bare ground, rust on the sun-scorched rocks. In the same way, the human being becomes the reflection of those around him; aware of the impressions of others, in spite of himself he borrows the color of their ideas[3]." This agrees with the proverb: "Tell me the company you keep, and I will tell you who you are."

Former Christian symbolists, among the learned, the clerical, or simple country-folk informed by popular tradition of the mantis' claim to the power of divination and its charitable use of this gift to help travelers, saw in it as in several other creatures an image of the "Good Guide," for whose divine aid the Catholic liturgy appeals: *Tu dux ad astra et semita sis meta nostris cordibus*[4]: "Mayst thou, our guide and path toward heaven, be the goal of our hearts' desires."

Thus, according to the imaginations of our forefathers, the mantis goes to the help of those who have strayed and gives them counsel: its long arms are lifted first as if to mean that all help comes from heaven; then their tips join as if in ardent prayer, and finally extend and point in the right direction. It is the image of Christ, the guide of souls.

Fig. 2 Mantis making gesture of pointing the way. From nature, ⅔ life size.

On the other hand, the hideous spider presents itself as the antithesis of the pious mantis: the spider places its treacherous ambushes everywhere, stopping the joyful flight of winged insects, paralyzing them in its web, in order to kill and devour them. All spiders have underneath their mouths two organs provided with sharp hooks and a groove through which comes the poison with which they numb their victims before killing them. The Ancients sometimes exaggerated the gravity of the spider's bite, but it is nevertheless true that it is always harmful to people, and sometimes fatal. The spider that causes the most fear in Europe is the tarantula, which is sometimes four or five centimeters long, and is common in south and central Italy and in Sicily, Albania, and western Greece. Actually, its bite is not as dangerous as was formerly supposed. There was an odd treatment for those who were ill with its poison that used to prevail in Italy: the victims had to dance without stopping to the repetition of music of a stirring rhythm, known as the *tarentella*, until they dropped from exhaustion. This however was not the only remedy used against the tarantula's venom: the ancient Greeks, very reasonably I think, preferred the juices of the herb *phalangion* which was thought to cure the hallucinations and delirium brought on by the tarantula's bite. Aelian says that deer cure themselves of this poison by eating wild ivy[5].

Fig. 3
St. Fiacre spider, from nature; maximum life size.

There are two other kinds of spider in France that have an evil reputation: one is called the death spider, the victims of whose bite are said never to survive more than five or six months; and the St. Fiacre spider, a handsomely marked gray and black insect with a white cross on its back (Fig. 3), which it carries exactly as the scarab does the Tau symbol that is venerated as portraying the Christian cross. In the case of the unfortunate spider, however, the cross is said to be "upside down" and consequently "the devil's cross." So the St. Fiacre spider, which almost never bites, and is much less evil than its reputation, receives a large share of the dislike which people have in general for spiders.

Ancient oneiromancy or divination by dreams declared that to dream of a spider spinning its web foretold an error of judgment that could endanger the dreamer's honor, fortune, or very existence[6]. And among the country folk of France, at least, spiders are definitely associated with evil spirits. Mystics like Anne-Catherine Emmerich affirm that insects for whom people feel an instinctive aversion are often connected with troubled or maleficent spirits[7]. What is incontestable is that these beliefs have played a real role in popular symbolism.

Other spiders in various other countries must have been the subjects of beliefs founded partly on fact and partly on superstition; throughout Christianity, this insect has been regarded as an image of Satan, the treacherous pursuer of souls which are represented (exceptionally, but in this instance as in the symbolism of the swallow) by the small flying creatures that stray into his toils. Seated in the center of his web or hidden in a dark corner, he awaits his victims who are hopelessly lost the moment they are caught. In the thirteenth century, Pierre le Picard says in his *Bestiary* that the spider is the image of the devil who weaves and tends his webs, and works to take and destroy the souls of those who through lust, drunkenness, murder, or covetousness fall into his traps[8]. In ancient iconography, the spider most often represents the demon of lust and more especially its customary agent, the seductive and provocative prostitute; it is she who is represented in those jewels in whose design the spider is at the center of the web (Fig. 4). Sometimes a naked woman replaces the insect (Fig. 5), recalling the fabled Amazons described by Pomponius Mela, whose chief weapons are nets in which they entangle their adversaries and then drag them to death behind their chariots[9].

In Christian spirituality, the spider web itself represents in the first place "vain works," such as have no value in God's eyes. "Pray for us personally," St. Paulinus of Nola wrote in the year 405, "that we may not be misled into weaving spider

Fig. 4 19th-century ornament in gilded silver, from the author's collection.

Fig. 5 "The Seductress." An engraving from the time of Napoleon III.

webs, accomplishing works without merit[10]." The delicate tissue of the spider web was also the image of human frailty; as a puff of wind, a flying cockchafer, a falling flower can tear the web, so a trifle can destroy the life or health of a human being, and nothing is more fragile than the integrity of his conscience or the duration of his happiness.

Another idea makes the spider web represent heterodox teachings, in which souls become entangled and cannot free themselves. This symbolism was widely used in the Catholic Church, especially at the beginning of the spread of Protestantism.

From a different point of view, the symbolists of India and its sacred books were interested in the connection of the spider and its work with the symbolism of weaving. According to René Guénon, their webs, composed of threads patterned in concentric circles and others radiating from the center to the edges, were considered images of the pattern of the cosmogonic sphere, and the spider itself in the middle of this planisphere they took as the representation of the sun, the heart of the world[11].

Referring to the treacherous cruelty of the spider, which embraces other insects in order to inject its fatal poison, the European heraldists saw the insect as a symbol of traitors like Judas. In the West, the medieval heraldic science took the spider and its web as images of the dishonest judge who makes exceptions for different persons. A later echo of this idea comes from Vulson de la Colombière: "It is the symbol of the corrupt judge and of the inequality of the laws, as the wise Solon said, who compared the laws with spider webs because they hold small flies but are not strong enough to retain the big ones which pass through them; as in the same way it is the little people who are enslaved by the harshness of the law, of which the great ones of the world take no account[12]."

The mantis and the spider are equally ferocious; the embrace of either is fatal. But the former has the advantage of the latter because of two fortunate gestures which recall that which is most uplifting in the human being: prayer and charity. And people make of it the image of Christ, the savior and guide of mankind; and the other becomes the emblem of Satan[13].

NOTES

Title Figure: Great mantis on watch; ½ life size. From nature.

1. Cf. R. Drouault, *Le Loudunais*, p. 1, *Les Paysages et Monuments du Poitou.*
2. *Grande Encyclopédie*, T. XXII, p. 1178.
3. M. Beule, "Journal de mes Fouilles" in *Gazette des Beaux-Arts*, April 1872, p. 287.
4. Roman breviary, Office of *Ascent. Domini.*
5. Aelian, *Hist. Div.*
6. Cf. Mme. Lenormand, *Les Clef des Songes*, p. 24.
7. Cf. Argos, in *Le Voile d'Isis*, T. XXXV, 1930, #132, p. 902.
8. According to Charles Cahier, "Bestiaires," in *Mélanges archéologiques* (*Le Bestiaire de Pierre le Picard*), T. II, p. 212.
9. Pomponius Mela, *De Situ Orbis*, Book I, 19.
10. St. Paulinus, Bishop of Nola, *Correspondence*, XXXVI.
11. Cf. Guénon, "Le Symbolisme du Tissage," in *Le Voile d'Isis*, T. XXXV, 1930, #122, p. 68; also *The Symbolism of the Cross*, ch. XIV, p. 68.
12. De la Colombière, *La Science héroique*.
13. *Editor's note*: The interested reader can find much more about the mantis in the African religions, and about the spider in Native American mythology, notably Iktomi among the Sioux and Spider Woman among the Navajo.

VII

FABULOUS BEASTS

THE UNICORN

Few animals, real or fabulous, have been such favorites as the unicorn in the whole field of symbolism in the arts, literature, and practices of the Middle Ages, among mystics, symbolists, artists, doctors, even magicians and sorcerers of all kinds. This unusual preference could only have grown up from very ancient roots; so it should not be surprising to find the unicorn's image in the art of the oldest civilized nations. I have found it in Chaldean and Babylonian artifacts, notably a cylindrical seal engraved on semiprecious stone, reproduced by Soldi[1]; two winged unicorns rear on hind legs on each side of the sacred Tree (Fig. 1).

Fig. 1 The unicorn on a Babylonian seal.

Perhaps from equally ancient times, Chinese sacred art shows a fabulous animal of the deer family with a single frontal horn, called *ki-lin*; the male is called *ki*, the female *lin*. The appearance of a *ki-lin* in China was cause for national rejoicing, because it was said that it could only happen during the reign of a sovereign who was perfectly just and beloved by heaven, and that it opened an era of prosperity for the country[2]. Even today it is said there that it is unicorns that bring human babies to their mothers, and their images are much-used luck-bringers in the family[3]. The Chinese unicorn, however, sometimes lacks the grace and elegance of its occidental counterpart, as shown by the unattractive monster whose faithful likeness is reproduced by Doré[4].

Four hundred years before our era, the Greek Ctesias, physician to Artaxerxes, King of Persia, lauded the supposed medical properties of the unicorn's horn[5]; Philostratus copied him[6]; and among the Latin writers, Aelian[7] and Pliny[8] spread and amplified the fantasies that Ctesias had gathered from the Persians and the Medes. Here is Pliny's bizarre description of the unicorn: "It is an intractable beast with a body similar to that of a horse, a head like a deer, feet like an elephant, and a tail like a wild boar; it makes a low-pitched bellowing sound, and has a single black horn two cubits long in the middle of its forehead. It is said that this beast cannot be taken alive."

In the Bible, the unicorn is spoken of as if it were several different animals: Moses and David, for example, sometimes give it several horns, and European translators have added to the confusion. The Vulgate says: *Salva me ex ore leonis, et a cornibus unicornium humilitatem meam*: "Save me from the lion's mouth; and my lowness from the horns of the unicorns[9]," while Crampon translates literally from the Hebrew: "Save me from the lion's mouth, take me from the horns of the buffalo[10]." In other passages from Judaic writings, the unicorn was identified with the onager of India, with deer and zebras, and especially with the oryx[11] as in the case of the sculptor who in the twelfth century fashioned the monster column in the monastery of Souvigny, in Allier (Fig. 2). Finally we can refer to Tertullian to whom the unicorn was the one-horned oryx of the Ancients[12]. However, the most essential characteristic of the unicorn is the horse-shaped body and the long, straight, forward pointing horn, often spirally grooved. The oryx, on the contrary, is usually represented in medieval art with its single horn curved backwards.

Fig. 2 The oryx designated as a unicorn on the 12th-century Souvigny Monster Column.

Artists of the later medieval period, especially the her-

Fig. 3 The death of the unicorn; from a 14th-century English manuscript.

aldists, often endowed the unicorn with a goat's beard which their predecessors had never given it. Those who looked among various kinds of onagers for the prototype of the fabulous animal have relied on what Philostratus wrote in the second century in his life of Apollonius of Tyana, that in the marshes near the river Phasis there are wild asses that have one frontal horn with which they fight as furiously as bulls[13].

In any case, before our era people of almost all countries thought of the unicorn, in spite of the elegance of form generally attributed to it, as an invincible and very dangerous animal. It was fancied that it could never be captured by any hunter, but that a pure woman, virginal in spirit, heart, and body, attracted it irresistibly and that she alone could lay hands on it. It was said that when the animal found her, it would kneel down in front of her and lay its head against her breast and caress her gently; and at this moment, the huntsman treacherously hidden nearby would spring out and give the unicorn its death blow, or bind it with ropes by which it could be led away captive (Fig. 3).

The ninth-century book, the *Roman d'Alexandre*[14], tells us that "if she is not a virgin, the unicorn, far from lying in her lap, kills the corrupted girl who is not a maiden . . ." We find the same imaginings in the fifteenth century, in the writings of Brunetto Latini[15].

Strange fantasies also arose involving the astonishing virtues of the unicorn's horn, going even farther than the tales spun by Ctesias; it was said that if filings of the horn were swallowed, or simply applied to wounds, this was a sovereign remedy that would counteract the venom of the most dangerous reptiles, and would cure madness, the plague, epilepsy, gangrene, etc. Vessels made of this horn were a protection against all sorts of evils and rendered the worst poisons harmless, so they are often listed in royal inventories and described as richly ornamented: "A unicorn horn ewer adorned with gold and surrounded with a number of small gemstones . . . a goblet of unicorn horn adorned with gold . . .[16]" In the *Inventory of Charles V*, mention is made of two goblets of unicorn horn, richly mounted and decorated with diamonds and precious stones; and all these listings include a large number of different vessels described as containing fragments of the horn[17].

In actual fact, this rare and almost universal panacea was simply the ground horn of a cetacean of the dolphin family, the one-horned narwhal that inhabits the seas of Europe and Asia. This fact explains why unicorns were nearly always depicted with horns twisted like screws, and immensely long. La Colombière[18] gives a precise measure: six and a half feet, or two meters twenty; a bothersome appendage for a quadruped the size of a deer. So it is not surprising to see that the sword-handle of the emperor Maximilian of Austria, called "The Unicorn's Blade," is made of narwhal horn[19]. The ancient treasure of the Abbey of St. Denis, now in the Cluny Museum in Paris, which was taken for a unicorn horn, is that of a narwhal. It looks like a long twisted Easter candle in pale wax.

"It is easy to see," says Professor Hippeau, "why the unicorn appears so often in Christian iconography[20]." The *Divine Bestiaries*, following the ancient *Physiologus*, dedicated the noble animal to the symbolism of Christ, and the *Bestiaries of Love* compared it to that other lord of suffering, which is the poor humble human heart. For the former, the old legend of the unicorn, the virgin, and the hunter was a theme eminently suited to represent the Incarnation and the redemptive sacrifice of the Son of God. Thus the unicorn became the symbolic image of Christ descending through his bodily birth into the bosom of humanity, represented by the maiden in the legend; and the hunter was the counterpart of the Jewish people who put the Savior to death[21]. Among many other medieval writers, Honorius d'Autun, who died in 1140, saw in the maiden of the legend the double image of humanity and of the Virgin Mary[22]; others emphasize her complicity with the hunter and hence humanity's role in causing Christ's death by treachery. Here is William of Normandy:

Ihesus-Crist, nostre Sauveor	Jesus Christ our Savior
C'est l'Unicorne espiritel	Is the spiritual unicorn,
Qui en la Virge prist ostel,	Who made his dwelling in the Virgin,
Qui est tant de grand dignité;	He who is of such high dignity;
En ceste prist humanité	In her he put on his humanity
Par quei au munde s'aparut;	Through which he manifested himself to the world:
Son peuple mie nel quenut	His people did not recognize him[23]
Des Jeves einceis l'espièrent	On the contrary, the Jews spied on him
Tant qu'il le pristrent et lièrent.	Finally they took him and bound him
Devant Pilatre le menèrent	They led him before Pilate
Et ilec a mort le dampnèrent.	And soon condemned him to death[24].

In the medieval bestiary quoted by de Caumont[25], the unicorn is also the emblem of Christ, the maiden is Mary, and the hunter represents the Jewish people.

In the last years of the fourth century St. John Chrysostom formulated another symbolic motif according to which "unicorns are the righteous, above all Jesus Christ who fights his adversaries with his cross as if it were a horn; this is the horn in which we put our trust[26]." Nevertheless, this interpretation was not retained by the medieval symbolists, for whom the unicorn's horn meant the Savior's divine force and power; in the words of David, "But my horn [my force] shalt thou exalt like the horn of an unicorn[27]."

Another aspect of this symbolism relating Christ and Mary is brought out in *Parnassus*, the magazine of the College Art Association of America, where Mrs. E. C. Marquand points out that in the fifteenth-century "unicorn tapestries" as they are called, there is always a central tree, like the Tree of Life, whose "axial" significance is in accordance with that of the

Fig. 4 The death of the unicorn; 12th-century sculpture from Strasbourg Cathedral.

single horn[28]. In fact, the presence of this central tree goes much farther back in time in its artistic relations with the unicorn than the fifteenth-century tapestries. It is present, for instance, in a Strasbourg sculpture pictured here (Fig. 4) and in many others. The tree, when it appears singly in works of art relating to Christian symbolism, most often has the significance of world-axis, which is one of the aspects of Christ; and it is always the case with the "cross-shaped tree" whose branches form the sign of the cross, as we often see it in the Roman catacombs.

In connection with the Tree of Life as it was considered in the *Parnassus* article, Guénon points out that if one recalls Virgil's *Iam redit et Virgo*, a connection may be glimpsed between the unicorn and the virgin with quite a different meaning from any given by the habitual interpretations[29]. It is possible that certain medieval masters may have pursued the symbolism of the unicorn to this point, but certainly such a depth of interpretation would have been limited to a very small number of people.

In the same period, in the mystical "Triumphs," unicorns drew the chariot of Chastity[30]. Earlier, because of its links with the idea of virginity, writers of sacred texts such as St. Bonaventure in the thirteenth century made the unicorn symbolize the Virgin, the mother of Christ, the "All-Holy" of the Byzantines[31].

A variation in the symbolic representation of Christ's Incarnation through the unicorn legend took place in the last period of the Middle Ages, which has been preserved in some very interesting pieces of art. In an English work we find this quotation from the French: "It is well-known that in the sixteenth century (and earlier) the mystery of the Incarnation was often represented by the following allegory: a unicorn taking refuge in the bosom of a pure virgin, four hounds rapidly pursuing it, a winged huntsman sounding a horn. The mystical zoology of the time helps to provide an explanation: The fabulous animal whose single horn wounds only to cleanse of all poison whatever part of the body it touches is the image of Jesus Christ, the physican and savior of souls. The hounds are given the names of *Misericordia, Veritas, Justitia* and *Paz*, the four reasons which induced the eternal Word to emerge from his repose; but as it was through the Virgin Mary that he chose to descend among men and put himself in their power, it was thought best to choose the fable of a maiden serving as a trap for the unicorn by the attraction presented to him of the charm and perfume of her virginal breast; finally the angel Gabriel, taking part in the mystery, was easily recognizable beneath the appearance of the winged huntsman urging on the hounds and blowing his trumpet[32]."

The names of the mystical hounds vary; sometimes they are the *mercy* and the *love* of Christ for human beings, his

Fig. 5 The pursuit of the unicorn by the angel hunter. A copper disk of the early 16th century.

spirit of *justice* and *obedience* in relation with the Father; and in an engraving made about 1440 in the Bibliothèque Nationale in Paris, the dogs have the names *Castitas, Veritas, Humilitas*[33]. On a sixteenth century copper medallion reproduced by Cloquet, the dogs are not given any names (Fig. 5). There are other striking representations of the archangel huntsman and his dogs[34].

Many learned Christians, notably Hippeau in his edition of the *Bestiaire divin*, have taken note of the moral, but altogether human, meaning that the *Bestiaries of Love* attached to this same legend of the unicorn and the maiden. They have seen in it the allegory of a man who through his loyal love of a woman puts his trust in her and is deceived and betrayed. Throughout the Middle Ages, "our singers and story-tellers have often compared to the unicorn the cavalier defeated by Love and by the Lady[35]."

Fig. 6 Armorial bearings of the Duvals, lords of Mondrainville, 16th century.

The unicorn was one of the favorite subjects in the heraldic art of the Middle Ages; it was seen in helmets and shields, on banners, on seals, in the decoration of knightly tourneys and of "courts of love." In all these different roles, it always meant faithful attachment to purity of life, the shunning of vice, and the attraction to beauty. In those days, since the bestiaries were everywhere, the unicorn was generally known as a symbol of Christ and appeared as such on the coats of arms of certain priests and nobles (Fig. 6).

Although it was perhaps in reality the natural prototype of the unicorn, the rhinoceros became its antithesis in Christian symbolism. It seems to be what Job describes under the name of Behemoth, the evil monster that is the brother of Leviathan, who eats grass like the ox, who carries his sword in front of him and lives hidden "in the covert of the reed, and in moist places[36] (Fig. 7)."

Fig. 7 Antique bronze rhinoceros from Novo-Tekerkask; actual size.

Contrary to the unicorn who, it is said, searches for sweet smells and pure things, the rhinoceros wallows in the mud and slime of the marsh; it stands for filth as the unicorn stands for purity. Its horn was taken to be one of the emblems of the demon of pride[37]. Let us say in its defense, however, that some ancient mystics regarded it as the image of the force of God's wrath because of the terrifying violence of its anger.

NOTES

Title Figure: The unicorn on the Cassard coat-of-arms.

1. E. Soldi, "Cylindres babyloniens," in *Revue archéologique*, 3d series, T. XX-XVIII, 1874. Plate XIV, #2.
2. Cf. C. de Harlen, "La Lampe de la Salle obscure," in *Revue de l'Histoire des Religions*, 1893, p. 295.
3. Cf. Doré, *Recherches*, Part I, T. l, pp. 2 & 4.
4. *Ibid*, Part I, T. II, Vol. 4, p. 440, fig. 209.
5. Ctesias, *Indica*, XXV.
6. Philostratus, Bk. IV, ch. 1.
7. Aelian, *Hist. Anim.*, Bk. IV, ch. 52.
8. Pliny, *Natural History*, Bk. VIII, 31.
9. Psalms 21:22, Douay-Rheims version. See also KJV, Psalms 22:21.
10. Crampon, *La Sainte Bible*: Psalms 22:22 (from the Hebrew text), p. 684.
11. *Le Bestiaire divin*, Hippeau ed., p. 127.
12. Tertullian, *An Answer to the Jews*, X.
13. Cf. Philostratus, *Lives of the Sophists*, Bk. III, 1.
14. *Traicté des Proprietez des Bestes*, from *Roman d'Alexandre*, Book IX.
15. Latini, *Li Livres dou Tresor*, Bk. I, P. V, CCI.
16. *Inventaire des Ducs de Bourgogne* (15th century), Nos. 2359 & 5292.
17. Cf. Léon de Laborde, *Glossaire français du Moyen-âge*, pp. 359-365.
18. De la Colombière, *La Science hèroique*, p. 275.
19. Cf. *Gazette des Beaux Arts*, 1875, p. 215.
20. *Le Bestiaire divin*, Hippeau ed., p. 128.
21. Cf. Mâle, *L'Art religieux* (3), p. 56.
22. Honorius d'Autun, *Sermo de Nativit. et de Annonciat.*
23. Reference to St. John 1:10-11: "The world was made by him, and the world knew him not; he came unto his own, and his own received him not."

24. *Le Bestiaire divin.*
25. Cf. de Caumont in *Bulletin monumental*, T. XXI, 1816, p. 385.
26. St. John Chrysostom, *In psalm. XCI*, Montfaucon edition, T. VII, p. 778.
27. Psalm 92:10.
28. *Parnassus*, October 1938.
29. Guénon in *Études Traditionelles*, December 1938, p. 464. [*Editor's note*: The quotation from Virgil is from the *Eclogues*, IV, 4:

    Ultima Cumaei venit iam carminis aetas;
    Magnus ab integro saeclorum nascitur ordo
    Iam redit et Virgo, redeunt Saturnia regna;
    Iam nova progenies caelo demittitur alto.

    Now is come the last age of the song of Cumae;
    The great line of the centuries begins anew.
    Now the Virgin returns, the reign of Saturn returns;
    Now a new generation descends from heaven on high.
    (Tr. H. Rushton Fairclough)

    The Cumaean Sybil prophesied that a new cycle of ages would follow the Iron Age and be heralded by the reappearance of Astraea (Justice), "The Virgin," who was the last of the immortals to leave the earth and would be the first to return in the new Golden Age.]
30. See Franc. Filalfo, Petraca, Franc. Canzoniere; *Canzoniere*, Ed. Codeca, 1493.
31. St. Bonaventure, *Sermo IV*, *In Nativitate Domini*; also d'Autun, *op. cit.*
32. *A descriptive catalogue of early prints in the British Museum*, p. 127.
33. Bibliothèque Nationale, *Catalogue de l'Exposition du Moyen-âge*, 1926, p. 93, #130.
34. See de Saint-Laurent, *Guide*, T. III, p. 148; *Revue de l'Art chrétien*, 1888, fasc. I, pl. 2; L. Cloquet, *Éléments d'Iconographie chrétienne*, p. 352; Ch. Cahier, *Caractéristiques des Saints*, p. 45.
35. J. Bedier and P. Hazard, *Histoire de la Littérature française illustrée*, Part I, Ed. Larousse, p. 44.
36. Job 40:10-18, Douay-Rheims version.
37. Fel. d'Ayzac, *Le Taureau*; gloss on MSS. in the Bibliothèque Nationale in *Revue de l'Art Chrétien*, T. XXV, 18800, p. 15.
37. Cf. Cloquet, *op. cit.* (note 34), p. 336.

End Figure: The treacherous virgin capturing the unicorn; 16th-century sculpture from the Comynes chapel.

THE WINGED HORSE

THE HORSE IN its real shape, but provided by human imagination with great wings, is one of the most elegant creations of symbolic art. Many centuries before the Christian era, the winged horse was engraved on the cylindrical seals of the Babylonians, and in and around the part of Asia they inhabited it was sometimes shown with a human face[1]. The Median and Persian artists depicted winged horses long before the classical myth was thought of, and characterized it with a kind of dotted band crossing the wings[2]. Perhaps it was this influence that carried the winged horse motif across Asia to appear in China in the early epochs[3]. The graceful silhouette of the air-borne horse also pleased the very early European artists, and upon it the Greek poets built the legend of Pegasus (Fig. 1). Its image was engraved on the coins of numerous cities that were under Grecian influence; the Romans followed suit, and so did the Gauls. Among the Scandinavians, the name of *Falke* (falcon) which was given to the horse of the hero Thedrek leads one to suppose that this was a winged horse[4]. And in the world of literature, the Bible speaks of the horses of fire who drew up to heaven the flaming chariot of the great prophet, Elijah the Tishbite[5].

It must be remembered that the Ancients believed in the real existence of winged horses which they said came from that same land of Ethiopia whence came also the hippogriffs and the centaurs. According to Pliny, these Ethiopian horses had not only wings but horns like those of bulls[6], which led

Fig. 1 Bellerophon on Pegasus, fighting the Chimera. Worked in silver by Jannière in 1878.

Joannes de Cuba to describe them in that form and as objects of terror to other animals[7].

But hear the poets: Born from the blood of Medusa flowing from the sharp edge of Perseus' sword, Pegasus as he sprang to birth struck Mt. Parnassus with his hoof and thus caused the fountain of Hippocrene to gush forth; later the Muses plunged into its waters and found inspiration there. Perseus, going to the rescue of Andromeda, mounted Pegasus who carried him in swift flight to the place where a sea-monster held her captive[8]. Bellerophon also captured Pegasus in the fields of Hippocrene and rode on his back to conquer the terrible Chimera and then to vanquish the Solymians and the Lycians; whereupon, blinded with pride, he attempted to mount into the sky, but Pegasus in full flight threw off his rider who fell tragically to his death, and the beautiful animal swiftly lifted itself into the sky and took its place in the group of stars that bears its name.

With the victories of Perseus and Bellerophon over monsters and barbarians, this myth lends itself to certain allegories that the early symbolists, especially in Greece, might have been tempted to apply to Christ and the Christian; but on the other hand, the fall of the presumptuous Bellerophon presented a difficulty, and the mystics who tried to make use of the myth did not arrive at anything very satisfactory. It was rather by attributing to Pegasus the role of mount to Phoebus-Apollo, god of pure light and pure beauty, and by making it often the image of *Apollo Conservator*, the Preserver[9], that ancient art and literature managed to include the winged horse in the symbolic fauna of the Savior. In Rome itself, from the first Christian centuries, it can be seen how "the Sun-god becomes Christ who lifts himself from the earth with the sun's glory[10]."

Fig. 2 The winged horse on a 4th-century Christian lamp from Carthage.

The winged horse took his place in the ivory mosaics of Roman Christianity, on the Christian lamps of Carthage[11] (Fig. 2), and elsewhere, about the third or fourth century, or later; it was represented, by itself, in the center of a circular medallion in the Roman catacombs[12]; it was painted in the crypts of those of Palestine[13]; and in the Christian necropolis of Antinoë in Egypt, a Sassanid silk fabric, embroidered with images of the winged horse, was used as a shroud for a buried body[14]. This was surely not a random choice; and certainly it was with Christian meaning that the Middle Ages introduced the winged horse into ecclesiastical and monastic art: it is depicted, for example, in the Romanesque frescoes of the ancient Abbey of Saint Savin in Vienne[15] (Fig. 3).

Islam also created two winged horses which carried two human beings to the kingdom of heaven. It is the Moslem belief that God created for our first father Adam a horse made of amber and pure musk which he named *the horse Mamoun.* He gave it two wings made of precious stones and brought it to life. Mounted on this winged horse and guided by the archangel Gabriel, Adam in his lifetime visited the heaven of the Angels, and it was there that he learned the words of praise that are for the Moslems the greatest of all prayers: "God is great and contains in himself all the greatnesses that can be imagined![16]"

Fig. 3 The winged horse in the 12th-century Romanesque frescoes of Saint-Savin in Vienne.

The other winged horse of Islam is *Buraq*, the silver-gray mare on whose back Moahammed made his famous "Night Journey" from Mecca to Jerusalem, and thence to heaven[17]. The scholars of Islam say that Buraq will be the first quadruped that God will bring back to life on the last day; angels will place on its back a saddle made of shining rubies, and put in its mouth a bit of pure emerald, and lead it to the prophet's tomb. God will then revive Mohammed who, after speaking with the angels, will mount Buraq and be carried into the heavens[18].

NOTES

Title Figure: The winged horse on a coin from Tauromeion.

1. Cf. L. Delaporte, "Catalog des cylindres orientaux" in *Annales du Musée Guimet* (1909), p. 72 and plate 77, #16.
2. Cf. Em. Guimet, *Les Portraits d'Antinoë*, p. 6.
3. See the winged horse from the Ming dynasty at the Jacquemart Museum in Paris.
4. De Gubernatis, *Mythologie*, T. I, p. 361.
5. II Kings 2:11.

6. Pliny, *Natural History*, Bk. VIII, XXX.
7. Joannes de Cuba, *Hortus Sanitatis*, 2nd part CXIV, 1491 & 1539 editions. See the engraving of the *Hortus Sanitatis* in Part I above, "The Bull," page 15.
8. See Marie Meunier, *La Légende dorée des Dieux et des Héros*, pp. 278-290.
9. Cf. Renel, "Le Lion mithriarque . . . " in *Revue de l'Histoire des Religions*, 1903, p. 45.
10. Leclercq, *Manuel*, T. II, p. 579.
11. *Revue archéologique*, 3d series, T. IV (1884), p. 385.
12. Dom Guéranger, *Ste. Cecile & la Societé romaine aux deux premiers siècles*, IV, pp. 51 & 576.
13. Leclercq, *op. cit.*, T. I, p. 123.
14. Em. Guimet, "Symbole asiatique des nécropoles d'Antinoë," in *Annales du Musée Guimet*, 1903, p. 25.
15. See A. de Caumont, *Abécédaire archéologique*, p. 172.
16. Cf. Echialle Mufti, *Religion ou Théologie des Turcs*, T. I, p. 16.
17. Cf. Savary, *La Vie de Mahomet*, p. 20.
18. Mufti, *op. cit.*, T. I, XXVII and XXVIII, pp. 173-181.

End Figure: The winged horse on a Corinthian coin.

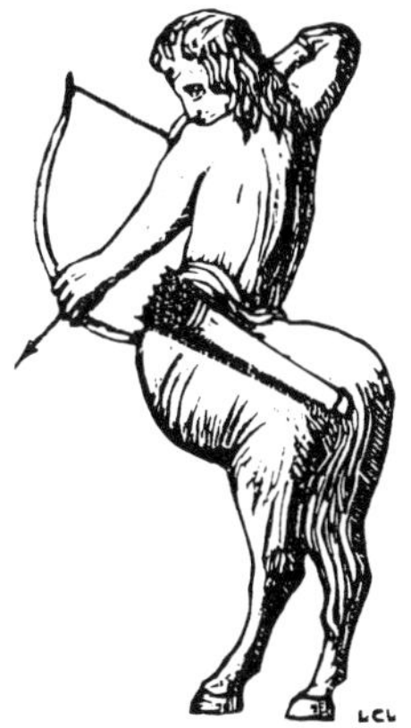

THE CENTAUR

MOST AUTHORS THINK that the fabulous creature with the torso of a man and the lower body of a horse was the product of the poetic and artistic imagination of ancient Greece, where it was said that a whole race of these creatures lived in the mountains of Thessaly between the massifs of Ossa and Pelion, where they were finally exterminated by their enemies the Lapiths[1]. However, the Egyptian centaur engraved on a basalt tablet now in the Bologne museum opens the question as to whether this mythical creature was not a Greek borrowing from the more ancient art of Egypt.

Putting aside the Greek fable that placed a nation of centaurs at the foot of Mt. Pelion, it seems probable that the centaur, taken singly, was in the earliest times a symbol that put the principal qualities represented by the horse, especially strength and speed, at the service of the intelligence of man. This idea is reinforced by the pieces of Etruscan art that show not only the horse-centaur but also the even swifter deer-centaur[2] and dog-centaur[3], both thought to be images of the diligent and devoted servant (Fig. 1).

Fig. 1 The deer-centaur and the dog-centaur; Etruscan bronzes.

Bronzes of Etruscan manufacture often depicted a strange creature with not only the torso but the complete body of a human, also having the hindquarters of an animal, as is the case with the deer-centaur and dog-centaur pictured above; and the Greeks themselves sometimes adopted this curious notion. The centaur in its ordinary form appeared on some of their coins; and on the gold coins of the Gauls of what is now Poitou, it became the androcephalous horse in which the human element was reduced to the head alone. This seemed to symbolize the activity of the nation's intelligence, and perhaps even a Druidic idea of a higher order—its equine character doubtless maintaining the role of animal of light which we recognized in the horse's symbolism[4], since the man-headed horse was on the other side of the coins from the head of Belenus, the god of light[5] (Fig 2).

Fig. 2 Gold coin of the Gallic Picts, from the author's private collection.

But if in the ancient world the centaur symbolized the valuable qualities of activity, speed, and strength at the service of conscious human intelligence, above all and more frequently it symbolized these same qualities at the service of evil human passions: of pride, represented by the man's head, of lust by his torso and greed by his hands. In several cults, centaurs were looked upon as genies, secondary "daemons" of the lower world. Only one—their king, Cheiron—was not included in this unfavorable regard. Nevertheless, especially among the Greeks, the centaurs had some higher qualifications: on funerary monuments, for instance, they often appeared as the mount of Psyche, the soul; sometimes they rose up on the storm clouds, carrying souls to the kingdom of the just[6].

Simply from the fact of its role as psychagogue, conductor of human souls to the divine and happy regions, the centaur could claim a place in the front rank of creatures emblematic of the Savior, from the beginning of Christian symbolism. Nevertheless, owing doubtless to the low esteem in which it was held, the centaur was almost completely excluded from the first thousand years of Christian art; however, during the first centuries of the second millennium, the attention of contemplatives was arrested by the centaur's double nature whose two parts, taken separately, were regarded sympathetically in Christian symbolism as an allegorical image of the double nature of Christ, in the same way as in other myths of hybrid creatures. The centaur's human part represents Christ's divinity as Man made in the image of God; and the animal part represents his humanity, attached with four feet to the earth which is man's kingdom and which gives him his physical food.

Fig. 3 The centaur Cheiron carrying Eros; antique marble statue.

An exception to the low opinion in which the centaur was generally held was always made in favor of the most famous member of their race, Cheiron; mythology sets him above and apart from all the others and presents him as a being of high intelligence, moral quality, wisdom, and goodness.

The Greek story says he was the son of Kronos and of Philyra, the linden tree. St. Justin, in the second century of our era[7], wrote that he was the friend and counselor of Phoebus-Apollo, and the friend also of Heracles, Aesculapius, and Jason. He became the loved and respected teacher of Achilles, of the Dioscuri, Palamedes, and Theseus; and finally, it was at his side that the divine Dionysus learned sacred science.

The school of Pythagoras made much of these qualities of

educator attributed to Cheiron, and drew from them some useful examples and lessons; so it is not surprising to see the master and one of his most famous pupils represented in the rich decoration of the Pythagorean basilica of the Porta Maggiore in Rome[8]. Pindar, writing some five hundred years before our era, claimed that after twenty years of study with this incomparable teacher, his pupils could be certain of never committing or uttering a reprehensible act or word[9]. It is said by some that Cheiron sometimes took care of that *enfant terrible*, the child Eros (Fig. 3).

The fable tells us that it was Cheiron who taught men the medical secrets of plants, who restored the sight of blind Phoenix, the son of Amyntor[10], and brought Peleus the king of Thessaly back from the dead. At last, though born immortal, Cheiron chose to die. Homer eulogized him as "the only just Titan[11]," thereby explaining how the good centaur became the object of a cult among the Magnesians of Thessaly, and justifying the beautiful works of pagan art that glorify him. Among these is the fine painting of the villa Iten, in Pompeii, which shows him teaching Dionysus the divine ritual, and the famous fresco at Herculaneum where we see him teaching the art of melody to the young Achilles on the seven-stringed lyre.

Christian art of the first millennium also made an exception of him in its otherwise rigorous exclusion of the centaurs. A large bronze tablet from the sixth century in the Cairo museum is decorated with several scenes of Thetis entrusting the young Achilles to Cheiron's care.

Later, the medieval mystics would connect the good centaur, the incomparable physician, who could restore the sight of the blind and bring the dead back to life, with Christ who said of his own work: "The blind receive their sight, and the lame walk, the lepers are cleansed, and the deaf hear, the dead are raised up. . .[12] During the same period, medical science consecrated to Cheiron a plant called "centaury," whose juice, according to the old books of magic, mixed with the blood of a hoopoe and put in the oil of a lamp, produced marvelous visions and inspirations[13].

But the vices which antiquity attributed to the centaur made it a natural symbol of the evil passions and so of Satan. Origen, in the second century, compared the depraved man to the centaur, with the same concept which made the horse and the mare emblems of lust[14]. St. Basil, in the fourth century, made it the image of the devil; and the Coptic life of St. Paul the hermit tells that Satan showed himself to St. Anthony in the desert "in the form of a centaur, half man and half horse[15]." With the same idea of a satanic image, Giotto painted a centaur on the fresco at Assisi where he represented St. Francis's triumph over his passions and over hell.

Fig. 4 The female centaur; sculpture from the basilica of St. Denis, 13th century.

The female centaur was the image of the woman who forgets her dignity due to excessive curiosity. It also represents, like the mare with the woman's face of our twelfth-century Roman sculptors[16], the voluptuous woman in general and especially the seductress (Fig. 4).

A later echo of medieval symbolism in Italy is given by *The Divine Comedy*, where Dante places all the centaurs in Hell, including Cheiron[17]. It need hardly be added that in his immortal masterpiece the poet made no claim to interpret the symbolism of the myths of which he spoke in perfect accord with the traditional opinions of his day.

The gods of light, who were always at the same time gods of love and of beauty, have forever been the best-loved and the most readily served. And all of them, or almost all, have been represented by the figure of an archer loosing an arrow, or by a foot soldier skillfully hurling a javelin. We see this archer-god on the most ancient Chaldean monuments. On a seal in the Duke of Luynes' collection, the Babylonian god Marduk fights thus with the monster Tiamat[18]; this struggle at the world's beginnings, according to Babylonian mythology, ensured the triumph of the benevolent gods over the powers of chaos. Among the Assyrians, the Sun-god was shown on the solar wheel with his bow in hand (Fig. 5)[19].

Among the Persians, the god Ormuzd was represented by the image of an archer, sometimes on horseback; and on the coins of the Achaemenid kings, he wears a crown. In India, Karna, son of a virgin and the Sun, whose myth goes back to at least the fourth century before our era, becomes a skillful bowman when he grows up[20].

Ancient Greek artists represented Apollo and his female counterpart, Artemis, as two archers, because the Sun and the Moon, which are consecrated to them, shoot their rays to the earth like luminous shafts [21].

Fig. 5 The divine archer; Assyrian Sun-god.

The bow, which ancient symbolism thus placed in the hands of the gods of light, is the hieroglyph of energy or force, and the arrow is that of speed. Because of this symbolism, and because the equine body of the centaur is equally the symbol of swift strength, and also because according to the myth the fabulous centaurs of Thessaly were particularly skillful bowmen, at an early date the Greeks made the centaur-archer the symbol of Phoebus Apollo under the name of *Apollo Conservator*[22]. In Europe, the Gallic Belenus, god of all light, was envisaged, like the Sun-god of Sardaigne, in the form of an archer[23].

The Romans followed the example of the Greeks and frequently gave the centaur-archer the symbolic meaning of Apollo as the Sun. In Rome itself during Constantine's reign, Christ replaced this god in all his aspects that could be reconciled with the Christian teaching, and this substitution was often celebrated in art. It is thus that the archer and the centaur-archer gained entrance among the personal symbols of Christ. "Because I have bent Juda for me as a bow," says Zacharias "... And the Lord God shall be seen over them and his dart shall go forth as lightning[24]." And David: "He hath bent his bow, and made it ready. And in it he hath prepared the instruments of death, he hath made ready his arrows for them that burn[25]."

It is in the role of triumphant vanquisher of his and his Church's enemies that Jesus Christ has always been recognized in the enigmatic image of the archer; and this symbolism is authenticated by the Book of Revelation which says of the divine rider on the white horse: "He that sat on him had a bow; and a crown was given unto him; and he went forth conquering, and to conquer[26]."

Fig. 6 Christ armed with sword and bow; from a 12th-century French manuscript.

A twelfth-century French miniature, reproduced by the Abbé J. Corbelet in *L'Art Chrétien*, represents not Jehovah, god of combat, but Christ haloed with his cross, holding the two weapons which the Book of Revelation attributes to him, the sword and the bow with its arrows (Fig. 6). Earlier, toward the end of the fourth century, a Christian woman of Vermand (Aisne) wore on her finger a superb gold ring which she carried to her tomb; the monogram of Christ, X and P superimposed, which decorates the setting, is formed by a bundle of arrows, a reminder that the Savior is the divine archer who looses his shafts in all directions[27].

In Christian symbology, archers whether humans or centaurs, are always hunters of souls; often they represent Christ himself fighting against evil, or taking possession of souls. Medieval art frequently presents images of centaur-archers. When they are seen directing their shafts against an evil mon-

Fig. 7 12th-century sculpture from Parize-le-Chastel, Nivernais.

ster, they can be seen as representing the divine Archer in his war against Satan. If on the other hand the arrow threatens a harmless creature like a deer or a non-rapacious bird (Fig. 7), then it is the divine hunt for souls which seeks to take possession of them even by means of the painful dart of suffering, for their ultimate happiness. But when the archer, whether human or animal, directs his shaft toward heaven, it is always the symbol of Satan. It is then represented with a hideous body and a horrible face (Fig. 8). Equally disturbing and not to be taken in a good light are the centaurs, whether archers or not, whose peculiar features are so exaggerated as to accentuate their monstrous character—such as one in the cloister of St. Aubin of Angers, of the seventeenth century, which has a woman's torso on a four-footed masculine body[28].

Fig. 8 The demon archer. 12th-century French art, from de Caumont.

In the Greek language, the words for *bow* and *life* are connected. The Christ-Archer was thus regarded as the propulsive force of life, and medieval hermetism preserved this connection with the archer as a symbol of Jesus, and with his weapon, the bow, in accordance with the Jewish Kabbalah which makes the Hebrew letter *kaf* the ideogram of the impulsive force[29], because this letter is shaped like a bow. The expansion of this force, in action, is the full manifestation of life.

A word should be added on the meaning of the bowman in medieval astrology, because it agrees in a way with that of the centaur-psychagogue that has been spoken of. The constellation of Sagittarius whose conventional sign is the arrow[30] governs the ninth month of the astronomic year which begins on the first day of spring; so it rules what astrology calls "the ninth house," which corresponds to the ninth part of its cycle of the year and to the month of November. The old astrologists said that the astral influence of this constellation of Sagittarius had among other effects that of lifting toward God the thoughts and affections of numerous human beings; thus it led spirits from the lower, material plane toward higher regions.

NOTES

Title Figure: The satyr archer, Italian.

1. Homer, *The Odyssey*, XVI; *The Iliad*, I and II. Also Virgil, *The Aeneid*, VIII, 293, and Ovid, *Metamorphoses*, XV.
2. Cf. Reinach, *Répertoire*, T. II, Vol. II, p. 692.
3. *Ibid.*, T. III, p. 285, #4.
4. Charbonneau-Lassay, "Le Cheval," in *Regnabit*, T. XIV, #9, Feb. 1928, p. 145.
5. Cf. M. Lecointre Dupont, *Essai sur les monnaies du Poitou*, p. 6.
6. Cf. P. Biardot, *Explications du symbolisme des terres cuites grecques . . .*, p. 43.
7. St. Justin, *Apolog. pro Christian.—De Monarch.*, VI.
8. Cf. Carcopino, *Basilique*, II, 126.
9. Pindar, *Pyth.* (trans. Puech), T. III, p. 45.
10. Propertius, Bk. II, ch. I, 60.
11. Homer, *The Iliad*, XI.
12. St. Matthew 11:5.
13. Cf. du Roure de Paulin and C. de Gassicourt, *L'Hermétique dans l'Art héraldique*, p. 84.
14. See Charbonneau-Lassay, *op. et loc. cit.*; & above, Part II, "The Horse," p. 103.
15. Cf. L. Amélineau, "Histoire des Monastères de la Basse Egypte" in *Annales du Musée Guimet*, T. XXV (1894), p. 4.
16. See above, Part II, "The Horse," fig. 6.
17. Dante, *The Divine Comedy*, Inferno, canto XII.
18. L. Delaporte, "Les Cylindres orientaux de la collection de Luynes" in *Aréthuse*, XII, 1926, p. 97.
19. Layart, *Monument*, first series, Plate 21.
20. P. Saintyves, *Le massacres des Innocents*, p. 30. Also Frazer, *Folklore in the Old Testament*, II, 451.

21. Cf. Cornutus, *Traité de la nature des dieux*, XXXII.
22. Cf. Renel, *Revue de l'Histoire des Religions*, 1903, p. 45.
23. Cf. A. J. Reinach, *Itanos et l'Inventio Scuti*, III.
24. Zacharias 9:13-14 (Douay-Rheims version).
25. Psalms 7:13-14 (Douay-Rheims version).
26. Revelation 6:2.
27. M. Deloche, *Les Anneaux des premiers siècles du Moyen-âge*, p. 150, # CXXIX.
28. See A. de Caumont, *Abécédaire ou rudiment d'Archéologie*, 1851, p.162.
29. Dante, *op. cit.*, Paradiso, canto I.
30. Made of a cross whose shaft ends in a dart.

End Figure: An astrological centaur-archer from the Grant Kalendrier des Bergiers.

THE LION OF THE SEA AND THE MANTICORE

IN THEIR INSATIABLE hunger for marvels, our fathers created impossible lions which held a place in the ranks of more or less symbolic monsters and, being almost always placed on the side of evil, were often employed as evocations of the Lord of Hell.

One of the most ancient Christian depictions of the lion of the sea shows up on the sarcophagus of Theodosius, at Cividale in Italy, from the first half of the eighth century. There the creature appears to unite in itself the principal species of animals: by its lion's head and forelimbs, it is a quadruped, a fish by its fins, a reptile by its tail, a bird by its wings (Fig. 1). On the monument which displays it, its image is sculpted on each side of a sort of tree of life, in a posture which recalls the oriental tapestries of the time of the Sassanids[1]. Might this depiction perhaps, by a happy exception, signify that the whole animal kingdom draws its life from the Tree of Life?

Fig. 1 The lion of the sea on an 8th-century tomb at Cividale, Italy.

In the arts of the Middle Ages, and especially in heraldry, the image of the lion of the sea is more simple, more decorative, and less sympathetic than on the tomb of Cividale[2]; it presents only a lion's front quarters joined to its fish-shaped body. In the sixteenth century, the engraver of the works of Ambroise Paré made it simply a quadruped covered with scales, a monster who is a "strange beast" but who had no symbolic meaning[3].

By contrast, the manticore is a sort of lion-centaur whom the Middle Ages regarded as a veritable antithesis to the Christ-like lion which restores its young to life; for it is an inexorable destroyer. Its birth in the world of legend goes back quite far; Aelian, who lived in the third century, says that Ctesias asserts that there is a very powerful animal in Asia that resembles a great lion and has three rows of teeth, which is called *Marticoras* or *Manticoras*, that is, one who devours men[4].

At the end of the thirteenth century, Dante's teacher Brunetto Latini described the fabulous creature this way: "The Manticore is a beast in this land (of India), which has a man's face and a blood red complexion, yellow eyes, a lion's body, and a scorpion's tail, and which runs so hard that no beast can escape it. But above all meats, it loves the flesh of man[5]."

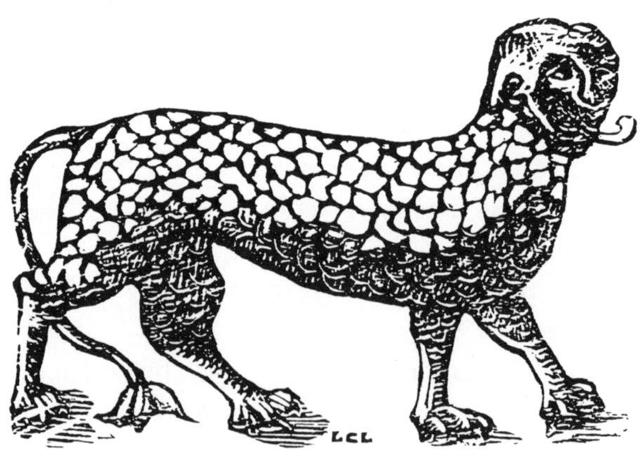

Fig. 2 The lion of the sea according to Ambroise Paré, 16th century.

And Rabelais completes this frightful portrait by telling us that "Mantichores are very strange beasts: they have a body like a lion, red skin, face and ears like a man, three rows of teeth each one running inside the others as if you interlaced your fingers; in the tail they have a barb with which they sting as scorpions do, and they have an extremely melodious voice[6]."

The celebrated monster column at the monastery of Souvigny in Bourbonnais, which dates from the twelfth century, bears the image of the infernal lion-centaur, under the name: MANICORA[7].

NOTES

Title Figure: The lion of the sea on a medieval German coat-of-arms.

1. See Leclercq and Marron, *Dictionnaire*, Fasc. LXXV, col. 1800.
2. De la Colombière, *La Science héroique*, p. 264, # 89.
3. Paré, *Oeuvres*, Bk. XXV, *Des Monstres*, p. 1052.
4. Aelian, *De natura animalium*.
5. Latini, *Li Livres dou tresor*, Bk. I, CXCV.
6. Rabelais, *Pantagruel*, Le Duchat edition, 1782. T. V, p. 191.
7. Cf. Mâle, *L'Art religieux (2)*, p. 324, fig. 189.

End Figure: The manticore on the Souvigny monster column.

THE HIPPOGRIFF

IN A VERY old initiate group in Asia the Sanskrit translation of St. John's Apocalypse is regarded as the holiest of scriptures, and the horseman in red and his mount as the most sacred of all symbols. The rider is designated by the title "He who is promised on the last day"; the white horse has the head of an eagle and wings of gold, and flashes of gold issue from its eyes. This is the hippogriff. It is pictured in full gallop on a very ancient Greek ivory discovered in Sparta[1], and its image adorns several Greek and Gallic coins. We see it striking an evil beast with its head, and its spirited action fills the disk of a Roman lamp found in Poitou[2] (Fig. 1).

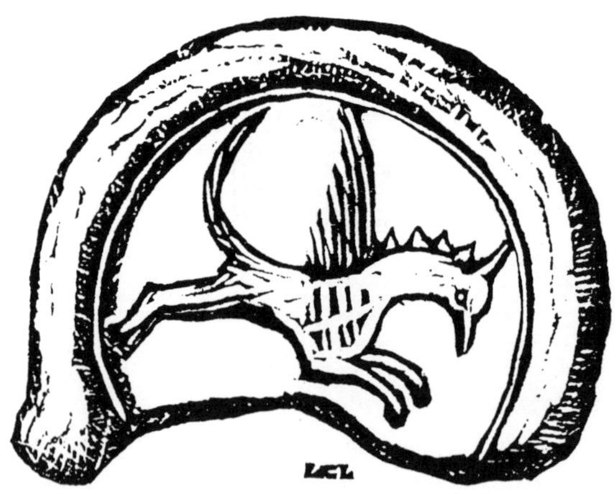

Fig. 1 The hippogriff on a piece of a Roman lamp, in the Musée des Grandes-Écoles at Poitiers.

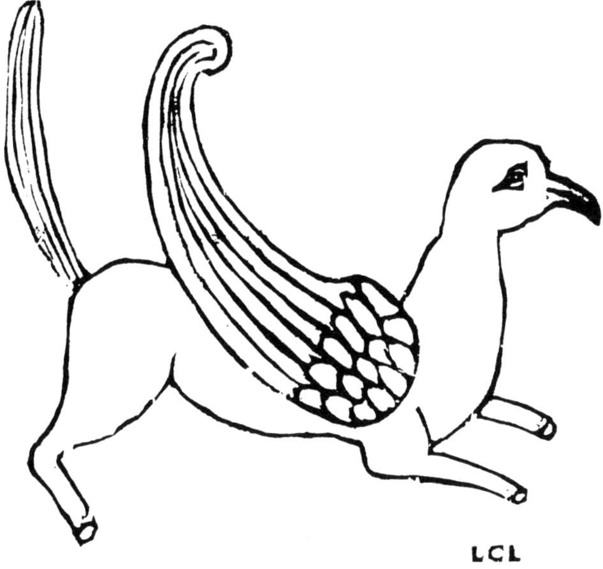

Fig. 2 The hippogriff on a 12th-century sculpture at the Prieuré du Bas-Nueil-sur-Dive in Vienne.

In the era of Greco-Roman supremacy as well as since, the qualities of the eagle and the horse were joined in the hippogriff, and in Christian symbolism, like its brother the griffin, it is the image of Dante's "two-natured beast"—the divine and the human natures united hypostatically in the unique Person of Christ. As with the griffin, the quadruped hindquarters represent Christ's humanity, and the breast, head, and wings of the eagle his divinity.

I reproduce here a Roman depiction of the hippogriff from the capital of a twelfth-century pillar in the old chapel of the Benedictine priory at Nueil-sur-Dive, near Loudun, in Vienne (Fig. 2). Images of the hippogriff are much less frequently seen in medieval Christian art than those of the griffin, the unicorn, and the winged horse; it is however quite wrong to suppose, as do some modern encyclopedists, that it was an invention of the fifteenth-century Italian poet Bojardo[3], who was the governor of Reggio and was later popularized by the *Orlando Furioso* of Ariosto.

NOTES

Title Figure: The hippogriff on a coin of the Gallic chief Pixtilos.

1. See Reinach, *Répertoire*, T. IV, p. 444, #3.
2. Société des Antiquaires de l'Ouest, Musée des Grandes-Écoles, in Poitou.
3. See Bojardo, *Le Roland amoureux*, 1494- (unfinished work).

End Figure: The hippogriff on a Gallic coin.

THE GRIFFIN

WITH THE CENTAUR and the hippogriff, we have introduced the fabulous "biformed" animals, to use Dante's word—hybrid creatures out of the abyss of time, chosen by Christian symbolists to represent the nature and excellence of Christ; but of these their favorite was the griffin.

Some scholars believe that griffins were conceived in the imagination of those Assyrian artists who were such extraordinary portrayers of animals during the twenty centuries preceding our era; or perhaps in some part of Chaldea near Babylon. The griffin is indeed found in the ancient art of these areas. I present here a drawing taken from a Babylonian cylinder seal engraved on semiprecious stone, where we see the griffin between the sacred symbol of the Tree of Life, surmounted by the solar globe and the lunar crescent, and a winged spirit attacking with a curved blade[1] (Fig. 1). A very ancient Chaldean sculpture shows two griffins who have come upon a gazelle; they have exactly the same aspect that has come down to us through the centuries[2]. The lintel of the entrance door to the palace of the Assyrian king Sennacherib, seven centuries before Christ, was decorated with two griffins drinking from a vessel placed between them[3]. The myth of the griffin was also known to the Persians at what was certainly an even earlier time; I reproduce here the beautiful

Fig. 1 The griffin on a Babylonian cylinder seal.

Fig. 2 Bronze head of a griffin; from Persepolis.

head of this animal found on the banks of the Araxes at Persepolis[4] (Fig. 2).

In the fifth century before our era, the Greek Ctesias who was mentioned before, the physician to King Artaxerxes of Persia, believed in the existence of griffins inhabiting some far-distant place which he describes as four-legged birds the size of wolves, whose backs were covered with black feathers and their breasts with red ones[5].

Ancient Indian art certainly recognized the griffin, before and at the beginning of our era, and made use of its image[6]. Modern scholars think that the Orient borrowed it from very ancient Greece, and that it must have reached Asia by means of the art of Cyprus, which would have received it from Mycenae[7]. Sir Arthur Evans says that in Greece this kind of hybrid animal goes back at least as far as the sixteenth century before Christ[8]. In Crete, in the rediscovered palace of King Minos at Knossos, on each side of the throne, huge griffins lie in fields of lilies, which were the emblematic flower of the Cretan royalty[9] (Fig 3).

Fig. 3 The griffin among the lilies; in the palace of Minos at Knossos.

The soil of Greece has yielded metal griffins of very archaic appearance[10], as for instance in Schliemann's excavations at Mycenae; and the griffin's image is seen on some beautiful Greek coins. Pliny describes the "griphis" with his customary richness of fancy and declares they come from the country of the Scythians, that is, northern Russia[11], while Aeschylus locates them among the Ethiopians[12].

"Like all that legion of monstrous animals depicted in oriental art," says Dom Leclercq, "the griffin was not a simple flight of fancy; it had a symbolic significance, and played a religious role[13]." This is certainly true; but we do not know what different meanings it was given in the ancient East: the

Babylonian cylinder seal reproduced above shows it as an evil-doer, as Satan, the adversary of the Tree of Life; but who can say what celestial liquor, what divine soma of apotheosis the griffins were drinking from the sacred vessel in the palace of Sennacherib? Then again, the griffins guarding the throne of the Cretan rulers at Knossos could only have had a positive connotation—however mysterious the diversity of these regions and of the religious and symbolic ideas of their inhabitants. In any case, in the earliest civilizations griffins usually represented some of the allegorical meanings of the lion and the eagle, equally kings of earth and air, whose natures they shared.

In Greece and Rome, the best known role in which the griffin was cast by religious thought was that of guardian of tombs[14]. Part of a second- or third-century Gallo-Roman sarcophagus, showing Greek influence, found at Vertou (Lower Loire)[15], shows one of the most magnificent of the known images of the funerary griffin (Fig. 4). There is another on the two Christian sarcophagi at Arles, in Provence[16], on one at Nîmes[17], etc.

Fig. 4 2nd- or 3rd-century funerary griffin from Vertou.

Another concept made the griffin, among the Greeks, an animal of light. This explains why it sometimes sits at the feet of statues of Apollo, and why two griffins flank the statue of the god in his temple at Delos[18]. An old coin from Smyrna has on one face the head of Apollo crowned with laurel, and on the reverse side a crouching female griffin with its paw on the solar wheel[19].

In consequence of this dedication to Apollo, the god of light and beauty, the griffin represented to the Ancients poetic inspiration, which carries the mind far from the common things of this world, as in the griffin the winged foreparts of the eagle lift the heavy hindquarters of the lion[20]. Sometimes also we see the griffin's image not at the foot of the god's statue but on his lyre itself[21]. It remains to be seen whether this aspect of animal of light was not in fact borrowed by the Greeks from oriental fables: the griffin drinks flame from the cup of the fire altar in archaic Persian and Assyrian art. The scholar Schliemann says that some ancient writers claimed that the Hindus believed griffins to be hitched to the Sun's chariot[22].

But it was not only by pure light and poetry that the Greeks connected the griffin to Phoebus-Apollo; they regarded it also, according to Herodotus, as the vigilant and invincible guardian of the god's treasures, and on a higher plane, "the guardian also of the ways of salvation[23] (Fig. 5)."

Fig. 5 The griffin fighting with the serpent; antique Greek bronze.

It would seem that the griffin, endowed with such a wealth of symbolism of a high order, must have been adopted from the beginning by Christian symbolism. It was not so, however. The griffin is not included among the animals pictured in the catacombs, and when it appears on some fourth- and fifth-century Christian lamps, it seems to be with an evil aspect. It was not until the coming of the Middle Ages that the symbolism of the griffin was definitely connected with Christ and his saints; at this time the learned monks revived the forgotten legend of griffins carrying aloft Alexander the Great, and this scene was sculptured in cloisters and in the stone decorations of great churches. Here is the story of Alexander's ascension, translated from an old French text of the period: "The soldiers of the great king Alexander came upon a strange deserted country called Sixtus. In this land lived huge and hideous birds called griffins. The king had several of these attached to a cabin of wood and new leather which he had had built and in which he took his place. He then raised above the cabin a piece of meat attached to the point of his lance, and immediately the griffins rose in the air, drawing Alexander upward as he pointed his lance. He ascended to the heaven of fire, where the excessive heat at last forced him to descend, which he accomplished by lowering his lance[24]."

According to other, better known authors, he captured two griffins and made them go without food for three days; then he attached them to the two sides of his throne, and lifted above their heads two long lances carrying roast meat on their points; the hungry griffins took flight trying to reach their prey and flew upward thus for seven days, carrying Alexander to God's dwelling. He would have crossed the threshold were it not for an angel who said to him: "O king, why do you wish to know what pertains to heaven, when you do not yet know what is of earth?" The king recognized his presumptuousness, lowered the lances, and the griffins brought him back to our world[25].

Fig. 6 The ascension of Alexander the Great, on a 12th-century capital at Basel.

Ancient Persia attributed a similarly presumptuous undertaking to King Kai Kaous, who made use of giant eagles whose flight carried him to what heights only God knows, for he was never seen again[26].

The ascension of Alexander was represented in the twelfth century particularly in Italy in the cathedrals of Otranto and of St. Mark's in Venice[27]; it is also seen in Basel (Fig. 6), in Freiburg, etc., and in France in several towns, especially in Mans and Thouars in Poitou.

In thus depicting the griffins lifting Alexander to heaven, medieval art clearly intended to make this king, in spite of the failure of his audacious enterprise, the image of the soul carried toward heaven by the eagle-lion creature; moreover, in so doing it was in perfect agreement with ancient art and ideas. In the center of a painted stucco ceiling on the Via Latina in Rome, a veiled figure, which can only be the soul of a dead person, is carried up toward the sky by a griffin psychagogue[28]. In ancient Egypt, the griffin, called Sefer, transformed itself into the burnt offerings of the sacrifices, and by means of their smoke carried toward heaven the souls of the dead for whom the sacrifices had been made[29]. As we have said, medieval Christian mysticism saw emblems of Jesus Christ in all the animals who in pre-Christian symbolism carried souls upward, especially in connection with the symbolism of the eagle.

Émile Mâle has given the following explanation of the medieval depictions of Alexander's legend: "Alexander," he said, "is human pride, human knowledge that tries to snatch God's secrets from him. Man ascends, he boldly enters the place of mysteries, but it is a limitless region, and at last he is forced to stop in front of new mysteries."

It is indeed very likely that in the Middle Ages some minds understood in this way the legend of Alexander and the griffins; but the interpretation which makes the griffin one of the symbolic animals who lift souls to God is also in full agreement with Christian symbolism, because it is in harmony with the attachment of the psychagogic role to the eagle, the falcon, the panther, the winged horse, etc., on the same pre-Christian bases.

Joining in itself the two natures of eagle and lion, the griffin is one of the most satisfactory emblems of Christ's dual nature. "*Aquila, Christus . . . Leo, Christus,*" says the *Clavis* attributed to St. Melito[30]. Similarly to other hybrid creatures, the eagle foreparts depict Christ's divinity and the lion hindquarters his humanity[31]. Dante and the mystics of his time accepted this Christ-symbolism in the griffin, and thus presented "the double-natured animal," the "biformed beast"

Fig. 7 The griffin on the paneling of a choir stall in the Poitiers cathedral, 13th century.

whose "wings stretched beyond human sight": the members of the eagle-shaped part of its body were golden, and those of the lion part were white mixed with purple[32]. And the beautiful animal which pulled the symbolic chariot was greeted by the great poet in the following words:

> Blest art thou, Gryphon, that with beak and bite
> Thou tearest naught from this sweet-tasting wood[33]
> Seeing how ill the belly gripest from it[34].

Alchemists, who have taken the griffin as the symbol of the "chemical hermaphrodite, sulphur and mercury," recognize that "Catholic commentators have chosen to see the symbol of Jesus Christ, God and Man, in the double nature of the griffin[35] (fig. 7)." Its aquiline-leonine body makes it also the symbol of two of the four elements, earth and air, and thus of the two kingdoms of Christ, heaven and earth.

The Ancients looked upon their beautiful animal of light also as one of the signs of wisdom, which is the highest light of the mind, and in this way again it represents Christ. It is in this aspect that the griffin appears on the shield carried by Wisdom personified on the north door of the thirteenth-century cathedral of Chartres[36].

Fig. 8 The griffin, from a 12th-century Leviticus in the Bibliothèque Nationale in Paris.

From another angle, because the eagle and the lion are both strong creatures and consequently nothing can stop the griffin in its powerful flight or its irresistible charge, the hermetic symbolists made it represent Christ's power (Fig. 8). In accordance with this little-known theme, a fifteenth-century ring bearing the image of the griffin shows also the text from St. Luke: "But he passing through the midst of them went his way [37]." A talismanic potency was attributed to this gospel text in the Middle Ages, as witness King Charles V's fine cameo, at Chartres, and certain coins from Brabant[38]. It was said also that arrows shot from bows made of the griffin's big wing-feathers were irresistible in their flight[39].

Because of this symbolic connection with Christ's invincible power and the magical protection proceeding from it, the credulity of the times sought for what it believed to be "griffins' eggs," without pausing to consider that that part of the animal that would normally contain the organs of maternity was that of a quadruped and not of an egg-bearer. Not withstanding this detail, people of rank had such eggs richly mounted as cups, which were considered (like vases of pseudo-unicorn's horn) to make the beverages they contained particularly healthful. Without going into the question of what large exotic birds these eggs might have come from, I shall only say that from the twelfth to the sixteenth century they were highly prized, especially in England where they were called "grypeseye[40]." They are mentioned in the inventories of princely and noble houses.

The imagination of the ancient world established dragons and griffins as the guardians of hidden treasures; griffins were especially the custodians of the most beautiful and precious of colored jewels, the emerald. At the end of the fifteenth century, Joannes de Cuba said that the finest emeralds were those taken from the nest of griffins who guard them "with great cruelty[41]." And his editor, Philippe Le Noir, in 1539, accompanied this text with a woodcut which shows the griffin arriving at its nest (a bird's nest!) where its little ones are nestling on top of the emerald (Fig. 9).

Medieval Christian symbolism adopted the old fable of the griffin and the emerald. Among the concepts which it added to it we only know that, as rubies were taken to symbolize Christ's blood, the emerald was also connected to the symbolism of the redeeming blood because, it was said, the cup in which Jesus blessed the wine at the Last Supper, saying "this is my blood," was made of an enormous carved emerald. This is the Holy Grail of our forefathers, which the epic of the Round Table says was made from an emerald that fell from Lucifer's brow at the moment of his rebellion. It is also the Holy Cup of Genoa, unquestionably ancient, but made in green molten glass which was long thought to be emerald.

Fig. 9 The griffin and its nest, its young, and the emerald. From the Hortus Sanitatis.

The griffin was the symbolic image of the saints, thanks

again to its double nature; because the saints are eagles on account of the high regions where their thoughts and affections dwell, and lions on account of the moral courage which they prove in the battle between good and evil. Tradition has it that in the year 509, King Clovis found himself at Moissac and conceived the desire to establish a church there where monks could celebrate the holy rites. The night following this decision, the king dreamed he saw two griffins holding stones in their beaks and carrying them to a neighboring valley. And in this valley Clovis had a church and an abbey built[42]. The hagiological legend says that the two griffins represented the two monks who were to become the two first abbots of Moissac, St. Amand and St. Ausbert[43].

Along the same lines, the artists who decorated the ancient Byzantine cathedral in Athens, about the ninth or tenth century, carved on the facade two griffins eating the fruit of the Tree of Life. Now, this tree and its fruit are only for the saints, according to the inspired text which the Church has made its own: "To him that overcometh will I give to eat of the tree of life, which is in the midst of the paradise of God[44]."

Here we must return to the scene of griffins drinking from a mysterious cup, and look at it this time as simply as did the medieval Christian folk in France. Surely, along with Dom Leclercq who spoke for the Merovingian epoch, with Charles Cahier[45] and Émile Mâle[46], we must recognize that the griffins drinking from a cup are a decorative subject directly inspired by oriental religious motifs having nothing to do with Christianity. To be even more exact, we shall say that this was a twelfth-century copy, in French Romanesque style, of a decorative motif imported from upper Lebanon and northern Syria by the crusaders and other travelers. It is, in fact, the chalice of the Mazdean fire altar from which drink birds, lions, griffins, and dragons; it can be seen in embroideries, in jewelry, on the metal dishes imported in such quantities from the Orient in this period. But in religious art, on the capitals of pillars and the ornamental brackets of our Romanesque churches, for instance, the people of that time, who interpreted everything in accordance with the ideas of their faith, could not have seen anything else, in the griffins who quenched their thirst in the chalice, but holy souls asking for the grace necessary for earthly life from the sacrament of Christ's eucharistic blood.

In the symbolic iconography of the Middle Ages, the griffin, with its rapacious beak and the huge claws of a predator, often symbolized Satan; the three bestiaries studied by Charles Cahier[47] speak of it only under this name, which seems to suit it well, especially in those images of it which show it with a dragon-like rear ending in a reptile's tail (Fig. 10). It is surely on account of this satanic character in contemporary symbolism that formerly in the Sainte-Chapelle in Paris there was hung like a trophy what was supposed to be a griffin's paw; that of some big predator. It was said that a knight who had vanquished the animal in single combat had placed it there in the royal chapel as an ex-voto offering[48].

Fig. 10 The griffin-dragon, heraldic symbol of Satan, from a 17th-century coat-of-arms.

But all the heraldists recognized that the griffin, noble in both its aerial and terrestrial natures, often represented Christ on coats-of-arms[49]. This is especially the case when it serves as "allusive arms" (those which suggest a play upon the bearer's name or title) for great families: for example, the Griffa in the kingdom of Naples, the Griffen in Silesia[50], the Griffon in Saintonge and Poitou[51]. When a heraldic figure takes on the function of "allusive arms," it always carries the noblest meaning that can be attributed to it, which also then contributes to the luster of the owner's family name.

In other cases, the griffin means the alliance of speed and

vigilance with strength and courage[52]. Elsewhere, especially in the armorial bearings of cities, the griffin takes back its old significance as incorruptible guardian. But in the medieval religious heraldry and sigillography (the study of seals), when the griffin appears alone it must be regarded as the image of Jesus Christ, God and man. The "griffin-dragon" of heraldry, which is opposed to the usual "griffin-lion," and whose body ends like that of a reptile, always represents an abominable enemy—in a word, Evil.

NOTES

Title Figure: The griffins of Paradise; from a marble tank at Charenton-sur-Cher, 4th to 6th century.

1. Taken from L. Delaporte, "Cylindres orientaux" in *Annales du Musée Guimet*, 1909, p. 88, Plate VIII, #114.
2. Cf. Gustave le Bon, *Les premières Civilisations*, fig. 308, p. 596.
3. Cf. Perrot and Chipiez, *Histoire de l'Art*, T. II, p. 148.
4. Taken from Chas. de Linas, "Les origines de l'Orfèvrerie cloisonnée," in *Revue de l'Art chrétien*, T. XXIII, p. 34.
5. Ctesias, *Indica*, XII: Herodotus, III, 102; Aelian, *Hist. Anim*, IV, 27.
6. See in the Salle Lenart in the Musée Guimet in Paris.
7. See René Dussaud, "Le Sarcophage peint de Hagia Triada" in *Revue historique des Religions*, 1908, p. 170.
8. Evans, *Académie des Inscriptions*, meeting of Sept. 25, 1925.
9. Cf. Glotz, *Civilisation égéenne*, p. 143, fig. 20; and Jean Charbonneaux, *L'Art égéenne*, passim.
10. Schliemann, *Mycènes*, p. 257.
11. Pliny, *Natural History*, VII, 2; and XXXIII, 4-21.
12. Aeschylus, *Prometheus Bound*, 803.
13. Leclercq and Marron, *Dictionnaire*, T. VI, Vol. II, col. 1822.
14. Cf. Rich, *Dictionnaire*.
15. L. Mâitre, *Vertou*, p. 6.
16. Ed. le Blant, *Étude sur les sarcophages chrétiens de la ville d'Arles*, p. 3, #6 and p. 68, #67.
17. *Idem.*, *Les Sarcophages chrétiens de la Gaule*, p. 109, #123.
18. Cf. Déchelette, "Le Culte du Soleil aux temps préhistoriques" in *Revue archéologique*, 4th series, T. XIV.
19. A. de Barthélemy, *Album de Numismatique ancienne*, #286.
20. Philostratus, *Life of Apollo*, III, 4-8.
21. Cf. Héron de Villefosse, "La Statue colossale d'Apollon ... à Entrains (Nièvre)" in *Revue archéologique*, 2nd series, T. XXXI, 1876, p. 37.
22. Schliemann, *op. et loc. cit.*
23. Carcopino, *Basilique*, pp. 38 and 299.

24. Cf. Lambert le Cors and Alexandre de Bernay, *Li Romans d'Alixandre.*
25. Cf. E. Talbot, *Essai sur la légende d'Alexandre le Grand...*, p. 160; also Mâle, *L'Art religieux (2)*, p. 271.
26. Cf. *Shah Nameh*, Ed. Molh., T. II, p. 45; also *Shah Nameh*, Eng. tr. by Helen Zimmer, p. 117.
27. Barbier de Montault, *Traité d'Iconographie chrétienne*, T. II, p. 80 and Plate XXIV.
28. Cf. Fr. Cumont, "L'Aigle funéraire des Syriens," Fig. 22, in *Revue de l'Histoire des Religions*, T. XII, 1910, p. 154.
29. Cf. Lefébure, *La Vertu du Sacrifice funéraire*, II.
30. Cf. Dom Pitra in *Spicilège de Solesmes.*
31. Barbier de Montault, *op. cit.*, T. I, p. 131.
32. Dante, *The Divine Comedy*, Purgatory: Canto XXIX.
33. The tree of the knowledge of good and evil. Cf. Fr. Hayward, *L'Aigle et la Croix dans la Divine Comédie.*
34. Dante, *op. cit.*, Purgatory: Canto XXXII.
35. Dr. Probst-Biraben, "Allusion à l'Alchémie et à l'Astrologie de la Divine Comédie," in *Le Voile d'Isis*, T. XXXIV, 114, June 1929, p. 409.
36. Cf. Barbier de Montault, *op. cit.*, T. II, p. 193.
37. St. Luke 4:30. The text refers to the attempt by the Nazarenes to throw Jesus from the top of a cliff.
38. Cf. *Catalogue de l'Exposition du Moyen-âge* in the Bibliothèque Nationale in Paris, 1926, p. 122, #204; p. 116, #169; p. 137, #338.
39. Joannes de Cuba, *Hortus Sanitatis*, "Du Griffon."
40. L. de Laborde, *Glossaire français du Moyen-âge*, p. 335. [*Editor's note*: The obsolete English word *grypeseye* meant *gripe's* (griffin's) *egg*.]
41. Joannes de Cuba, *op. cit.*, 2nd part, IV, *Des Pierres*, ch. VIII.
42. Cf. *Bulletin archéologique*, T. III, p. 130.
43. Barbier de Montault, "Les Portes de bronze de Bénévent," in *Revue de l'Art chrétien*, 1883, p. 51.
44. Revelation 2:7.
45. Cahier, "Bas-reliefs mystérieux" in *Nouveaux Mélanges archéologiques*, 1874, p. 178.
46. Mâle, *op. cit.*, (note 25 above), p. 67.
47. Cahier, *Mélanges archéologiques*, T. II and III.
48. Cf. Berger de Xivrey, *Tradition tératologique*, p. 484.
49. De Gassicourt and de Paulin, *L'Hermétisme dans l'Art héraldique*, p. 109; also O'Kelly de Galway, *Dictionnaire*, p. 281.
50. Cf. de la Colombière, *La Science héroique*, p. 270.
51. R. Pétiet, *Armorial poitevin*, p. 71.
52. De la Colombière, *op. cit.*, p. 271.

End Figure: A Mycenaean griffin in bronze: from Schliemann.

THE DRAGON

THE DRAGON OF contemporary naturalists, *draco fimbriatus*, is only a little reptile no more than thirty-five centimeters long, which lives on the coasts and islands of Malaysia, Sumatra, Java, Borneo, and Celebes (now Sulawesi). It has membranes attached to both its flanks which act as a parachute when it leaps into space from a tree or a high rock (Fig. 1). But it is not this harmless little creature that concerns us here. If one reads the accounts of the first teachers of the Christian doctrine, it would seem that in the first thousand years of Christianity, "dragon" meant only the accursed dragon of Hebrew scripture and of St. John's *Revelation*[1] — a fabulous animal that seems to have sprung from an exaggeration of the crocodile, well before the time of King David.

It was not until later, during the Middle Ages, that the Nile hydra was represented as a veritable small dragon, sometimes with wings[2]. But at the same time there arose in certain particularly fertile imaginations a belief in the existence of another, different sort of Nile hydra, with a beneficent nature. Old memories from classical times supported this notion: the Ancients had spoken of dragon-like beings well-disposed to humans, and Suetonius said that the dragon is "of divine essence," *Divus Draco*. This kindly spirit

Fig. 1 The dragon of the southern coasts of Indo-China.

was supposed to have lived (of course!) under the burning skies of Ethiopia and in the countries on the coasts of the Indian Ocean, the Erythrian Sea of the ancient world.

Ceaselessly attacked by the "evil dragons," the "good dragons," it was said, were often overcome by the terrible teeth and claws of their adversaries; but then their blood, falling on the hot desert sand or the burning rocks of the mountains, took on a resinous appearance, dark crimson in color, and became one of the most precious remedies known to man: *dragon's-blood*, which healed the often frightful wounds suffered by knights in combat, and the bites of wild animals[3], as effectively as dittany and better than any other medication. Blood that could cure so miraculously could surely flow only from the heart of a beneficent creature; and in the thoughts of some, a relation was even made with the healing blood of Christ—a boldness of symbolism no greater than many to which the bestiaries of the epoch were already accustomed. But in fact, this symbolism, like many others, seems not to have gone beyond the circle of alchemists, seers, and apothecaries whose inner councils, especially until the Renaissance, were more than discreet in matters concerning their professional secrets and traditions.

It was not until the beginning of the seventeenth century that the mystery of the true nature of dragon's-blood was revealed by the Andalusian scholar, Nicolas Monardes[4]. Here is what an important French medical journal wrote recently on the subject of the remedy so much prized by our forefathers: "The word dragon's-blood was given to it not because of its red color, but because the Ancients thought that it came from the dried blood of the dragon, a fabulous animal in whose real existence they believed. Dioscorides denied the truth of this notion, without however stating the true provenance of the substance. The Spanish physician Nicolas Monardes was the first to indicate its vegetable origin. He states that the tree that gives this sap is called *dragon* because nature has printed this animal's track on its fruit. But it is much more probable that the sap received the fabled name which was then passed on to the tree that produced it and which was unknown to the Ancients[5]."

This is a very judicious statement; the dragon's-blood that the Ancients collected came, without their knowledge, from the dried fruits of different palm trees, especially the fruit of the *calamus draco*, growing on the banks of the Persian Gulf and in the basin of the Erythrian Sea, Hindustan, and Indo-China. Dragon's-blood is also produced by the *dracoema draco* of the Canaries and the Azores, and by the *pterocarpus draco* of the West Indies and South America, regions that were known to Nicolas Monardes. Pliny, for his part, as we shall see in the next chapter on the basilisk, attributes a magical power very similar to that of dragon's-blood to the blood of the basilisk, the dragon-cock.

It might be added that a careful study of the heraldry of the nobility of this epoch and its later developments[6] indicates that the dragon did not always play a villainous role on the armorial bearings, but sometimes represented vigilance, and also ardor; for it was said that the dragon "goes to battle like an impetuous torrent sweeping down from the mountains" and that from its lungs issues a breath so fiery that "it sets the air ablaze[7]."

Another concept of the dragon, which seems to have arisen in the Far East well before Christian times, is one which connects it with the divine Word, as in the Egyptian religion the ibis was related to the "Word of Creation." This idea was probably familiar to the ancient Christian communities of Syria, upper Armenia, and the more eastern Nestorian centers, for communications between the Near and Far East in the first thousand years of the Christian era were much more frequent than is generally imagined[8]; and it was a current notion in the regions that are now known as Khorassan, Afghanistan, and the Punjab. At the present time, in Lamaism and Indo-Tibetan Buddhism the dragon is still looked upon as the symbol of life and the divine Word, the creative and preserving utterance of life on earth[9]. "The dragon," says René Guénon, "was the ancient Far Eastern symbol of the Word, but it awakes only 'diabolic' associations in the minds of modern westerners[10]."

In Burma and the provinces of the neighboring Blue River Valley, the dragon is represented in its creative aspect as expelling from its mouth the flood of the first waters which contained the Fish, symbol of life on earth; and without doubt, this function of its mouth connects it with the Word of God the Creator.

Fig. 2 The sacred Great Dragon of China, protector of the Emperors and the Empire; from H. Doré.

All the people on earth who have had faith in one supreme divinity, the creator of all the worlds and the life upon them, have worshipped the all-powerful utterance which declared throughout space the laws which rule the gravitation of these worlds and the germs of life developing upon them. The Word of Creation to the pontiffs of Egypt, the Logos to the Greeks, the mouth of Ogmios to the Druids of Gaul, the voice of God or the uncreated speech to the lamas of Tibet and the bonzes of China and Indo-China; whatever it may be, the divine Word—however poorly known, ill-defined, or badly served—remains no less the Word of God which was in the beginning, without which nothing would have been made, and which is the very light and life of men[11]. For the Christian, all homage, all worship, directed toward the divine Word rises directly to Christ, the eternal Word of the Father, as anything thrown into space, in spite of itself goes straight to its true center of gravity.

In Annam, as the emblem of power, the dragon depicts the person of the emperor (Fig. 2); it is also the guardian of hidden treasures[12]. It might be added that in regions such as India and Tibet, the dragon is often looked upon as a psychagogue, since it is on its wings or its back that the souls of the holy ascetics are lifted and carried toward the Compassionate One after the death of their bodies. It is thus that the blessed soul of Milarepa departed from this world into the immensity of bliss.

It is an historical certainty that the first apostles of Christianity in China did not anathematize the image of the dragon of the region, for at the top of the Christian monument at Jinxian which was raised in 1625, a sort of crowning cupola surmounting the cross is held up by two dragons[13].

The Chinese see the sacred image of the dragon nearly everywhere—in the vines enlacing the tree trunks, in the foam of waterfalls, in clouds, in the smoke of funeral pyres and in that of their cooking pots[14]. Among these many dragons, some are good spirits, others are fearsome and maleficent. They become, as Father Doré says, hopelessly confused. The greatest of them all "is a mysterious, supernatural creature, the reptile-spirit specifically designated in Chinese books as the Dragon above all others." This Great Dragon, it is said, appears only in extraordinary circumstances, and in particular marked the reign of the very early, perhaps legendary, emperor Fu Xi, who claimed it made frequent personal appearances which exerted great influence for his governing policies[15]. The image of the Great Dragon in China is like the symbol of sovereign nobility and divine power; that is why it is embroidered on the emperor's coat and tunic, and often is shown as the mount of gods and goddesses. Above all the cult is related to the prosperity of the ruler and of his people.

The secondary dragons were divided into four families by the religious learned men of China: (1) dragons that rise into the sky; (2) dragon-spirits; (3) terrestrial dragons that cannot rise into the sky; and (4) underground dragons that guard hidden treasures and precious substances buried in the ground. The liturgy of the secondary dragons is extremely complex and its principal ceremonies are practiced to obtain rain or fine weather, or good crops of grain and fruit, and lead to the traditional annual "Growth Ceremony" (Fig. 3). Petitions for successful stock-raising and for all material goods are also part of this cult[16].

In all that Father Doré recounts of the draconic traditions in China, there is nothing which connects the dragon clearly with the creating and preserving Word. It is true that he speaks only incidentally of the high points of Chinese theology, and more especially of the simple superstitions of the people. He does say however that the dragon "is the active principle of *yin*, or in other words, it is the *yang* of the *yin*[17]."As is generally known, the *An Liang* (dark-light) or *Tai-ji* (great ultimate) of central Asia and China is composed of two cosmic principles, masculine and feminine, *yang* and *yin*, which are complementary and necessary for all activity and all life in the whole universe. Certainly this idea can be related to that of Christian theology, of the Spirit creating and animating the world, of the creative and preserving Utterance of life, the divine Word[18].

Fig. 3 Talismanic image of the Chinese "Dragon of Growth," from H. Doré.

Very old stories often describe the dragon as jealously guarding immense treasures in inaccessible caves, or on mountain peaks surrounded by precipices, which can be reached only by one dangerous path, full of pitfalls. In other legends, the dragon guards the entrance of a paradise that contains happiness, the most precious and fragile treasure of all. To taste it, or to possess the riches of any of these fantastic storehouses, a man must put to death the guardian monster; thus Hercules had to fight and conquer the dragon keeping the gate of the garden of the Hesperides where grew the golden apples of felicity. The blade reddened with the blood of the guardian of these places is thus the key that allows one to enter. For centuries and up till now, groups based on initiatic principles have kept the symbol of the defending dragon, and his title of "Guardian of the threshold" has passed into their vocabulary. It is the figurative death of this guardian-dragon which allows access to the Holy of Holies of the group, and participation in its life and secrets.

Fig. 4 The infernal winged dragon, from a 14th-century manuscript.

To the ordinary thought of the majority of Christians nowadays, the dragon stands for Satan, the spirit of evil, king of hell, and for nothing else (Fig. 4). This opinion, which leaves out too much of the ancient symbolism, conforms however with that of the medieval bestiaries[19], and is based on scriptural texts such as that about the Babylonian dragon-idol which Daniel destroyed[20] (Fig. 5), and the Apocalypse of St. John: "... and behold a great red dragon, having seven heads and ten horns, and seven crowns upon his heads. And his tail drew the third part of the stars of heaven, and did cast them to the earth: and the dragon stood before the woman which was ready to be delivered, for to devour her child as soon as it was born...[21]" And St. John adds that this great dragon, this "old serpent" is indeed he who is "called the Devil, and Satan...[22]"

Fig. 5 Daniel poisoning the Babylonian dragon; from a 14th-century English manuscript.

In accordance with these texts, the early artists made the dragon symbolize Satan, the Antichrist, the lord of all evil. They also present it as the ruler of all the agents of evil on earth, wherever or whoever they might be; thus we see in an old stained glass window in the church of St. Nizier of Troyes that the beast is worshipped by a king, a bishop, a monk, and a woman; from on high, God in the guise of a pope leans down with a reaping hook to cut off the monster's horrible crop of seven heads.

But opposing the sovereignty of the dragon over human beings, many hagiographic legends describe the victory of the saints over the spirit of evil, represented by the dragon. First, there are the two heavenly warriors, St. Michael and St. George, armed and equipped, mounted on war-horses; then a great number of the blessed who have no weapon but the strength of their virtue, which brings them a particle of the divine power. Among these are St. Andrew of Aix-en-Provence, St. Victor of Marseille, St. Armentaire of Draguignan, St. Martha of Tarascon, St. Radegund of Poitiers, and many others. The legend of Tarascon is well-known: a monstrous beast, a huge reptile "with a lion's gullet" described by Mistral, following the traditions of Provence[23], brought terror throughout the Rhône valley below Avignon. St. Martha went out alone to meet it and took it captive in Tarascon, binding it only with her fragile girdle—the image of paganism conquered in this region by the first apostles of the Christian faith.

In the sixth century, St. Radegund founded a convent in Poitiers where she lived with her companions in the practice of virtue. But a winged dragon of enormous size came to take up its abode in an underground tunnel of ancient origin that opened into the convent. Any imprudent nuns who came too near its retreat were devoured by the monster, but Radegund punished it; although it took flight to escape her approach, the saint struck it down with one sign of the cross (Fig. 6).

Formerly, in the old cities where such tales were told, rep-

Fig. 6 St. Radegund's dragon; now at the Musée de l'Hôtel de Ville at Poitiers. A 17th-century wood carving.

resentations of the conquered dragons were carried in solemn processions. Immediately following the cross in the processional order, these dragon-images symbolized Satan conquered and following his conqueror, as the enemy kings in the Roman triumphs followed with bound hands the chariot of the victorious Caesar.

According to Eusebius, it was with this image of vanquished paganism that the emperor Constantine had himself represented on foot, piercing with his lance a bristling dragon[24]. And with a similar thought, medieval artists sometimes placed a serpent, sometimes a conquered dragon, under the foot of the Virgin Mary, as an echo of the biblical curse: "She shall crush thy head, and thou shalt lie in wait for her heel[25]."

In the Salle de Baouit in the Louvre museum, there is an astonishing and very fine Egypto-Roman sculpture representing the god Horus, on horseback and dressed like a Roman legionnaire, who tramples under his horse's feet and pierces with his lance the Typhonian crocodile, one of the Egyptian symbols of evil.

NOTES

Title Figure: The dragon of the Hortus Sanitatis, *1491 edition.*

1. Cf. Leclercq and Marron, *Dictionnaire*, T. IV. Col. 1537 et seq.
2. See Part III above, "The Crocodile," Fig. 1.
3. In the last century, dragon's-blood still entered into the composition of various pills and unguents used for excessive bleeding, such as Tisserand's hemostatic lotion and Dubois' powder for bedsores.
4. Monardes, *De las cosas que se traen de las Indias occidentales.*
5. *Aesculape*, 2nd series, T. XVI, #3; March 1926, p. 102. See also Matthiolus, [Mattioli], *Comment. sur Dioscoride*, Bk. V, ch. LXIX.
6. Cf. de la Colombière, *La Science héroique*, p. 320.
7. Cf. Albertus Magnus, Bk. XXXV, *De Animalibus.*
8. Cf. J.B. Chabot, *Histoire de Mar-Jabahala III, patriarche des Nestoriens*, Paris, 1895.
9. Cf. J. Marques-Rivière, *A l'ombre des Monastères tibétains*, p. 125.
10. Guénon, "Seth," in *Le Voile d'Isis*, T. XXXVI, 1931, #142, p. 504.
11. St. John 1:1-4.
12. Cf. H. Gordon, *Conférence sur les religions indigènes en Indo-Chine*, Paris, April 14, 1932.
13. See Leclercq, *op. cit*, T. III, Vol. I, col. 1353-1385, fig. 2.802.
14. Cf. Doré, *Recherches*, passim.
15. *Ibid.*, Part I, T. II, Vol. IV, pp. 449 & 461.
16. *Ibid.*, Part I, T. II, p. 200.
17. *Ibid.*, Part I. T. II, Vol. IV, p. 452.
18. Note that the Great Dragon holds in his coils the Flame, the image of life (Fig. 4).
19. See William of Normandy, *Le Bestiaire divin*, XXV, *De Dragon.*
20. Daniel 14:22-27, Douay-Rheims version.
21. Revelation 12:3-4.
22. *Ibid.* 12:9.
23. Mistral, *Mireille*, canto XI.
24. Eusebius, *Histor. eccles.*
25. Genesis 3:15, Douay-Rheims version.

End Figure: One of the dragons from Queen Matilda's tapestry at Bayeux, 11th century.

THE BASILISK

THE BASILISK IS shown in medieval Christian art so often that we must take a moment to examine its legend and its monstrous image. Following Linnaeus, naturalists gave the name of basilisk to several kinds of medium-sized saurians chiefly inhabiting America and naturally having nothing to do with the famous basilisk of the Ancients, who designated with the name *basilikos*, "the royal one," a snake whose head carried a row of scales placed in the shape of a crown. Charles Cahier thinks that this historic basilisk is the uraeus of the Egyptians, the viper Haje[1], whose sacred image guarded both the sun's golden disk and the crowned forehead of the pharaoh; and Horapollo, writing in the fourth century of our era, was of the same opinion[2]. On a Roman lamp of this period, Christ is represented standing with the accursed beasts beneath his feet, and among them the basilisk in the shape of the viper-asp[3]. That coincides with the theory of Pliny, who describes the basilisk of Cyrenaica as a small snake with a white spot shaped like a crown on its head. He also states that the basilisk's breath kills shrubs, burns the grass, and breaks stones, and that the horseman who kills it with his lance dies also, and his horse as well, because the basilisk's venom flows back up the shaft of the lance . . . and he adds: "Nevertheless, this fearsome monster cannot resist weasels; this is nature's law: everything has its counterbalance[4]."

The Egyptians made the basilisk, their uraeus, symbolize the idea of eternity, says Horapollo, because "it is a member of the only race of serpents that do not die." He adds that the basilisk "with nothing but its breath, strikes dead any other animal, without even touching or biting it[5]." Because of this terrifying faculty, several nations of former times, where this was talked of, saw in the basilisk the ruinous power of evil. From the time of David, the basilisk was considered one of the four monsters who reflect this evil power: the asp, the basilisk, the lion, and the dragon, which the future Messiah must triumphantly crush beneath his feet: "Thou shalt walk upon the asp and the basilisk, and thou shalt trample underfoot the lion and the dragon[6]." Isaiah is even more explicit. In the first chapters of his prophecy he announces two mysterious future events: the coming of the Messiah, lord and principle of good: "And there shall come forth a rod out of the stem of Jesse, and a Branch shall grow out of his roots: And the spirit of the Lord shall rest upon him. . .[7]" The other event is the appearance of the accursed Antichrist, the lord of all evil: "out of the serpent's root shall come forth a cockatrice [basilisk] and his fruit shall be a fiery flying serpent [dragon][8]."

Among the pre-Christian peoples of the Mediterranean basin, the basilisk was in no better repute: some among them, says Pierius, declared it was born from an egg which was formed in the body of a very old ibis from the concentrated venom of all the snakes swallowed by the bird during its lifetime[9].

Pliny sums up thus the Greek and Roman legends on this subject: "As for the basilisk, which even serpents flee from, which kills by its odor alone . . . its blood has been greatly celebrated by the sages; this hardens like resin, and is of the same color; when water is added to it, it becomes redder than cinnamon. It is said to have the power to cure maladies and to prevent evil spells. Some call it the blood of Saturn[10]."

In Assyria, the god of war, Nergal, a mythic being more ferocious than the Greek Ares or the Roman Mars, was shown as a more or less dragon-like cock, which Éliphas Lévi (without identifying the piece of ancient art that was his authority for it) has depicted as a medieval basilisk, both cock and snake[11] (Fig. 1).

The cock itself was often the image of the Savior, but the basilisk, combining cock and snake, was quite the opposite. After having been the sign of Evil and Death in pre-Christian cults, in Christian iconography the basilisk became the emblem of Satan. This mythical creature had a cock's body ending in the tail of a lizard or a snake, like the *caladre*[12] which expresses an entirely different idea. Christian symbolism made use of all the earlier fables about the basilisk to make it the image of the Spirit of Evil, and the authors of bestiaries and similar works in the Middle Ages added still more to what has formerly been attributed to it. The Dominican Vincent de Beauvais, who wrote in the reign of St. Louis[13], concludes thus: "It is reliably said that the cock, when it becomes very old, lays an egg, out of itself ('*facit ovum ex se*[14]'), and that under certain conditions the basilisk is hatched from this marvelous egg. When the egg is laid in a manure heap, with the help of the heat generated there, after a very long time a little animal emerges... This animal has a tail like a viper and the rest of its body is like a cock. Some writers say that this egg has no shell, but a kind of skin that is so tough that it cannot be torn even with the most violent effort. Others say that the egg is hatched by a viper and an owl, but that does not seem assured. The writings of the Ancients limit themselves to affirming that there exists a kind of basilisk that is engendered from the egg of an old cock[15]."

Fig. 1 Kabbalistic image of Nergal, from Éliphas Lévi.

The Florentine Brunetto Latini, who was a contemporary of Vincent de Beauvais, adds a detail not mentioned by the latter: that through its eyes, the basilisk discharges waves of its inner poison so powerfully destructive that with its look alone it kills whatever human or beast it sees[16].

Some medieval artists emphasized this characteristic of terrifying malignity which their times attributed to the basilisk by representing the creature with eyes at the tip of its tail which sometimes ends in a serpent's head—which meant that it was thus equipped to see and to deal out death both before and behind. A Romanesque capital in the cathedral of Mans provides an example in sculpture of this hyperbolic symbolism[17].

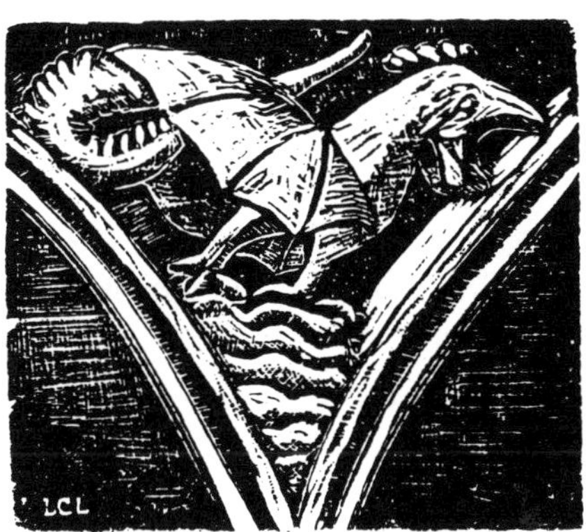

Fig. 2 The basilisk; a 13th-century sculpture from the Poitiers cathedral.

Fig. 3 The basilisk; 12th-century sculpture from the abbey church of Vézelay.

The half-cock, half-snake basilisk is seen not only in the sculpture of the great cathedrals such as those of Mans, of Amiens, Sens[18], and Poitiers[19], or of abbeys such as Vézelay (Figs. 2 & 3), but also in numerous rural churches, so popular in former times was this symbolism. The little country church of Claunay, near Loudun, in Vienne, contains a Romanesque capital decorated with the image of a knight on foot striking a helmeted basilisk with his sword. It is the struggle between Good and Evil, so often and variously depicted, and could be seen as Christ fighting with Satan. But the local legend, ignoring a flagrant anachronism, chooses to see in it the image of the valiant knight Frettard, the lord of Claunay, who in 1350 drove away the English from Loudun

Fig. 4 Capital of a pillar in the church at Véniers, in Vienne.

where they had been laying siege for three months to the town's impregnable fortress. The legend says that on returning to his manor house of Turzay in Claunay, he went in to the church to give thanks to God for his victory, and on leaving it, whom should he meet outside the door but Satan in the form of an armed basilisk, barring his passage. A terrible fight ensued which lasted till morning, during which the knight Frettard forced the monster to retreat, step by step, for three leagues, to the courtyard of his house at Coulaines-en-Mouterre; just as they arrived there, one of the barnyard cocks greeted the first light of dawn with his ringing voice. At this sound, the basilisk suddenly gave way completely and hurled itself into the well of Coulaines. Only once every ten years is it permitted during the night to come up to the well's curbstone.

It is clear that even when the popular imagination deflects these legends of the satanic cock from their mystical meanings, in the remote countrysides of France they remain within the context of the old themes expressed by the religious writers of the Middle Ages. I have lingered over the Claunay legend because it presents so well both the satanic character with which the basilisk was popularly endowed and that of the guardian who frightens away nocturnal demons and monsters, which is attributed by a tradition many thousands of years old to the voice of the basilisk's virtuous antithesis, the cock, saluting the dawn.

A curious capital from the very last period of Romanesque

Fig. 5 12th-century Romanesque capital at Mans.

art, which is in the church at Veniers, near Loudun, expresses a very different theme from that of the basilisk, showing the foreparts of a cock attached to the body of a bull (Fig. 4). Should we see in this hieroglyph the union of intelligence and of courageous strength, the one guiding the other? Possibly so, for in Christian symbolism the cock—when it does not represent the Christian, or on the other hand a vice—everywhere remains one of the symbols of intelligence because of the sacred text which bears on it: *Quis dedit gallo intelligentiam*? "Who gave the cock understanding?[20]" But in the basilisk, this precious faculty is placed at the service of evil. The hybrid creature at Veniers however is not necessarily one of the servants of the Evil Spirit.

The basilisk also sometimes symbolized the perverted Christian who stops at nothing; this is doubtless the meaning of the capital in the cathedral of Mans where two basilisks, in the words of St. Paul, drink "their own damnation" from the chalice (Fig. 5). And this allegory, evoking the sacrilegious communion, is the opposite of the theme of the capital in Henri Aymard's collection, where two cocks drink from the cup of life.

In the Kabbalah, the basilisk is the mount of the infernal angel Azazel, because this monster kills not only with its look but with the germs of the pestilences and contagious maladies it carries[21].

NOTES

Title Figure: Medieval image of the basilisk.

1. See Cahier in *Mélanges archéologiques*, T. II, p. 215. (It is the serpent Naja).
2. Horapollo, *Hieroglyphica*, Books I and II, 60.
3. *Dictionnaire archéologique chrétienne*, fasc. 84, col. 1173-4, #8.
4. Pliny, *Natural History*, Book VIII, XXIV. See also Part III above, "The Weasel," p. 149.
5. Horapollo, *op. et loc. cit.*
6. Psalms 90:13, Douay-Rheims version.
7. Isaiah 11:1-2.
8. *Ibid.* 14:29.
9. Cf. Buffon, *Oeuvres complètes*, 1835, T. IX, III, p. 203. Also *Le Bestiaire divin*, Hippeau ed., p. 120.
10. Pliny, *op. cit.*, XXIX, 19.
11. Lévi, *Les Mystères de la Kabbale*, p. 57.
12. *Editor's note*: *Caladre* is a French word for *pluvier*, the plover, a small wading bird whose various species appear in many parts of the world. It is also called *caladrius* or *charadrius*. In the Middle Ages a fabulous version of the *caladre* was popular: snow-white, sometimes endowed with horns, and often represented with a snake-like tail. It was thought to cure illnesses, and was taken as a symbol of Christ.
13. *Editor's note*: Louis IX of France, who ruled from 1226 to 1270.
14. In the same epoch, Albertus Magnus refuted this notion (*De Animalibus*, Book XXIV, 1).
15. De Beauvais, *Speculum majus*, Book XX. See also Part IV above, "The Egg," pp. 285-286.
16. Latini, *Li Livres dou Tresor*, Bibliothèque Nationale, #7068, folio 44.
17. See A. de Caumont, *Abécédaire archéologique*, pp. 105 and 267.
18. Mâle, *L'Art religieux* (3), pp. 61 and 74.
19. Cf. Elisa Maillard, *Les Sculptures de la Cathédrale de Poitiers*, p. 15 and Plate XLIII.
20. Job 38:36, Douay-Rheims version.
21. Télesphore, *Description hiéroglyphique du Rempart mystique de la Santé*, from Robert Fludd.

THE OUROBOROS AND THE AMPHISBAENA

THE OUROBOROS IS a snake curled in a complete circle and holding the end of its tail in its mouth; thus its name, for in Greek *oura* signifies "tail," and *boros* means "devouring," or "that which devours." Hence the Greek word *ouroboros* and the Greco-Latin *ourovorax* which is used by some writers.

The ancient Greeks borrowed this symbol from the Egyptians who had connected it, according to Olympiodorus and Plutarch, with planetary movements, and had given it various metaphysical meanings that in the process of centuries have widened considerably. After the Romans, various Christian and heretical sects, such as the Gnostics and the Ophites, adopted it with added meanings that we do not know with exactitude. During the height of the Middle Ages and thereafter, even up to the present time, the practitioners of alchemy, hermetism, and then of religious heraldry and that of the nobility held it sacred.

The most familiar of the meanings given the ouroborus by the Ancients is that which associates it with Time—time, which alone with God has had no beginning, and will have no end since it is the thread on which eternity is woven. The ouroboros also, curved in a circle, joining together the two ends of its body with the pressure of its jaws, makes an unbroken whole; reuniting in itself the beginning and the end, it comes to possess the essence of the eternal[1].

The Egyptians invented divisions in the starry and planetary movements that give us our times and seasons, in a way which allows us to measure the irresistible flow of time[2], or as Virgil calls it, its "irreparable flight." However, it seems that the original meaning of the ouroboros symbol related primarily to cyclic perpetuity, this inescapable, orderly renewal of cycles whose uninterrupted succession constitutes eternity. Probably to the Ancients these renewals were represented by the snake's characteristic of periodically changing its skin; for it was thought that in thus creating a new skin, the reptile also renewed its life. As Tertullian explains it, the snake "changes its skin and its natural age. As soon as it is aware of the approach of old age, it shuts itself into a narrow passageway and at that moment drops its wrinkled skin, and, stripped of itself, leaves its hole shining and rejuvenated[3]."

Classical mythology and its iconography made the ouroboros an attribute of Saturn, the son of Coelus, who represented time and was called Kronos by the Greeks. He was shown as an old man holding a scythe in his right hand, and in the other, the ouroboros, because in the succession of the years, the last month of each joins the first month of the next, like the tail and the head of the circular serpent. It is from this aspect that we see the kinship of this symbol with the image of Janus, under whose skull are joined the two figures of the future and the past which show the profile of an adolescent and that of an old man[4]. Eternity dwells in their perpetual union. On another plane, philosophers such as Alcmaeon[5] have applied the ouroboros emblem not only to the cyclic perpetuity of time but also to that of the human soul.

The second meaning of this emblem among the Ancients was that of symbolizing movement, and the continuous force which activates it—not only because its circular form can roll like a wheel or a child's hoop, but especially because the snake, in its natural state, not having the limbs to propel it with which other animals are endowed, nevertheless moves as they do, and with great speed, simply by means of the inner action of its flanks and of its ventral plates, an action producing a series of lateral and forward undulations. This inner power of self-propulsion caused the Egyptians to take the serpent as the image of cosmic movement, of the procession of the stars through space and consequently of the course of time and the uninterrupted succession of its phases.

It was surely when envisaging it in its circular form that Plutarch said of the snake that the Egyptians compared it with the heavenly bodies[6]. When the sacred uraeus, the viper Haje, coils itself in a circle on the falcon head of Ra or of Horus, the rising sun, it represents the sun's daily setting forth and return on its dazzling course; however, in this case the head and tail of the sacred asp emerge from the line of the circle, and it is no longer strictly the ouroboros (Fig. 1).

Fig. 1 The viper Haje on the head of Horus or Ra; a sculpture from Thebes.

Fig. 2 Sundial dated 1625, at the presbytery of Serverette (Lozère), from a 19th-century drawing.

But we find it again sometimes, in spite of the passage of centuries, on sundials of relatively recent date, where it imprisons within its circle the hours marking the sun's course. Here is a slate dial, dated 1625, whose inscription reminds the human being how little his life can resist the action of time, measured by these hours: *Memento quia pulvis es*: "Remember that thou art dust!" (Fig. 2).

It seems that we have now good authority to believe that in

some places in the ancient world, the ouroboros also represented the circulation of blood in the human body. This movement, which is a flux and reflux, would in that case have been recognized long before the time of Harvey (1578-1658), who explained its mechanism better than anyone had done before.

The symbol's most esoteric meaning comes from a notion cherished by the Ancients that "the serpent enjoys an unrivaled longevity; it is rejuvenated by growing old, and reborn in itself at the moment it attains its full growth and should begin to decline[7]." In fact, as its name indicates that it feeds on its own flesh (*Boros-oura*, "it devours its tail"), it is with the substance of itself that the serpent renews itself, according to the old fable, in the measure in which it is depleted by the force of time and events. In some provinces, our French peasants say that if one cuts a snake in two, between the end of its tail and the vital organs, the part that is destroyed will grow again and re-create itself as it was before. I do not know if this is true of snakes but it is certainly so with saurians, such as the wall lizard. Thus the Ancients could believe in the existence of a vital and rebuilding principle in the tail of reptiles that the serpent would absorb and assimilate, to procure its own longevity, by biting into the tip of its tail. This capacity of self-restoration made the ouroboros the symbol in the ancient world of the perpetual renewal of life, "the eternal beginning again of everything[8]."

The philosophy and symbolism of former times looked upon the circle as the image of the universe, of the infinite cosmos which includes divinity and all its works. And since the world's oldest myths made the serpent, like the dragon (which is itself a huge, hybrid serpent), the natural guardian of all kinds of treasure, the scholars of the time connected the name of the ouroboros snake with another Greek word *ouros* which means all at once "the guardian of a storehouse," "the savior," and "the leader"; and the circle's representation of infinity came to include the idea of the circular serpent enclosing everything within its ring and under its watchful eye. We find this theme persisting in the medieval Greek alchemists; this is proved by an eleventh-century Byzantine manuscript which is now at St. Mark's in Venice, which in the chapter on Cleopatra's gold work shows an irregular, naively traced, circular ouroboros holding within it the inscription *En to pan*, "the All in One[9] (Fig. 3)."

Fig. 3 The ouroboros from Cleopatra's chrysopee.

This agrees with what Olympiodorus says of the ancient Egyptian symbologists of the sacred, who, wishing "to represent the universe on monuments or express it in sacred characters, inscribed the serpent ouroboros[10] (Fig. 4)." Like the amphisbaena, this ouroboros was half black and half white.

Laden with other meanings from the distant past as well as the principal ones mentioned above, the ouroboros was immediately seized upon by the first proponents of ideas arising within the Church that its leaders considered heretical, and received from them still other significations, some of which were clearly contrary to Christian dogma. The Gnostics in particular used this symbol; it is found on a great number of their mystical inscriptions associated with letters or signs that

Fig. 4 The black and white ouroboros of alchemy.

have been diversely interpreted by numerous scholars, but none of these enigmatic expressions tell us its real meaning in the sense in which the Gnostics so frequently employed it. We know only that they made it the emblem of the annual cycle, of movement, and of the renewal of matter in a pantheistic sense. In the *Pistis Sophia*, an Alexandrian work generally attributed to the Valentinian Gnostics but which some consider to be the work of the Ophites, the body of the mysterious serpent is divided into twelve parts, twelve "eons" which correspond to the twelve months of the annual cycle.

It seems probable that the Gnostics, like Olympiodorus[11] and the Ancients, saw in it the image of the "Agathodaimon," the good spirit which helps and saves; and perhaps it is through this avenue that it approaches a relation with Christ, the Savior. The wide usage given it by the Gnostics hindered its representation in the decorative art of the catacombs by orthodox symbolists of the early Christian epoch, and although it appeared in later Christian iconography, its depiction never became common practice.

In the times of the first Roman emperors, the state on one hand and the new-born Church on the other both disapproved the practices of those who dedicated themselves to the occult sciences. Tiberius banished from Italy "magicians and mathematicians"; Claudius and Vitellius reaffirmed the edicts that proscribed astrologists and sorcerers. Tertullian for his part protested against those who sought to understand and explain the enigmas of an old apocalyptic Hebrew work, and accused them in particular of betraying the secrets of gold, silver, and other natural phenomena[12]. Threatened thus on all sides, the adepts of these investigative disciplines hid their work in mysterious formulas and under ancient symbols to which they gave special meanings whose key they guarded jealously. Chief among these symbols was the tail-biting snake.

The origins of alchemy, which was connected especially closely with the mysterious properties of metals and stones, have been admirably studied by Marcellin Berthelot[13]. He tells us that in its general sense as well as in alchemy "the circular serpent was the guardian of the temple of Knowledge, and only the one who has conquered it can cross the threshold of the holy place[14]." In making the ouroboros the guardian of their secret knowledge, the alchemists again established the connection mentioned before between the name of the symbol and the Greek word *ouros* taken in the sense of "guardian." This is very probably the origin of using the shape of the ouroboros for numerous door knockers in France in the eleventh and especially the nineteenth centuries (Fig. 7).

Practically speaking, in alchemical theory the ouroboros was the hieroglyph for "the dissolution of the body by fermentation[15]." Alchemy also made it the emblem of the active and of the passive elements, the former represented by the tail and the latter by the mouth of the snake—as in the ancient idea, the first giving to the second the substance for a new growth. Perhaps it is in this hermetic context that a symbolic connection was first made between the ouroboros and the "elixir of long life." On another plane, the circular serpent was the image of eternal wisdom and of its perpetual action in the world.

The Kabbalah considers the serpent Nahash, the tempter of Eden, as "the symbol of primordial egoism"; but the ouroboros represents even better the mysterious attraction of the self for itself[16], since the body's end moves in a circular trajectory away from its beginning only to return and fasten itself there; it does not depart from itself.

Modern occultists also look upon it as the symbol of the "full" and the "empty[17]"; and it is moreover from this aspect that it has always been connected with the hermetic symbolism of the generative organs of man and woman.

The medieval authors have scarcely mentioned the symbol of the ouroboros except in a completely exoteric way; those of them who like Albertus Magnus were involved in the study of alchemy certainly knew of other meanings, but kept this knowledge to themselves. In the thirteenth century, the bishop of Mende, Guillaume Durand, says simply that "before the invention of letters, among the Egyptians, the year was designated in the following way: They drew a dragon that bit its tail, because the year curves back upon itself. And it is thus that it is still marked by some[18]."

In the case of a number of these more or less hermetic groups which formed everywhere during the Middle Ages, their traces and testimony about their kind of spirituality and asceticism, methods and rituals, have become very rare. Nevertheless testimony like that found in the Carmelite monastery of Loudun and the notebooks of the *Estoile Internelle*, both of the fifteenth century, prove that there was quite a profound knowledge, which has now almost disappeared, of the old traditional symbols that were full of rich spiritual nourishment, and that they were interpreted in a perfectly orthodox way, although most often in closed groups. In the above-mentioned notebooks of the *Estoile Internelle*, the ouroboros encloses the gothic monogram of the name IHsuS, reduced to the consonants IHS, and above the sacred name stand the three crosses of Golgotha (Fig. 5). The snake's closed ring shows the old symbol of the perpetuity of the sacrifice and the redemption.

The drawing of the monogram of Christ placed inside the serpentine ring has been presented as "the symbol of his eternal dominion." In fact, in this composition the sacred monogram plays the role of the hub and spokes of a wheel whose rim is replaced by the snake—the rim beneath which the wheel's course takes place. The symbol of the perpetual renewal of Christ's action is more exactly expressed in this way by the two ideas that the ouroboros and the wheel both suggest: perpetuity and movement—the latter equivalent here to action.

In the sixteenth century the ouroborus sometimes represented the everlastingness of the future life. In this same century Jehan Frellon, taking the snake as a symbol of the earth, curved it into an oval shape in which he placed the hornet (French *frelon*) and the crab as images of air and water,

Fig. 5 The ouroboros of the 15th-century Estoile Internelle.

Fig. 6 Trademark of Jehan Frellon, 1549.

thus joining images of the three domains of living beings in the world[19] (Fig. 6).

On a Hermetic—not Masonic—seventeenth-century bookplate, on the trunk of the Tree of Life the ouroboros frames an image of the pelican, seemingly as an emblem of Christ, reviving its young by the ablution of its blood; and the circular serpent testifies to the everlasting continuation of this merciful compassion (Fig. 7). On a panel of painted wood of the eighteenth century, it haloes the head of the phoenix which encloses the alchemical sign for sulphur[20]. It is shown here that the two symbols, the reptile and the fabulous bird, have been endowed from the distant past with two privileges very close to one another: one renews its life with its own substance, the other is reborn from its own ashes; both live forever.

Fig. 7 17th- to 18th-century bookplate from the author's collection; hermetic (not specifically Masonic) design.

The jeweler's art sometimes made use of the circular snake. A child's bracelet on this model, made of yellow and brown twisted wires, was discovered some time ago in a Frankish burying ground in Vailly (Aisne). I remember too an eighteenth-century silver bodice-clasp, and also a beautiful gold ring. The clasp and the ring perhaps symbolized the constancy due to conjugal fidelity. In armorial bearings of the church or the nobility, again it is the idea of the everlasting that the ouroboros almost always represents.

It is certainly a symbol of the Trinity, it seems to me, that must be seen in the three images of the ouroboros which are sometimes found interlocked, with their circles penetrating each other as in the pattern called in symbolism the *Scutum fidei*, the shield of faith. The ancient image of perpetual duration, thus tripled in a single whole, accords with the idea of three eternal beings which together make One (Fig. 8).

Fig. 8 The triple ouroboros; from a 16th-century Italian painting.

During the Middle Ages, the whole structure of social life was based on ascending scales whose degrees were sometimes discreetly veiled; chivalry, the monastic order, the corporations and guilds of artisans, the universities, brotherhoods of all kinds, even the brotherhood of vagrant beggars, were founded on this pattern which came to them from the most ancient times. The priesthood itself from the Church's infancy had its minor and major orders leading to the episcopate, its culmination. Before the thirteenth century, hermetism made of the ouroboros the symbol of the successive stages which rise to the dignity of the episcopate, that is, the full development of the priesthood. We find in an alchemical document what the ecclesiastical writers of the time failed to say on this subject: "The priest, at first a man of copper, has changed color and nature and has become a man of silver; a few days later, if thou wishest, thou wilt find him changed to a man of gold[21]."

In the same sphere, from another angle, the ouroboros symbolized the successive revelations of science, of the knowledge reserved for the chosen few, and of the silence that is imposed on the initiate; for coiling itself mysteriously into a closed circle, of its own accord it closes its mouth. Perhaps it was in this sense that the famous printer and editor of the seventeenth century, Sebastian Mable-Cramoisy, who may have been the heir of the great brotherhoods of *Agle*[22], magnificently encircled his trademark with its image.

De Gassicourt and du Roure de Paulin say that in Freemasonry the ouroboros is frequently shown head downward[23]. I do not know what that was intended to express, but usually the reversal is unfavorable to the subject the symbol represents.

Fig. 9 Gold plaque from the sword belt of King Caribert, 6th century.

Another singular symbol in the serpent form is the amphisbaena. This fabulous reptile, whose Greek name means "one who walks on both sides," was taken for granted as really existing by the classical naturalists, which means that the idea was already old and familiar when their lives began. Pliny describes it thus: "the amphisbaena has a double head; that is, a head at its tail, as if one mouth were not enough to spew its poison[24]." Medieval writers simply repeated what Pliny had written.

This strange reptile, this impossible creature composed of

two bodies joined together and condemned to pull forever against each other, or else to coil one against the other in an inevitable duel, represented among the Alexandrian Neoplatonists the two principles of good and evil which struggle for mastery in the world, the mastery of human souls. With its two parts, it was both the "agathodaimon," the spirit of good, and the "cacodaimon," the spirit of evil. This is the meaning the amphisbaena has retained during the course of the following centuries (Fig. 9).

Several of its medieval, and more recent, representations show the amphisbaena as composed of a black serpent and of one of silver, or of gold. In medieval heraldry, the superior of the two serpents was often endowed with an elegant pair of wings[25], and the inferior one sometimes had paws.

Fig. 10 The amphisbaena of l'Estoile Internelle.

It was during the decline of Rome that the symbol of the amphisbaena spread from east to west across the countries of Europe, where it was already known but now came into general use and was Christianized; the old emblem of good and evil became "the double-headed serpent, one of whose heads represents Christ and the other Satan[26]."

The notebook of symbols of the fifteenth-century *Estoile Internelle* shows us a marvelous black and white amphisbaena (Fig. 10). The upper serpent has wings and wears a crown decorated with the royal fleur-de-lis; the lower one, entirely black, has saurian feet and crouches on the ground to resist the upward flight of its divine part.

Let us say in conclusion that in the world of real snakes, there exist two varieties which move equally frontwards and backwards. Modern naturalists have given them the names of *Amphisbaena alba* and of *Amphisbaena fuliginosa*; they even possess the characteristic that their very small heads and very thick tails resemble each other. However, they could not have served as prototype for the mythical two-headed amphisbaena of the ancient world, since their habitat is strictly confined to the southern part of America[27].

NOTES

Title Figure: The amphisbaena, in a woodcut from the Hortus Sanitatis.

1. Cf. Alcmaeon, *De rerum naturis.*
2. Cf. Horapollo: sec. Plutarch, *Isis and Osiris.*
3. Tertullian, *De Pallio*, III.
4. See Macrobius, *Saturnalia*, Bk. I, ch. XX.
5. Alcmaeon, *op. cit.*
6. Plutarch, *op. cit.* (note 2), p. 74.
7. Carcopino, *Basilique*, p. 310. Cf. Philon de Biblos, F.H.G. III, p. 572.
8. P. le Cour, *A la recherche d'un monde perdu*, p. 47.
9. See Marcelin Berthelot, *Collection des anciens alchémistes grecs*, p. 132, fig. 11.
10. Olympiodorus, *On the sacred art of the Philosopher's stone.*
11. *Ibid.*
12. Cf. Leclercq and Marron, *Dictionnaire*, T. I, Vol. I, col. 1065-1072.
13. Berthelot, *op. cit.* and *Les Origines de l'Alchémie*, Paris, 1885.
14. *Idem.*, *Collection*, Bk. I. The true alchemists, without denying the possibility of the transmutation of metals by the Philosopher's stone, were looking for something quite different, leaving the material research to "souffleurs" whom they treated with contempt. The latter however were the fathers of our present-day chemistry, and it is to them that the works refer which Berthelot studied. [*Editor's note*: See John Nelson Stillman, *The Story of Alchemy and Early Chemistry*, pp. 165-6, 171-2.]
15. Berthelot, *op. cit.*, Bk. I., translation, p. 32. [*Editor's note*: Or see Stillman, *op. cit.*, p. 171.] Also see above, Part III, "The Salamander," Fig. 2, this reptile curled in a circle like the ouroboros. The salamander was the alchemical symbol of calcination.
16. D. Thorion, from Maurice Barrès, *Stanislas de Guaita*, p. 241.
17. Cf. Papus, *Traité élémentaire des Sciences occultes*, p. 172.
18. Durand de Mende, *Rational des divins offices*, Bk. VIII, ch. III, 1.
19. Frellon, *Les Images de la Mort*, 1549 edition.
20. From the author's private collection. See below, "The Phoenix," Fig. 6.
21. Berthelot, *op. cit.*, Bk. I, p. 23. [*Editor's note*: Or see Stillman, *op. et loc. cit.*]
22. A secret group drawn especially from the Book Corporations at the end of the 15th and in the 16th centuries: printers, booksellers, workers in parchment, bookbinders, and engravers.

23. De Gassicourt and du Roure, *L'Hermétisme dans la Science héraldique*, p. 137, fig. 4.
24. Pliny, *Natural History*, Bk. VIII, 35.
25. De Gassicourt and du Roure, *L'Hermétisme dans l'Art héraldique*, p. 110.
26. Guénon, *Le Roi du Monde*, p. 35; also "Seth" in *Le Voile d'Isis*, T. XXXVI, 1931, #142, p. 585.
27. See J. Trousset, *Nouveau Dictionnaire encyclopédique*, T. I, p. 159, 3rd col.

End Figure: Bronze door knocker from the Prédhumeau garden at Pasquin, Loudun, in Vienne.

THE PHOENIX

FOR THE EXPLANATION of the phoenix's presence among the personal signs for Jesus Christ, once again we must turn to mysterious and prophetic Egypt, for though it cannot be thought that this symbol itself originated in the Nile Basin, its myth was born there—the singular myth that still clothes it and makes it the most marvelous bird ever created by the human imagination. It would seem that the phoenix was known in ancient Asia much earlier than in Egypt: the oldest known Chinese art shows a phoenix often in conjunction with the Nile lily or the lotus, and sharing their symbolic meanings. Surrounded by its long tail feathers like the heart of a rose by its petals (Fig. 1), its image has been revered since time immemorial[1]. In Assyrian art contemporaneous with the highest period of Egyptian culture, a sacred bird follows or precedes the galloping horses of the king's chariot, just as the falcon accompanies that of the pharaoh in Egyptian art; and this tutelary bird of the Assyrians resembles a phoenix much more closely than a falcon.

Fig. 1 The "lucky" phoenix of China.

The sparrow hawk, falcon, vulture, ibis, and swallow which we find in the religious art of Egypt are birds which are born and dwell in that country; the phoenix does not accord with any real species of Egyptian bird, which accounts for the hesitation in identifying it shown by many nineteenth-century scholars. De Rouge sees it as "a kind of heron[2]," and Champollion-Figeac calls it "a lapwing with plumes[3]." Its Egyptian name of *bennu* (a name which reflects an idea of splendor, and which seems, Lefébure suggets, to be related to the Assyrian word *banu*, meaning brilliant) hints at the vivid color which the Greeks translated as *foinix*, "crimsoned," from *foinikes*, "the color crimson"; *foinix*, which the Hellenist scholar Planche translates as "fire bird[4]."

There is no wading bird which corresponds to this color description, not even the flamingo as some have proposed. This is why, after having considered a number of depictions of the phoenix which coincide with the one on an obelisk at Cairo (Fig. 2), most Egyptologists have supported Cuvier's theory which sees the phoenix's natural prototype in the golden pheasant of Asia. This opinion is supported by the important role played by this bird in the symbolic art of Asia and especially that of China. In China, the *jinji* (the golden game-hen) and the pheasant *fu-wu* are sculpted, embroidered, engraved, painted, or drawn everywhere, with various but always positive meanings[5].

Fig. 2 The phoenix on a basalt obelisk in Cairo.

Canon Davin has written many learned pages which are in agreement with what I have just said, and which come to the same conclusion about the close kinship between the fabled Egyptian phoenix and the real golden pheasant. The latter was not known in Rome until the time of the first emperors, and was very rarely shown in Christian art; however, Dom Leclercq, who should always be consulted in connection with the art of early Christianity, shows a mosaic of Furni in which the cock pheasant appears beside his hen[6].

It seems clear that in the "Celestial Empire" of China the phoenix of fable was also no other than a poeticized version of the pheasant. Among the three hundred and sixty species of birds known in ancient China, it was the phoenix, *feng huang*, that wore the crown. *Feng* means male and *huang* female; the phoenix, it was said, is born in the Kingdom of the Wise, to the east of China, probably on some imaginary island. It eats nothing but the fruit of one sort of bamboo and drinks only the purest water. All the birds of heaven pay homage to it when it appears, and if it sings, all the cocks in the world echo it. Its song is a melody of five notes. It is six feet tall and its plumage is of five glowing colors[7].

This divine bird is born, it was said, from the sun or from fire. Son of the flame, and issuing thus from the great active principle *yang*, the phoenix exerts a decisive influence on the conception and birth of children, and in company with the unicorn it brings their souls to their mothers from above[8]. It is also an active factor of life in springtime germination and growth, and its image, like that of the dragon, takes part in the solemn rites of the "Growth Ceremony[9]."

Fig. 3 The stylized bennu *from a Book of the Dead.*

The phoenix, protector of emperors, was thought to appear to some holy man or great one of the empire in times of prosperity, when heaven bestowed special blessings on its children; in bad times, it withdrew to blessed solitudes far from the Chinese ocean and the Blue Sea. It was also said that the holy souls in heaven are fed divine dishes, among them the livers of dragons and the marrow of the phoenix, which keep their immortal state in a condition of unequalled bliss.

In the Egyptian religion, the *bennu*, shown in the hieroglyphs in the conventional aspect of a wading bird crowned with a plume (Fig. 3), was connected with the interwoven cults of Osiris and Ra. Virey tells us that it was "the symbol of periodic appearances, and so of sunrises; that is to say—let us take this into account at once—it was a symbol of the resurrections of Osiris[10]." All the images of the *bennu* are in general connected with the sun, whether at the tomb of Osiris in Abydos, at Anteopolis or Koptos or Edfu. At Koptos as at Anteopolis, the *bennu*, its breast provided with two human arms, stretches them out toward the star Sothis (our Sirius), which appears in the sky before the sun rises[11].

In a text found in the funerary coffer of an Egyptian queen of the eleventh dynasty, Osiris entrusts to the *bennu* the secrets of eternity. In the *Ritual of the Dead*, which is so interesting with its ideas of Purgatory and of Hell, Osiris says: "I am the *bennu*, the great one who is in Annu (Heliopolis); I am the law of existence and of beings" (birth, death, and resurrection[12]). This identification of Osiris and the bird sacred to him is found from very early times, but it seems that it was only rather late, in the last millenary before our era, that in the temple of Heliopolis the *bennu* was honored with its own legend. (This was doubtless due to the Heliopolitan priest's anxiety to hide, under indecipherable enigmas, from the priests of Memphis and Thebes the astronomical discovery that he had made of the "Sothic period[13]" and the "circular cycle[14].") This legend said that there never existed more than one *bennu* on earth. When it felt its five hundredth year approaching, it took flight, passing first by Arabia, to Heliopolis, where the priests were divinely forewarned of its coming. There on the altar of the Sun temple it built a funeral pyre of precious Arabian spices, upon which, when the sun's rays set it on fire, the phoenix itself was consumed. But from its ashes was immediately born a little worm that before the end of the day was transformed into a new and fully vigorous *bennu*.

According to Herodotus, Hesiod lived in the time of Homer, and others make him the contemporary of Solomon; in any case, Pliny, Plutarch, and Ausonius[15] claim that he was the first to speak of the legend of the *bennu* in the classical countries, where it was called by the Greek name of *foenix*, phoenix.

"If this bird," says Herodotus, "is like the portrait that has been drawn of it, its wings are part golden and part red, and the shape of its body is like the eagle's."

It was in 480 B.C., the same year in which the famous battle was fought at Thermopylae, that Herodotus visited Egypt; his travel accounts are quite confused[16]. Pliny, in his *Natural History*, and Ovid who wrote his *Metamorphoses* at the time of Christ's birth, were more exact. Pliny, attributing his information to Manilius, says of the phoenix: "No one has ever seen it eat. In Arabia it is dedicated to the sun, and it lives five hundred years; when it comes to the end of its life, it makes a nest of bits of cinnamon bark and of rosemary, fills it with perfumes, and dies upon it. From its bones and their marrow comes a worm which becomes a new phoenix, whose first act is to arrange a worthy funeral; it carries the whole nest to the City of the Sun [Heliopolis], and places it on the altar there. This same Manilius says the turning cycle of the Great Year is accomplished with the Phoenix, and that then the same signs reappear of the seasons and the planets. This renewal takes place at noon on the day when the sun enters the sign of the Ram."

A little later Tacitus also, in speaking of the phoenix, brought proof that in his time the secret of the "Sothic period," whose discovery the priests of Heliopolis had cloaked in mystery, had been unveiled.

Pomponius Mela on his side expresses himself thus: "The phoenix is always alone, for it has neither father nor mother. After having lived five hundred years, it lies down on a pyre which it has built of heaped up spices and lets itself be consumed. Then when the liquid element of its parts solidifies, it engenders itself from itself and is reborn. When it has gathered enough strength, it carries the bones of its former body wrapped in myrrh to a town in Egypt called the City of the Sun, places them in a sanctuary and consecrates them with special funerary rites[17]." And the Greek poet of Egypt, Nonnus, in the fourth century, in his *Hymn to the Sun*[18], spoke in much the same way. Nonnus wrote these lines before his conversion to Christianity, but nevertheless expresses in them the same thought as Pomponius Mela's in the passage quoted above: that the phoenix brings about its rebirth from itself, and not from any other source; and this above all is the reason why Christian symbolism chose the fabulous bird as one of the most perfect symbols of the risen Christ.

The legend of the phoenix, set forth more or less clearly by the authors I have mentioned, as well as others, was soon known in all parts of the vast Empire. Christian symbolism, finding it everywhere, made it into one of the principal symbols of the Resurrection. Human life is short, and often exposed to undeservedly harsh circumstances, as well as to the evildoing of other people. The thinkers and theologians of ancient Egypt believed that the divine powers, in the name of justice to mankind, must resurrect the human being after death so that he might at last be dealt with, in body and soul, according to the inviolable laws of an all-encompassing justice, in a life untouched by accidents. They proclaimed this real faith in the restoration of the human being after death by the symbols of the phoenix, the frog, deciduous trees and others, all symbols that the Christian religion accepted as appropriate for the person of the resurrected Christ.

The early monuments of Christian art are characterized by the common root-idea of hope, liberation, and immortality. "But now is Christ risen from the dead, and become the firstfruits of them that slept. For since by man came death, by man came also the resurrection of the dead. For as in Adam all die, even so in Christ shall all be made alive[19]." This dogma, so clearly affirmed by the new faith, needed symbols to manifest itself to the eyes of the world. For this glorious role, the priests and teachers of the newborn symbology chose first of all the Egyptian phoenix; all the other symbols of resurrection were adopted after it. The phoenix, always the only one of its kind on earth, reborn from its own ashes under the burning rays of the sun and in the sweet-smelling fire of spices, is one of the most beautiful symbols of Christ. The Church Fathers of the early centuries celebrated it, some naively believing the naturalists of their time, others, the majority perhaps, accepting the legend with wise reservations; all, however, drawing from the miraculous bird the same conclusion of the certainty of the resurrection of the body, and making it the image of the resurrected Christ. St. Clement, one of the first of St. Peter's successors as Bishop of Rome, about the year 79 wrote to the Church at Corinth: "Behold this paradoxical prodigy which takes place in the East, in Arabia: there is a bird called the phoenix, the only one of its kind, and it lives five hundred years..." and the pope told the legend as Pliny, Ovid, and other classical writers had done. He concludes: "Shall we judge it a great and astonishing matter that the Artisan of the Universe should bring about the resurrection of all those who have served him in a holy manner, with the confidence of a valiant faith, when he shows us with so small a thing as a bird the magnificence of his promise?[20]" Many others of the same time and in succeeding centuries spoke in the same way[21].

Fig. 4 The phoenix on the palm tree; a mosaic from St. John Lateran in Rome.

Made use of thus by teachers of the faith, the phoenix was bound to appear often in Christian art, as a symbol of this teaching or as an image of Christ. In either role, it remained in accordance with the spirit of the ancient Egyptian *bennu* who represented the reappearance of the dead, the resurrections of Osiris, and finally the idea of the reanimation of the human body after death. When it reflected the image of Christ, it was often shown perched on the palm tree (Fig. 4). Martigny remarked that "When St. Paul is shown on any ancient monument, the phoenix on the palm tree is always behind this apostle" who was the principal herald of the doctrine of Christ's Resurrection. Bosio applied to the phoenix perched on the palm the words of the Song of Songs: *Ascendam in palmam et apprehendam fructus ejus*: "I will go up into the palm tree, and will take hold of the fruit thereof[22]."

Often the phoenix bears the palm of the conquerors because of its conquest of death, or like the dove it holds the branch of peace. "It is Christ saying to Christians: Peace be unto you[23]."

Like the eagle and the falcon, the phoenix is closely connected with the idea of the sun and of light, and it is frequently seen on Christian lamps of Roman times[24] (Fig. 5).

Because it was supposed to be reborn from its own destruction, and thus to prolong its existence indefinitely, it was looked upon as one of the emblems of cyclic eternity by Christians just as it had been in the times preceding them. This is its significance on the coins and medals of the non-Christian Roman emperors, such as a coin of Augustus inscribed AETERNITAS. AVG—FEL. TEMP. REPARATIO: "The eternity of Augustus—Happy renewal of time," and the phoenix dominates the inscription. Alchemists from medieval times to the present day sometimes have placed the phoenix on the alchemical sign for sulphur, which is a triangle carrying an inverted cross at its base. I reproduce here one of these representations of the phoenix on the sign for sulphur (Fig. 6). This eighteenth-century work is painted on a wooden panel and rather faded, but the design is still quite clear: on a brown background, the golden triangle of sulphur is outlined by a red band, and the scarlet image of the phoenix fills it completely; the bird's head stands out against a sky-blue aureole framed by an ouroboros, the serpent curled in a circle and biting its tail, which clearly defines the character of the phoenix as an image of perpetuity through the continual renewal of cycles.

Fig. 5 The phoenix on the palm tree, on a 4th- or 5th-century Carthaginian lamp.

Above the point of the alchemical triangle are the four Hebrew letters of the holy tetragrammaton:

YOD-HE-VAV-HE
The Most High

Medieval writers explained as best they could the myth of the burning up and the rebirth of the phoenix. The bestiaries of the Romanesque period, including that of William of Normandy, sang its praises. Mystics of the Middle Ages also made a connection between the phoenix and Christ, because the former is born without obeying the ordinary laws of reproduction, and because only one ever exists on earth; thus, said the symbolists, Jesus came into the world without a terrestrial father, and never has the world known another man like him. The *Armenian Bestiary* published by Father Cahier[25], and others, tell the legend of the phoenix in much the same way as William of Normandy. They all emphasize that the symbolic bird, like Christ, comes back to life exactly three days after its death.

Fig. 6 The divine Phoenix on the alchemical sign for sulphur. 18th-century painting on wood, from the author's collection.

In French heraldry, the phoenix was and is one of the emblems of hope, as a human feeling as well as one of the theological virtues. It is also a symbol of purity of conscience, and sometimes, in the Middle Ages and by extension, of chastity. An Egyptian hieroglyphic text of the funeral liturgy has the dead person say in the presence of Osiris, the judge of the dead: "I am pure, I am pure, I am pure! My purity is that of the *Bennu*, the Great One[26]."

Fig. 7 The phoenix symbolizing fortitude and chastity; a 15th-century medal.

This ancient Egyptian concept passed through time and is found again in the Middle Ages; according to Huysman, the image of the phoenix we see in the sculptures of Chartres Cathedral is the attribute of chastity and more especially feminine chastity[27]. A medal struck at the end of the fifteenth century, in honor of Julia Astalia, has on its reverse side a phoenix surrounded by flames, and by the inscribed words: *Exemplum unicum for.(titudinis) et pud.(icitiae)*: "Unique example of fortitude and chastity (Fig. 7)." The same meaning of chastity is to be noted in the phoenix of the rose window of the Cathedral of Paris and the sculptures at Amiens[28].

In the same way that the Far East associated the phoenix as the protector of human births with the lotus which is the flower of life, Western art sometimes related it to the nenuphar or water lily, especially the white *nymphea* which is an emblem of chastity and of virginity, because in former times (and still today) the *nymphea* plants were used to make

Fig. 8 The phoenix in a wreath of waterlilies, from a 15th-century woodcut.

antiaphrodisiacs. Figure 8 shows the phoenix in a wreath of blooming water lilies, from a fifteenth-century wood carving in the collection of W. Mitchell, now in the British Museum[29]. The symbolism of the water lily is not a new one, for in ancient times this plant was dedicated to the nymphs, and Pliny recommends it as a remedy favoring continence: *Venerem in totum adimit nymphea*: "The nymphea completely takes away desire[30]."

NOTES

Title Figure: The phoenix in the flames; from the Hortus Sanitatis.

1. Cf. G. de C., "Vue générale de l'Art chinois," in *Gazette des Beaux-Arts*, T. V, 1872, p. 116.
2. Em. de Rouge, *Notice des Monuments du Louvre*, 1860, p. 85.
3. Champollion-Figeac, *L'Égypte ancienne*, p. 259.
4. J. Planche, *Dictionnaire grec-français*, p. 1198, 3rd col.
5. Cf. Cesar Cantu, *Histoire universelle*, T. III, p. 318.
6. Leclercq and Marron, *Dictionnaire*, T. V, vol. 1, col. 1.080.

7. See Doré, *Recherches*, Part I, T. II, vol. IV, pp. 442 *et seq.*
8. *Ibid.*, Part I, T. I, pp. 2 and 4.
9. *Ibid.*, Part I, T. I, vol. II, p. 200.
10. Virey, *Religion de l'ancienne Égypte*, p. 143.
11. Canon Davin, "La Capella greca" in *Revue de l'Art chrétien*, 2d series, T. X, 1879, p. 379.
12. *Ibid.*, p. 384.
13. *Editor's note*: *Sothic* from the star Sothis (Sirius). A Sothic period was a cycle of 1460 Sothic years of 305 days.
14. Davin, *op. cit.*, p. 388. See also Dausson, *Cours d'études historiques*, T. III, pp. 255 *et seq.*
15. Pliny, *Natural History*, Bk. VII, ch. 48; Plutarch, *De oraculum defectu*; Ausonius, *Eydyll.*, XVIII.
16. Herodotus, *Euterpe*, LXXIII.
17. Pomponius Mela, *De Situ Orbis*, Bk. III, ch. 8.
18. Nonnus, *Dionysiaca.*
19. I Corinthians 15:20-22.
20. St. Clement of Rome, *Epistolae ad Corinthios*, XXIV, 6.
21. Cf. Davin, *op. cit*, T. XI, 1879, p. 70. See also Commodianus, St. Cyprien, Lactance, etc.
22. Canticle of Canticles, 7:8, Douay-Rheims version.
23. Davin, *op. cit.*, p. 540.
24. See R. P. Delattre, "Lampes de Carthage," in *Revue de l'Art chrétien*, 1890; also Leclercq, *op. cit.*, fasc. LXXXIV, col. 1.140.
25. Ch. Cahier, S.J., in *Nouveau Mélanges archéologiques*, 1874, p. 125. Honorius d'Autun, *Specul. Eccles.*, Vincent de Beauvais, *Specul. majus* and *Miroir historiale.*
26. *Rituel des Morts*, ch. 83. [*Editor's note*: E.A. Wallis Budge, *The Egyptian Book of the Dead, The Papyrus of Ani*, ch. 83, p. 339.]
27. Huysmans, *Cathédrale*, T. II, p. 265.
28. Mâle, *L'Art religieux* (3), pp. 147 & 145, fig. 58.
29. *Catalog of early German and Flemish woodcuts, British Museum*, Vol. I, p. 130, Pl. III.
30. Pliny, *op. cit.*

End Figure: Miniature from a medieval bestiary of the phoenix on its nest.

THE SPHINX

THE SPHINX IS the best known of all the hybrid creatures, made up of two bodies of natural animals. In Egypt—where the magnificent Great Sphinx is far older than the pyramids, which were constructed in the third millenary before Christ[1]—it is formed of a human head and breast, almost always masculine, and the body of a lion. In Greece it is more often shown with the head and breast of a woman. In Mycenaean and Etruscan art[2] (Fig. 1), the animal-body is often so slender that it suggests some swifter and less sturdy species than the lion, and sometimes even seems to have the feet and tail of the greyhound, while in some other representations, the hind legs are those of a bull.

Fig. 1 The Etruscan sphinx from the Campana tomb.

Following the example of Pliny, Pomponius Mela speaks of the sphinx as a strange animal that actually lives in the mountains of Ethiopia, the country that the Ancients made the home of such a horrific fauna. Both writers describe them as dark-skinned animals with female teats on the belly[3].

The sphinx had many meanings in Egypt. In its masculine aspect it represented Harmakhis, "Lord of the Two Horizons," a concept that linked it with Anubis and perhaps Amon-Ra, symbolic entities that relate to the sun's daily course, the image of human life.

From the religious aspect, the sphinx was the emblem of divine sovereignty, wisdom, and force, expressed in impassive majesty and inviolate repose. It always represented a god or a king—which amounts to the same, as the pharaoh was the emanation or earthly incarnation of the Sun-god Ra[4]. The Sphinx was also regarded as a solar divinity and one of the symbols of abundance[5]. From the philosophical aspect, and in the tradition of the Egyptian hermetic works (said to be inspired by the god Thoth, the thrice-great Word, "Hermes Trismegistus"), the sphinx was the symbol of unity, of truth, and of the Absolute[6].

And from still another aspect comes the familiar Greek story of Oedipus and the sphinx. At Thebes, in Boeotia, a huge female sphinx propounded a riddle to the passersby, and tore in pieces those who could not solve it: What animal is it that in the morning goes on four feet, on two at noon, and in the evening on three? Oedipus replied that it was man, who in his childhood crawls on all fours, walks on two feet in the noon of his life, and when he is old needs a staff as well as his two legs. Having thus thwarted the sphinx, Oedipus drew his sword and killed it. This abominable sphinx, which the mythologists say was born of Typhon and Echidne in the wilds of Ethiopia[7], was always and everywhere regarded as an evil monster: the antithesis of the Egyptian sphinx, which is the symbol of divine light and wisdom.

Of all the mysteries which engaged the thought of the Ancients, the most vital was the enigma surrounding the ending, the beginning, and the flowering of life. Every egg, every seed, bears within it a germ which in favorable conditions brings forth a being resembling its producer. The people of the ancient world showed a lively and sincere gratitude to God the Creator, however they conceived of him, for this gift. Among the Egyptians, the sphinx was linked to the symbolism of the concern their wise men felt for life's mystery. It was one of the symbols of the life-giving sun, and the female sphinx was the image of Isis, mother of Horus; the ram-sphinx represented Amon, "considered as the power that begets and maintains the life of creation[8]." Sacred sculpture placed two sphinxes, one on each side of the Tree of Life, "to symbolize the double idea of fertilization and of conception[9] (Fig. 2)," and the same is true in Aegean art of the Mycenaean epoch[10], and in many other places. In Greece, certain coins from Chios show the sphinx and the amphora placed beside each other[11], reminding us that for the ancient world woman was "the vase of life" and the amphora one of the symbols for a pregnant woman. It seems that the Druids, in Gaul, related the many-breasted sphinx with the Egyptian sphinx as a symbol of fertile maternity.

For the ancient Egyptians, human life on earth was only a pre-existence. Nut, the mother of Osiris, was said to cause unceasingly those who died each day to be born to a new life; the death bed "is the cradle of the deceased[12]." A vignette from *The Book of the Dead*[13] represents the phases of rebirth after the death of the human being. Sphinxes take part in this transformation, and one of them, reclining on a bed, personifies Harmakhis, the rising sun, divine symbol of resurrection.

Although the sphinx was a solar divinity among the Egyp-

Fig. 2 Egypto-Cypriot pillar capital.

tians[14], it had no wings, at least not before the Hellenistic period; but the region of the northern shores of the Mediterranean and its islands shows us winged sphinxes in flight toward the sun. In his famous excavations at Mycenae, Schliemann found sphinxes in the tombs of princes[15] and in the first Christian centuries the old custom was preserved of placing in the shadows of sepulchers those ancient symbols of solar light which later became symbols of Christ.

"It is the light of the sun," says Éliphas Lévi, "that is represented by these gigantic sphinxes with the bodies of lions and the heads of magi[16]." For the ancient priests of Egypt, this was the divine light in its most divine conception.

If we turn to the other side of the earth, unexpectedly we find the sphinx again in the archeology of the Aymara Indians of Peru, where once more it turned its great stone gaze toward the beneficent course of the sun[17] (Fig. 3).

In spite of all distortions attendant on its wanderings, even in Rome the sphinx preserved its character as a hieroglyph of light. The sphinx that decorates the top of a cornice in the ancient frescoes of Livy's house on the Palatine carries on its forehead a lamplike flame[18].

Fig. 3 Pre-Colombian Peruvian sphinx.

According to Eusebius[19], there existed in Alexandria, from the beginning of Christianity, an important school for the instruction of neophytes and the preparation of the clergy. This institution, called simply the Didasculum ("the school"), which was at the height of its powers in the third century, succeeded in reconciling earlier religious ideas with the dogma, morality, and spirit of Christianity. These ideas included the old Egyptian theory of the creative Word[20], the more recent thesis of the Logos, the divine Word intermediate between God and humanity, a concept propagated by Philo and the Hellenistic philosophers; the divine spirit which breathes life into the soul; the immortality of the soul, etc. Certain ancient Egyptian symbols which could be reconciled with the new religion were applied to Christ, to the Christian mysteries, or to the faithful soul: the sacred scarab, the ibis, the falcon, the frog, the mongoose, the palm tree, the lotus, etc.

It could indeed be that the sphinx was first used as a symbol for Christ by the Alexandrian Gnostics, and accepted as such by the Didasculum in spite of its usual antagonism to their viewpoint; the ancient meanings attributed to the sphinx lent themselves so well to this adaptation: Jesus, like the Egyptian Harmakhis, was "Lord of the Two Horizons"—of the East, which from earliest Christian times represented his birth, and the West, which symbolized his death; he is the God of light, but also of the kingdom of shadows. He is conceived as sovereignty, all-powerful force, and divine wisdom; further, as the divine Sun, the source of abundance, and the repository of eternal secrets.

Fig. 4: Stone engraving of Oedipus and the sphinx.

The following centuries preserved this first reconciliation between Christ and the symbolic meanings of the Egyptian sphinx. In ancient Egyptian, le Cour says, "the word Christ means the possessor of the secret[21]." For the only point in which the Sphinx of Egypt resembles the evil sphinx which Oedipus slew in Boeotia (Fig. 4) is that it also guarded a secret, as the Theban sphinx guarded its riddle—a secret of supreme wisdom for the direction of human life, summed up in four verbs: *To know—to dare—to will—to be silent.*

These were now applied to Christ, for the Christian teachers believed that he exemplified to its fullest degree the sphinx's precept. When a man governs his life by these four verbs in connection with each other, he receives from them the maximum force that he is capable of using. They must be looked at thus:

To know—to dare—to will—to be silent.
To know how to dare, to know how to will, to know how to be silent;
To dare to know, to dare to will, to dare to be silent;
To will to know, to will to dare, to will to be silent;
To be silent about one's knowing, to be silent about
the goals of one's daring, to be silent about one's will.

The characteristic which placed the sphinx in contact with the mystery of life only enhanced its value as a symbol of Jesus Christ; for Christianity, even more than earlier religions, proclaimed in its sacred art as in its liturgy a profound gratitude for the gift of life to the one constantly invoked as "Author of life," whom it called "our life": *Jesu, auctor vitae—Jesu, vita nostra*[22]. So it should not be surprising to see the Tree of Life standing between two sphinxes on a bas-relief in the *Catholicon*, the cathedral of Athens, just as it was in ancient Egypt and in Crete[23]. Whether or not this bas-relief was an old work of pagan art, its use in this place is no less significant.

Jesus was the "light which lighteth every man that cometh into the world[24]"; and the sphinx, solar god of the intense, pure light of the Egyptian desert, was a suitable symbol to represent it. So it is difficult to doubt that the first Christian symbolists of Alexandria, who were so deeply attached to the ancient Egyptian symbols, were the first to reconcile Christ as light of the world, with the sphinx, symbol of the Sun, the god of their country.

Like the griffin and the centaur, the sphinx has represented the union of the divine and human natures in the figure of Christ, and his two-fold sovereignty over the spiritual and material worlds. In the sphinx as in the centaur, his divinity is represented by the human head and breast, because this part is animated by the soul, created, according to Genesis, in the image of God[25]; and the body of the quadruped represents his humanity, attached like ours to the earth during his earthly life. All that I have said about the symbolism of the centaur relating to this union of two natures is equally valid for the sphinx.

The two-fold nature of the sphinx suggests the presence within it of two different hearts: one belonging to its human breast and the other to its animal body. It is "the animal with two hearts." The same should apply to the centaur, but I do not believe that the ancient Christian symbolists ever gave this their attention. For them, everything arising from the spiritual element and the higher functions of the human soul was related to the first of the two hearts of the sphinx, to the heart of the human breast. In their eyes, it was from this heart that intelligence, knowledge, will, and all the noble faculties and feelings were derived. In this they agreed with the Ancients—the Assyrians and especially the Egyptians, who placed the seat of the soul and reason in the heart, and not in the brain.

To the second part of the sphinx, they related everything concerned with the physical life of man and his lower appetites—lawful or sinful—his earthly goods, his ordinary preoccupations.

As a result they compared to the first heart the spiritual man whose thoughts dwell in the more elevated realm of religion, and who gives precedence in his life to the concerns of a higher level over the mundane interests of the material world. The heavy, sensual, and commonplace man was compared with the second heart: the man who carries his life like a leaden weight and never raises his head higher than the edge of his field, his dining table, or his cash box.

But there is something else: certain images of the sphinx have the head and upper body of man, the wings of the eagle, the forepart of the lion, and the hindquarters of the bull; and it was above all this sphinx that engaged the attention of the Christian mystics, because it evoked the four sacred animals in the visions of Ezekiel[26] and St. John[27]. As we have seen in speaking of the Tetramorph, the combined totality of these four animals was, in Christian symbolism, one of the great, mysterious emblems of Christ, which condensed in itself all the individual meanings of each of the separate animals. So the sphinx, which was made up of one part of each of the four, was a true tetramorph. The occultists of today, remote as most of them are from early hermetists, recognize this: "The sphinx displays to the Christian," says one of them, "the angel[28], the eagle, the lion and the bull[29]," and Schuré [30] says that the entire evolution of the animal nature can be seen in the human and bovine parts while the divine nature is visible in the eagle's wings. The eagle has indeed, in certain themes in Christian iconography and symbolism such as the griffin, represented the divine nature; however it is the human part that represents it in the sphinx.

NOTES

Title Figure: Sphinx on a gold plaque found in Cyprus; Mycenaean art.

1. Maspéro, "Les Secrets des Pyramides de Memphis," in *La Liberté*, May 14, 1893. Also cf. Moret, *Mystères égyptiens* (Chronologie luminaire).
2. J. Naire, "Une plaque d'or mycénienne" in *Revue archéologique*, 3rd series, T. XXX, 1897, p. 333; and J. Martha, *Manuel d'Archéologie étrusque et romaine*, p. 73, fig. 32.
3. Pliny, *Natural History*, Bks. VIII and XXXI. Pomponius Mela, *De situ orbis*, Bk. II, ch. IX.
4. Cf. A. de Rouge, *Notice sommaire des Monuments égyptiens, exposés au Louvre*, p. 34. Also Virey, *La Religion de l'ancienne Égypte*, pp. 90 and 142, and Moret, *op. cit.* in note 1 above, p. 285, etc.
5. Cf. M. Pluche, *Histoire du Ciel*, T. I, p. 50.
6. Cf. Papus, *Traité élémentaire des Sciences occultes*, p. 186.
7. Cf. Grasset-Dorcet, "Cypria et Paphos," in *Gazette des Beaux-Arts*, T. XXV, 1868, p. 340.
8. Virey, *op. cit.* in note 4 above, p. 182.
9. G. Colonna-Ceccaldi, "Un Sarcophage d'Athiénau," in *Revue archéologique*, T. XXIX, 1875, p. 23.
10. Cf. Glotz, *La Civilisation égéenne*, Bk. III, p. 278.
11. Cf. Louis Menard, *Histoire des Grecs*, T. I, p. 199.
12. Moret, *op. cit.* in note 1 above, p. 58, note.
13. Naville, *Le Livre des Morts*, Pl. CLVII, and p. 186.
14. Virey, *op. cit.*, p. 179, note.
15. Schliemann, *Mycènes*, pp. 43, 263, etc.
16. Lévi, *Histoire de la Magie*, p. 61.

17. See A. d'Orbigny, *L'Homme américain*, Bk. I. Cf. *Magasin pittoresque*, T. XXVI, 1858, p. 33 and Pl. II.
18. Cf. S. Blondel, "La Perspective dans les Beaux-Arts de l'Antiquité," in *Gazette des Beaux-Arts*, T. XVII, p. 33.
19. Eusebius, *History of the Church*.
20. See Moret, *op. cit.* in note 1 above, *Le mystère du Verbe Créateur*, II, pp. 103 *et seq*.
21. Paul le Cour, *Atlantis*, #10 and #21, p. 2.
22. Litanies of the Holy Name of Jesus.
23. See Freeman's engraving in *Magasin pittoresque*, T. XXIX, p. 265.
24. St. John 1:9.
25. Genesis 1:26.
26. Ezekiel 1:10 and 10:14.
27. Revelation 4:6-8.
28. It is not the angel, but man furnished with wings like the three other animals; the texts of Ezekiel and St. John are explicit.
29. Papus, *op. cit.*, p. 187.
30. Schuré, *L'Évolution divine: du Sphinx au Christ*, p. 33.

End Figure: The Egyptian sphinx, from a drawing belonging to the Abbé Leroux (Deux-Sèvres, 1914).

EPILOGUE

AND EVERY CREATURE which is in heaven, and on the earth, and under the earth, and such as are in the sea, and all that are in them, heard I saying, Blessing, and honour, and glory, and power, be unto him than sitteth upon the throne, and unto the Lamb for ever and ever.

And the four beasts said, Amen.

Revelation 5:13-14

Illustration composed from medieval motifs by the author.

BIBLIOGRAPHICAL APPENDIX

Where names of authors quoted do not appear in this list, all available information has been contained in footnotes.

Aelian (Claudius Aelianus). *De Nature Animalium.*

———— . *Varia Historia.*

———— . *Historia Divina.*

Aubin. *Les Diables de Loudun* [*The Cheats & Illusions of Romish priests & Exorcists —Discovered in the History of the Devils of Loudun*, 1703].

Barbier de Montault, Javier (Msgr.). *Traité d'Iconographie chrétienne.*

Carcopino, Jerome. *La Basilique pythagoricienne de la Porte-Majeure, (Rome).* Paris, 1927.

Diehl, Charles. *Justinien et la civilisation byzantine au VIe siècle*, 1901; a new edition in French published by Burt Franklin, New York, 1969. [There are two English titles: *Byzantium, Greatness and Decline*, tr. by Naomi Walford, Rutgers Univ. Press, 1960; and History of the Byzantine Empire, AMS Press.]

Diodorus Siculus. *Bibliotheca Historia* [*Library of History*].

Dionysius the Areopagite (St. Denis). *Traité de la Hiérarchie* [*The Ecclesiastical Hierarchy*].

Déchelette, Joseph. *Manuel d'Archéologie préhistorique, celtique et gallo-romaine.*

Doré, Henri, S.J. *Recherches sur les superstitions en Chine.* 18 vols.

de Galway, O'Kelly. *Dictionnaire archéologique explicatif de la Science du Blason*, 1901.

de Gubernatis, Angelo. *Mythologie zoologique ou Légendes animales*, ed. Durand & Lauriel.

de la Colombière (Marc de Vulson, sieur de la Colombière, d. 1665). *La Science héroique.*

de Morgan, Jacques. *L'humanité préhistorique* [*Prehistoric Man: A General Outline of Pre-History*. Norwood Editions, 1924].

de Saint-Laurent, Grimouard. *Guide de l'Art chrétien.*

——— . *Manuel de l'Art chrétien.*

Gevaert, Émile. *L'Héraldique, son esprit, son langage, et ses applications*. Brussels and Paris, 1923.

Glotz, Gustave. *La Civilisation Égéenne* [*The Aegean Civilization*, tr. by Dobie & Riley, London: Routledge & Kegan Paul, 1968].

Guénon, René. *Autorité spirituel et pouvoir temporel.*

——— . *Introduction à l'étude des doctrines hindoues* [*Introduction to the Study of the Hindu Doctrines*. London: Luzac, 1945].

——— . *L'Ésotérisme de Dante.*

——— . *L'Homme et son devenir selon la Vedanta* [*Man and His Becoming According to the Vedanta*, London: Luzac, 1945].

——— . *Le Roi du Monde* [*The King of the World*. London: Luzac, 1945].

——— . *Le Symbolisme de la Croix* [*The Symbolism of the Cross*. London: Luzac].

Hippeau, Célestin. *Le Bestiaire divin de Guillaume, clerc de Normandie*. Caen: Nardel, 1852.

Huysmans, Joris-Karl. *Le Cathédrale*, Cres. ed. [*The Cathedral*. London, 1898].

Joannes de Cuba (presumed author). *Hortus Sanitatis*. Philippe le Noir edition, 1539.

Jouveau-Dubreuil. *Archéologie du Sud de l'Inde* [*Iconography of Southern India*].

Latini, Brunetto. *Li Livres dou Tresor*, 13th century.

Leclercq, Dom Henri. *Manuel d'Archéologie chrétienne: Depuis les origines jusqu'au VIIIe siècle.*

Leclerq, Dom Henri and Marron, Henri. *Dictionnaire d'Archéologie chrétienne et de Liturgie.*

Lévi, Éliphas. *Le Clef des Mystères* [*The Key to the Mysteries*, Weiser, 1990].

——— . *Les Mystères de la Kabbale* [*Mysteries of the Qabalah*, Weiser, 1974].

Mâle, Émile. (1) *L'Art religieux de la fin du Moyen-âge en France* [*Religious Art from the Twelfth to the Eighteenth Century*, Princeton Univ. Press, 1982].

——— . (2) *L'Art religieux du XIIe siècle en France* [*Religious Art in France: the Twelfth Century*, Vol. I, Bollingen Series # 90, Princeton Univ. Press, 1978].

——— . (3) *L'Art religieux du XIIIe siècle en France* [*Religious Art in France: the Thirteenth Century*, Vol. II, Bollingen Series # 90, Princeton Univ. Press, 1984].

Maspéro, Gaston. *Bibliothèque égyptologique.*

——— . *Études de Mythologie.*

——— . *Histoire ancienne des peuples de l'Orient classique.*

Mattioli, Pietro Andrea Gregorio (16th cent.). *Commentarii in libros sex Pedacii Dioscoridis.*

Moret, Alexandre. *Du caractère religieux de la royauté pharaonique* [*In the Time of the Pharaohs*, Putnam, 1911].

——— . *Mystères égyptiens.*

——— . *Rois et dieux d'Égypte [Kings and Gods of Egypt*, Putnam, 1912].

Moret, Alexandre and Davy, George. *From Tribe to Empire: Social Organization among Primitives and in the Ancient East.* Knopf, 1926.

Pausanias. *Voyages historiques en Corinthe.* [From *Periegesis*, the collected works of Pausanias in Latin. There are two English translations: *Description of Greece*, tr. J.G. Fraser, and *Guide to Greece*, tr. Peter Levi, Penguin Classics, 2 vols., 1984.]

Philostratus. *La Vie des Sophistes* [*Lives of the Sophists*].

——— . *La Vie d'Apollonius de Thiane* [*The Life of Apollonius of Tyana: The Epistles of Apollonius and the Treatise of Eusebius/Philostratus*, Harvard Univ. Press, 1960].

Pitra, Jean-Baptiste-François. *Spicilège de Solesmes* [Latin, *Spicilegium Solamense*].

Plutarch. *De Iside et Osiride* [*Isis and Osiris*].

——— . *Moralia: Praecept. conjug, & Quaestiones conviviales* [French, *Propos de table*; English, *Convivial Questions* or *Table Talk*].

——— . *Parallel Lives* — (Brutus, etc.).

Pomponius Mela. *Cosmographia: sive de situ orbis.*

Rasmussen, Knud. *Du Groenland au Pacifique* [*Greenland by the Polar Sea*, 1921. Abridged ed., *Across Arctic America*, 1927].

Reinach, Salomon. *Cultes, Mythes, et Religions* [*Cults, Myths, & Religions*, tr. Elizabeth Frost, London, 1912].

——— . *Répertoire de la Statuaire grecque et romaine.*

Rich, Anthony. *A Dictionary of Roman & Greek Antiquities* [*Dictionnaire des antiquités grecques et romaines*].

Ross, Alexander (1591-1654). *Pansebeia*: or, *A view of all religions in the world; with the several church-governments from Creation, to these times. Together with a discovery of all known heresies, in all ages and places.* London, 1653. [French translation by Th. La Grue, 1666.]

Schliemann, Heinrich. *Mycènes* [*Mycenae: a narrative of researches and discoveries at Mycenae & Tiryns*, New York, Scribner, 1880].

Schuré. *L'Évolution divine: du Sphinx au Christ* [*From Sphinx to Christ*].

Steiner, Rudolf. *Le Mystère chrétien et les Mystères antiques* [*Christianity as Mystical Fact and the Mysteries of Antiquity*. London, Rudolf Steiner Publishing Co.].

Tabouis, G.R. *Nabuchodonosor* [*Nebuchadnezzar*].

Tertullian. *Ad nationes* [French, *Au Nations*; English, *To the Nations*].

——— . *Adversus Judaeos* [French, *Contre les Juifs*; English, *An Answer to the Jews*].

——— . *De Baptismo.*

——— . *De Pallio* [French, *Du Manteau*; English, *On the Ascetic's Mantle*].

——— . *De Poenitencia.*

——— . *De Scorpiace* [French, *Scorpiaque*; English, *Antidote for the Scorpion's Sting*].

Theodorus Lector. *Historia Tripartita* [French, *Histoire ecclésiastique*].

——— . *In Leviticus.*

Vellay, Charles. *Le culte et les fêtes d'Adonis-Thammouz dans l'Orient antique.*

William of Normandy. *Le Bestiaire divin de Guillaume, clerc de Normandie*, 13th cent., Paris (Caen), Hippeau ed., 1852.

FOR THE BEST IN MYTHOLOGY, LOOK FOR THE 

☐ **THE RAMAYANA**
R. K. Narayan

One of India's supreme epics is the heroic tale of the courtship, exile, and battles of Prince Rama, here told in a brilliant modern prose version by the novelist R. K. Narayán.
172 pages *ISBN: 0-14-004428-0*

☐ **GODS AND MYTHS OF NORTHERN EUROPE**
H. R. Ellis Davidson

Davidson, a specialist in Norse and Germanic mythology, describes both the familiar gods of war and fertility and the more puzzling figures of Norse mythology, such as Heimdall, Balder, and Loki.
252 pages *ISBN: 0-14-020670-1*

☐ **MIDDLE EASTERN MYTHOLOGY**
S. H. Hooke

The source of much of Greek, Roman, and even Celtic mythology may be found in the traditions and legends of the ancient Near East, now called the Middle East—from the Egyptians and Assyrians to the Canaanites and Hebrews.
200 pages *ISBN: 0-14-020546-2*